# Scholarium

Claudia Gross

# Scholarium

TRANSLATED BY

Helen Atkins

*The* Toby Press

The Toby Press
First English Language Edition 2004

The Toby Press LLC
POB 8531, New Milford, CT. 06676-8531, USA
& POB 2455, London WIA 5WY, England
www.tobypress.com

*Das Scholarium* © 2002 Deutscher Taschenbuch
Verlag GmbH & Co KG, Munich, Germany

The publication of this work was supported
by a grant from the Goethe-Institut

ISBN 159264 056 7, *hardcover*

A CIP catalogue record for this title is
available from the British Library

Typeset in Garamond by Jerusalem Typesetting

Printed and bound in the United States
by Thomson-Shore Inc., Michigan

*For my parents*

# I

*Cologne, Anno Domini 141*

n this city everyone had a secret. The apprentice had something to hide from the journeyman, the journeyman from the master, the master from his wife and she from her mother. The city exuded an aura of secrecy, and rumours gathered like dense clouds above its hundreds of rooftops.

One man had failed to come home last night, and was feared to have been attacked by robbers; another had been seen creeping along Lintgasse, dragging a club foot and cursing angrily to himself, while a third had apparently fallen into the Rhine, for it was said that his corpse had been sighted farther downstream....

People knew perfectly well that no more than half of all this talk, conjecture and tittle-tattle was true. But this deterred no one from relating what he had seen, heard, smelled or sensed.

From the day when Pope Urban VI had granted the city's petition to found a *studium generale*, the new university provided people with a new subject for their gossip. Truth to tell, none of them had a very clear idea of what went on there, except that it involved a great deal of teaching and studying. Of course teaching took place at monasteries and cathedral schools too, but the *universitas* was not quite the same. It seemed to consist of a huge conglomeration of scholars who spent their time arguing about how many angels could perch on the point of a church steeple without falling off. The city fathers loved their *studium generale* because it filled the coffers and raised the prestige of the city; but to the ordinary burgher those fine fellows, the students, brought little benefit. And so it was not long before the most outlandish rumours began to circulate concerning the *universitas* and its halls and colleges. They were trying to prove that God existed, some declared, even though everyone, man or woman, knew that God's existence was not a matter of proof. Perhaps, whispered others, they were all unbelievers whose studies served merely to mask their ungodliness. And yet the Pope himself had paid tribute to the high renown of each of the Faculties, and this had set tongues wagging all the more. Could it be that those learned gentlemen, the philosophers, were required to provide proof of God because in fact he did not exist at all?

Meanwhile each citizen of Cologne anxiously guarded his own secret, be it some trifling matter unlikely to cause a great stir, or one that might have the direst of consequences if dragged out into the light of day. Behind every house-front lurked a cloven hoof, behind every wall a pair of illicit lovers, at every confessional a motley gathering of tormented souls threatening to cast off the burden of their furtive sins and load it instead onto the heart of the listening priest.

Those priests ministering to their flock were true artists in the handling of life. Obliged to bear home with them such mountains of personal confession, and powerless to do more than instruct the penitent to say a rosary, they guarded each confidence like a priceless treasure and quickly tried to forget where they had found it. But these were treasures that they would have preferred not to find at all, so distasteful, so absurd, or so dreadful were they. There was little harm in the cheating husband who visited a *gemeyn doichter*, a harlot; nor in the widow engaging in an *amour* with a man twenty years her junior and lasciviously rejoicing in a second springtime. Far graver were the wicked acts of heresy into which a hitherto blameless burgher might have strayed before finding his way back to the fold; or the offence of an alchemist who had thought to find God in wine, even though everyone knew that wine might bring forth truth—*in vino veritas!*—but nothing more.

Still worse things were told, sins that were enough to make the father confessors' ears curl. A man might admit to having killed his friend. Respectable women confessed to unsatisfied lusts of the flesh. Men of supposed good character talked freely of their amorous dalliances. The priests could only exhort them, one and all, to do penance.

In the evening they bore their heavy burdens homewards. Then darkness descended, bringing with it a little peace and quiet. But appearances were deceptive. As night fell, mischief grew. By the light of flickering torches people felt safe from watching eyes, since little could be seen but shadows flitting from one dark corner to another. Most murders were committed at night, and most acts of adultery too—anything that needed to be done stealthily and surreptitiously was carried out under the cloak of darkness. Night took charge of all secrets, she held them safe and carried them with her to the grave. And the morning pretended to have seen nothing at all.

# Lectio

**H**is head lowered between hunched shoulders, looking neither left nor right, Laurien Thibold made his way through the streets of a city that was almost wholly unfamiliar to him. True, his father had brought him to Cologne once, some years ago, and had pointed out to him the great city wall, the churches, convents and monasteries, the town hall and the markets, and Laurien had looked in amazement on all these wonders. But today he was more interested in reaching his scholarium unscathed. Back at home, on the Lower Rhine, he had been told that in Cologne students would lie in wait for a newcomer and drag him off to their own institution, for the *bursae* and colleges were not exactly overflowing with wealth, and each new student brought much-needed cash to replenish their empty coffers. Although Laurien had a place reserved for him in one particular scholarium, these tales had made him uneasy, and now he was positively afraid. What if someone, identifying him as a prospective student, should seize him by the sleeve and drag him off across the city? On the other hand, if he kept walking along like this, with his eyes fixed on the cobbles and on the planks laid across the streets, he would never find his scholarium. He must gaze confidently ahead and give the impression that becoming a new member of the university was the last thing he wanted. And if someone did accost him, he would say that he was looking for a friend of his.

Now he had reached a market-place where the farmers and dealers had herded their cattle together. It reeked of dung and urine. Whips cracked on the hard, dusty earth, cows bellowed, market women screeched. Laurien timidly asked one of the cattle-dealers the way to St. Gereonstrasse, where his scholarium was supposed to be. The man pointed with his whip to the far end of the market-place and told him to cross over Schmierstrasse, go past the hospital on The Katzenbauch, and then turn left.

Laurien mumbled his thanks. Unconsciously hunching his shoulders again, he hurried on beneath the blistering sun. They smash your teeth in, his cousin had whispered maliciously at a family party. They dress up a new student in an animal skin, throw him into the water and leave him to flounder until he is almost drowned before fishing him out. They would force Laurien to swallow excrement, concealed in a pie, so that he would only realise at the second or third mouthful what it was that had just gone into his stomach....

'You shouldn't believe everything you hear about students. Don't worry, they'll leave you in peace, and besides, Domitian will put in a good word for you—I've already seen to that,' his father had reassured him when Laurien, greatly agitated, had repeated the horror stories to him that evening. Laurien's health was delicate. A dipping in the cold river water would instantly give him influenza, and his stomach would certainly never recover from the faeces. He shuddered at the mere thought. If these tales proved true, then he would not stay at the university but would go straight back home and become a plain copyist like his father.

He looked up. The city frightened him. He already felt desperately lonely, and torn between his unbridled terror of the unknown and his ardent wish to go to university. But no one was taking any notice of him. The bells were pealing, everyone was just walking past him, women were carrying on conversations from one window to another, children were running up and down the alleys, and a hundred reflected suns shone from the water in the wells. Just one more inquiry to make sure that he was going the right way, and then he would feel the boundless relief of knowing he would soon be there. But another shock awaited him in Schmierstrasse. Here there were alehouses one beside the other, and heaps of filth, each higher than the last; scavengers rooted around in the refuse, pulling out all manner of bones and other disgusting objects and thrusting their trophies under his nose. 'Now look at this leg of pork here, pity there's not a scrap of meat left on it, but it'll still fetch a penny or two, eh?' A fat old woman leaning out of a window was bawling across to the other side of the street in language unintelligible to Laurien, and this made him go still faster; soon he was rushing along, no longer daring to ask anyone whether he was nearly there. At last he spied a narrow street. That must be The Katzenbauch, for there on the left-hand side was the hospital, with a few beggars huddled on the ground outside its gate. Relieved, Laurien turned off to the left.

The lane was narrow and dirty, but quiet. Not many people passed this way. Right at the near end were the ruins of a house that had collapsed. Next to these remains stood an ungainly building with narrow metal-grilled windows and a heavy door with iron fittings. Judging by his father's description, this must be the Scholarium. Not much light was likely to find its way to the desks here, Laurien thought, or into the heads of the scholars either. His heart was in his mouth, and before ringing the bell he listened for any sounds from within. But all remained quiet, and only the noisy bustle of Schmierstrasse came echoing into this dismal, cramped little spot. He tugged on the bell-pull.

The canon who opened the door to him was of dwarfish stature, scarcely reaching to Laurien's shoulder. An attractive face, fine blond hair, and a slim build. His eyes were restless, and his scrap of a body was constantly in rapid motion, continually drawing attention to itself despite its meagre size.

Laurien perceived a certain forcefulness around the mouth, and suspected that a sombre temperament lurked behind the high forehead. Introducing himself as Marius de Swerthe, the cleric explained that it was his role, as the elected Prior, to oversee the

Scholarium and maintain its proper spirit, and above all to ensure that the students spoke Latin at all times. Conducting Laurien along the corridors, he showed him his dormitory and the refectory, which also served as a *paedagogicum* for those who, like Laurien, needed to catch up on part of the syllabus. Laurien felt uncomfortable. In order not to seem impolite he had to look downwards each time he answered a remark of de Swerthe's, and he found this constant tilting of his head embarrassing. However, de Swerthe appeared not to notice. His manner was kindly but firm and he fairly flew through the rooms on his short, spindly legs, like some aerial sprite, pointing to this or that, his thoughts seeming always to be darting on ahead of his slight frame.

'In winter we get up at five, and in summer at four, because lectures start early,' he explained in Latin, already turning the next corner into another corridor. '*Prandium* is eaten at sext, *cena* at vespers…'—de Swerthe stopped and looked up at him—'and there is a tankard of beer to go with it. The main door is locked at compline. There are strict penalties for staying out at night without permission. Oh, yes, and another thing that I meant to tell you: Frederico Casall, one of our Faculty Masters, will give you extra tuition in the afternoons to cover what you have missed during these past months.'

They had reached the end of a corridor, and de Swerthe opened a door. Outside, a garden lay bathed in the seductive warmth of the sun.

'There is no time for idleness here,' declared the undersized Prior, with a note of contempt in his voice. 'However, should you at any time feel a need for contemplation, it is permissible to sit out here or to take a walk along these paths. Your father was a copyist?'

Laurien was startled. 'Yes, he was a scribe.' What was the connection between his father and the need for contemplation? The dwarf's thoughts seemed to be as disjointed and unpredictable as his gestures.

'You know, of course, that Moritz von Semper, the lawyer for whom your father has done copying work, has made the necessary arrangements for you to live and study here. Domitian von Semper also lives in this Scholarium, even though his father could easily have afforded to rent private lodgings for him. So if you have any further questions, put them to him. And now unpack your belongings. I will go and fetch you an Arts Faculty coat, which you are expected to wear at all times. And in the next few days you will have your matriculation.'

A little later Laurien was sitting alone in the rather dark and cheerless dormitory, gazing around him. There were five plank beds here, and the Prior had told him there were ten more in the adjoining room. Attached to the wall was a crumpled piece of parchment bearing the motto, '*Homo res naturalis est.*'

Laurien felt physically and mentally exhausted. He had been on the road for two days, had slept little during the intervening night and had hastened on his way again at first light. His feet were painfully sore, and even his thoughts flowed sluggishly and were in need of rest. The coat that the Prior had given him lay across his bed, a brown ankle-length garment with a girdle and hood. Laurien stood up and hung it on a nail in the wall. Then he lay down on his straw mattress and looked out through the narrow, barred window. There was no sky, no sun, nothing at all to be seen but stones piled on top of each other, a whole windowful of broken masonry—the remains of the house next door.

Someone was shaking him gently by the shoulder. He must have fallen asleep, for as he opened his eyes he saw a youth of about his own age, dressed in the sombre Arts Faculty coat, leaning over him. It must be Domitian. Laurien sat up.

The student planted himself on the only stool in the room and propped his head on his hands. Beneath his fair, curly hair his bright blue eyes were laughing in silent mockery. He enquired whether Laurien had slept well.

'I'm still a little weak.' Laurien was embarrassed and attempted to justify himself. 'I was laid up with a fever for several months. That's why I wasn't able to be here for the start of the semester. Are you Domitian?'

'Yes, who else?' came the reply. 'You must have made an excellent impression on my father, for him to be helping you like this.'

'I've only attended grammar school,' said Laurien quietly.

Domitian laughed. 'Well, from what I've heard you're a bright spark. What are you planning to study? Jurisprudence?'

Laurien shook his head. Law? No, all he wanted was to graduate in the Faculty of Arts. The seven liberal arts, the *septem artes liberales*. That had the ring of freedom about it, his father had said.

'I only want to take the Bachelor's degree,' Laurien mumbled, lowering his voice as if he felt that this did not show the right attitude.

Domitian nodded, and then stood up. Turning towards the window, he stared at the ruined walls. 'One of the Magistri will be sure to go over with you what you've missed so far, but I can tell you straight away what *I've* picked up here, after being stuck in this Faculty for over a year like an ox in the mire. Here everything is divided and separated, broken down into its component parts and then, if it's lucky, put back together again. But generally it isn't so lucky and it's left in pieces. Did you know that everything can be divided and separated, even things that belong together? As though someone were to pull your arms and legs off, and then say, this is an arm and that's a leg, and you're a human being. I mean, can you understand that?'

Laurien, still sitting on his bed, was staring at his coat hanging on the wall. The symbol of the Faculty.

'Can you understand it?'

He gave a start. No, why should he be able to understand it? He had only been to grammar school.

Domitian gave him a searching look. 'As a new student you have to hold a feast,' he said, abruptly changing the subject. 'I've already mentioned it to my father. He'll give you the money for it. And now get dressed. It's the *hora vespera*, time for supper, and afterwards we go to divine service in St. Boniface's chapel. I must be off now: it's my turn to be *hebdomadarius*, so I have all sorts of duties this week. I still have to feed the goldfinches and set up the tallow candle in front of the statue of the Holy Virgin.'

At the long tables there was no speaking during the meal, which consisted of gruel with almonds and a vegetable pie, washed down with a tankard of *Gruitbier*. At the head of the largest table sat Marius de Swerthe, trying, with obvious difficulty, to keep his jerky movements under control. Next to him, bending over his plate as he ate, was his *lupus,* a wiry red-haired fellow with sharp eyes and a hungry belly, whose function it was to keep the students under surveillance. The meal was accompanied by readings from works in Latin. Laurien glanced surreptitiously around. To the right of the *lupus* he recognised Siger Lombardi, one of the Magistri, who also lived in the Scholarium. He was a young man still—Laurien judged him to be in his mid-twenties—with dark colouring. Just outside the refectory he had greeted Laurien pleasantly, and then had held back, leaving the rest to de Swerthe. The Prior had confined himself to introducing Laurien very briefly to the assembled students of the Scholarium before the kitchen-maids began to place the plates and the steaming dishes of food on the tables. But when the meal was over, de Swerthe rose to his feet and in Laurien's honour recited, as he had done many times before, the rules of the institution.

It was forbidden to make any loud noise or to sing at any hour of the day or night, to go in or out after the door was locked, or to have unseemly relations with the female kitchen staff. It was forbidden to play at cards or dice, to throw things at fellow-students, or to bring women onto the premises...

And so it went on for some considerable time. Laurien sat on the hard bench, his head bowed and his face rigid. You were not allowed to do anything here but sleep, eat and study. It was just like his grammar school.

Immediately after mass they would be expected to withdraw to their dormitories, though Domitian confided in a whisper that even there you could never really feel free, because the Prior and his *lupus* would come creeping along the corridors and put their ears to each of the doors.

However, when the service was over, de Swerthe beckoned to Domitian and instructed him, late as it was, to hurry over to Magister Casall's house and pick up a book for him. He might as well take Laurien with him, he added, so that the new student could introduce himself to his teacher straight away. They must be back, though, within the hour.

The city had given Casall the use of a house close to St. Andreas's hospital, which was only a short way from the Scholarium. They walked briskly, as the Prior had instructed them to, and in less than a quarter of an hour had reached the house, which was bathed in evening sunlight. Once there, they pulled on the bell-rope, but there was no response. All at once they heard a shrill scream. As they gazed up, startled, at the closely fastened windows, more cries followed in rapid succession, clearly audible even through the glass.

'That's a woman, surely,' whispered Laurien, shrinking into the doorway.

Domitian nodded. 'Yes, it's his wife, Magister Casall's wife. Ignore it, pretend you haven't noticed. Any moment now they'll open the door, and everyone will act as if they hadn't heard a thing.'

Sure enough, the door now opened. A servant admitted the two students and, showing them into Casall's study, asked them to wait there for a few moments. Then she shuffled back into the kitchen. Laurien gazed around. On a desk there was a stack of at least twenty books. He did not dare to take a closer look at the titles, and simply stood motionless. And there they came again, those dreadful cries.

Domitian, bolder than his companion, stepped over to the desk and ran his index finger along one of the spines. 'This is Cicero, *De inventione*, do you see, and these,' pointing to another volume, 'are Boethius's writings on logic.'

Laurien nodded absently. How could Domitian pretend not to hear those piteous cries coming from right above them, as though descending straight from heaven? Then suddenly all was quiet. Now they heard footsteps on the stairs, and a moment later the study door opened.

Casall stood before them. 'Ah, the young gentlemen who have come for the *Orator*. And you must be the new student, Laurien, is that correct?'

Laurien gave a start. Casall had a waxen face, which looked puffy and almost mask-like, as if he had given his skin a dusting of white powder. His eyes, which were scrutinising Laurien closely, were black and deep-set.

'I shall be instructing you in the *trivium*: grammar, rhetoric and logic.'

Casall turned away from them and hunted among the books on the desk for the *Orator,* eventually extracting it from the pile and handing it to Domitian with an enigmatic smile. 'Be very careful with the *Orator.* Normally he's chained up in the library, like a dog...' He laughed. 'Anything that has to be chained up is dangerous, either because it may bite or because it sows confusion in people's minds. And now be off with you.'

They turned and went out of the room. As they left, Laurien listened for any sound from above. The cries had ceased.

They stepped out into the street. At that moment, all the city's bells started pealing simultaneously. It was deafening. Two maidservants were quarrelling outside the house opposite, and a group of nuns were singing a hymn as they passed by on their way to St. Andreas's church. Laurien put his hands over his ears. The town where he had attended grammar school had been quite small. Cologne was such a contrast that he found it unnerving, with all its hustle and bustle, and its hordes of people producing a babel of voices as bewildering as the clangour of the bells up there in the countless church towers.

Domitian clasped the book tightly to his coat as they walked back to the Scholarium.

'Well, what do you make of him?' Domitian asked, his voice unmistakably tinged with sarcasm.

'Make of whom?'

'Casall. Do you suppose you could learn a great deal from him?'

'I don't know...Domitian...' Laurien stopped walking and clutched at his companion's sleeve. 'Was that his wife—was he really beating her?'

Domitian nodded, and suddenly Laurien saw a look of bitter resentment in his azure eyes.

'Yes. It's common knowledge here. That's his way of bringing truth and lies out into the open. But he is within his rights. Thomas

Aquinas speaks of the threefold inferiority of woman, and says that it is right and proper to chastise her, because she has a will but no understanding, like the animals. Do you see?'

Laurien did not see, but Domitian told him sombrely that he would find out soon enough—that living in Cologne would give him a whole new view of the world. Laurien nodded. No doubt he didn't properly understand it as yet. That was, after all, the purpose for which he had been sent here—to gain a proper understanding of the world.

A little later, as he was tossing and turning restlessly on his plank bed, listening to his roommates' breathing, all the different sounds of the day ran through his mind again. The bells, the screams, Casall's voice. Only now did he register that it was this voice that kept re-echoing in his memory. A peculiar voice, like a musical note that, having once started, never varies.

'Laurien? Are you asleep?'

Domitian, in the next bed, had rolled over to face him.

'No.'

'When you can't get to sleep, ask yourself what you have learned during the day. That helps you to round off the day in your mind.' Domitian pulled the blanket up over his head.

Laurien gave a nod, although Domitian would not be able to see it in the pitch darkness. Had he learned anything today that would enable him to round off the day in his mind? The host of impressions he had received were racing around madly in his head like chickens let loose in a field. No, he had not learned anything. He had arrived here at last, which was all one could say. Wait, there *was* one thing, he thought, as he felt himself gradually yielding to fatigue: he had learned that he had not yet acquired the right way of looking at things. He yawned and rolled over onto his side. But what *was* the right way of looking at things?

After the two students had left the house she sat quite still and waited, trembling, for what still lay in store for her.

But he did not return. She could hear him moving about downstairs and kept her eyes fixed on the door. If Barbara, the maidservant, set a bottle of wine before him now, he would get drunk, and then before long he would be sure to fall asleep over his books in the study.

Sophie began to relax. The window was open, and she heard the bells start ringing again. She also heard the nuns singing about the miracles performed by Christ—that same Christ who seemed to have forgotten all about her, Sophie, as she sat here on the edge of her bed, feeling the blood on her back soaking through her shift, seeping warmly into the fabric. She must take it off, because blood would not come out unless it was rinsed off straight away with cold water. Nevertheless she continued to sit there motionless, listening to the voices of the bells. Now their ringing was joined by a peal from below. The doorbell.

It must be one of her sisters. But Casall would say that his wife was tired and had already gone to bed. Sophie stood up and slowly began to unlace her dress. When had the beatings and humiliations begun? She could still dimly remember a Casall who had been kindly, if stern. But that had been more than two years ago. An eternity.

Sophie Casall could speak and write Latin as if it were her mother tongue, because when she was young her father had given her every opportunity to study as much as she liked. And so, at some point after her marriage to the Master of the *septem artes liberales*, who was considerably older than she was, she had taken to reading the books that he left piled up on the desk in his study when he went out to his lectures and disputations. Indeed, he was often out for the whole day, so she was able to devote many hours to reading. Seneca, Cicero, Aristotle, Porphyry…the whole gamut of ancient philosophy, and the commentaries by Albertus Magnus and Boethius and the rest. Casall had all the books she needed to satisfy her thirst for knowledge. At first Sophie had kept her reading a secret. She had inserted bookmarks to remind her of the pages at which the books had been left open, so that Casall should not notice how she was spending her time. One afternoon, however, Casall had been sitting over one of the volumes, wrestling with a problem. Hunched over a work by Thomas Aquinas, which he peered at through his eyeglass, muttering to himself and then glancing up as a thought struck him, he had suddenly turned his head towards her and quoted in Latin: 'Not he who has a good understanding is considered a good man, but he who has a good will.'

Sophie froze. This was the first time he had ever spoken to her in Latin.

'Is that a question?' she asked cautiously.

He was so lost in thought that he was not conscious that it was she whom he was addressing. Perhaps he thought he was in discussion with one of his students.

'There is a contradiction here—listen. That is the view that he expresses in the *Questiones* on the virtues in general, yet in another passage—where he expresses agreement with Aristotle—he maintains that the understanding is nobler than the will.'

'Then "good" cannot be equated with "noble",' said Sophie. 'What is the difference between "good" and "noble"?'

'There is no difference,' replied Casall in astonishment, as though unsure which amazed him more, her answer or the contradiction itself. 'There is no difference,' he repeated in a puzzled tone, then abruptly closed the book and left the room.

From then on she read quite openly. She left her bookmarks in the books, and asked him when he came home what texts they had covered that day. His replies were brief and grudgingly given, but he never actually refused to answer. He would mutter that they had been studying the *Analytics*, or *On the Soul*, and, content with that, she would resolve to read the relevant chapters the very next day. But what became obvious, more so even than the bookmarks that she left in the books, was that the more she read, the more easily she could follow what he said, and to him this was intolerable, as disgusting as a rotten fish. One day, as if to test her, he set her a direct question to answer, and she, proud of her learning, ventured out unsuspectingly, like a sleepwalker, onto the tightrope that he had prepared for her. Returning to the contradiction in Aquinas that he had previously remarked on, he said casually, at supper:

'Which do you think is nobler, Sophie, the power of the understanding, or the will? We had a disputation in the Faculty about this today, and I think that the position of those who give precedence to the understanding is closer to Aristotle's view…'

Sophie looked down at her plate. 'You are aware that I read your books.'

'Of course. But you intend me to be aware of it. So tell me your opinion on this matter.'

As fearless as a sleepwalker, she was balancing in the very middle of the rope. Beneath her yawned the terrifying abyss, but her eyes were still shut fast, and it was as if she were in the realm of dreams. She looked up and smiled. 'If you really want to know my opinion, I believe that there must be something else between the understanding and the will.'

'Something else? What do you mean?'

'To me the question of which is the more noble is of no real significance. I am interested in what forms a link between the two.'

'You have not answered my question.'

'A person who is able to understand a thing does not necessarily also have the will to act in accordance with that understanding.'

'Hm,' growled Casall, and returned his attention to the bream on his plate, cutting off the heads and tails and carefully detaching the two halves of each fish from the bones. Then at last he pronounced his judgement: 'The understanding is the force that drives our actions, and therefore it is nobler than the will.'

'If your understanding told you that a woman possessed every good quality that you could possibly imagine, then you would marry her, would you not?'

Casall had a morbid fear of one day choking to death on a fishbone, and yet he loved nothing better than a well-boiled fish. With meticulous precision, and with a murmured prayer to St. Blaise, he pushed the bones to the side of his plate. Only then did he look up.

'But suppose you did not actually love her,' Sophie continued, 'but in fact loved another woman who did not have half of those good qualities, would you marry her all the same? Or would not love lead you to the one who possessed your heart?'

At the very moment she spoke these words, she saw Casall's expression harden. For it was precisely this that had happened to him, long before he met Sophie. He had been supposed to marry one woman but had loved another. Only the offer of the post in Cologne had finally extricated him from this dilemma and resolved his conflict of conscience at a stroke. But worse than this, it seemed, was that he had suddenly become aware of the manner in which Sophie was conducting her argument. It was wholly inadmissible to introduce concrete examples from real life into a discussion of scholastic ideas: that would be like trying to compare cats with trout.

'Is that the "something else" that you were talking about?' he asked harshly. 'Feelings?'

Sophie nodded. 'Yes. Anxiety and fear and anger—and love.'

Casall went on eating slowly and deliberately, and ran his tongue around his mouth to make quite certain that no stray bone had become lodged between his teeth.

Suddenly words burst forth from him. 'I do not wish you to read my books in future,' he said coldly. 'I forbid it. Do you hear? That is to stop once and for all.'

That was when she woke up. Teetering half-way along the rope.

From that day on she reverted to reading in secret, but Casall must have given the servant instructions, for she evidently reported to him that Sophie was still sneaking into his study. He had taken to striking her, trying to beat the knowledge out of her, almost breaking her bones in his efforts to break her will.

Thus it had all started, and thus it would remain to the end.

From then on she entered his study only when expressly directed to do so. It had become the realm of forbidden books and of her lost respect for her husband. She hated him. She knew that he could not bear the fact that she was his equal and that she held up a mirror to him in which he saw two Casalls: the learned Magister and teacher of metaphysics, and the pathetic, stunted human being who shunned feelings as the Devil shuns the cross.

On the third day after his arrival at the Scholarium, Laurien had his matriculation interview. Domitian had recommended he go to Magister Konrad Steiner, whom he considered to be an intelligent, objective man who showed no preference for the modern or the traditional philosophers, but was receptive to the ideas of both.

In outward appearance Steiner resembled a prophet. His full, light grey beard hung down over his chest, while only a few remaining hairs adorned his head. He conducted the interview in one of the big colleges in the city, one that boasted an extensive library which he lost no time in recommending to the new student. Then he asked him about his family background and his financial situation, and learned that Laurien came from a town on the Lower Rhine that he himself happened to know well. He also established that the famous advocate Moritz von Semper had used his influence on Laurien's behalf and obtained a *bursary* for him. Steiner assessed the new student's seriousness of intent: this was in fact the chief object of such an interview, for students could not be allowed simply to drift from one university to another, leading a life of pleasure and conviviality. Once he had satisfied himself of the lad's firm resolve to prove himself worthy of Cologne University, Steiner escorted Laurien into the presence of the Rector, before whom he was required to swear oaths to the Faculty, to the Rector and statutes, and lastly to the Empire. And when Laurien had paid over his matriculation fee he was at last entitled to call himself a *scholar simplex* of the Arts Faculty of Cologne.

The following Sunday was a week before the feast of St. John. Every resident of Cologne knew of a certain meadow down by the river where St. John's wort, which could bring such blessed relief to the sick, was in flower. The bushy plants grew there in profusion, capturing the sunshine in their golden-yellow blooms. During the night preceding St. John's Day people skilled in the art of healing would harvest the flowers, from which they brewed a wondrous remedy that had rescued many a sufferer from the toils of melancholy.

In fine weather, large numbers of people would come here to stroll along the river-bank and enjoy the sight of those billowing clouds of yellow flowers. Casall, who had been living in Cologne for only three years, agreed to let Sophie take him down there. She had packed a basket of fruit and wine so that later on they could sit down in the meadow and take some refreshment. As they sauntered along, the pebbles beneath their feet hot from the fierce midday sun, a group of five students, led by Siger Lombardi, the Master from the Scholarium, approached from the opposite direction. Laurien was among them, as was Domitian von Semper. Greetings were exchanged, and they decided that it would be pleasant for the whole company to spend the afternoon together. De Swerthe had given the students leave to go out for three hours, impressing upon them that they must return punctually at the appointed time.

They sat down in the meadow, and Sophie unpacked her basket. Pears, apples, a loaf of bread and a simple local Rhine wine were handed round, with Casall taking good care to ensure that Sophie received nothing. Predictably, the students soon began to discuss scholarly matters with the two Masters. To avoid appearing to show the slightest interest in this masculine conversation, Sophie pretended to be watching the seagulls wheeling above the water. Then she focused her gaze upon a small red beetle that was scuttling to and fro in the sand; but all the while she was listening intently.

Casall's pet subject was Aristotle's *Ethics*. This was his favourite reading, and he never permitted a free disputation on it, but only one in which argument and counter-argument were expounded in standardised propositions that could not depart in any way from what was taught. In his view, even the commentary by Siger of Brabant—who, though now rehabilitated, had once been considered a heretic—was unworthy of being cited, and if any mention of it did come to his ears he would grimace as though he had just bitten into a lemon.

Sophie meanwhile had been gazing up at the seagulls once again, and dazzled by the sun, she had closed her eyes. When she re-opened them a few minutes later she found herself looking at the two students seated to Casall's left. There was Domitian, and the new student, Laurien. And now she noticed how the latter was staring at her. Was there a big hole in her dress, or something of that kind? In confusion she put her hand to her throat and drew the collar closer. He was a quiet, reticent lad, this Laurien, perhaps seventeen years old, and too new to the Faculty to be able to join properly in the discussion. He had short brown hair poking out from under his cap, brown eyes, a pale face with a diffident expression. Domitian was quite different—fair-haired and blue-eyed, with long, luxuriant curls and laughing eyes, and an air of self-confidence and experience, as though he had been to the end of the world and back again and knew all its ways. It was not to be wondered at: after all, his father was an eminent lawyer who regularly frequented the Imperial court, and something of that aura of power was bound to rub off on the son. Slightly to one side, a blade of grass between his lips, Lombardi sat in silence with his knees drawn up, listening to the others with a condescending smile. And while Casall expatiated on the 'double truths' of the *doctor subtilis*, Duns Scotus—a subject on which Sophie too might have had something to contribute—she returned Laurien's gaze quite openly and was rewarded with a shy smile.

A blush spread over his face. Timidly he looked away and lowered his eyes. Sophie seemed to him like a shaft of sunlight breaking through the clouds, clear and radiant, banishing all darkness. But then he remembered her screams, and a feeling of profound compassion came over him. How gladly he would have torn her from that monster's clutches, like the hero saving the maiden from the jaws of the dragon. But he was just an insignificant young student, and not only was she married to that brute, but he was fully entitled to chastise her.

Laurien raised his eyes again and looked straight into Sophie's. He would willingly have drowned in those depths of tender blue.

'We are leaving,' Sophie suddenly heard Casall's voice beside her. She nodded submissively, gathered up the remnants of food and rose to her feet. Feeling the pressure of Casall's hand on her shoulder, she did not dare to bid the students a warm farewell, but merely gave a silent nod all around.

'Perhaps your wife would like to stay a little longer.' Laurien managed to force out the words, stammering with shyness. Casall eyed him with astonishment, and an amused smile played about his lips.

'Perhaps you would like to stay?' Casall put the question to Sophie, who shook her head in embarrassment.

'As you see,' said Casall with a self-satisfied smile, 'she would rather come home with me.'

He seized hold of her arm roughly and she allowed herself

to be pulled along, her face set like stone as though transfixed by a gorgon. Laurien averted his eyes.

'You've fallen for her,' Domitian observed softly, lying back on the sand.

'I just couldn't help thinking of the other evening, when we collected the *Orator*,' Laurien responded. 'She's so lovely. She looks like the Virgin Mary. Her hair is as blonde as overripe wheat.'

'And you're a dreamer, Laurien. She's married. If you cross swords with Casall, you'll live to regret it, I can tell you.'

The other students laughed in agreement. Lombardi felt sorry for the new student; he did not want the lad to find himself the butt of the others' mockery right from his first week, and so he rose to his feet, beckoned Laurien over to him, and took him down to the edge of the Rhine. There he sat down on the bank, close to a birch sapling, and said, 'Well, Laurien, what do you see? I'm sure you have already asked yourself what sort of things you will be learning here. So tell me, what do you see?'

Laurien sat down beside him and replied in surprise, 'Water. And the reflection of the tree.'

Lombardi tossed a pebble into the river. The contours of the image rippled and dissolved. He nodded. 'Exactly. You look into the water and think that that looks like a tree. Yet if you were to dip your hand in, you would realise that it wasn't a tree but just its reflection, or, as we philosophers would say, the idea of it. That is what you will learn here. You will learn to consider a thing in its own right but also as secondary to the idea of it. In other words, in the latter case things are not real but are merely images of something.'

'But how is it possible, for instance, for me to have an idea of something that doesn't exist in reality?'

Lombardi grinned. 'That's a good question. But if you distinguish between idea and reality, then it is possible. Our premise is that behind every individual thing the idea of it must exist. Whether that explains the essence of things, though, is something that not even a philosopher can tell you.'

'It's all the same to me what I learn,' Laurien declared, leaping to his feet. 'I don't want to become a Master of Arts. I'll be quite satisfied to be a Baccalaureus.'

'You won't get far here with that attitude,' murmured Lombardi as he watched the lad sauntering away along the river-bank, every so often plucking playfully at the tall grasses.

The first weeks passed. There was much to learn, infinite amounts. So much that Laurien sometimes feared it was beyond his powers. The more so since for days he had been feeling unwell. Today he could barely stand upright, his head ached, and he was prone to a shivering that came from within. He had therefore gone back to bed after the midday meal, but had been unable to sleep. With an effort he dressed himself again. As he emerged from the dormitory he bumped into Domitian and three other students. 'Tomorrow evening we're going to the Ox tavern with Casall, Lombardi, Steiner and all the other Masters,' Domitian announced in his usual cheerful manner. 'Will you come?'

Laurien nodded. If only this shiver would stop running up and down his spine as though he was sitting on an ants' nest. And this persistent headache. At that moment the dwarfish Prior came along the corridor, half-buried under a pile of folio volumes that he was carrying. 'Well now, my fine young scholar,' he said with a grin, peering at Laurien from behind the books. 'Will you soon have caught up on all that you missed?'

Again Laurien nodded.

'Tell me, does he beat you too?' Domitian asked unexpectedly. Laurien looked at him questioningly.

'Casall. Everybody knows that he's given to lashing out on occasion.'

'No, he doesn't. But I still don't like him,' muttered Laurien. 'As far as I'm concerned he can roast in Hell. I hate him!' He was thinking of Sophie. In fact these days he did nothing but think of Sophie. By night she haunted his dreams, by day he was lost in thoughts of her. He sat, stood or walked he knew not whither or where, continually having to drag himself back down from the soaring flights of his imagination.

The others roared with delight, and only the faces of de Swerthe and Domitian remained serious. It seemed to Laurien that a swift glance of understanding passed between them, and then de Swerthe commented bitterly that Casall was indeed a most unpleasant specimen of his kind and would have done better to have stayed in Paris. The others laughed again, but Laurien was in no mood for jollity. He felt so weak that he was afraid he might lose his balance at any moment and collapse in a corner.

The following evening it poured with rain. People retreated into their homes and went early to bed, except for those with something to celebrate. Through the darkness came the muffled sound of a creaking cart. That was the *goltgrever,* the 'gold-digger', who had emptied the cesspools and was now pushing his steaming load down towards the Rhine. He was only allowed to shovel out the 'gold' in the evening, and to transport it only at night. It was well-paid work; others showed little inclination for it, but to him the generous wages were incentive enough to go about his evil-smelling business. His nose had become inured to the pungent stench that assailed him when he opened the pits and loaded his freight first into the barrels and then onto his handcart. Privately he considered that the smells that wafted around a knacker's nose were no better, and in any case the good folk of Cologne deposited their excrement wherever and however they felt like it.

With his head tucked down between his shoulders he pushed the cart along in front of him. He had the rain at his back, pelting mercilessly down on him, and his cloak, which he had pulled up over his head to keep the water off, almost completely blocked his vision. All at once his progress was checked: the cart would not budge. When he walked round to the front to see what it was that had caught between the wheels, the hazy illumination of a hastily lit tallow candle showed him the shadowy outline of a pair of feet protruding from a tangle of elder bushes. 'I might as well load him up on my cart too,' the gold-digger muttered to himself, stepping closer to look at the body. Pushing the elder branches apart, his hands encountered a figure in a dark-coloured garment similar to a monk's habit. A priest? The gold-digger hesitated. Then he resolutely straightened up and pulled the cloak over his head again; the rain was getting heavier all the time. *What's it to me*, thought the gold-digger, who had seen plenty of corpses in Cologne before now. At his own measured pace he carried on pushing his cart-load of barrels down to the Rhine.

The rain drummed monotonously on the roofs of the city and beat against window-panes. The master of the fullers' guild had already retired to bed with his wife, put out the lamps and closed his eyes.

Suddenly he heard a scream. It was so piercing, so terrible, that he sat bolt upright in bed, listening. That was the scream of a human being—of a man. Then a few brief words rang out in the street, 'Help, help, he's going to kill me!' And then another scream followed, this time breaking off abruptly with a choking rattle, as though a life were indeed swiftly departing. Leaping out of bed, the fuller slipped into his hose and jerkin, pulled on his boots and rushed downstairs. He lit a torch hastily, then unlocked the door and stepped out into the street. A window opposite had been thrown open and someone was peering out.

'Did you hear that too, neighbour?'

In the next house a door opened. Widow Notsiedel cowered fearfully in the doorway.

'Down there, look…'

She pointed towards the end of the street, where, in the light of a wall-torch, a figure with flapping coat-tails could be seen just turning the corner. That way led to the gardens of St. Ursula's, after which there were only a few more houses. The fuller started running in that direction, but stopped short after a few steps. There was something dark lying on the ground. He bent to pick it up: it was a book. Then a little further on he found a boot. Now more and more neighbours roused by the commotion emerged from their houses. They all began to trudge along the street, which was muddy from the downpour, scouring the gutters and the boards that lay across the roadway. Soon they came upon a second boot, and Widow Notsiedel, who had joined in the search, discovered a torn-off sleeve. The fuller examined it by the light of his torch. 'That looks like a sleeve from one of the coats the Arts Faculty people wear,' he muttered thoughtfully. Before long they saw the other sleeve lying under a tree, and then a biretta of the kind worn by a Master of Arts. And now yet more neighbours came rushing towards them with a coat that they had found. With no sleeves. They went on a little further, but finding nothing more they turned back again. Searching the street in the opposite direction, they finally discovered the likely owner of this strange collection of garments. He was lying behind a well belonging to a small house in Marzellenstrasse. Lifeless, and as naked as God had created him. And his shirt, hose and underclothes, drenched by the rain, were draped over the stone rim of the well.

The fuller drew closer to the body and bent down. Taking hold of the dead man's hand, he felt for a pulse but found none. He caught sight of a pool of blood on the ground, and rolled the dead man slightly over, onto his side. At once they all saw a gaping wound in the back of his head, suggesting that the man had been struck down with a heavy object. Deathly pale, Widow Notsiedel crossed herself.

'He is past saving,' the fuller said quietly. 'He cried out for help, but to no avail. The murderer was too quick for us. I was already in bed when I heard the screams, and by the time I had put my clothes back on...but what puzzles me is why the killer laid such an obvious trail leading to his victim. We would never have found him so quickly if he hadn't spread those clothes around...'

'Though the trail actually seemed to point the other way, towards St. Ursula's,' commented the widow. Her neighbours nodded in agreement.

'This house belongs to one of the Masters attached to the Faculty,' one of them volunteered. The fuller promptly turned towards the house and tugged at the bell-pull, but no one answered.

'We ought to notify the Cathedral Provost. After all, he's Chancellor of the University,' said Widow Notsiedel, whereupon they all set off *en masse* for the cathedral precincts, where the Provost was fast asleep and snoring lustily. Their clamorous ringing dragged him unceremoniously from his slumbers.

They accompanied him back to the corpse, recounted the whole course of events, and held their torches close to the dead man's face. On seeing it, the Chancellor gave a start. 'In the name of God, you are right, it *is* one of the Masters of the Arts Faculty,' he stammered, the colour draining from his face. Then they showed him the objects they had found in the street, and explained again, all speaking at once, how a trail of items had been laid as though to guide them to the victim. Two boots, two severed sleeves, a biretta and a mutilated coat. And the book. The Chancellor took this and asked the fuller to hold his torch closer. The light fell on the pigskin binding. The Chancellor said nothing, but clasped the book to him. The good folk clustering around him would have been none the wiser in any case, given that it was Aristotle's *De Interpretatione* with Boethius's commentaries. Presumably it had belonged to the dead man.

'I will have the body removed,' the Chancellor said at last in a subdued tone, and urged the neighbours to go back to their beds. He went to fetch the magistrate's officers and instructed them to convey the body to the city mortuary, and only then did he himself return home.

The following morning he convened all the Masters of the Faculty to give them an account of the night's events and to inform them that the dead man now lying in the mortuary and awaiting burial was one of their number.

There they sat around the table, the remaining twenty-one Magistri of the *artes liberales*, their lectures cancelled because a colleague had been horribly murdered during the night. It was not difficult to deduce his identity, for look as they might, the one nowhere to be seen was Frederico Casall.

'This morning Casall's wife paid a visit to one of the magistrate's officers to report that her husband had not returned home last night,' Konrad Steiner told them. 'It seems that she had not been notified of his death.'

The Chancellor nodded. 'That is true. But the officers disclosed it to her. I had intended to withhold the unhappy news for a little longer, and, to be honest, I was not sure how to tell her, given that it all happened in the middle of the night...'

'Well, now she has heard it from a different source,' Steiner murmured, lowering his eyes.

Lying on the table in front of the Chancellor was the book. 'In addition to Casall's clothing, this was also found in the street. It is Aristotle's *De Interpretatione*, and it belonged to him. What is strange, however, is that a piece of vellum was tucked into it, with some writing in Latin.'

He opened the volume, drew out the parchment, which by great good fortune had remained dry during the night, and in a low voice read out its contents:

> *You separate everything that belongs together, yet you do not recognise what does not belong together. Solve this riddle and you will have come a little closer to him who has brought Casall a little closer to Hell.*

'Somebody—presumably the murderer—must have placed this parchment in the book. I have spent the whole night brooding over that strange first statement, but I can make no sense of it. The murderer must have intended us to find his victim soon, for even though the trail led in the opposite direction, he had laid out the items in such a way that someone was bound to come upon the body. There is method behind it. A physician who came to the mortuary this morning at my request confirmed that Casall was killed by a blow to the head, but we have not found the murder weapon anywhere. And the master of the fullers' guild saw a shadowy figure hurrying away...'

They all looked at each other in bafflement. This was indeed a strange business, with the separated items of clothing and that philosophical conundrum.

'A joker,' said Theophile Jordanus, frowning. Jordanus was one of the Masters of Arts, who had transferred from Paris to Cologne two years earlier. 'A fool who thinks he can put us to the test. This is his way of showing us what kind of a man he is.'

'A fool? I am more inclined to think that we are dealing with a cold-hearted villain. Yes, certainly he is trying to tell us something, because he thinks he is cleverer than we are. And he is evidently a man of education, since he has a command of Latin. In fact, that should make our task of unmasking him somewhat easier. It can only be someone capable of writing in that language. And that, gentlemen, points to...us.'

At this they all lowered their eyes. Out in the corridor they heard footsteps approaching, then receding. They were waiting for the Rector of the university to join them so that a decision could be made about what should happen next. But the Rector was probably still closeted with one of the criminal court magistrates.

'Casall went to the Ox tavern last night with the students from the Scholarium in St. Gereonstrasse. It was close to midnight when they all set out for home together...' the Chancellor mused.

Steiner nodded. 'Yes, we were all at the Ox. Which means that we,'—his eyes took in all his colleagues around the table—'cannot be suspected of having anything to do with this heinous crime. When the murder was committed we were all still sitting there together. Casall left the inn at around ten o'clock, saying that he wanted an early night. He must have been somewhere else up to the time when he encountered his murderer. The master of the fullers' guild states that he heard the cries shortly before eleven. Where had Casall been until then? Surely he can't have been walking the streets all that time, especially in the pouring rain!'

'Casall was not exactly given to fanciful behaviour,' observed Jordanus in a sarcastic tone. Everyone present knew that he had not had a very high regard for the dead man. Casall had been an unpleasant individual, such was the thought in all their minds, and the Chancellor needed no powers of clairvoyance to be aware of it. 'There are plenty of people who might welcome Casall's death. First and foremost his wife. I'm sure I don't need to enlarge on that...'

No, indeed he did not. They all knew that Casall had beaten his wife regularly. It was even rumoured that he had sometimes put her on a chain, like the books in the library, to prevent her from leaving the house, and that she was like a bitch on heat, always on the look-out for new lovers.

'Nobody knows whether these tales about her are true,' put in Niklas Moribus indignantly. 'It was only Casall himself who was always saying that he could not let her out of his sight because if he did she would immediately jump into bed with another man. He constantly denigrated her, but I have never seen her out alone in town. We ought to take care not to blacken her reputation even further.'

'He is right,' said Steiner sternly. 'Why are we so eager to declare someone guilty before we even know the meaning of that strange statement on the parchment—let alone its originator? It is possible, but by no means certain, that it was written by Casall's widow, who does know Latin, as we are all aware. But something else has just occurred to me…Domitian von Semper also left the inn before eleven, because he had to run an errand for the *lupus* of his Scholarium. And his route could well have taken him straight along Marzellenstrasse…'

For a few moments they were all too taken aback to speak.

Then Jordanus, looking enquiringly round the table, asked: 'Had Domitian any possible motive for killing his teacher?'

'Casall gave him such a thrashing recently that he was unable to attend lectures for two days. Nobody knows why. Apparently Domitian had not prepared his lessons, but that by no means explains Casall's use of such extreme violence.'

'Murder as revenge for corporal punishment? Do you consider Domitian von Semper capable of such a thing?' the Chancellor now interposed, a sombre expression on his face. He decided not to wait for an answer but to bring the discussion to a close: this affair was making him extremely uneasy. He turned to Steiner. 'Here, take the book with you and think hard about that message. When you have solved the riddle, come to me and we will have the murderer arrested.'

Steiner laughed wryly. Perhaps the writer was a madman whose thought-processes were more confused than logical. If, however, he was indeed a person who thought logically, then it must be possible to turn his own weapons against him. Steiner pulled the book towards him and once again scrutinised the parchment closely.

'We could start by trying to identify the handwriting,' he murmured.

Sophie had been sitting on the stool for hours, stunned and motionless. In front of her, on the stove, the meal prepared by the servant had long since grown cold. The loud ringing of the doorbell made her start.

She opened the door, and there stood Konrad Steiner. 'Oh, it's you, Magister Steiner…you're the last person I would have expected.'

Steiner smiled. 'Well, I am here on a mission of my own, as it were.'

She led him into her husband's study and invited him to sit down at the table. She herself leaned against the window-seat.

'So whom were you expecting?' asked Steiner curiously.

'One of the magistrates. I hear that they have begun their enquiries. Whether there is anyone who is without witnesses as to where he was between ten and eleven last night…anyone who might have had an interest in killing my husband…and a knowledge of Latin…'

Steiner made no reply. He gazed at her as she stood there before him with her arms folded. A ray of sunlight fell across her hair. Her black gown accentuated her pallor and made her eyes seem as hard as stone.

'Where were you at the time in question?' he asked, making his voice as gentle as he possibly could.

Sophie nodded. 'Yes, you may well ask. I was fast asleep, but no one will be able to vouch for that.'

'Everyone in the Faculty knows that your husband did not give you very much occasion to respect and honour him. That is something you must consider…'

'Oh,' she said with a mocking laugh, 'I have considered it, I assure you.'

Steiner stood up. There was something in her manner, in her stony expression, that troubled him. It was not his responsibility to come here and question her. Nevertheless, he asked her to sit down at the table and write down a sentence for him. Surprised, she fetched a quill pen and paper and wrote, at his dictation: 'You separate everything that belongs together, yet you do not recognise what does not belong together.'

Steiner drew the parchment towards him. Her handwriting was small, upright and painstakingly neat, whereas the writing found in the book sloped to the left and had an arrogant flourish to it. It is possible to disguise one's hand, Steiner thought dubiously; handwriting is like a piece of clothing, it may conceal more than it reveals.

'What was the purpose of that?' asked Sophie, curiously.

But Steiner made a noncommittal gesture and, with a slight nod to her, left the house without another word. His stomach was rumbling, but in half an hour lectures would resume. There was no time to eat. He strode across the Neumarkt and turned off towards the College. A few students were already standing outside. He caught sight of the Rector, who seemed to be waiting impatiently for his arrival.

'I must talk to you,' the Rector began, taking Steiner by the arm and drawing him aside. 'I have come straight from seeing the magistrate. Although the dead man was a member of the Faculty, the location of the murder puts it within the jurisdiction of the city authorities. However, in this case, the magistrate needs our help, because he can make nothing of that puzzling statement left inside the book. They are only just embarking on their investigations—the questioning of witnesses and so on and so forth—you know the procedure. Only one thing is certain: the students and Masters associated with the Scholarium, yourself included, were all together in the Ox. The wife—one of the magistrate's officers told me that he questioned her this morning—has no witnesses to confirm her whereabouts. But there is one further person, besides Domitian von Semper, who has no alibi. At the time in question he could easily have climbed out of the window...'

They were mounting the College steps. The Rector paused outside the door and looked Steiner in the face. 'He was lying ill in bed with a fever, in the sickroom of the Scholarium in St. Gereonstrasse.'

'Whom do you mean?'

'Laurien. Laurien Thibold. You know him, he attends your

lectures. And he had lessons with Casall too. According to some of the students he once said that as far as he was concerned Casall could roast in Hell. And he has only been in Cologne for four weeks.'

Steiner could readily call Laurien to mind. He had last seen him three days ago, at his lecture. A quiet lad, an impecunious student who made no very strong impression, either favourable or unfavourable. He could not possibly have killed Casall.

'How can you say such a thing?' he asked the Rector, aghast. 'It's unthinkable!'

'If you have such strong preconceptions, I will find someone else to send…'

'No, no, let me look into it. Will you take my lecture for me?' Steiner asked him. 'Poor fellow, the shock will turn him into a pillar of salt!'

He turned to leave. The Rector looked thoughtfully after him. Steiner presided over all the Magistri, and this status fully entitled him to make some enquiries of his own. But he had too high an opinion of mankind, and an unwillingness to see the obvious might well impair his judgment.

This morning Laurien had managed to rise from his sickbed and walk around the room a little. The physician had told him he might do this, as the fever seemed to have subsided and he was feeling noticeably better. All the same, the doctor had added just before leaving, he should continue to rest in the sickroom for one more day. There would be no afternoon lesson for him in any case, since his teacher was no longer of this world. Domitian had crept surreptitiously into the room and told him of Casall's death. It was causing a tremendous stir, he said. The whole Faculty was talking of nothing else, and the Chancellor had asked Steiner to take charge of the affair.

'I'm not shedding any tears for him, the swine,' had been Laurien's only comment, and his thoughts had at once turned to Sophie. Then Domitian had slipped out of the room again, and Laurien had gone back to bed.

There was a knock at the door. Sitting up, Laurien saw Magister Steiner enter. What could he want of him?

'Are you still unwell?'

'No. But I'm still not supposed to go to classes today.'

Steiner stepped over to the window and looked out. Yes, it would have been quite easy to climb out of here unobserved in the pitch dark, when rain was falling and people had already gone to bed. Outside there was just the empty lane, and from here to St. Ursula's or Marzellenstrasse was no great distance.

'I should like to dictate something to you. Fetch some paper and ink.'

Somewhat surprised, Laurien left the room and returned with the materials. Then, seated at the rickety desk by the window, he wrote down the sentence that Steiner dictated. *He writes an elegant hand*, Steiner thought, *very legible, neither too big nor too small*. But it was nothing like the writing of the man he was seeking.

'A suspicion has been voiced,' said Steiner casually. 'This may mean nothing at all, but you and Domitian are the only ones who have no witnesses as to where you were between ten and eleven last night, and I'm told that you once proclaimed for all to hear that as far as you were concerned Casall could roast in Hell...'

Laurien stared at him. 'They suspect *me*? Why? And why suspect Domitian?'

'Domitian came back earlier than the others, and as for you, you could have climbed out of this window, and a person can still run, even with a fever. I don't believe you are guilty, but I should like to be sure. What was the problem between you and Casall? All I know is that he was giving you extra tuition in the afternoons.'

Laurien nodded. And then he related how he had gone to fetch the book from Casall's house on his very first day in Cologne. Steiner listened, letting his eyes wander over the paper with Laurien's handwriting. Then he looked up. 'But you didn't even know her.'

'No, I didn't. But do I need to know a horse to feel sorry for it when it's beaten? You're right, I didn't know her, but I still felt sorry for her. And that's all there is to it.'

Steiner nodded. It was just as he had supposed. A suspicion with feet of clay, born of desperation, because at present there was no other suspect in sight. Even so, that kind of suspicion was like the Devil's shadow: once it had appeared it took time and patience to get rid of it again.

'I believe you, but that's neither here nor there,' said Steiner as he was leaving. 'We must find the murderer, that's all that matters. Don't worry now, the truth always comes to light, because it shuns the darkness.'

Next Steiner went to find Domitian. Astonished to be asked about the route he had taken back to the Scholarium, Domitian denied having passed through Marzellenstrasse. He had left the inn at around half past ten and been back at the Scholarium soon after that—he had run, in fact, because of the rain bucketing down. He had no witnesses though, because of course the other students were still out, and the Prior had been visiting his mother on the other side of the city. When Steiner asked him about his relationship with Casall, Domitian admitted his strong dislike of him, but insisted that that on its own was hardly a reason to kill someone.

'Why did he give you such a thrashing a few weeks ago? There surely must have been a reason for that.'

Domitian stared at him. 'A reason? Certainly there was, but it seems to me that you're looking for a reason to accuse me of this murder. I had failed to prepare my lesson, that was all. So he started hitting me. You know yourself how readily he used to lash out.'

'With such violence that you had to stay in bed for two days?'

Domitian withdrew into silence, and Steiner said nothing more either. Was that really the whole story? Or was there something more behind the punishment, something of which he had no inkling? He asked Domitian to give him a handwriting sample, and watched him form the words in a bold, sweeping hand. Domitian's writing, like the other samples, bore little resemblance to the writing on the piece of parchment.

The *lupus*, whom Steiner questioned next, claimed that he had inad-vertently dozed off, only waking up again when the students had arrived back. As for Domitian, who had been fetching a book for him from a student in another college and had therefore returned earlier, he had unfortunately not heard him come in.

In the adjoining kitchen, little de Swerthe could be heard giving orders. In his angelic voice, he was reprimanding the kitchen-maids and finding fault with the cleaning of the cooking pots. Steiner halted in the doorway and watched as, mounted on a stool, he took the pots one by one from the shelves and looked inside them, cursing aloud to himself as he did so. Suddenly he noticed Steiner waiting, and smiled.

'Oh, Magister Steiner. What brings you to my kitchen?'

'I wanted a word with you. About Domitian von Semper.'

The dwarf nodded, clambered down from his stool and led Steiner into his study, where he offered him a seat and swung himself up onto the edge of a table.

'What would you like to know? Whether he could have murdered Casall? You realise what a serious accusation that is…'

'Yes, but he left for the Scholarium before all the others did, and I want to know at what time he actually arrived back here last night. You were not here, so I am told, and your *lupus* had apparently nodded off. So he says, at any rate.'

De Swerthe smiled. 'Does that put him under suspicion? Perhaps he was in league with the student, who knows? No, that is absurd…but to return to Domitian. Do you know about the beating? Casall has seldom given any student such a thorough thrashing as he gave him. Even from the start they didn't get on well, because young von Semper always had a haughty and arrogant manner. Casall came from a humble background, as you know. But a student is still only a student, even if he is of noble birth, and his supercilious manner so infuriated Casall that he took the first opportunity to show Domitian who was in charge. And when the lad was lying in the dormitory afterwards, bruised and battered, he shouted out in his pain and fury that he would make Casall pay for what he had done. I heard him distinctly.'

'That would be a possible motive,' Steiner said thoughtfully. 'Did anyone else hear him say that, besides yourself?'

'He may have said it to others too, I don't know. But he nursed an implacable hatred towards Casall, that much is certain.'

Steiner nodded. 'You know Domitian better than I do. What is he like?'

The dwarf's short legs were dangling in the air, and he swung them back and forth. 'One of fortune's favourites, I would say. Born with a silver spoon in his mouth, charming, obliging, but in his own particular way unscrupulous too, yes, undoubtedly so. Whatever he wants, he takes, because he believes his rank entitles him to it. People of his stamp are born at the zenith, at the highest point of the heavens' vault. They regard themselves as being very special, if you take my meaning...'

'Do you think him capable of committing murder? Out of wounded pride?'

'Oh, I think anyone is capable of murder. What do we know of the hidden depths of a fellow creature who seeks to conceal his true feelings? I tell you, nothing at all.'

Steiner made no reply, and the dwarf climbed down from the table and began to pace up and down the room, apparently deep in thought.

'You were out visiting your mother?' Steiner suddenly asked.

De Swerthe nodded. 'Yes, until midnight, the *lupus* can vouch for that. She is old and sick, poor soul, and is always glad of a little company...'

Steiner stood up and took his leave. The hot day was drawing to a close, but a certain sultriness still remained and he loosened his coat as he stepped outside. It was all rather odd, he reflected, as he walked in the direction of Marzellenstrasse. The *lupus* dozing off and not waking up until past eleven, and the Prior visiting his mother, so that there was nobody who could confirm the exact time of Domitian's return to the Scholarium. Was that mere chance, or had someone given chance a helping hand? But that would presuppose that Domitian had two accessories to his wicked crime, two people who refused to say when he had finally come back because they were shielding him.

Steiner had returned to his house in Marzellenstrasse and had gone to sit in the garden to think matters over. Ever since his sister's death there had been no one to keep the garden under control. The roses had vanished from sight, engulfed by rampant weeds of every description that poured forth in all directions like a storm tide, spreading all the way to the spot where Steiner liked to sit. He did not interfere, but simply observed how some plants thrived and others gave up the struggle. It struck him now that it was the really beautiful flowers, the ones with large, colourful blooms, that were gradually disappearing. What a strange caprice on the part of nature, he thought, to suppress beauty and favour simplicity. Man alone could halt and to some extent reverse the process by pulling up the weeds and giving the roses room to grow. Was it the same with people? Pensively Steiner shook his head. How could he venture such an analogy? On his lap lay the parchment bearing the strange riddle. The longer he pondered on the meaning of the words, the more confused he became. What, in God's name, did they not see that did not belong together? And who was meant by they? Those who now had the task of investigating Casall's death? What if the parchment had only accidentally found its way into the book? And what was one to make of the shadowy figure seen by the master fuller? Had that been the murderer?

With a sigh Steiner rose to his feet. He had to go over to the mortuary, where the physician who advised the magistrate's court was expecting him.

The coffin was already closed, but the physician who had carried out the autopsy was more than willing to tell him about his findings. Casall had suffered a large wound to the back of the head, inflicted by a blow from a heavy object, which had also caused a fracture of the skull. In the hair, which was matted with blood, some tiny fragments had been found, splinters of earthenware, suggesting that the murder weapon could well have been an earthenware vessel.

'He was killed by a blow?' repeated Steiner. 'From behind?'

'Yes, in all probability. Perhaps Casall was sitting by the well, on the rim of the basin, and the killer came up behind him.'

'But what in Heaven's name was Casall doing in Marzellenstrasse in the middle of the night, and in the pouring rain, too? And, what's more, right outside my house?' Steiner broke off, as a thought struck him. 'Could he conceivably have been killed somewhere else?'

'Oh, certainly. Anywhere at all, in principle. That can no longer be established beyond doubt. Any traces have been washed away by the heavy rain that fell all night.'

'And what about the time of the attack?' Steiner wanted to know.

'Well, the fuller has stated that he heard the screams shortly before eleven o'clock, and then it was perhaps something under half an hour before Casall was found.'

'What reason do you suppose the murderer had for removing Casall's clothes?' asked Steiner.

'Perhaps he was attempting to obscure the circumstances of the death,' the doctor speculated.

'Casall screamed, and the screams must have been intensely loud and piercing—the neighbours say they were the cries of a man who knew that his life was at stake. The sound quite literally made them fall out of bed. But why did the murderer go on to lay a trail leading to his victim? Admittedly he made it lead in the wrong direction, but it was obvious that people would hunt around in the immediate vicinity. I accept that he was trying to confuse us. But perhaps he also wanted to divert our attention from something else entirely. Let us just piece together everything that we know. Casall encounters his murderer, who strikes him down from behind with a heavy object, possibly an earthenware pot. So Casall, already gravely injured, screams for help at the top of his voice, but his assailant strikes a second blow and Casall is dead. Then the killer puts the parchment into the book that Casall was carrying, pulls off his clothes and boots, and detaches the sleeves from his coat. After that he drops the individual items of clothing at intervals along the street. Between the terrible cries for help and the appearance of the first of the neighbours there is a gap of five, or at the very most ten minutes. Five to ten minutes, during which he has time to lay his trail. When the master fuller emerges from his house, he just catches sight of him disappearing round a corner. Strange behaviour for a murderer, don't you think?'

The physician gave a low chuckle. 'It seems to me that a really crafty devil was at work there. He thinks he's vastly cleverer than you are. Have you taken handwriting samples?'

'Yes, but handwriting can be disguised. I can't rely on that.'

'So what are you relying on?'

'I wish I knew,' grunted Steiner. 'But I haven't the faintest idea. That philosophical riddle has me thoroughly puzzled. It sounds like a sentence from a scholastic dispute. Is the murderer someone from the Arts Faculty? The parchment would suggest that. But he may be deliberately trying to lead us onto the wrong track. He appears to be saying, look, I think like you, therefore I am one of you. Whereas in reality…'

'Well?' The physician was curious to hear more.

'In reality he may be some poor devil who was thrown out of the Faculty, for whatever reason. Such things are apparently not unknown.'

'A former student with a grudge? Plotting his revenge?'

'It's possible,' murmured Steiner. But if that were the case, where should he start looking for him? Was he still in the city at all? He had had ample time to make himself scarce.

'If a student was expelled from the Faculty there must be some record of it, mustn't there?' the physician said thoughtfully.

She had lit a candle to the Holy Virgin, and when Laurien came upon her she was kneeling in prayer before the statue, a veil covering her face. He only recognised her when she stood up again and passed him on her way out of the church. He followed her outside and across the market-place, where she stopped briefly to buy something at a stall. She had an attractive way of walking, dainty and graceful, and the black of her dress stood out among the bright colours worn by the market-women and the Cologne housewives. Then she moved on, and Laurien kept on walking behind her, past St. Andreas's and all the way to the street where her house was. Suddenly she turned round and looked him calmly in the face. Had she known all this time that he was following her? He came to an abrupt halt.

'Why are you creeping along behind me?' Sophie asked. He tried to say something, but his voice would not obey him. He gazed mutely at her, his expression a mixture of devotion and embarrassment.

'You were one of my late husband's students,' she said, smiling. He was able, at least, to produce a nod. And suddenly he found his voice again. 'Yes. I'm so sorry.'

'Really?'

What kind of a question was that?

'Would you like to come in? I've had some cakes baked and ordered some wine. The funeral feast is tomorrow, you know.'

He was so confused that he did not know what to do. Go inside with her? But that would make the worst possible impression. He could not simply enter her house like that. He ought to return to the Faculty.

But he followed her all the same.

'Tomorrow we'll be at the Ox. The house is too small for all the people who will be coming. And it will cost me a fortune, I can tell you.'

This was not how he had imagined a grieving widow. Now she tossed her hat on to the table, swept the veil from her face and flung open the windows. The door to Casall's study was ajar, and Laurien looked in. Every one of the books was lying open. There were even some spread out on the kitchen table, and others on the broad window sill. It was as if she had decided to decorate the whole house with his books. Now the rumours that Laurien had heard about her started to race around in his head. She's like a bitch on heat...she deceives her husband the moment he leaves the house...she reads his books...she enjoys it when he beats her...that's what she's like, there are women like that, so they say...

He gave a start when she placed a tankard of *Gruitbier* in front of him and invited him to sit down.

'N-no, I have a lecture starting soon,' he stammered almost

inaudibly. But she only laughed. 'Whatever the lecture is about, I'll explain it to you. What is it he's lecturing on, your Magister?'

'Thomas Aquinas's ethics.'

'Very well then, tell me: which is of greater worth, the faculty of understanding, or good will?'

He did not reply.

'Well? Don't you know the answer?'

'I think that he who has a good will is considered a good man,' he recited at last.

She nodded and sat down opposite him. Never in his whole life had he felt so helpless and intimidated. Her presence set him shivering as though he were in bed with a fever. And yet he could have gazed for hours at that beautiful face and into those cornflower-blue eyes that were watching him with such amusement.

'But you know that that's all nonsense, don't you?'

He nodded. It must be nonsense if she said so. He would have believed anything she told him, even if she had asserted that the whole world was as yellow as a lemon.

'He gave me a sentence to write down,' she suddenly burst out angrily. When she was annoyed there were creases on her high forehead and dimples at the sides of her chin. 'You separate everything that belongs together, but fail to recognise what does not belong together.'

Strange, he thought. So she too had been made to write out that sentence. That implied that she was also under suspicion.

'It sounds like a sentence from a scholastic text. Do you know what's odd about it? That whoever wrote it is right. For how can you separate the understanding from the will? Casall always said that in order to investigate something you have to break it down into its component parts. I wonder if you think so too?'

He no longer thought anything at all. He felt like a star that had slipped from its prescribed path and was tumbling aimlessly around in the universe. In a daze, he got to his feet.

'I must go now.'

'Yes, off you go. But first tell me your name.'

'Laurien. Laurien Thibold.'

'Goodbye for now, Laurien. We're sure to see each other at the funeral feast. The students Casall taught personally are invited.'

He nodded and thanked her, blushing, and then hastily left her house. Once out in the street he took a deep breath before setting off, confused and yet oddly elated, for the Scholarium.

Sophie had booked a whole room in the Ox, and a good-sized one, for more than fifty people were expected—the Magistri, the students that Casall had had the most to do with, the Chancellor and the Rector, and some prominent citizens. Casall's family, on the other hand, had not made the journey from Padua, for his body was to be transported to Italy.

That morning Sophie had been to the Provost's House to see the Chancellor, and had received some unwelcome news: since her house had been rented by the Faculty, now that Casall was dead she must vacate it. Suddenly she was a poor woman again. Her father, God rest his soul, had never been very successful; true, he had been a free burgher of the city and had made an adequate living as a simple copyist, but there had never been money to spare for luxuries. When Casall had asked for Sophie's hand in marriage—her father sometimes undertook writing tasks for the Faculty—she had felt as if the skies had cleared and she would bask in sunshine for the rest of her days. So much for that, she told herself now, as she walked home from the Provost's House. But at least the misery of her life with Casall was over. There were so many other men she might have married! Men had swarmed around her like bees around sage blossom but, avid for learning, she had thought nothing better could come her way than a Master of the Faculty.

She saw the leaded glass windows of the Ox sparkling in the sunshine. The inn sign swung slowly to and fro in the light breeze. A black dress, the funeral meal, a year of mourning, and then she would be free to do exactly as she liked.

But Sophie did not intend to wait as long as that.

At the funeral meal all the guests helped themselves liberally to food and drink. Sophie's mother was there, together with her stepfather and her two sisters. The Chancellor gave a short address. He said nothing of the mysterious circumstances of Casall's death, but instead spoke of what an extraordinary man Casall had been, a Magister first at the College of the Sorbonne in Paris and then at the University at Prague, before he had come to Cologne, where some of the most eminent scholars had taught even when the city had had only monastery schools. Then he praised the way in which Casall had upheld traditional teachings, and closed with the promise that the Faculty would have masses read for the dead man's soul and make the customary distribution of bread to the poor. At last the Chancellor resumed his seat.

Sophie was sitting with her sisters, who were members of the women's yarn-spinning guild. They were having an amusing time trying to marry their elder sister off again, even though they themselves were still single. There were such nice Masters who would surely be happy to marry her, and the young students weren't so bad either...

Sophie listened unmoved: let them laugh and joke if they liked. She looked across at their mother, whose face wore an anxious expression. Only twenty and already a widow. A bad omen, even if the men were already stealing covert glances at her. But Sophie knew that none of them would want to have her as a wife. More likely one of the students—but they had not a penny to bless themselves with, they were poorer than the mice in St. Ursula's.

'Do you see that one over there?' her sister Marie whispered into her ear. Sophie followed her gaze. She did not know which one Marie meant, for they were all sitting close together on the opposite side of the table: Laurien, Domitian and Siger Lombardi. The first quiet and shy, slightly built and with delicate features; the second the son of a wealthy advocate, an arrogant lad who did not know the meaning of poverty; the third, Siger, dark, with an untamed look about him, friendly enough but with an inscrutable, diabolical smile which he wore on his unshaven face as another man would wear a beard.

'Which of them do you mean?' Sophie whispered back.

'Which do you think?'

Domitian? No, he would not interest her. Too bright and sunny, a superficial and yet calculating character. 'The small one? He's quite a pretty fellow...'

Her sister shook her head.

'Surely not the dark one? He's one of the Masters.'

Yes, she did mean him. Casall had once said that he possessed an almost alarmingly keen intellect. A mind as sharp as a knife. He had studied in Paris and then taught at Prague and Erfurt. Erfurt, Casall had fulminated, his mouth twisted with contempt. The Faculty at Erfurt was dominated by the nominalists, with their radical views: it was because of them that faith was in danger of becoming divorced from pure scholarship. They were godless, those nominalists, for if objects alone possessed reality, then there was no longer a place for God in this world! Something about this colleague of his had always troubled Casall. His obscure past? The cynicism that leapt from his eyes like a snarling dog? His air of friendliness? That was certainly false—you could be sure that Lombardi held a knife ready to stab anyone in the back. His mother was from Brittany, it was said, his father an apothecary from Berne with a past as dubious as his son's. Was he the one, Sophie wondered, to help her start a new life?

'I'll ask him if he would like to have one of Casall's books,' Sophie murmured to herself as she waited impatiently for the party to break up at last. Gradually the guests began to disperse. The Masters remained for a while, talking quietly in a group, while most of the students were already leaving the room. Sophie's mother and sisters were going to come back to her house with her, but they could not leave while the Masters were still there. The students who were still standing with Lombardi thanked her for the meal, Domitian in his usual easy manner, Laurien with a timid nod. Lombardi merely smiled, whereupon she asked him straight out whether perhaps he would like to have the *Theologia summi boni*. He stared at her.

'I can't keep all of the books,' she explained, her cornflower-blue eyes gazing at him, all innocence, 'and I'm sure you can find a use for it.'

Domitian cast a quick glance at Lombardi. 'Yes, I am sure he can. He can always find a use for truths that haven't come from our clerics.'

Lombardi merely laughed. 'If you were to give me the book, I would yield to no one in my admiration of your generosity.'

Then she knew that she had not been wrong about him. He was not serious, but she had not expected that so soon. She was merely trying to make a new start, and as she fished in new waters, he was the hook she needed.

She had invited him into the garden at the back of the house and had laid the book, open, on the wall. He had bent over it and was turning the pages. A book like that cost a fortune—it had to be hand-copied—and it also had Casall's annotations in the margins, in his small, slightly crabbed handwriting which leaned first one way and then the other, apparently unable to settle on a single orientation.

He could feel her eyes fixed on him from behind. They were like sharp little darts, but he had the hide of an ox, not easily penetrated.

'Have you read it?' he asked, without looking up. He heard a clear 'Yes, indeed,' and nodded. Of course she had read it, her passion for books was well known.

'You are said to have claimed that there are no more godless places on earth than the Faculties of Arts,' came her voice once again from behind him.

'Who says that?' Lombardi swung round.

Strange, she had never noticed that below those dark locks he had blue eyes. A harmonious face, one might almost have called it Grecian, in the classical mould, had it not been for those piercing eyes.

'My late husband.'

All this time she had been sitting on the opposite wall. He now went over and sat down beside her. His hair smelled of rose water.

'Yes, there is nowhere more godless. If it is God you are looking for, then keep away from the Faculties of Arts, where we all constantly speak of God but no one believes in him.'

'You seek proofs of his existence.'

He laughed. 'Yes, but we don't find them.'

'That is not true. These books are full of proofs, ontological, hermeneutic, metaphysical…'

He looked at her with a smile. Did she really want to have

a discussion with him about ontological proofs of the existence of God? That was not what he had read in her eyes after the funeral meal a few days ago. She had been looking for proof of something quite different then.

'If you are prepared to give me this book, that will give me great happiness. But now I had better go, before people start to gossip.'

'Don't worry, you can stay. No one will cast aspersions on my character. I told all my neighbours that one of the Masters from the Faculty would be coming to take a look at my late husband's books.'

It would have been perfectly simple, she thought. But he hesitated. Had she been mistaken after all? It was certainly not the fear of God that was holding him back from going upstairs with her. Fear of wagging tongues? Perhaps.

'You won't be angry with me if I leave now?'

She laughed. No, she would not be angry. 'Will you come again?'

'Certainly.'

He stood up and took the book from the wall. She saw him to the door and let him out. And then she caught sight of Domitian and Laurien waiting on the other side of the street. She quickly closed the door.

At this late hour, when the night watchmen had already called ten o'clock, the streets were almost deserted. Steiner was on his way to see the Chancellor. In the moonlight he could make out the silhouette of Cologne's cathedral. The vague outline of a bat flitted past his lantern. Within the monastery walls there were hundreds of the creatures, hibernating under the old roof timbers of the former barn in winter, and in summer flying into the novices' hair when they retired to their dormitories after Compline.

Steiner quickened his pace and passed through the gateway. The monk who unlocked the gate for him murmured that the Provost was already awaiting him. In the inner courtyard his lantern was reflected in the basin of a well. Another monk promptly opened the door to him before he had even rung the bell, and he found himself in a bare white entrance hall. To the left was the refectory, to the right the chapel. There was a smell of fish and of sweat—the cold sweat of young novices terrified of the Devil.

Now Steiner knocked on a massive oak door and went in. The Chancellor was standing at his desk, writing something on a piece of paper. Steiner sat down and stared into the fire of pine woodchips.

'The magistrate has been making enquiries in the town to establish whether, apart from the people who found Casall, anyone else saw or heard anything that could help us clear up this murder,' the Chancellor said without preamble, interrupting what he was doing. 'I told him all I knew about your investigations so far. But I would like you to continue to keep your eyes and ears open. Pick up what information you can, and analyse the matter logically. After all, that is your *forte*. Find out the meaning of that statement on the vellum...' He laid down his pen and pushed the paper aside. 'You went to the archive and looked at the documents there. Why?'

'There have been students who have left the Faculty under a cloud. I wanted to look up their names.'

'And what did you find out?'

'There was no one among them who had any quarrel with Casall.'

Outside they could hear the trees rustling in the wind.

'I have made certain individuals give me samples of their handwriting,' Steiner went on. 'Laurien Thibold, Casall's widow and Domitian von Semper. Though of course anyone can disguise his handwriting if he wants to...'

The Chancellor shook his head and moved across to the window, standing with his back to the courtyard. 'It could have been the wife, of course, but do you seriously think she would kill her husband? Creep out of the house at night to commit an act of which she would immediately be suspected, since everyone knows how much she hated him? And Laurien? After only a month in the Faculty, would he really be likely to kill his teacher? Or Domitian von Semper? To be sure, Casall's beating must have deeply wounded his pride, but is that sufficient motive? We know far too little about what was really behind it all...'

Steiner leaned forward. 'That piece of vellum was not in the book merely by chance. But what does the murderer hope to achieve by it? What do we not see that does not belong together? I simply cannot make sense of it.'

'Perhaps we need to understand first of all what he means when he writes, "What belongs together, you separate, but you do not recognise what does not belong together." Whom does he mean by that "you"?'

Steiner laughed softly. 'Oh, I'm afraid he means us. And does he not have a point? Let us suppose that he has, or has had, something to do with the Faculty. What did he learn here? That to investigate things one must first take them to pieces. *Ratio fide illustrata* is a fine thing, but it does not help us here. I am only repeating what is common knowledge if I say that there are not a few who dislike this kind of scholarship—who would dearly love to see someone like William of Champeaux excommunicated. You know what Robert de Sorbon said: "Nothing is perfectly understood until it has been ground between the teeth of disputation."'

The Chancellor frowned. 'You are surely not suggesting that the riddle has something to do with our method of scholarship?'

'I am suggesting precisely that. Our murderer may be one of our sharpest critics, someone who is familiar with our form of disputation, who has practised it himself, or perhaps still does, but who thinks that the intellect is by no means capable of understanding everything—someone who would like to put human beings and objects back together again, who feels that we have torn them from their organic context, leaving them to wander about like lost souls…'

The Chancellor had turned away, and said nothing. After glancing briefly out of the window, he came back to his desk. Absently he groped for his pen. 'Lost souls,' he repeated under his breath, and then looked up. 'Do you think so too, Steiner? That we turn everything into lost souls? Including human beings?'

'Yes, I think we do. And I think that that is not the way to get closer to God. But that is not relevant to the matter at hand. We are concerned with the murder of Casall, and I am simply trying to understand the murderer's thought processes. Why did he cut the sleeves off Casall's coat? Why did he take the coat off him at all?'

'Do you know why?'

'No. I am just considering various possibilities. Assuming that he believes that our method is wrong, then he must regard the exact opposite as being right. But he also writes that we do not recognise what does not belong together. That is absurd, is it not? For is there anything that we have not yet torn apart?'

Outside it began to rain again. A warm, gentle shower on a summer's night. The rushing of the wind outside was replaced by the soft patter of raindrops. The Chancellor rested his head in his hands.

'Steiner, you are my only hope. I don't want a scandal.' He turned and went to fetch a candle from the sideboard, as if it might shed light on the case. 'What did you just say was the second part of the riddle? We do not recognise what does not belong together? By heaven, that really is pure sophistry…'

'What does not belong together?' Steiner asked insistently. 'Let us start with quite trivial things. Do the sleeve and the coat not belong together? Or the biretta and the coat? Or perhaps the boots and the sleeves? Or did the book not belong with the coat? It's useless. We shall get no further this way, and yet there must be some significance to it. The murderer cuts off the sleeves. He pulls off Casall's boots. He puts his book down in the middle of the street where it is sure to be found. The book belonged to the victim, there is no denying that. But perhaps the coat was not Casall's?'

'It was his coat,' the Chancellor replied gloomily, 'his wife identified it. She had only recently mended a tear in the shoulder.'

'Then the sleeves did not belong to it.'

The Chancellor shrugged his shoulders wearily. 'Even if that were the case, does it get us any further? Supposing that he cut Casall's sleeves off his coat and threw them into a pond. Then he cut the sleeves off a different coat and left them for us to find. I ask you, how does that help us? That cannot be what does not belong together. It must be something quite different.'

Steiner was suddenly overcome with fatigue. Perhaps the

Chancellor was right, and he was cudgelling his brain to no purpose. He was probably on completely the wrong track. He rose heavily to his feet, said goodnight, and let one of the monks show him out. The warm rain was refreshing and revived his flagging spirits. Steiner stopped and looked upwards. Behind him the gate in the monastery wall was being locked. Now he was alone in the street. The sleeves had been lying over there, just a few steps away, and if one took the turning towards St. Ursula's, there was his house, and Casall's body had been found in front of it. Steiner walked along the street. On the left were more walls, with gardens and orchards behind them. The shadowy figure seen by the fuller must have climbed over one of those walls. But what exactly had been the sequence of events? The murderer had killed Casall in front of Steiner's house, left him lying there, cut the pieces off his coat, scattered the garments around and also laid the book on the ground; he must have had the piece of vellum ready in his pocket beforehand. Casall's cries for help had roused people from their sleep, and at that point the murderer must still have been in the street. When the master fuller opened his door he was just running off. No one had chased after him, because they had stumbled upon the sleeves and the book. All the same, how was it possible that after carrying out the grisly deed he had had time to spread the various items around? How long would it take? Five minutes? Ten?

What did they not see that did not belong together? Steiner was so engrossed in his thoughts that he almost walked straight past his own house. Shaking his head, he turned back and took out his key.

The Master was standing at the lectern. The students were sitting on low stools before him, while the Licentiates and Baccalaurei sat on the benches, except when they took a turn at reading. Jakobus started to read from the *Summa Theologiae*. He read slowly and clearly, indicating new paragraphs, punctuation and capital letters, so that each student could write it down correctly. In this way he taught them about Thomas Aquinas's proofs of the existence of God, and as though God were watching him with approval, a ray of sunlight shone through the arched window straight onto the page.

'The existence of God may be proved in five ways. The first and most obvious way is that derived from movement…'

And so on, up to the fifth proof. The students' heads were bent as they industriously wrote down the text. Then Jakobus paused and passed the book to one of the Licentiates, who continued the reading.

Laurien raised his head. His hand hurt from writing so much, his neck was stiff from keeping his head bent, and so was his back from sitting crookedly on the stool. The movement of pens on paper made a scratching sound that filled the room, while in a monotonous, slightly nasal voice, the Licentiate began to give a commentary on the text that had been read. Laurien cupped his head in his hand and closed his eyes.

He's asleep, thought Steiner when, a little later, he softly opened the door and looked in. A delicate boy, but gifted. I ought to do something for him now that Casall isn't here any more. Who, he wondered, was giving him the *paedagogicum* now?

He tiptoed in and leaned against the wall. A Baccalaureus was standing beside him. 'Who is tutoring him now?' Steiner asked him in a whisper, jerking his chin in the direction of the tired boy.

'Nobody, so far. I thought Lombardi might do it. After all, he lives in the Scholarium. And he is in desperate need of a few pennies, the poor devil.'

Steiner looked at him doubtfully but made no reply and slipped out again. A cold draught gusted along the windowless passage and under his coat. Lombardi? In his lectures he had to conform to the statutes. What was to be presented in the lectures, how and for how long, and what commentaries at what time—there was no aspect of the lectures that was not governed by the statutes. Even the answers to the questions were prescribed. A donkey could learn in that way, Steiner thought with amusement. He himself would have welcomed a little more freedom in how they taught. But if Lombardi gave Laurien individual tuition there would be no witnesses, and Steiner did not trust Lombardi an inch. His father was from Berne and his mother from some God-forsaken place in Brittany. And besides, it was quite obvious that he was a follower of Ockham, whereas this university regarded itself as committed to Thomism.

Steiner stopped. Here the wind, trapped in the inner courtyard, whistled even more sharply around him. What nonsense, Steiner told himself reprovingly. Just because someone held a different view, that was no reason to harbour suspicions against him. And what kind of suspicions? That he might fill Laurien's head with strange ideas?

'Magister Steiner, may I have a word?'

Steiner turned round. Behind him stood Theophile Jordanus, with his shiny bald pate, clutching his billowing cloak and looking very worried.

'Jordanus? What is it?'

'Something quite disturbing, Steiner. A suspicion has arisen...'

Jordanus seemed extremely ill at ease. 'You know how on that evening we were all in the tavern together, and we all used each other as witnesses—reciprocally, as you might say. But now someone is claiming that Lombardi left the tavern for about half an hour during that time...'

Lombardi? Steiner looked at Jordanus in astonishment. Had he not just been thinking of Lombardi? But not in this connection. 'He left the tavern?'

'Yes. Magister Rüdeger remembers suddenly noticing that Lombardi had vanished. Like a ghost, without a word to anyone—and then he reappeared just before eleven. He says he was gone for at least half an hour.'

Steiner could not help laughing. 'Like a ghost? Perhaps he was just answering a call of nature.'

'For half an hour? Hardly! As soon as Rüdeger mentioned it to me, I remembered it too. Lombardi was not in his seat for quite some time.'

As Steiner tried to focus his memory, a sudden puff of wind danced round a little niche in the cloister occupied by a statue of the Virgin Mary, and blew out the candle in front of it.

'I am sorry, but I can't remember. I only know that he was

there, and if he was absent for half an hour I probably simply didn't notice.'

Theophile Jordanus turned pale. 'It would be a good thing if you had noticed, though,' he said softly.

'Yes, it would, but that cannot be helped. Did anyone else notice it?'

'Only those who were sitting immediately around him.'

Steiner nodded. That also explained why he himself could not remember, for he had been sitting at the other end of the table. 'I will have a word with him,' he said, patting Jordanus on the shoulder.

Then he left the College and hurried off in the direction of the market-place.

While the lectures were going on the Scholarium was a hive of domestic activity. The women who worked there cooked and washed, swept the rooms and brought in firewood. They exchanged banter with Steiner, for he had an air of paternal kindliness about him, quite unlike the dwarf, who ran his Scholarium with rigorous discipline. Steiner came upon him in the refectory, drinking a solitary tankard of beer. Seeing him come in, de Swerthe self-consciously pushed it aside and stood up.

'Is Magister Lombardi in?'

'No, he has gone out to buy some paper. But he will be back very soon. Have you come about Laurien?'

At this very moment the door opened and Lombardi entered. Looking slightly surprised, he took off his cloak and tossed a bundle of paper onto the table.

'I need to talk to you,' Steiner said curtly.

There were not many books in Lombardi's room. Generally he had to borrow the texts he needed, and some people said that he was even poorer than his students.

'You have it in you to study to a higher level if you so chose,' Steiner began, sitting down on a stool near the window. 'Why do you stay on here as a Master of the *septem artes liberales* when you could gain a professorship in *ius canonicum*?'

Lombardi laughed and leaned back against the wall, folding his arms. 'It suits me this way. I don't care to be confined like a horse in a pen.'

'The reason I'm here is, er…' Steiner began, searching for the right words, '…well…on the evening when Casall was killed, you left the tavern for a while. Is that true?'

Lombardi said nothing. He looked out of the window, at the debris of the ruined house. After a while he nodded.

'That's right. For about half an hour.'

'You should have told me that from the start. Now I am hearing it from others, which is not good. Where were you?'

'Well, let's say I was with a woman. Is that enough for you? I am certainly not Casall's murderer, because in half an hour I could not possibly have gone from St. Kunibert's to your house, murdered Casall, cut up the coat and got back to the tavern. That's obvious, isn't it?'

It would have been difficult, Steiner thought, but not impossible. If one sliced the half-hour into three like a cake, there would be ten minutes to get there, ten to commit the murder and scatter the things, and ten to get back. Though in that case he could not have escaped over the wall, for then he would have taken considerably longer. Five minutes just to get through the gardens and orchards. Steiner shrugged his shoulders. 'You know the text that the murderer left lying near the body. Does it suggest anything to you? Have you any idea what he is trying to tell us?'

Lombardi pushed himself away from the window sill and came closer. Now there was a flash of mischief in his blue eyes. 'I'm sure you yourself have given it a great deal of thought.'

'Yes indeed, I think of nothing else these days. I believe the murderer is someone belonging to the Faculty, someone with a poor opinion of our method. That is one aspect of the riddle. But I can't make anything of the other aspect. What does he mean by saying that we do not recognise what does not belong together? The sleeves were separated from the coat…but after all, we could see that.'

Lombardi nodded. 'Why did he cut off those parts? Do you know what I keep wondering? Might he in fact have had an urge to mutilate the body—to cut off the head and arms? Perhaps at the last moment he shrank from such a gruesome deed and mutilated the coat instead? I'll tell you what I think. The murderer was in a sense holding a mirror up to us, because in our disputations we divide everything into its component parts. Including man: here is his will, here is his intellect, here is his heart, and somewhere or other is the rest of him. All neatly gutted and filleted like a trout for the table. That is why the murderer cut up the coat.'

Somewhere a door closed with a thud. Then the quick steps of the students came clattering along the corridor: lectures were over. Every now and then the voices of the kitchen-maids could be heard as they served up the meal.

Lombardi is right, thought Steiner. But this did not bring them any closer to discovering what it was that they failed to recognise as not belonging together.

'Very well,' he said thoughtfully, 'we know why the murderer acted precisely in that way. He is opposed to our method and has demonstrated the fact in his own peculiar manner. But that is only the first part. We still don't know what it is that does not belong together.'

'Were the boots Casall's?' asked Lombardi.

'Yes.'

'And the coat?'

'Yes.'

'The sleeves?'

Steiner did not answer. How could you tell?

'The biretta?'

Again, no answer.

'The book?'

'Yes, unquestionably.'

'Find out whose the sleeves were.'

Steiner stood up. They could hear the rattle of spoons from the refectory.

'You mean that I should have every Master's coat checked?'

'Yes, why not? Perhaps the sleeves really didn't belong to Casall's coat and can point us towards something that might be important.

Suppose that one of the Masters has a coat that has lost its sleeves. That might suggest that the murderer was acting on his instructions...'

Steiner opened the door. This would mean asking each of the Masters to show him every coat he possessed. 'They would all feel that I suspected them,' he muttered as he left. Behind him Lombardi laughed aloud. 'Why don't you start right away, with me?'

Steiner had not started with him. No doubt he would consider carefully whether to tar them all with the same brush, whether to stigmatise them all in this way. And yet, Lombardi knew the idea would give him no peace, squeezing out all other thoughts, so that in the end he would do it out of sheer desperation.

Deep in thought, Lombardi stirred his spoon around in his soup. All around him there was no talking, only the slurping sound of the students eating. The Prior had already finished his meal and was sitting with his hands folded together on the table. My God, Lombardi thought, I shall go mad if I have to live in this dreary Scholarium for much longer. Here everyone creeps around like sin incarnate in the kingdom of God, while the city is full of pleasures and amusements. The atmosphere is gloomy, the food meagre, the rooms dirty, and in winter the cold seeps in through the doors. Domitian and Laurien spoke little, because their lack of an alibi was weighing on their minds. They were now even closer than before. Laurien carried Domitian's books, cleaned his shoes and seemed humbly devoted to him. The thought suddenly struck Lombardi; what if they were both in it together? What if the one had claimed to be sick and the other had gone home early—what if it had all been an ingenious plan? But he dismissed the idea. Laurien was no killer. He could more readily believe it of Domitian: ambitious, clever, devious, blue-blooded, arrogant at times, he would be capable of anything. And then there was that business of the thrashing—the story had gone the rounds of the whole Faculty. Was it possible that the much-lauded son of the famous lawyer had never come to terms with that beating, that insult, and had nursed an implacable hatred in his heart ever since?

'You are to take over the scholar Laurien's *paedagogicum*,' said a high, clear voice close beside him. Lombardi had not noticed the diminutive figure of de Swerthe coming up behind him.

He looked up. 'Is that an instruction from Magister Steiner?'

'Yes. He gave me the message for you just before he left. You can start straight away.'

At least it meant ready money, something that he was not unduly blessed with. Outside the sun was shining in a clear blue sky, the colour of liverwort. If only he could be down by the river, stretched out in the sun, looking at the barges lying at anchor in the harbour, where the stench of fish alternated with the aroma of spices, depending on what had just been unloaded.

Instead he summoned Laurien to come to his meagre quarters and dictated Aristotle to him.

The room in which Laurien was now to receive his lessons was every bit as dingy as the rest of the Scholarium. He sat on a stool and Lombardi stood at his lectern, reading aloud or giving explanations. Laurien wrote down what Lombardi dictated, leaning close to the burning taper, for the narrow windows let in virtually no light. Lombardi had begun by explaining that he would instruct Laurien in all the subjects—not only grammar, rhetoric and logic, but also music, arithmetic, geometry and astronomy. The *trivium* and the *quadrivium*. As Laurien had no books of his own, Lombardi would have to lend some to him. But he could also try to study in the mendicant monks' library, using the chained books there. Lombardi listed more and more titles that would be relevant to his studies. *De consolatione, Summa theologiae, De amicitia*, and so on, endlessly.

During one of these lessons Lombardi read part of Aristotle's discussion of categories to him. There was a long-standing and unresolved controversy over this in the Arts Faculties, with the result that two distinct camps had formed. In Erfurt the nominalists were in favour, while elsewhere the realists dominated. But if Laurien had been asked what his own view was, he would not have been able to say. One group believed only in the existence of individual things, the other in the concept, the idea of things. How could one distinguish between a thing and the idea of a thing, Laurien wondered.

Lombardi's voice was making Laurien drowsy. Had he not

been obliged to write the text down, which kept his mind alert to some extent, he would have fallen fast asleep. Furthermore, he had difficulty in grasping it all. What were these categories over which the philosophers felt the need to fight such bloody battles?

Lombardi first read out the text and then provided a commentary, in which he drew upon other commentators and translators. As he piled commentary upon commentary, a tangle of questions began to form in Laurien's mind, becoming ever more impenetrable until in the end he could only stare at Lombardi open-mouthed.

'Now,' said Lombardi at last, managing a smile, 'now, the issue is obviously the nature of things and of concepts. Which, then, are of higher value: universal ideas or individual things? What do you think?'

'I think individual things are of higher value, for if we did not have them we could also have no inkling of the general concept of them,' Laurien stammered, unsure of himself.

Lombardi gave a bittersweet smile. 'So you would give precedence to the individual things. That would be the position of the nominalists. Aristotle himself does not adopt a clear position on this. Let us pursue our questioning. William of Champeaux maintains that even if no white thing existed, the colour white would exist all the same.'

'But that's absurd!' Laurien exclaimed. 'How could the colour white exist if there were nothing of that colour? Besides, white is a quality, not a thing.'

'That may be so,' replied Lombardi. 'But each thing has qualities in order that it may be recognised and distinguished from other things. Thus the quality white belongs to the thing. No thing without a colour and no colour without a thing. What is the difference?"

Laurien had nothing to say. Now he could no longer see the difference either. Was there nothing that could manage without colour? But he could tell that this was not what Lombardi had in mind, and so he replied cautiously:

'You separate the idea from the thing. You take the white away from the white lily and say, "There is the lily, and there is the white." Is that right?'

'Yes, more or less. But we will talk about that tomorrow.'

Lombardi closed his book. Giving Laurien no more than a cursory nod, he left the room. Laurien remained seated and scribbled down the last sentence. Suddenly he thought again of the reflection of the tree in the water. Was that what Lombardi had been trying to explain to him? The image in the water and the tree growing in the earth? But were they not one and the same? Domitian was right. Here things which belonged together were separated, for did not the thing and the idea of it belong together? Here, it seemed, they chopped the whole world up into pieces and placed them in a series of boxes just as other people sorted their clothes into different chests. But what did they do with the doubtful bits that were left over?

'A peculiar way of thinking,' Laurien muttered as he gathered his papers together and stood up to go.

Steiner was standing by the harbour, looking pensively out onto the river. They had shown their trust in him by asking him to investigate the matter of Casall's death, so that they could tell the city council and the magistrates that they had people of their own to deal with what might be called the philosophical aspect of the crime. And here he was, going back to them and demanding to inspect their coats. For philosophical reasons, naturally! Because that was what method demanded. There was nothing more important than method. Even here at the harbour it was clearly in evidence, providing a well-defined framework. Harbourmaster, bailiff, customs official, each had his function. Today the bustling throng of traders, bargemen and officials irritated him, although normally he loved the harbour and its lively activity more than almost anything else. Except perhaps his studies. They were all he had. Now and then he would visit a bath-house, but never a brothel, nor did he indulge in other pleasures. He had never possessed a woman, except perhaps for *Sapientia*, but she was not of flesh and blood—she was an ethereal being hovering above him. A union of that kind was extremely complicated. So he needed a counterpoise, and when he saw these people in their colourful clothes—he himself wore his dark coat at all times, which could not be said of some other Masters—he shared their pleasure in the simple things of life. He sometimes went out in a boat to watch the fishermen at work, and thought: this is the kind of contemplation that suits me.

Now he sat down on a low wall and watched the people who were standing in front of the corn beam. A bell struck six. In an hour's time the gates would be closed, and then it would be expensive to get into the city. Or out of it. He thought of Domitian von Semper. If the investigation of the coats yielded nothing he would have to take another very serious look at that young nobleman.

Altogether there were twenty-one Masters of the seven liberal arts. Eleven of them had rooms in the colleges and the rest lodged in houses rented from the city. Steiner started with the colleges; then came the *bursae*, which had a more worldly ambience, and lastly the *hospitium*, where only one Master resided and where the poorest students lived in an almost monastic atmosphere of discipline and quiet. Finally Steiner approached the Masters living in rented houses. Always with the same question: 'Could you show me your coat? Have you more than one?'

He was met with incomprehension or open resentment; hardly any of his colleagues could understand why he was doing this. He did not enter into lengthy explanations, but merely offered hints or observed that he was simply trying to establish the truth. Twenty-one Masters and twenty-one coats, all complete with sleeves and a biretta. And as he was about to make his last visit, he could only silently shake his head over his own inadequacy and think, what nonsense this is.

Lombardi, whom he had left till last, received him with a grin and immediately produced his coat. He said he had no other.

'So the sleeves are not what we're looking for, nor are the birettas,' Steiner murmured, discouraged, though if the truth be told, he had never imagined that the answer could be anything so banal.

He went to the Provost's Residence to see the Chancellor, and requested that a search be made of the two student dormitories in the Scholarium in St. Gereonstrasse. Perhaps something might be found there that would confirm the suspicion relating to Domitian von Semper. Though sceptical, the Chancellor let himself be persuaded to authorise the search.

'He asked to see all the Masters' coats.'

Griseldis laughed as she put the white marguerites into a jug. Sophie stood beside her, gazing gloomily at the dazzling white of the flowers.

'When are you moving?'

'Tomorrow.'

She had to leave Casall's house, which the city had rented for him. Fortunately she had been offered a small room. But that was not the worst of it. Her family refused to support her unless she lived at home with them, and she could expect nothing from Casall's family. So where was she to find the money to live on? True, there were charitable houses, and the city gave some support to poor widows, but this was not what she wanted. What she wanted was something that was not open to her. Women might study in convent schools, but not at the university. Women could not gain a licentiate qualifying them to teach and lecture, for how could it be considered proper for women to impart knowledge to men?

'Listen,' Griseldis now said in a low voice, 'if the idea horrifies you, then forget I ever mentioned it. But give it some thought, because it's a discreet way to make some money. You're young and pretty, and men would like you...'

Griseldis had been doing it for months. She knew an innkeeper who procured women for men. She earned good money, and because she was not a whore but a respectable citizen she could demand whatever amount she happened to need. And the men paid up. Whores might be prepared to sell themselves for no more than a handful of cherries—Griseldis would have scorned to be like them.

'You couldn't have done it here, living in this house,' she said now, looking intently at Sophie's face, which remained fixed and expressionless. 'But in your new room no one will know you and you can slip out without anyone noticing. The place where you can have the assignations is not too close to the centre. And the men conceal their faces, and come late at night. So long as you take a little care, no one will ever know.'

'I'm not a whore,' was all that Sophie said.

'No, of course not. You simply earn a bit of extra money and stop when you've got enough. The men are respectable, well-dressed and free with their money.'

'And what if it gets out?'

'If you're careful it won't.'

Sophie looked around. Tomorrow she would be moving out. Most of the furniture would have to be left behind, because the house had been let furnished. All she could take with her were Casall's books, the crockery, her bed, a chest for clothes, and a table and chairs. She could have sold the books, but that was out of the question. They were the only things of value that she possessed.

'Shall I ask him?'

She was startled. 'Who?'

'The innkeeper! Shall I ask him whether he can do anything for you?'

'No, for heaven's sake, no!'

They left the house and headed towards the Holy Apostles. So as not to leave a Master's widow in complete penury, one of the city's wealthy families had offered her a room in their big house on the Heumarkt. A flight of stairs led from a back entrance to the upper floor. The room, which was light, was situated at the front of the house; cattle were traded down below, so that the noise of beasts and dealers travelled straight up to the window. As yet the room was empty. As empty as Sophie, who stood forlornly in the middle of it, covering her ears.

'It'll be better tomorrow,' Griseldis said, 'when the room's furnished.'

Sophie nodded. Tomorrow.

It had been his first disputation, and now he was leaning against the wall exhausted, his back aching. Even on a Saturday they did not leave you in peace. But he had not been called upon to say anything, for he was a mere *scholar simplex* and was expected to keep quiet. The ones who spoke were the Masters, the Licentiates and the Bachelors. The Masters were all obliged to attend this event, and to wear their coats. The same procedure was followed each time. One of the Masters proposed a thesis, and the Bachelors then had to find the arguments and counter-arguments which, on the basis of *ratio* and of tradition, necessarily followed from it.

This time it was Steiner's turn. 'Not he who has a good understanding is considered a good man, but he who has a good will. That is the issue that we are about to examine.'

Laurien looked up.

'Now,' Steiner continued, 'how can it be that the will is superior to the faculty of understanding?'

One of the Bachelors, a fat fellow with a bloated face, raised his hand. Everyone knew that he would dearly have loved to study for a Master's degree but had not the necessary means, and he always pushed himself forward. He announced that he would like to comment on the subject.

'A different passage states that the understanding is nobler than the will. It seems to me that Thomas himself was not quite sure which should have precedence.'

Steiner nodded but said nothing. Now another Baccalaureus took his turn, while Laurien's eyelids again began to droop. He had very different matters going through his mind. He needed money for paper and for the women who did his washing. He had done the sums over and over again, money for paper, for wine, for the baths, the cook, the barber, the beds...at this rate he would end up begging for alms in the market place...

'...and yet it is the same. The will is the highest virtue, but what is it without the power of understanding? He says that reason is perfected in the contemplation of truth, for man is man insofar as he is rational. Thus the understanding is also superior to love, he says, and the understanding ranks higher than moral...'

And so it went on for some time, until Laurien's head was spinning. Steiner's next question related to the Thomist proofs of the existence of God.

'Now, I maintain that something unmoved cannot exist at all, for how should it then move anything else?'

The fat Baccalaureus answered: 'But there must be a constant that moves things. This is the first effective cause, as Thomas demonstrates in his second proof. Thus we have to distinguish between the movement and the cause, for the two things cannot be one and the same.'

And the next student continued, 'There is something that has its necessity in itself, just as it has its movement and its cause in itself. And that is God. So God is…'

Laurien, who had just been thinking of his unpaid bills, silently shook his head. How was it that he could think about the barber and at the same time follow the disputation? But he could. And it annoyed him exceedingly that he was condemned to silence.

'How am I supposed to wash myself if I have no water?' he whispered to Domitian, who was sitting beside him.

How could something that was unmoved create movement, Laurien wondered, confused. How could God, as the Unmoved, create movement? Everybody knew that movement only took place if a thing acquired momentum. But it could only acquire momentum if it came into contact with something that also had momentum. Could something immobile produce momentum? The wind produced waves, and waves produced more waves. But what if there had been no wind? Where would the waves come from then? From God, would have been the answer given by those at the front who were still carrying on the disputation. Whenever they were stuck for an answer they had a magic formula on the tip of their tongues: God. God was there to plug every gap—God, a construct that was like a ghostly presence flitting through the disputation.

Suddenly he heard Lombardi's voice. 'There is no first entity that is moved by nothing else. On this level of reasoning one cannot reach any conclusion. Suppose we compare God to an apple tree. It stands fixed and rigid, and yet there is enough life in it to produce apples. Have you ever heard it do that? I mean, the way that the tree gets its apples—is it audible? Can one smell it? Can one taste it? Can one feel it? No, it simply happens. Certainly we can prune the tree so that it produces more and better apples, but its mystery remains hidden from us. God said to the tree: furnish man with apples, just as he said to the hen, furnish man with eggs. You cannot make movement the basis of your argument: that may be appropriate for the fall of a stone, but not for the mystery of life.'

A murmur arose, low and disquieting. No one had ever argued in this way during a disputation.

'The mystery of life?' repeated the fat Baccalaureus in astonishment. 'Does that not also have to be moved in order to come into being?'

'Yes, indeed,' said one of the Licentiates, amused, 'that really does require some energetic movement.'

There was a ripple of laughter. Even Steiner smiled.

'If everything were in a circle, there would be no need of a beginning,' said Lombardi. 'Then the last mover would also be the prime mover...'

'And where would this circle be?' asked the Baccalaureus in a venomous tone.

'It would be everywhere,' Lombardi answered calmly. 'It would be the principle of the world and of the universe.'

'And God? Where are you going to put God? At the beginning or the end?'

'There would be no beginning and no end. That is the principle of the circle.'

He proceeded no further with his answer. But it was clear what its logical implication would be. Steiner brought the disputation to an abrupt close.

That evening two men acting on the Chancellor's instructions arrived at the Scholarium in St. Gereonstrasse and inspected the students' dormitories. They also searched the chests in the corridor in which their clothes were kept, leafed through the books, perused the notes, rummaged in the beds and pulled off the blankets, but apart from a quantity of fleas hopping about they found nothing. Steiner stood at the door watching them. Had the murderer—had Domitian von Semper or perhaps even Laurien—left no traces at all? Where might the murderer have been when he wrote his message?

'I could just as well have written it in the College,' came Domitian's voice, suddenly, from behind Steiner. He joined him, smiling. 'I wouldn't be so stupid as to leave my incriminating notes here.'

'No, I'm sure you wouldn't,' Steiner replied equably.

'So you do still suspect me?'

'Yes, I do.'

'And Laurien? Might he not equally well have done it?'

'Possibly. Yes, that is also possible.'

'I didn't do it,' said Domitian curtly. 'And Laurien wouldn't hurt a fly. This is absurd.'

Steiner said nothing. Yes, it was absurd, but there was nothing to point him in any other direction.

Now, in the evening, it was quiet outside her window. The cattle traders had gone, and there was a pungent smell of urine in the air. Some heavy clouds which had drifted across the sky as the sun was setting now hung there, obscuring the moon. A sign creaked on its hooks as a wind came up.

Sophie was freezing. The cold had enveloped her like a second skin, like a coating of frost. Holy Mother of God, what was she doing here? Why was she not training for some respectable occupation? Was she too lazy? Too indolent? Too proud? They would never let her, a woman, study at the university—the very idea was laughable. So she'd show them what she was capable of. Griseldis had said that that was a good and easy way to earn money. Just one now and again, no more than that. Each client would cover the cost of a book, and she would read until the letters came popping out of her eyes. She had no practical use for her reading, and yet she wanted to know everything. Where had it come from, this thirst for knowledge that was like a curse?

And yet she had told Griseldis that *that* was something she would not even consider. Perhaps she should seek employment as a copyist. This thought made her feel a little calmer. Wrapping her cloak around her, she went downstairs. The first drops of rain were already falling. Outside the house she hesitated; she did not like walking through the streets alone at night, but Griseldis was expecting her. After crossing the Heumarkt, she received a sudden shock. Might he accompany her, asked a cheery masculine voice, and there behind her stood Lombardi. He was wearing a doublet and hose and pointed shoes, and there was no biretta covering his dark curls. If he were not wearing that dark cloak he would look like a Greek god. They walked on together.

'Is there any new information about the murderer?' asked Sophie.

'He is thought likely to be either a student or a Master in the Faculty of Arts,' he replied. 'Who else would think of setting us a philosophical riddle?'

'And have you solved it, between you?'

'No.'

'I heard that Magister Steiner had inspected all the Masters' coats. That won't have made him popular.'

'Oh,' Lombardi said, mockingly, 'the accepted version is that he was only trying to eliminate us as suspects. And he has succeeded in doing that.'

'It couldn't have been the Masters in any case,' Sophie murmured, 'since they were all together at the inn. One for all, all for one.'

Suddenly the heavens opened, and the street was running with water, window shutters were blown open, branches snapped off trees. 'Come on,' shouted Lombardi, taking Sophie by the hand. Further on in the direction of the Berlich they came to a tavern where the host was struggling to close the door that the storm had flung open.

They sat down on a bench and ordered wine. Outside the windows thunder and lightning raged. The innkeeper crossed himself. Innumerable church bells began to peal. Rain and hail beat against the windows, and soon water was washing under the door. Yet more bells started pealing, and the roar of thunder echoed through the streets. Once again the storm tore the door open, and a small knot of men pushed their way in, seeking shelter from the storm. Lightning has struck the Church of the Apostles, one of them cried, and in no time the magistrate's officers came rushing along the street.

There was pandemonium. Someone said that a bunch of ragged villains had looted a goldsmith's shop after the hail had smashed his windows. At the cathedral building site some scaffolding had collapsed, burying two women as they were hurrying past. By now the inn was so packed that there was barely enough room left for a mouse. But still a group of men pushed and shoved their way in—fellows whom the innkeeper had never seen before. He would have liked to get rid of them, but they shouted for beer and clearly had no intention of going back out into that hell. At some point one of them took hold of an axe and held it to the innkeeper's throat. If he did not bring them beer that instant he would make a handsome corpse—and, after all, they were willing to pay, their pockets were full of money…

Sophie wanted to leave. Better to endure rain and thunder than stay here. The innkeeper had hurried out to the back to fetch beer for the waiting ruffian who still stood there with the murderous tool glinting in his hand. Lombardi got up and drew her through the crowd and out into the street. As they left the inn they saw lightning strike a tree diagonally opposite, in front of the ladies' convent.

Later Sophie could not remember how it had all started. One of those men from the inn must have grabbed hold of one of the ladies from the convent and danced around with her in the street. And then suddenly a fight had broken out. With Sophie in the midst of it. In unspeakable terror she had pressed herself against the convent wall, which was being showered with splinters of wood. Because of the rain the tree was no longer burning, but now all at once it came crashing down. And then, right beside her, she saw the fellow trying to dance with the convent lady, who, no doubt thinking that the end of the world had come, was screaming and doing her utmost to fight him off. With a laugh he placed his powerful hands around her neck and begun to squeeze. The lady sank to her knees, but instead of letting go he squeezed harder and harder, with a deadly calmness. No one moved, everyone just stood around, gaping. And then suddenly he himself fell to the ground. Dead. Felled as though by another bolt of lightning. And there behind him stood Lombardi, holding in his hand a knife dripping with blood. Sophie closed her eyes.

'He saved the lady's life,' the people shouted to the constable who now came running up and bent over the dead man. The lady was breathing with difficulty and fingering the strangulation marks on her neck, the red imprint of the hands with which he had tried to throttle her because she would not dance with him. The dead man, as everyone could now see, had an ear missing. Might he not be a thief and murderer, a fugitive from justice? The thunderstorm had probably lured him from his hideout in the hope of some looting. But why should a fellow like that want to force a convent lady to dance with him?

Sophie opened her eyes again. The body was still lying there, and Lombardi was talking to the constable in a calm, matter-of-fact manner. Where had he got the knife from, the constable asked. Lombardi replied that he always carried it when he went out after dark. He was Siger Lombardi, a Master of the seven liberal arts, and lived in the Scholarium in St. Gereonstrasse. The officer nodded. By the light of a lantern the other ladies of the convent had gathered around their maltreated sister, who now came forward, still trembling at the knees, to thank Lombardi. He gave her a smile, and she silently pressed his hand and turned away.

The Feast of St. John had gone by, the yellow flowers had been harvested. Now poppies and cornflowers were blooming in the fields, and the wheat stood tall. Waves rippled along the sandy shore, and sunbeams floated on the water. Further down the river, Steiner could see a small house offering refreshments. Only a few customers were sitting there. He was hungry and thirsty. Even from here he could see the fish being grilled on skewers over a fire.

Jordanus was already waiting for Steiner. He too had come on foot, though on the other side of the river, and from the landing jetty to here had been another hour's walk. As a result the soles of his feet were excruciatingly painful. Steiner ordered one of the grilled fish and a beer. Then he looked at Jordanus's weary, suffering face and laughed. Some way to the west, on the opposite bank, the city could be seen glowing in the heat.

'I'm getting old,' said Jordanus, taking off his shoes. 'I feel as if I've been on a pilgrimage to Santiago de Compostela, whereas all I've done is one walk along the other side of the river, and I even came half the way by boat.'

'But if we spend all our time sitting over our books we shall quite forget what the real world looks like, Magister Jordanus,' Steiner said jokingly.

'Haven't we done that anyway? Sometimes when I listen to the disputations I have the feeling that we are losing ourselves in dreams and fantasies. That out there…' he pointed at the fields round about, 'surely that is reality. Could you cultivate a field? I mean properly, sowing the seed and later harvesting the crop?'

Steiner shook his head. 'No. I'm not a farmer. And neither are you. That's just the way it is, some till the fields of nature and we till those of the mind.'

'But perhaps nature's fields are better…' murmured Jordanus.

'You really are in low spirits.'

Suddenly Jordanus leaned forward and took hold of Steiner's sleeve. 'You shouldn't have done that, asking the Masters to show you their coats. That creates bad feeling.'

'I know, but I wanted to be sure. Now I am. Every one of us is above suspicion.'

'Except for Lombardi.'

'Yes, possibly. But he would have to be a magician to get to my house and back in half an hour and murder Casall in between. And he swears that he was not gone for more than half an hour.'

'He may be mistaken. I tell you, Steiner, Lombardi is an equation with two unknowns. I think there is something suspect about him. Did you hear that the evening before last he saved the life of a lady from the convent? By plunging a knife into her attacker's back? You know what happens in such cases. The good people of Cologne are hailing him as a hero—in fact he has considerably enhanced the prestige of the Faculty!'

'But the fellow was only trying to dance with her,' Steiner said.

'He almost strangled her. She is still confined to bed in a thoroughly weakened state. And nobody else was prepared to come to her aid. They all just stood by, looking on.'

'Until Lombardi came along.'

'Yes, until Lombardi came along.'

'He's rather too quick to use a knife, don't you think?'

Jordanus shook his head. 'What if he is, Steiner? Whatever one may say against him, the fact remains that if he had not taken such prompt action the lady might now be dead. True, some will say what of it, she's only an old maid and well past her prime, but a life is a life.'

Steiner downed his beer. He stretched his legs out in front of him and squinted into the sun. 'Jordanus, I'm not getting anywhere. I admit that it was Lombardi's idea to check the coats, and it was quite a sensible one. But the coats are not the answer. I'm completely on the wrong track, and I can't see any solution however much I puzzle over it. I'm beginning to think it was a madman who left us that piece of parchment, and now he's killing himself laughing, watching us rack our brains and torment ourselves. Lady *Sapientia* has deserted me. I think I shall have to concentrate on Domitian von Semper—that seems to me the only line of enquiry I have, because on his way back to the Scholarium he could certainly have come along Marzellenstrasse. Perhaps he chanced to encounter Casall there and seized the opportunity—'

'Very well. Let us suppose that he was the only person in the street at the time. Sophie Casall and Laurien were asleep in their beds. Then *he* must have set the riddle and cut up the coat—'

'What was there apart from the coat?'

'The shoes, but they belonged to Casall. His wife can testify to that.'

'She also testified that the main part of the coat was his. What if she is lying?'

'And what if tomorrow the world stands on its head? Steiner, what *do* you have faith in? You must have *some* firm ground under your feet when you are hunting around.'

'That's just the problem,' Steiner muttered. 'But what if she really is lying?'

'Why should she lie? To protect herself?'

'What if they are all lying?'

'You don't mean that seriously.'

'No,' Steiner said quietly, 'I don't mean it seriously...what do you know about Lombardi?'

'Not much. That he is clever and gained his Master's degree when he was only twenty. In Paris. Then he went to Prague and later to Erfurt. That he has a weakness for Ockham and Bacon. That he kills men who try to attack convent ladies. That he is not exactly wealthy. That he is a handsome fellow and a cynic…'

'…and that he would be capable of leading us all by the nose,' grunted Steiner. For a while they were silent, watching some children playing on the bank, until Jordanus asked where Lombardi had actually been during that half hour. 'With a woman, but I did not ask her name. He thinks that if I can do simple arithmetic I'll know that he cannot be the murderer. So he doesn't need to tell me anything. But I should still like to know.'

From the opposite bank they could hear the church bells pealing in canon. The gates would be closing in an hour's time, and Jordanus thought with horror of the return walk. He put his shoes on again with a grimace of pain. 'I shall hardly be able to walk…'

Steiner grinned. 'Then you'll just have to spend the night here, my dear colleague. I hear that they have quite decent beds in their houses.'

Jordanus stood up. 'It's like fire,' he said almost reverently. 'It's as though I had a *thousand* fires burning under my feet. Now I know what it is like for martyrs to feel the fire, and not only under the soles of their feet. O merciful heaven, release me…'

They set off. Jordanus had decided to take off his shoes again, and he hobbled along, barefoot, at Steiner's side. Then in the distance he saw an ox-cart approaching across the meadows. Some trader or farmer on his way home.

'I must make him give me a ride,' Jordanus exclaimed joyfully. 'He must take me to the boat.'

Jordanus began to cry out as if he were in mortal agony. The cart stopped, and the farmer looked towards them. Jordanus beckoned and gesticulated. God be praised, thought Steiner with relief, as the cart at last turned towards them.

Jordanus offered the farmer a sum of money if he would take him to where the boat was moored that would convey him to the opposite bank. And so up he climbed into the cart, while Steiner continued on foot. He still had a good half-hour's walk ahead of him, and as he walked along, suddenly he thought he heard a voice.

'Steiner!'

He spun round. It could only have been Jordanus, but Jordanus was sitting in the jolting cart, bending over his aching feet again. Strange, there was no one else here.

With a shake of his head Steiner continued on his way.


Sophie had been born just outside the gates of Cologne. Some time later the city had engaged her father as a copyist, and the family had moved into the city and acquired the rights of citizenship. Now that Casall was dead and her father too had been in his grave for a year, her mother insisted that she return home. But Sophie refused. She was not a child any more, she made her own decisions. She had two years of hell behind her, a marriage full of beatings and humiliations. There would be no more of that. She did not intend to be handed on from one lord and master to another. Her sisters would like her to become yarn-spinners like themselves, saying that she could join the guild and earn her own living, but Sophie had about as much talent for making yarn as Griseldis had for marital fidelity. She had first met Griseldis in her sisters' yarn-spinning workshop, where Griseldis had worked for a time. Griseldis was the exact opposite of Sophie; she always knew what she wanted. And so Sophie was not surprised that she was able to become ever more affluent by selling her body, without any harm coming of it. Any questions from her husband she dismissed with a shrug, and she pretended that she was still employed at the spinning workshop. The fool did not even notice what was going on, since, being a trader, he was hardly ever at home.

Sophie wished she were like Griseldis, clear-headed and single-minded. But she lacked her unscrupulousness. She got caught up in complications and moral difficulties. It was more in her nature to think things through and examine them from every angle before taking any action. Now, instead of coming to a decision, she sat like one paralysed, staring out of the window, counting the horses in the market square below, and the cracks of the whips.

'How can you say you feel revolted by it if you've never tried it?'

Griseldis unpacked her basket. Cheese, bread, a bottle of wine.

She laid the change on the table. 'This won't last you long. I'm afraid you'll have to spin yarn after all.'

Sophie nodded. Yes, spinning yarn—at least that was a respectable occupation. Incredible drudgery, but respectable. As a yarn-spinner she would get a good husband. One like Casall—her father had said she would never make a better match than that. Perhaps they would give her some writing work at the university…she could at least ask, that could do no harm.

'Who is he?' she asked.

'I don't know. A young man, and he pays well. It would cover the whole of your rent for this month, and on top of that you'd get a lavish meal and a first instalment for your creditors.'

'Doesn't it make you feel dirty, Griseldis?'

No, Griseldis did not feel dirty. Griseldis had come from the gutter and slept her way up. Sophie pressed her face against the window-pane. Down below, the horse-dealers' whips cracked as they flicked through the air. One blow, and then another. Blows and beatings, life seemed to be full of them…

She did not even know the innkeeper's name. Nor did she know the name of the street to which Griseldis led her, heavily veiled. She felt nausea like a black, poisonous toad in the pit of her stomach. Her mother was pestering her to come home—she would not give her a penny if she refused. The new month loomed up before her, and she would not be able to obtain credit. Or would she? As the widow of an eminent member of the Arts Faculty? This was another thing she could have enquired about, but she hesitated. Her whole life seemed to consist of dithering and hesitating, and now, as she was taking the worst possible of all options, she advanced so timidly that Griseldis became impatient.

The house, a door, a staircase, another door, a room, clean and tidy. A good bed against the wall, curtains of a thin, dark material at the window, and a table with attractively decorated goblets and a bottle of good wine. It was very dimly lit, with only two candles burning. There was silence round about, as though no one lived in the house.

'One hour,' Griseldis said, 'and take your veil off. He's already paid, you'll get the money from me. Now, have a drink…'

Sophie lifted her veil and put the goblet to her lips.

When Griseldis had gone she lay down on the bed and closed her eyes. There was still time to leave. To go to her mother, who would welcome her with open arms and send her to the spinning workshop. She might even help her by going to the Faculty on her behalf to ask about copying work…

She swung her legs over the side of the bed: she must get away from here. Determined to leave, she stood up. Her heavy long skirts brushed against the goblet, which was standing on the floor, and some wine spilt over the floorboards. And then, rigid with shock, she saw the door slowly opening. He had not even knocked.

She stood still, hastily drawing the veil over her face. He came in and closed the door behind him. A slim, dark figure. Gloves which he took off and threw on the table. A vigorous gesture. By the meagre light of the two candles it was not possible to make out his face. Sophie began to feel frightened. Now it was not just the theoretical scruples, the vague despair, but concrete fear of this man. Close-fitting hose, a doublet, pointed shoes, a light, swirling cape.

'Are you going to keep your face veiled?'

She heard the ironic undertone in his voice. A voice that sounded familiar. Had she heard it before? But she did not know where.

'I don't mind,' he said in a friendly tone as he tossed his cape onto the bed. Then he stepped over to the window and pushed the material a little to one side. Now Sophie knew who it was. She must get away at once. She gathered up her skirts, desperately hoping that he would not move. But as she reached the door he turned round and took hold of her. Lifted the veil from her face.

'Lombardi…'

He let go and looked intently at her. The poor Master and the widow of his murdered colleague. How can he afford this, she wondered. For some moments they faced each other in silence, until at last he sat down on the bed. 'I had no idea…'

'No, of course not.'

It was infinitely worse for her than for him, for he was merely a man going to a whore, while she—she would be dishonoured and humiliated, a disgrace to the city and the Faculty, if he so much as breathed a word to anyone. He sensed what she was thinking. 'I won't say anything,' he murmured, staring down at the points of his shoes. 'But I would like to know why. Do you need to do this?'

'Casall left me nothing but debts,' she said quietly. 'Do you know how long it would take me to earn the money by spinning? I didn't want to go back to my mother.'

She was on the verge of tears. She felt unspeakably tired.

'Sit down beside me.'

The bed was soft. How she had wanted him, this man Lombardi, on that occasion when he had come to collect Casall's book. But now, under these circumstances? She could not bring herself to look at him.

'How long have you been doing this?'

'This is the first time. I didn't want to at first, but then it seemed the easiest way…'

He laughed softly. 'Will and understanding, do you remember? Casall talked about that conversation he had with you. You despised him, didn't you?'

'Any woman would have despised him. Just because I could read his books and was no less intelligent than he was, he beat me and humiliated me. The understanding is nothing, Lombardi, it dangles like a worm on the end of a fishing-rod…'

'And what is the fishing-rod?'

She turned her head towards him. Here they were, sitting and talking like participants in a disputation. 'The fishing-rod, Lombardi, is the heart. But none of you in the Arts Faculty wants to know anything about that.'

'You don't rate the intellect very highly, then? And what about the will? Does it dangle on the end of the rod too?'

'The will follows reason,' she murmured, and looked up. 'Thomas says that the will follows reason. But you don't believe that. You're not a Thomist.'

'No, you're right, I really don't believe that. I teach it because it is laid down in the statutes, but I think that the will is free. And I think that our method of seeking for truths leads us in totally the wrong direction; we might just as well wait for an earthworm to fly. It never will, so we'll wait in vain. And yet we never stop chopping up the world and looking for flying worms.'

'In Erfurt you lectured on Ockham and Duns Scotus...'

'Yes. They are more receptive to them there. What we are teaching now will still be parroted in five hundred years—aren't we teaching now what was thought five hundred years ago? Have you ever visited the Faculty of Medicine? I've heard about Persian doctors who see the human being as an entity and not as the sum of bones and organs and fluids and gristle...'

'And what is the human being as an entity? Not the sum of individual parts?'

'The understanding is a construct,' Lombardi said, amused, 'just like the will and your heart, of which you speak so delightfully. They are ideas that we form, just as we can form an idea of a flying earthworm.'

They said nothing for a while, and then he stood up and poured some wine into the goblets.

'I paid a large sum of money for this hour,' he suddenly said coldly. 'But not for a discussion with you.' He passed her one of the goblets.

The hour is over, she thought. Any moment now the night watchman will come and call it out. She stood up. 'I will return your money.'

But he shook his head. 'No, you will not.'

Was he trying to frighten her? 'You can destroy me,' she said softly, 'is that what you want?'

'No.' He laughed. 'I've already said that I won't betray you. But we have an agreement, Sophie, and I like you more than any other woman...'

He blew out the candles. She knew that scent of rose water on his hair, heavy and sweet. Down below the night watchman was passing. His voice died away as he went on down the street. The hour was over, but she could feel her inner repugnance ebbing away.

Lombardi was handsome, young and clever—she could hardly have wished for anyone better. She had been the first woman her husband had had relations with, and he had never done more than lie down with her, lift her skirt and take his pleasure in a pause between reading two books. Lombardi, coldly taking advantage of her situation, no doubt intended to enjoy to the full what he had paid for. He laughed into her ear, wanting to make her purr like the little pet cat that he had smuggled into the Scholarium. He wished that he could see her clearly, but the room was dark and it was too much of an effort to light the candles. So he imagined to himself what she must look like. Skin like magnolia petals, eyes like the azure sky with shimmering white clouds. Come here, my little pussy-cat, the hour may be over but I haven't finished yet, in fact I haven't even properly begun.

Outside there was the sound of footsteps. Drunken students rolling out of an inn, making a din and jolting the citizens out of their sleep. And as if that were not enough, now they were starting to play music. Two of them were playing the fiddle, a gypsy song. The residents would soon be throwing jugs and spindles at them and calling the constables.

Sophie listened intently. What if a constable were to come? She must get home. But Lombardi took hold of her arms and gently placed them around his neck. 'They'll soon be gone,' he murmured, and then, as if afraid that she might escape from him after all, he tried to pull her towards the bed. But when she realised that he was serious, the sense of revulsion arose in her again. The poisonous toad in her stomach turned over and wanted to get out. Pushing Lombardi away, Sophie rushed out of the room, and along the corridor, which was dark and narrow. There was the staircase, but the students were down below, playing their gypsy music.

But now they had moved on. Shivering in the darkness, she wrapped her cloak around her, pulled the veil down over her face and ran out into the street. It was empty now, fortunately. But where—Sophie looked around her—where was she? Blessed Virgin, help me! That church over there, that must be St. Cecilia's. The other way, then. Her feet were covered in mud and dirt. In her haste she had not been able to put on her shoes. Nothing but shadows everywhere. And hardly any light, only the moon showing fitfully in gaps between the clouds. At last she reached the Heumarkt. She crossed it, panting, ran to the back entrance of the house and raced up the stairs. The window of the room was open. She banged it shut and at last could put on a light.

'And even if the world were as blue as a lemon, you would want to try and prove it. You are familiar with Scotus's double truth, of course? That something may be true and yet not true? It just depends on one's standpoint. But my question is, where *do* you stand?'

Was it a matter of where you stood? One could cast doubt on anything, even on one's own standpoint. Steiner was looking for the motive, but there was no need. He had a motive: revenge, hatred, envy.

Steiner shook his head. Lombardi cast a sinister shadow before him, he was like a grey wolf. Basically it did not matter whether he believed in God or not—which of them did? Trying to prove something did not mean that you invested your belief or your heart and soul in it. And yet he felt a shiver of cold when he saw Lombardi. What was one to make of that business with the lady from the convent? Had Lombardi felt any qualms at all about sticking his knife into a man's back? He maintained a total silence on the subject. And everyone went to mass, even the grey wolves who believed in nothing.

He came close to asking him. But during mass, in the sight of God, he could not speak such a question. The aroma of incense hung heavy above their heads, and their ears were filled with the monotonous chanting of the choir of servers. Apparently there were sects whose members actually copulated on the altar. They violated nuns who, in a deluded frenzy, were only too willing to let themselves be defiled on the sacred stone. Someone had told him this; it was only a rumour, but a persistent one. Some flagellated themselves to death, some committed violence and murder, and some fornicated in churches—and to this last group, allegedly, Lombardi belonged. Steiner could not remember who it was who had whispered this into his ear, and he was not one to give credence to rumours. But all the same...

They were going to take communion. His knees ached, but what was that compared to the agony of Christ? The clerics in their dark habits were moving into the chancel and taking their places in the heavy wooden stalls.

Have you ever copulated with a nun on the altar? They are said to be compliant, but maybe they are not. Have you defiled them? Apparently the most unbelievable scenes take place…. There would be the devil to pay if he started making such accusations. Out of the corner of his eye he could see Lombardi kneeling beside him, his hands folded, his head bowed. What would happen if he asked him straight out? Would he be able to tell from his reaction what the truth was? Repeating malicious gossip was also a sin.

They stood up and stepped forward. The priest was murmuring almost inaudibly. He did not even look at most of the communicants, merely pushing the wafer mechanically between anonymous lips, but when it was Lombardi's turn he did look up. Only a brief glance; by the time Steiner was before him his eyes were already lowered again.

Ghosts. Wherever I look I see ghosts with empty eye sockets. The chorale, a tuneless chant, accompanied them on their way out. The late afternoon sun dazzled him. It was now or never.

'They meet in a church. *Avidissimum animal, bestiale barathrum, concupiscentia carnis, duellum damnosum*…that is their alphabet, but they give it a different meaning. The priest stands before the altar. Women offer themselves to him, lifting their skirts and showing him their breasts. He chooses a woman. When he has chosen her she lies down on the altar and he has intercourse with her. The novice monks are not allowed to copulate, that is a privilege reserved for the priest, who takes one woman after another…'

Steiner said nothing. Inquisitorial investigations were the preserve of the Dominicans. But there was no inquisitor in Cologne. As yet. He, Steiner, was not even a cleric, he was a member of the Arts Faculty. A scholastic who constructed edifices of the intellect. But now, though assailed by doubts, he was busy constructing a bad reputation for Lombardi.

'You know this only from hearsay?' Jordanus, who had stopped outside the church with Steiner, spoke so quietly that it was difficult to catch what he was saying. Lombardi had taken his leave of them and departed.

'Of course. Do you imagine that I've attended such gatherings?'

'And who was it who told you?'

'Someone who is in a position to know.'

A Dominican, then. In this town there were hordes of them, like flies. 'And what do they call themselves?'

'No idea. But does it matter?'

'No. All that matters is whether or not Lombardi is involved with them.' Jordanus shook his head. 'You still suspect him of having killed Casall…and now you're looking for a skeleton in his cupboard.'

'If he were involved with them, that would at least be a motive. A *magister in artibus* belonging to a heretical sect. That would mean that he was a deluded fanatic, and a man like that would be capable of anything.'

Jordanus shook his head. 'If it ever gets out that you have asked a single question along these lines, they won't let you go until they've found out everything. And you know how these things go: a mere suspicion is all it takes for a person to be put on trial. Or burnt. Is that really what you want?'

Steiner raised his hands imploringly. 'You misunderstand me. I don't want to accuse anyone, and so far I'm only putting these questions to you. Nobody else. But if you know anything or have heard anything, then in God's name tell me. Rumour had it that Lombardi left Erfurt because there was some doubt about his integrity.'

'And he was then allowed to teach in Cologne?' Jordanus replied, laughing. 'Who would have engaged him to teach here if there had been any truth in those rumours? No one. None of us knew anything of this. But how do you know about it? What you said about "someone in a position to know" was a lie, wasn't it? I fear that you are entering too completely into the role of an *advocatus diaboli*.'

Embarrassed, Steiner looked down at his feet. Students. Some students had told him. Students who had been drinking plentiful amounts of good wine. He could not even remember their names now. Children still, fifteen-year-olds. From one of the more prestigious colleges, where they had a sense of their own superiority.

'You see? Nothing but rumours,' Jordanus said, resting a hand on his colleague's shoulder. Then, turning on his heel, he walked off without another word.

After three months of living in the Scholarium, Laurien's pride in his new life and his high expectations of it had drained away. Three months spent in arduous study of Aristotelian logic, of arithmetic and geometry, and also of music and astronomy. Increasingly often Laurien found himself longing for home, but it was out of the question to think of simply throwing away his *bursary* and returning to what he had been. The title of *magister artium* would elevate him to the nobility, as it were, and so he must grit his teeth and see it through. Certainly the other students at the Scholarium also felt as he did. Students who had their own rooms in the town were better off, for at least once lectures were over for the day they could do as they pleased. In the Scholarium there was no freedom at all. The dwarf maintained a joyless regime in his small kingdom, which he governed with a firm hand. Meals, prayers, assemblies, the weekly confession—the time Laurien spent on his various duties in the Scholarium dragged more and more. The food consisted of gruel, soup, lean meat and vegetables; only rarely was there a roast, cheese or fruit. Confession was held in the Scholarium's own chapel, where even at the height of summer you still found yourself sitting in a cold cubby-hole of a place, your teeth chattering. Visiting the bath-house was at least a change, even if it offered no sensual pleasures. Sensuality was altogether problematic. Laurien had heard from those with their own rooms that they went to visit whores; somewhere in Cologne's twisting alleys there was a whorehouse that was open to anyone with enough money or other objects of value. Someone had even claimed, whispering behind his hand, that a student had managed to buy his way in with a bag of stolen apples! The alehouses and brothels were seething with lustful pleasure, but in the Scholarium you lived like a monk. Moreover, the dwarf felt himself fully entitled to use the lash when one of his boarders appeared to have strayed into some place where he had no business to be. Laurien listened to the others' speculations about what they did not actually know, and if there was one who did know more than the others, then he was king. A woman was to be had for a mere threepence, with the brothel-keeper providing food and good wine to boot, and so on and so forth. With the curiosity of the totally inexperienced, Laurien would listen closely. Against the old Roman wall there was supposed to be a convent where by crawling through a hole in the wall you could look in at a window at nightfall and watch the nuns undressing. In fact the nuns were said to have made the hole themselves so that they could be sure of being watched, and after undressing they would fall into each other's arms and fondle and kiss one another. But worse still were the reports of a sect which met together to celebrate the *sexum sacrale*. For them, God in his heaven was not close enough, and so they adopted a form of mysticism which did not stop at the word but demanded deeds. Deeds so dreadful and sacrilegious that Laurien could not bear to listen, but had to get up and leave the room. He did not want to hear these tales. All he needed to know was how much money it would cost to go to a whore, and that it was more than he had. When they whispered together, glancing at him—and the group always included Domitian—he pretended not to be interested, until Domitian suggested that he might come along with them the following day: it would be a good opportunity.

'What for?' Laurien had asked, but Domitian had just laughed and said that he would see soon enough.

They would feed the diminutive Prior some lie or other, and he would be sure to swallow it. He had always swallowed whatever they had told him in the past, so long as they made a great show of honouring his regulations. They were a threesome: Domitian, Laurien and a student from the College. It was this student, Marinus by name, who had made the suggestion in the first place, and when Domitian had objected that it might be better not to take Laurien with them he had just shrugged. 'Leave him behind, then, and we'll go on our own.'

But now all three of them were going after all. Out through the Hahnentor and then a good two hours on foot. The dwarf thought that they were visiting Domitian's father, and since he had a proper respect for *ius canonicum* he had no option but allow them their outing. So they would have no lectures today, and no disputation, but instead, as Domitian said with a chuckle, something far more stimulating to the mind. He and Marinus made a big secret of their destination, but in any case Laurien was not inclined to ask questions. Overjoyed to have escaped the Scholarium, he let them drop their hints, joined in their banter and revelled in the sun's warmth and the prospect of an unexpectedly delightful day. He would willingly have gone to an execution if it meant a few hours' release from the confines of his gloomy prison.

After an hour or so, however, he did ask where they were going, and Domitian replied laconically: to a church. Laurien was astonished. Why should they walk for two hours in the scorching heat when there were any number of churches in Cologne itself? This was a special church, explained Marinus, the student from the College. A very special one. And then they both split their sides laughing, and Laurien stood there sheepishly, not daring to probe any further. After another hour's walking they came upon a derelict courtyard, behind which could be seen the outlines of a solitary building that might once have been a church. But the side aisle had lost its roof and one wall, and there was no doorway by which to enter; the chancel was the only part of the church that still had its outer walls.

'A ruin,' observed Laurien, nonplussed.

Domitian looked up at the sky. In about an hour's time it would be sunset, he said: they would have to wait until then. It was on the tip of Laurien's tongue to ask what for, but he refrained. Marinus unpacked his bundle, and after some food and drink they lay down in the grass.

Gradually it grew dark, and the crossing tower cast its shadow over the chancel. Laurien began to feel drowsy. He must have dozed off, for suddenly he felt a vigorous poke in the ribs. Sitting up, he discerned a group of priests and novices, dressed in dark habits and carrying candles, advancing along the roofless aisle. Behind them came a line of nuns, also holding candles. 'A mass,' thought Laurien, feeling more and more confused.

'Come on,' whispered Domitian, starting to crawl on all fours towards the ruin. He kept his head lowered, and finally stopped, crouching down behind a clump of bushes.

'You mustn't make a sound. If they catch us here they'll kill us.'

'Why?'

Domitian made no reply, but kept his gaze fixed on the ruin. 'Here, have some of this, it'll do you good.'

He held out a bottle of wine, and Laurien took a good swig. 'I could have attended a mass in town,' he grumbled. Marinus laughed softly. 'Yes, but not one like this.'

The monks had reached the altar and they now placed their candles on the ground and folded their hands to pray, while the nuns who had followed them seated themselves on the dusty floor and began to intone a hymn, singing in low-pitched voices in what appeared to be an unintelligible kind of Latin that Laurien could not understand.

'That's not Latin, you dolt,' whispered Domitian, grinning. 'That language doesn't exist, or if it did it could only be the language of the Devil.'

One of the nuns had a sort of drum that made a bright, high-pitched sound not unlike the pealing of a little convent bell. With the drum-beat accompanying their singing, the nuns gradually rose to their feet. Laurien could not work out what this strange ritual might be, for he had never seen anything like it in a church. And when the nuns peeled off their habits, lifting them over their heads, cold shivers ran up and down his spine. Surely they were not going to...? No, that was impossible. Domitian held out the bottle to him. 'Come on, drink some more.'

By this time it was pitch dark. The candles on the ground flickered, lighting up the columns and the grotesque faces on the capitals. One of the priests, who was now standing before the altar, raised the hem of his habit. The first nun stepped up to him, naked, and received his blessing. The blood froze in Laurien's veins, and the bottle fell from his hand.

The nun lay down on the altar. Two of the priests—though Laurien was beginning to doubt that they really were priests—began to tie the woman to the massive stone slab with ropes and cords, so that soon she was totally unable to move. The others had resumed their singing in that incomprehensible language, their voices going up a note and down a note, never more than that, and they had linked arms and were swaying from side to side. Then the priest stepped forward, lifting his habit, and thrust himself between the legs of the captive nun. Laurien turned his face away. Never in his whole life had he seen anything so repellent. And never in his whole life had he felt so sick.

'He's as white as a shroud, even in the dark,' Domitian whispered into the ear of his friend Marinus. Laurien could not bear to look. Though his eyes were firmly closed, he could hear the nun's cries, the priest's panting, and the other women's tuneless chant, which was growing ever louder and more insistent.

'How long have you two been sneaking out here to watch this?' he hissed softly. He heard a suppressed laugh.

'Long enough to know what they get up to,' responded Marinus. 'But you mustn't breathe a word to anybody about it. You'll have to give us your oath on the Bible that you won't.'

Laurien ventured another glance towards the church. An oath on the Bible! After witnessing what was going on over there, how could he ever swear an oath on the Bible again?

The nun was now being untied, and two others were taking their turn. The one delivered from her bonds went staggering back to join her sisters, who had now started wildly leaping about. Of the two nuns now up at the altar, the first sank to her knees, her head disappearing under the priest's habit, while a second priest seized hold of the other and leaned her up against one of the columns. The nuns' singing had by now turned into a hysterical shrieking that hurt Laurien's ears, and they were all embracing one another and tumbling around on the ground like randy cats. One of the priests was still leaning against the column, his fingers digging like claws into the woman's shoulders. Beneath his habit his hips pounded back and forth, and above it all the light tone of the drum beat out the rhythm of these satanic revels.

Once more Laurien averted his eyes. Crawling a short way away from their clump of bushes, he vomited on the grass until not a drop of fluid remained in his stomach.

He felt a touch on his shoulder. 'Hey, what's wrong?'

He drew his hand across his mouth. 'That's disgusting, absolutely revolting. How could you two possibly imagine that I want to see things like that? Have you taken leave of your senses?' His whispering had turned to bitter sobbing. Again the bile rose in his throat, and again he was sick on the grass.

Domitian crawled back to Marinus, who was watching with a lascivious grin as two of the priests took up positions around a single nun, one in front and the other behind.

'I'm afraid we may have some trouble with him,' Domitian said under his breath. 'I had no idea he was so squeamish.'

Marinus nodded absently. This was quite different from when he just went to a whore in Cologne. This was the *sacrum sexuale*, the most shameful sin that a Christian could commit. He would dearly have loved to go over and lie down on the altar with one of those crazed women, but he was a student, he had a long career ahead of him and could not afford to fall foul of the Inquisition. Even sneaking out here, knowing what went on and keeping quiet about it was an extremely serious offence, but he was young and unwilling to forgo this voyeuristic gratification. Each time, on returning to Cologne, he had gone straight to a brothel and tried to recapture the sensation of depravity, of perverse wickedness, but it had never been the same as squatting here in the grass, watching. Once he had asked one of the whores to let him tie her up, but she had simply laughed at him and told him he had been studying the wrong books. As if anything like that was to be found in their scholarly texts!

'We'll have to go back, he can't take it,' he heard Domitian say. Marinus felt life stirring between his legs and put his hand under his coat. 'Not yet,' he murmured, 'later.'

Since the encounter with those followers of the Devil his life had changed. On the way back to the city he felt as though he had lost the power of speech. Hanging his head, his hands buried deep in his pockets, he had arrived back at the Scholarium and had promptly been made to swear on the Bible not to betray what he knew by a single word. Then Marinus had left for his own college, and Domitian for the cathedral. How could he calmly go off to mass like that? Was there something wrong with him, Laurien, that made him see more in that spectacle than simply a mirror-image of his own suppressed lust? Marinus and Domitian went along to watch and thought nothing of it. Why could not Laurien see it in the same light? Because he had never slept with a woman? In that case they could have taken him to a brothel. They had probably thought they were giving him a treat.

Laurien could not eat. Nor was he able to follow the teaching, because whenever he tried to concentrate he would see shrieking nuns on an altar and a priest's thrusting loins. Once he attempted to go to confession, but he turned back before reaching the confessional because he had, after all, given his oath on the Bible. He sensed that to talk about it would ease his mind. But he must not betray Domitian and Marinus, and so he would have to stay silent for ever and ever, until at last he fell silent for all eternity. On top of this there was the business about Casall, the suspicion that he might have killed his teacher. Domitian was also a suspect, and yet he seemed quite unconcerned, and laughed and joked about it. Increasingly Laurien found himself wondering what Domitian had in fact done on his way back from the tavern to the Scholarium. Had he been in Marzellenstrasse? Had he encountered Casall there?

As ill luck would have it, a friend of Domitian's father chanced to visit de Swerthe a couple of days later, and in the course of conversation innocently revealed that the lawyer had spent the past week in Würzburg. This made the Prior suspicious, for in that case he could not possibly have invited his son to supper.

The noose around Laurien's neck was being drawn tighter, as tight as the bonds around the bodies of the rabid nuns.

Convinced that he had been deliberately misled, de Swerthe

asked Lombardi to look into the matter. The two students, he said, had served him up a barefaced lie, and he wanted to know the truth. And so Lombardi summoned first Domitian and then Laurien. For this inquisition he had placed a stool in the middle of his room, while he himself remained standing behind his table; but in fact he did not consider the matter very serious. Students did lie and cheat and go drinking and whoring unless a very close eye was kept on them. And if they were constantly penned in, as they were here in the Scholarium, they snatched at every opportunity to experience the fascinations and the perils of a big city.

After Domitian, with every sign of deep remorse, had admitted to spending the time in question in a brothel, Lombardi sent for Laurien. He entered, sat down and at once lowered his eyes to the floorboards.

'Now, Laurien, it's quite clear that you've been lying to the Prior. Domitian's father didn't invite you to a meal on Sunday. So where were you?'

Laurien raised his head with a jerk. That same evening, after their outing, they had agreed on their story about visiting a brothel, so that they would give the same version of events should the need arise. The words were on the tip of Laurien's tongue, and yet none passed his lips. He simply must get the whole thing off his chest or he would suffocate. It was choking him, it was preventing him from breathing. Perhaps he could rid himself of those horrible images if he put them into words. But the very thought of describing it all threatened to turn his stomach again. On the other hand, if he continued to keep it to himself he would die of starvation, for his belly was so full of it that there was no room in it for anything else.

'We went to a brothel,' he breathed.

Lombardi nodded. 'Yes, so I have already been told once today.' He felt a sense of unease. Why was the boy sitting on the stool like that, so hunched over, so frightened?

'Was it so horrible?' he enquired gently.

Laurien shook his head.

'I'll have to punish you both. You lied to the Prior.'

Yes, punish me, sir. Punish me, Lord, for sitting here and holding my peace, even though the world is full of heretics and demons and I myself can no longer wash my hands in innocence.

'Is there something else?'

Lombardi's tone cut him to the quick. Yes, there is something else, but I have sworn an oath on the Bible.

'Laurien?'

Lombardi's voice grew ever softer, as soft as butter, as soft as the tender bleating of the mother ewe when she sees her newborn lamb. What Laurien heard in it was sympathy, and it burst all the restraining dams he had erected. Even the dams he had built to hold back his tears, which now started coursing down his cheeks.

'I, I...I can't say anything, I...I've sworn an oath on the Bible....'

Lombardi just nodded. So he had been right after all. The lad did have something on his mind.

'Sworn an oath on the Bible? To keep your mouth shut?'

A sorrowful nod.

'Then you're quite right not to say anything. But it's torment-ing you.'

'Yes.'

'What can we do to remedy this sorry state of affairs? You have sworn to keep silent, but you need to get it off your chest, even so. Is that how it is? Can you see a way out?'

No, none. There is none. I shall take those dreadful images with me to the grave.

Lombardi drew up a second stool and sat down facing Laurien. 'Then let's consider together whether there may not be some way out after all. You want to free yourself from something that is a torment to you. Why don't you tell me, and I will take the guilt upon myself by swearing on the Bible not to reveal anything?'

Laurien blinked, his eyes still brimming with tears. Everything looked blurred and distorted. He saw Lombardi's dark locks, his bright eyes. He is willing to take the guilt on himself? For me? Laurien nodded gratefully. 'How is it to be done, sir?'

'You tell me the truth, everything that's worrying you. Just like going to confession. Your secret will be safe with me.'

Laurien brushed the tears from his face. He was becoming more composed.

'Even if really you do not have the option of keeping silent, because you would be violating everything that is sacred to us as Christians?'

'How could that be?'

Lombardi was bewildered. What was this secret that was so terrible? What monstrous burden was the youngster carrying on his puny shoulders?

'Talk.' Lombardi's voice was suddenly ice-cold.

Then it all came pouring out. Laurien related how they had sat on the grass, eating and drinking and in the best of spirits. How the priests and nuns had appeared all at once from nowhere, and the priests had copulated with them on the altar, tying them down with ropes. Then his voice faltered and his tears flowed once more. 'They, they… they took me along because they thought I…I would find it as exciting as they do, but they're callous and have no feelings…the Demon is in them…the Evil One…' Now he could not speak for sobbing. His poor little soul was wrung with anguish, and the longer he wept the more those hideous images, that filled his head and his guts, came tumbling out. He had quite forgotten Lombardi, who was still sitting there, staring at him as though he himself were the Demon.

'Holy Mother of God,' he heard his teacher murmur at last. Lombardi had risen to his feet, averting his face.

Laurien raised his head. 'Will you…will you keep it a secret?'

Lombardi nodded. 'Off you go.'

Laurien stood up, pushed the stool under the table, and slunk from the room. As he closed the door behind him he suddenly thought he saw a shadowy figure hastily rounding the corner towards the refectory, as though someone had been listening at the door. He heard the rustle of fabric, of some garment; but was far too engrossed in his own misery to pay it much attention. Silently shaking his head he went into the dormitory.

Lombardi was very popular with the students; he was young, and was like a mirror that they enjoyed looking into because they hoped to be just like him one day. The fact that he was a nominalist troubled no one. Everybody here was something—Scotist, Thomist, saint or sinner. You just had to know where you belonged. All Masters, whether in Bologna, Paris or Cologne, taught essentially the same material, so the fascination that Lombardi held for the students had to have some other cause.

And he himself? He was aware that they were fond of him. He did not beat them or impose punishments, as other Masters did, for being late for mass, for asking inane questions or questions that should not be asked at all, or for giving answers that were not the ones envisaged in the statutory teaching plan.

On the evening following his conversation with Laurien, Lombardi went to Spielmannsgasse. Wanting to be alone, he stopped off at a wretched little tavern where the wine cost little and the women even less. It was a place only frequented by the worst kind of riff-raff, including perhaps the people he was looking for. It was a haunt of murderers, thieves, tricksters, flagellants, Amauricians, and renegade monks who could now indulge to their hearts' content in gluttony, drinking and whoring.

Lombardi took a seat in the furthest corner of the room, for this rabble revolted him. They stank of schnapps and urine; in the dim light one could only make out outlines, but even those were such that one would want to forget them again instantly. Screeching and bawling filled the air, since the wretched quality of the wine did not deter the customers from pouring quarts of it down their throats. Lombardi glanced about him. With a sense of bitter irony he recognised that he trod a fine line between opposite extremes, and that in order to ascend to the higher realms of the intellect he was often obliged to plumb the depths of vulgar reality. As he looked around—his throat already rough from the evil brew—he noticed that a short fellow, one of a group of ragged figures, was staring at him as though he were the Devil incarnate.

*You're taking a big risk*, the thought flashed through Lombardi's mind. *They know you, they just don't know what walk of life you're in now and where to find you. If you don't watch out you'll be dead in a gutter by morning.*

The small man approached him. 'Lombardi? Is it really you?'

Lombardi claimed to be just passing through on his way to Paris, and spun the fellow all manner of tales. The other laughed, slapping his thighs, and then leaned over towards him. 'So you're not with them any more?'

This was it. This was exactly what he had wanted to know. 'They're still around, then? I thought they'd all been burnt at the stake long ago.'

'Not all of them. Some of them, but not all. *I'm* still alive and kicking, as you see.'

'And are you still with them?'

'No. Our prior was the first to be consigned to the flames, and the rest scattered in all directions. Those were good times, but they're over now.'

'I heard that the ones who are left have found a new place, a ruin…'

The man nodded. 'Weilersfeld. There's an old church that burned down. But anybody going there is a fool. I for one am setting off for Flanders tomorrow.'

Lombardi had all the information he needed. He paid and left the tavern. As he strode through the streets he remembered that Weilersfeld had once been a Cistercian abbey. At some time it must have burned down: most likely God had lost patience with the monks' sins and had himself started the fire in which they had all perished. A devilishly apt location for such gatherings. Truly satanic. Don't go near it, he told himself, it's far too dangerous. It only takes one of them to betray you, and then you won't be wearing your doctoral hood any more, you'll be swinging by it. And yet…he needed to be sure. That abbey was so damnably close to town. Less than two hours' walk, and on horseback you were there in no time at all. How quickly a fire like that could spread to the city itself. Lombardi came to a halt. Nothing but darkness around him; only at the far end of the lane, which was clogged with rubbish, was there a torch fixed to the wall, giving out a feeble glimmer.

In the dormitory it was pitch dark. The other students' breathing, the faint rustle of blankets when one of them turned over, the muttering of another one talking in his sleep; every night the sounds were the same. Laurien stared at the wall. He could not have gone out even if he had wanted to. The main door was locked, and the dwarf slept with the key under his pillow. The windows were barred, and in any case the rubble of the house next door was piled up outside them.

The worst was over, and yet the memory still tormented him. He had transferred his burden of guilt to Lombardi, so it was up to him now what he did with it. But what if Lombardi were no better able to bear the weight of it than Laurien himself, and revealed everything? Perhaps it would be best to leave the university and start a new life somewhere else. Not today, nor tomorrow, but soon. Here he would always have to be on his guard in case Lombardi should talk. Then they would come and interrogate him. Domitian would turn against him; so, perhaps, would all the others in the Scholarium, and he would find himself completely isolated. He would be crucified by Domitian and Marinus for having betrayed them, and by the rest for having kept quiet. He felt as though he were suspended in mid-air, between heaven and earth. He wished he could be an angel.

In the morning Steiner was summoned to speak to the Chancellor. Asked if any progress had been made on the Casall case, he could only shake his head apologetically, whereupon the Chancellor nodded and gestured towards a piece of vellum lying on the table in front of him.

'Then read this. It was addressed to you, in any case.'

Steiner reached for the parchment.

'It was lying on my front steps this morning.'

*You are taking your time. You are right to do so. But do not wait too long, or someone else may be next.*

It was the same handwriting. And the same kind of parchment as before.

'A madman,' was Steiner's judgment. He was alarmed. 'Is he planning to kill someone else now?'

'Yes, and it could be you, Magister Steiner. It seems that you don't think fast enough for his liking. It's a race against time. Either you solve the riddle very speedily or he finds himself another victim. Yes, he is indeed a madman. Logic hardly seems the appropriate weapon here.'

Steiner made no reply. In considering this case they had over-looked something, that much was certain. If only he could work out what it was. He had to use logic, because it was the only weapon he possessed.

'The murderer knows that I proceed by logic,' he said thought-fully, 'and that is why, in his impudence, he chooses that particular line of attack. No, logic is the right weapon. So—let us start all over again. What is it that we have overlooked?'

The Chancellor grinned. 'Perhaps you should hold a discussion on it with your students,' he suggested ironically, although this new threat made the situation anything but a joke.

'Do you know, that is not at all a bad idea,' Steiner muttered.

It was dangerous to discuss the matter publicly, but he must do it, risk or no risk. Names could be changed, circumstances disguised. The students knew that Casall had not died a natural death. But surely they would not guess that it was he they were talking about if Steiner went about it the right way.

'A cow has been stolen. It moos loudly when the thief loosens its tether and drags it away with him. Its bellowing wakes the farmer, who gets out of bed and goes to look in the byre. The cow is gone. The farmer sees just the shadow of a figure running away. He sets off in pursuit, but on the path he finds the cow's tether. A little further on he finds its bell, and then a tuft of hairs from its tail. Until at last he finds the whole cow, done to death with a knife. These appear to be the facts. Now I would like you to tell me what can be proved and what cannot. There is something in the story that does not belong: either it does not belong to the facts of the case, or it does not belong specifically to the stolen cow.'

The students looked at one another and laughed. It was rare

for there to be anything to laugh at in class; there was no provision for that in the statutes. This story was utterly banal. But it must have some hidden significance.

'Perhaps the tether didn't belong to the cow,' one of the students conjectured.

'Yes, it did. That is proven.'

'The bell?' another called out.

'Yes, the bell was the cow's too.'

'The tuft of hairs,' a third suggested.

Strange, thought Steiner. That is exactly the procedure that I followed. There were no other pieces of evidence. Or were there?

'Perhaps the dead cow was not the one that was stolen,' said Laurien.

Steiner shook his head. 'Yes, it was, the very one. The farmer identified it.'

'Did he actually see the thief?' asked one of the Baccalaurei.

'No, only a shadowy figure running away.'

'But that wasn't necessarily the thief.'

'Quite right. That is only a surmise.'

'And the knife?' cried the *Baccalaureus*. 'Was it found at the scene of the crime?'

'No. He must have taken it away with him.'

'The people who were in the vicinity at the time must all be questioned, and checks made as to whether anyone can vouch for their innocence.'

'Yes, all that has been done. All the possible suspects have alibis for the relevant time.'

'That's impossible,' said the Baccalaureus, who was enjoying this. '*Somebody* must have done it.'

Exactly, thought Steiner, somebody must have done it. But apart from Lombardi, who cannot really have done it, Domitian, and lastly Laurien, sitting there so attentive and as much in the dark as anyone—and heaven knows he had no motive whatsoever—I can think of no possible culprit.

'The point of the puzzle is that there is some element or other in the facts of the case that does not belong,' Steiner reminded them. 'That is what I am interested in, rather than in witnesses or a *locus facti.*'

'If all the items that were found belonged to the cow, then it must be something else,' reasoned the Baccalaureus. 'Perhaps the cow wasn't stolen at all, but broke loose. It is only an assumption that the cow was stolen. Did anybody see it being stolen?'

'No,' said Steiner, 'no one saw that. All the same, the animal was found lying dead under a bush.'

'It could have broken loose and then fallen into somebody's hands.'

'And why should he have killed it?'

'Why should anyone have killed it? You're looking for a motive, but that doesn't solve the puzzle.'

Steiner was watching Lombardi and Domitian. But however closely he observed their faces, he saw not a flicker of reaction. No agitation, no mocking superiority, nothing at all out of the ordinary. What, then, if it was one of the others in the room? If so, that person would know exactly what this discussion was really about, and might very possibly be one of those participating in it. Or he might be sitting there in silence, listening and drawing his own conclusions. And what if he intended him, Steiner, to be his next victim? Because he felt superior to him, because he was, perhaps, a demented Arts student or graduate who was using logic as a means to gratify the desires of his own sick mind?

'Yes,' murmured Steiner, 'I am looking for a motive, but I believe I have already found it. It must be someone who hates cows and who, by committing this act, seeks to torment and humiliate those who like them and work with them.'

'He must be a very strange individual,' said the Baccalaureus with a shake of his head.

Steiner opened his book, indicating that this extraordinary discussion was at an end. He needed time to think. And while his eyes wandered unseeing over the lines of the text, he tried to recall a remark that the Baccalaureus had made. It was merely an assumption, he had said, that the cow had been abducted. It was indeed an assumption. Had anyone actually seen Casall being attacked and killed? And yet he had screamed, and he had been murdered, for he had most certainly not struck himself on the head with the heavy earthenware pot. It was true that killing oneself called for considerable skill and ingenuity, but he would surely have chosen a different means of dispatching himself to the next world. The very manner of his death pointed to murder. Steiner felt confused, and passing the book to one of the Licentiates he went to sit down on a bench against the wall. The Baccalaureus's objection was by no means a foolish one, but it was focused on the wrong *conclusio*. The question of whether or not the cow had been abducted was not the issue. But it pointed in the right direction. Perhaps this was where the solution was to be found. They must look at the start, at the beginning of the story, for that was where the fog was, where veils obscured the facts of the case. Not on the way to the body, nor at the scene of the murder. Because from the moment when the fuller had left his house there were witnesses aplenty who had followed events right to the scene of the crime.

When the class was over and Steiner was about to leave the lecture room, the Baccalaureus came up to him again. 'Were there any other cows nearby?' he asked.

'Yes, certainly. But they were probably all asleep.'

'So the cow's bellow could only have come from the cow itself?' The Baccalaureus was grinning. He had seldom had such an extensive conversation on the subject of cows.

'It bellowed because it sensed that the thief meant it no good,' replied Steiner, somewhat testily. What sort of stupid question was that?

'It must have been quite a clever cow,' laughed the *Baccalaureus*. 'It had a premonition, did it, that it was about to be killed?'

'No, of course not.'

'Then why did it bellow? Because the thief had interrupted its sleep?'

'Tell me, young man, where is this leading, exactly?' By now Steiner was really angry.

'I don't know myself, sir. I am merely pointing out that the start of your little anecdote is rather shrouded in obscurity and would benefit from having the light of reason cast upon it.'

Steiner nodded. That was perfectly true. But then one never could find independent witnesses to an act and the events immediately preceding it. If one could, there would be no need of investigators.

'Do you know the solution to the puzzle?' asked the Baccalaureus. Steiner did not answer. Such problems were not to be found in Aristotle or Thomas Aquinas. Nor in the statutory teaching programme. Steiner gave the Baccalaureus a smile and left the room.

Sophie had gone back to work as a yarn-spinner. Her sisters had put in a good word for her, and as a result the mistress had taken her on as an apprentice. Now, as she sat on her stool from dawn to dusk spinning blue thread, her spirits grew dull and she felt ever more weary and exhausted. Her name had been submitted to the spinners' guild and she had been formally entered in the register of apprentices. For four years she would have to sit like this, twisting the yarn onto the twiners. Then she would be able to set up her own business, but that was the very last thing she aspired to. Her mistress was impatient with her and had only taken her on because she was a respectable widow who needed to earn a living. The workshop did not even possess a four-spindle machine, because the city council had forbidden the use of such equipment.

Not long before, Sophie's mother had married a wealthy guild master. He was a burly fellow, a master shoemaker with lecherous eyes, who had sold his business because he had gout in every limb and now proposed to spend the rest of his life being waited on hand and foot by his wife and her maidservant. Nobody could imagine why Sophie's mother had tied such a millstone around her neck, for she had been mistress of her own affairs and no one could compel her to remarry. And yet she had fallen for the old fool's feeble blandishments and jumped into bed with him. He had never owned a house himself, being too mean and preferring to keep his money safely stowed away in a jar, and so Sophie's family had stayed in their own house and he had simply moved in. Now he spent every day sitting at the window, staring out at the street and being waited on. Once a day he went to mass, but he counted out the coins for the offertory box in advance, because every penny he possessed was recorded in the accounts which he drew up every few weeks, and would be released into the world, with wailing and gnashing of teeth, only when absolutely necessary. He was not much liked in the city, for avarice was a sin. Even the wedding had been a cheap affair. Essentially he was a sick old man who saved his money for the physician. Whenever his gout was especially bad and was preventing him from going out, a professor of medicine, no less, would be summoned as though by royal command. After the consultation he would count out the coins into the doctor's hand, his face contorted with pain—pain that had less to do with his bones than with the fact that a professor should charge such a damned high price for his quackery.

Sophie kept her distance from him. Usually he was dozing at the window when she visited her mother, and at mealtimes he ate alone in any case, plagued as he was by his gout.

'Whatever does our mother see in him?' she once asked one of her sisters. 'Wasn't she perfectly comfortable as she was? What nonsense did he fill her head with, to make her throw herself away like that?'

It remained a mystery. From time to time Sophie spent a night in the house, and from her room, which adjoined theirs, she could sometimes hear them in bed together. When he was on good form, sounds of gasping and groaning would reach her through the wall, and she thought that perhaps that was what he was after. It surprised her that he was still capable of it, though perhaps what she heard was only his unsuccessful attempts at intercourse. But he could not have been so very unsuccessful, because after four weeks her mother announced that she was expecting a baby.

Steiner had inadvertently been drawn into a student drinking party. They were sitting in an ale-house celebrating a Baccalaureus's graduation. As he was passing by in the street the new graduate came rushing out to urge him to share a tankard of wine with them. Deep in his own thoughts, Steiner smiled and, allowing himself to be dragged inside, sat down with them. Lombardi was there too, sitting in a corner, apparently slightly drunk. Steiner drank a good measure of the wine and then moved over to join Lombardi. Someone made a remark about Steiner's cow puzzle, jesting that cows had now at long last attained philosophical recognition. Lombardi, who clearly had no idea what they were talking about, asked to be enlightened.

'I set my students a problem,' Steiner replied, and repeated the story of the abducted animal. Lombardi listened, astonished and somewhat baffled until he realised that Steiner was alluding to the Casall case but had presented it in a different wrapping.

'Well?' he asked, amused. 'Were your students able to help you?'

'Very possibly. They pointed out an unfounded assumption that I had made.'

'An assumption?'

'Yes. Namely that we had always simply assumed that the cow that bellowed was the same cow that was killed.'

'So two cows were killed?'

'Well, only one was found dead. But there could possibly be a second one. It's just that we haven't looked for it yet.'

Lombardi was too surprised to answer. Where might one be likely to find a second corpse? But certainly it *was* a mere assumption, a wholly unsupported premise, that there had been only one body and that there was not still a second one lying hidden somewhere. But somewhere in this train of thought there was an element that disturbed him, some detail that did not belong. There had not been two bodies; the baseless assumption related to something else.

'The cow's bellowing,' he said in an undertone to Steiner, 'only tells us that it mooed. But we can't prove that it was this same cow that was killed. *That's* the point.'

The tankard was going the rounds, but when it reached Steiner he simply held it in his hands without drinking. Suddenly he set it down on the table, stood up and pushed his way out through the crush.

Once outside he hurried to the cathedral, to the Provost's House. There he pulled the bell-cord and waited.

That was the point! Lombardi was right, even if he could not see—could not yet see—its full significance. Now all that remained was to incorporate it into the puzzle as a whole, as though one were constructing a building. One of the maidservants came and opened the door. Steiner burst in and found the Chancellor eating his supper.

'Ah, Steiner, take a seat. Good heavens, you look as if the Devil were after you…'

Steiner subsided onto a chair. On the table were a selection of pies and a capon giving off a delicate aroma of saffron, but Steiner had lost his appetite.

'I think I know the solution to the riddle,' was all he said.

The Chancellor lowered his knife. 'You have…'

'Yes. If you start with that statement devised by our murderer, it suddenly becomes quite simple. In fact its brilliance lies in its utter simplicity. You see, when we kept pondering on what it was that did not belong to the murder, or did not belong to Casall, we were always thinking of visible things. Things we could see. The sleeves, the biretta, the book, the shoes. I even toyed with the extraordinary notion that the dead man might not be Casall at all, but someone else. His twin brother, perhaps. Anyway, those were all false trails. Man is, after all, a being who perceives the world primarily through his eyes.'

He stopped for breath, and the Chancellor took advantage of the pause. 'So the solution of the riddle relates to another of our senses?'

'Yes. Our sense of hearing. Casall cried out in mortal anguish— the witnesses told us so. But that is a wholly impermissible assumption, and I was incapable of distinguishing the illusion from reality.'

The Chancellor pushed away his plate. 'Distinguish illusion from reality? I don't think I quite follow you.'

Steiner nodded. 'We perceive reality in sequences of events that are familiar to us. A man screams because he is in fear of death. Shortly afterwards he is found dead. Why should it occur to anyone to suppose that the scream did not come from the murdered man? The scream is what does not belong. The scream was not uttered by Casall, but by someone else. And that alters everything. Including the position of the witnesses, because if the scream was not Casall's then he could have been killed considerably earlier.'

It took a while for the Chancellor to grasp the implications of Steiner's discovery. He rose to his feet and fetched a second goblet, which he filled with good Rhenish wine. 'You believe, then, that someone else uttered that cry? When Casall was already lying dead by your well?'

'You see, the murderer aimed to confuse us by misleading us over the timing of the different events. We thought that only a few moments separated the scream and the murder. But if the scream was uttered by someone else, when was Casall actually killed? Whether he lay naked in the rain for ten minutes or for an hour cannot possibly be established with certainty.'

'But what,' the Chancellor frowned, looking at Steiner, who was now drinking his wine with calm deliberation and a somewhat self-satisfied air, '... what can we conclude from all that? Why should someone have screamed when there was nobody threatening his life?'

'We can conclude, in my opinion, that the scream was either coincidental, which seems most unlikely, or a false scent purposely laid by our murderer. He cried out himself, thereby obscuring the time factor, or rather fixing it in such a way that we took the time of death to be a given fact.'

'*Incredibile*,' muttered the Chancellor. 'How did you come to think of that?'

Steiner laughed. 'Oh, I took your suggestion seriously and discussed the case in a lecture, which of course was hardly in accordance with the regulations. Naturally I changed the elements of the story. I used what you might call a bovine philosophical analogy. But the true significance only became apparent to me this evening.'

'This is bad,' the Chancellor said grimly, 'because even if we do appear to have solved the riddle, I mean, if it really happened as you say, then all the witness statements we have heard so far are worthless. Because if Casall was murdered much earlier...'

Steiner stood up. Yes, he had to start again from scratch. Who would be able to give him information about the time of the murder? How long had Casall been lying dead outside his house?

# Quaestio

# H

e looked around. There was no such thing as *the* Faculty. There were only colleges and halls and student houses. And students and Masters. It wasn't like in a monastery, where as soon as you went through the gates you could see everything at once: *ora et labora* all going on in one and the same place. But where was the Faculty? Scattered the length and breadth of the city. The theologians had their place somewhere or other, you were best to look for them near the monasteries; then there were the lawyers, but where they were to be found was a mystery to him. Or perhaps Cologne didn't have any. And finally the Arts people. Some of them lived in a college, and he had once even been given a meal there, but they were poor students, he wouldn't go to them. Who should you go to to make a statement? The constables? Or straight to the top, to the city council, that was run by the big guilds? He didn't want to go there. He was a gold-digger's son, a good-for-nothing, he was already a drinker and a thief and was not inclined to work at his father's trade. So who would believe him? And anyway, why should he get involved? His sort were better off staying in the background, out of sight. And yet…he had heard that the council was offering a reward for any information about the mysterious death of Magister Casall. He could do with the money, and after all he did know something, because his father had seen the body.

He wandered irresolutely through the streets and alleys. Looking at the houses and at the goods for sale in the market-place was certainly not the answer, but he needed to think. Who could he ask? A priest in one of the churches? That monk standing there in front of the meat hall?

The Raven—that was his nickname because his skin was as dark as a gypsy's—approached the friar as he was looking anxiously up at the sky, where heavy clouds were suddenly blocking out the sun. 'Beg pardon, venerable Brother, I'm looking for a Master from the Faculty. Can you tell me where I can find one?'

The friar, a Franciscan in a brown habit, looked down at the urchin, who could not have been more than fifteen, and frowned. 'What might someone like you want with the Masters? You're not a student, are you?'

The Raven shook his head. 'No, but I've got some information I'd like to pass on. Only I don't know where to go with it. Where's the Faculty?'

The Franciscan laughed. That was a good question. Everywhere and nowhere, that was where the Faculty was. Right now one of the *bursae* was nearest. There was sure to be a Master there. 'Keep going along this street, and then left until you come to a house with blue shutters.'

The Raven set off. But from the *bursa* he was sent on to one of the colleges, and from there along Judengasse and westwards towards St. Ursula's. Because he always said he wanted to speak to one of the Masters, they all thought he must mean Steiner, and so by the time he reached Marzellenstrasse it was noon and he was feeling increasingly hungry.

Steiner was not at home. The servant told the boy to wait, since he would not tell her the purpose of his visit. Keeping a suspicious eye on him, she gave him a bowl of soup, which he devoured greedily.

By the time Steiner appeared the Raven had dozed off in his chair.

'You are looking for me?'

The boy awoke with a start. He nodded eagerly and sat up straight on the chair. 'I've heard there's a reward for anybody that saw anything.'

'And what did you see?'

'Me? Nothing, but my father, he says he saw the dead Master.'

'And why have you left it so long? And why hasn't your father come himself?'

'I wasn't able to come before. I had some work for two months, so I couldn't. And my father doesn't want to.'

Steiner nodded. Yes, that made sense. If a boy like this had work for two months, that would be more important.

'But after that? You have found your way here now, after all. Why not sooner?'

'I didn't know who to come to.'

'Tell me, then, what your father saw.'

'Well, it was like this. That evening he was taking a load down to the Rhine—he's a *goltgrever*. He had to go down Marzellenstrasse. In front of the wall he spotted a man in a dark-coloured coat lying under an elder bush that was in flower. Afterwards it occurred to him that the Faculty people wear coats like that. Then when he came back up from the river the man under the elder had gone, vanished into thin air. And later I got to hear about the dead Master and I thought it might have been him.'

'A dark coat? Like those the professors wear?' Steiner repeated.

'Yes, like the professors wear.'

'When did your father see him lying there. At what hour?'

The Raven shrugged his shoulders. He did not know the exact time.

'Midnight?'

'No. Earlier than that. A lot earlier.'

'How much earlier? An hour?'

The Raven hesitated. Time was something you couldn't get much of a grip on, even though it was measured and the night watchman walked through the streets chopping it into pieces with his calls.

'No, maybe two hours.'

Around ten, then, thought Steiner, frowning.

'Was the man under the elder dead?'

'No idea. Could have been. He wasn't moving, my father said. But he didn't see his head. The twigs with the white blossom were hanging over him down to his chest.'

'He was dressed,' murmured Steiner.

'Yes, of course.'

'Did your father see sleeves on the coat?'

*What a funny question*, thought the Raven, and nodded. Yes, of course there had been sleeves on the coat. All coats had sleeves.

It crossed Steiner's mind that the lad could hardly be a more unsuitable witness. He was not even a citizen of Cologne, and was probably an occasional thief with a bad reputation. And strictly speaking he was not a witness at all. If his father would not give a statement himself, the whole thing was rather pointless.

'Did your father hear anything? Did he hear screams?'

The Raven shook his head. 'No, the man wasn't screaming, he was just lying there, quiet.'

Everything fitted. Casall had been killed at around ten o'clock, straight after leaving the tavern, and the murderer had hidden him under the elder. An hour later somebody had screamed—possibly the murderer himself—and had dragged the body from the elder bush to the well outside Steiner's house. It would take no more than five minutes from the wall to his house, even dragging a heavy corpse.

Steiner asked to be shown the bush. It already had the first of its purple-black berries, dangling in heavy clusters over the wall. The bush actually grew on the far side of the wall, but it was big enough for its branches to hang over and reach down almost to the ground. An excellent hiding-place in the dark.

'How was it that your father saw the man at all?' asked Steiner, puzzled.

'The feet had slipped down on to the roadway a bit. My father didn't see him at first, but his cart got stuck. And then he looked to see what had got in the way.'

They went back to Steiner's house. What about his reward, the lad wanted to know. But that was nothing to do with Steiner. The reward had been put up by the city council, and so, like it or not, the Raven would have to present himself there. However, he seemed very reluctant to do so and begged Steiner to approach the council on his behalf. Steiner nodded his assent and told the lad to come back the next day. After sending him on his way, he stepped out into his garden, deep in thought.

The murderer kills Casall and hides the body under an elder bush. No one was likely to pass by at such a late hour. Then he waits, and just before eleven he starts to scream and cry for help...

No, that's not right. Steiner was sitting on the wall of his overgrown rose garden, trying to introduce some clarity and coherence into his thoughts. First he has to take the dead man's clothes off him and spread his possessions around. Then he can cry out. He screams like a man at death's door, and as he does so he runs off in the direction of the convent gardens. No, that doesn't cover everything. Because there is the body—what about that? It's still lying under the elder bush. So first he drags the corpse to the well and strips it of its clothes. Of course, I wasn't at home to notice anything going on. Next he distributes the book and the clothing. And only then does he start screaming. That's how it must have been. There's no other way it could have happened. What a devious scheme!

And a risky one. How easily he might have been observed. And fancy leaving the dead man lying around for people literally to trip over his legs! That had perhaps been his fatal mistake, for now Steiner knew for certain that Casall had not died at around eleven o'clock, but earlier. And he knew that all the statements made by the witnesses were irrelevant. The question was where they had been an hour earlier.

Steiner stood up. He needed to talk to the magistrate.

'He had the audacity to set a *cow puzzle*. Just imagine: a *cow puzzle*! He even had the effrontery to refer to it as such. Not only was he in complete breach of the teaching regulations, but he wasted a full half hour of the lecture on it and to this day has not troubled to make up the lost time. What is taught, and when, is clearly laid down, and there is no regulation that says we have to fritter our time away on puzzles.'

They were standing in the corridor outside the lecture room, facing each other like two angry bulls: Theophile Jordanus and one of the Bachelors who had been at the lecture in question. His sympathy for the *moderni* was no secret. Jordanus, older and wiser, smiled quietly to himself. He was aware of the real meaning of the cow puzzle because Steiner had told him. And he also knew that the murderer's riddle seemed to have been solved as a direct result. So the fact that someone was trying to cause trouble over it was of minor importance.

'What do you propose to do about it?' he enquired placidly.

'What do *you* propose to do about it?' the Baccalaureus threw back at him, his eyes blazing.

'You are not really concerned about the lost half hour,' Jordanus pointed out mildly. 'You are looking for an excuse to undermine Steiner's authority because he consistently strives to achieve a compromise between the two philosophical schools of thought. If you object to that, why don't you leave this university and find a place at another one?'

'Yes,' snarled the Baccalaureus, 'I've heard that they want to go back to the old teaching method here and teach only the hoary old writers. Ancient relics gathering mould. The world is full of fresh ideas and new concepts, and yet you, Magister Jordanus, still think that your laughably inadequate devices can prove God's existence—that everything can be proved using that utterly antiquated methodology.'

'It is not really a question of methodology,' countered Jordanus gently. 'Much more a question of what I am trying to prove. Moreover, my position is not too far removed from that of the nominalists, as you know.'

'And what exactly are you trying to prove? If that's how you see things, I should like to know what it is you hope to achieve.'

Jordanus turned to go. A murderer identified beyond all doubt, that was what he hoped to achieve. For after all, the murderer was using the very same method. But he said nothing and with a mere nod tucked his book under his arm and walked off.

> *Now that you appear to have solved the first riddle, I will*
> *set you a second one that could show you the right path if*
> *you are clever enough. Think of the quadrivium and the*
> *following question: how can it happen that a dove kills*
> *a vulture?*

Steiner was beside himself with frustration. Casall's murderer was lurking somewhere close by, at his very elbow, and making a fool of him and everybody else. Setting them riddles and secretly watching them. How did he know that they had solved the first riddle? By rights he should not have heard that the new witness statement had led them to discover the true time of the murder, because Steiner was being deliberately reticent and had informed only the Chancellor, Jordanus, and the magistrate in charge of the case. One of those three must have told somebody else. Or was one of them the murderer? Steiner considered where each of them had been between ten and eleven o'clock on that night, but they had plenty of witnesses to clear them of suspicion. The magistrate was a garrulous man. A remark here, a hint there, and in no time the story would be borne on the breeze and would come to the ears of the murderer. Wherever Steiner went and whatever he did, he felt he was being watched. The new evidence had rendered the original witness statements useless; however, Laurien, Sophie and Domitian were still left without alibis. Lombardi could now be eliminated, but then Steiner had never seriously doubted his innocence. Three of the Masters who had not reached the tavern until after ten had no one to vouch for their whereabouts before that time because they had been at home. And what about the Bachelors and Licentiates? Steiner questioned them all. What about the other faculties, one of them asked. The theologians—they all began by studying the *artes liberales*, so they had to be considered too. It was a valid point. Assuming that the murderer was a person who had some connection with the Arts Faculty, the other faculties could not be ruled out. This greatly enlarged the circle of suspects.

But Steiner could hardly go and interrogate the theologians. That would only create bad blood and would rebound on him in the end. And what about the principals of the colleges and *bursae*? De Swerthe, for instance? His mother's house was in St. Johannisstrasse, and it was at least possible that the little Prior might have passed along Marzellenstrasse on his way there.

On the following evening Steiner went to the Prior's mother's house, where de Swerthe claimed to have been until shortly before midnight on the night of the crime. But Steiner's visit proved bitterly disappointing, for the old woman had fallen from a ladder a month before and since then had only been able to speak wildly and incoherently. She insisted that her son had never moved out, but still lived with her. She said that she had never heard of a Scholarium of which he was supposed to be the Prior. Her son studied at home, she maintained, a simple-minded smile lighting up her face: his books were all upstairs in his room, but neither she nor anyone else was allowed to go in there. Then, quite out of the blue, she flew into a rage and threatened Steiner with a broom, chasing him all round the house until at last he came within sight of the front door and managed to escape into the street. Shaken by this experience, the first thing he did was to find himself a seat in a tavern, where he planned to apply his logic to a tankard of *Gruitbier*. And to solve the second riddle.

How can it happen that a dove kills a vulture? I refuse to let him torment me, I refuse to solve his riddles. I will not play his game. His devious, macabre game of cat and mouse, in which I am supposed to be the mouse. But what if—just supposing it for the moment—he really does want to help me? If in his twisted mind he really thinks that I will accept his help—or believes that I will take up his challenge, seeing him as a worthy opponent? After all, I took the first riddle seriously and beat my brains out over it. So why not again this time? And what if the solution really does lead me to the murderer? He will know, because he knows everything, and before I can send the constables to seize him he will be gone. This can only be the Devil. The earth will open up for him and he will disappear.

Steiner felt an icy shiver running down his back. If he was up against the Devil, it was not a fair contest. But it really seemed that his opponent could be no one else. Surely this was no mortal man, who was everywhere and nowhere, and had such self-confidence that he even built his pursuers a bridge to help them catch up with him.

Steiner kept thinking of the demented old woman. What were those books that she had mentioned in her ramblings? Had that just been her madness talking, or was there a germ of truth in it? There was no question of her being able to provide the Prior with an alibi, and Steiner was annoyed with himself for not having gone there sooner to ascertain de Swerthe's guilt or innocence. But who could have guessed that she was about to lose her mind?

Steiner paid and set off again. Back to St. Johannisstrasse. All seemed quiet in the house. But how could he get inside without waking the old lady? The bolt on the door was heavy and immovable. Steiner hesitated and was about to walk on when he noticed that an upstairs window was open because of the late-summer sultriness that had descended upon the city. Resolved to act, he hitched up his coat and climbed onto a bench that stood in front of the house. Then he reached with both hands for the window-sill and tried to pull himself up. After several failed attempts he finally gained a purchase on the window-sill with his foot, and at last he found himself lying with his whole body in the window opening. He listened for a moment, holding his breath. Then he let himself down on to the floor inside the room and looked all around. The moon provided a little light, revealing the outlines of the furniture—a table, a bed, a chair. The door was open. As he crossed the room Steiner glimpsed some books lying on the table. He crept to the landing, where he could hear the old lady's loud snoring coming from behind another door. Back he went to the first room, where there were indeed three books lying on the table. Once his eyes had adjusted to the darkness, he was able to make out two of the titles: one was Aristotle's *Libri naturales*, the other Boethius' translation of the *Analytica posteriora*. But when he picked up the third book and took it over to the window so as to be able to read the title more easily, the blood suddenly froze in his veins. It was the *Libellus* de *alchimia*, one of the standard works used by alchemists! Steiner lowered the book and stared out into the street, which was bathed in the bright light of the moon. What did de Swerthe want with this book? And why was it here in this room? Did he read it when he came to visit his mother? Quite apart from the fact that this was hardly fitting reading for a prior, it amazed Steiner that he should have any interest in it. In general, de Swerthe presented himself as a strict traditionalist: Thomas Aquinas was his intellectual model, and for the nominalists he showed nothing but distaste and scorn. But what if that was just a sham, an assumed intellectual position rather than his true one? What if in reality he held unorthodox, heretical views and led a double life? The study of the occult was a two-edged sword and was only grudgingly tolerated.

Steiner replaced the book on the table and set about climbing back down. His old bones protested, but hundreds of ideas were cavorting about in his head like foals in a meadow, and when he was safely back on the ground he asked himself to what use he could put his new knowledge. He remained standing in the street and stared up at the window again. Next morning he would ask the neighbours whether they could confirm that the Prior had visited his mother on the evening in question.

Sophie knew that it would lead to a breach with her mother, but she was determined never to go back to the spinning workshop. The decision had come to her as suddenly as the idea underlying it. And that idea was so outrageous, so irresistible in its sheer absurdity, that she could not get it out of her head. She had been to the Crown *Bursa* to return a book that Casall had borrowed. There were not many women there. A few working in the kitchen or the laundry, a few doing copying work. She might have had some chance of being taken on as a copyist, but she hesitated. With her eyes cast down, she crept along the corridors to return the book to the librarian. She was conscious of the heavy odour of ink-stained linen rags. Her idea came to her little by little at first, like a wind that starts gently and gathers force until soon it is rattling the doors. She stopped in her tracks. Nearer the back of the building was a small cloister where she saw some students standing together, talking. She halted as inspiration struck her like a bolt of lightning. What if she simply went along and enrolled?

What future did she have as a yarn-spinner? Oh, certainly, it was an honourable calling, but she felt that she had been spoiled for it long ago by ideas and concepts, by pride and arrogance. She could not live that life. Enrol? For fun? Out of conceit? Should she just try it to see what happened? She knew the procedure from Casall. She had to go to a Master of her own choice and he would interview her to test the seriousness of her desire to study. He would ask her questions about her background and interests and also about the financial aspect of her application, and if his impression was favourable he would accompany her to the Rector. Then she would be required to pronounce the words of the oath, which might indeed be something of a hurdle, because an oath, once sworn, cannot easily be undone. She would pledge her loyalty to the Faculty, to its Rector and statutes, and to the Holy Roman Empire. Let them have their oath, thought Sophie, I shall be loyal, I shall merely not be the person I claim to be. It was impossible to enrol as Sophie Casall. True, it was not expressly forbidden, but she would have been met with incomprehension. A woman did not study, because there was no reason why she should. And what could she say when they asked how she was going to pay for her studies? Studying was expensive, it cost a great deal of money unless you received a *bursary,* and if you were poor your only way was either to beg in the market place or to carry books for more senior students, polish their boots, sharpen their quills....

She walked on, round the cloister where the students were standing, still talking. One gave her a quick glance and she lowered her head. At the end of this passage was the librarian's room. She handed in the book and walked back the way she had come.

But how would she pay her matriculation fee and all her other expenses if she did not go back to spinning, she asked herself, and the euphoria that she had been feeling up to that moment became overlaid with doubt and anxiety. She walked faster. And faster still. Soon she was running along the corridors, picking up her skirts and running as if for dear life. She must get out of here, and then think things over calmly.

The solution seemed quite simple. The old miser had his bulging purse hidden under his bed. It was a simple matter to creep into the bedroom and shake a few coins out into her palm. Then she went to a tailor who did not know her, and pretended that the doublet and hose she bought were for her husband. Next she purchased an ugly black horsehair wig and beard from a showman, and returned to her room where, without further ado, she cut off her hair to shoulder length so that it would fit under the wig. But where could she obtain the coat, the symbol of her student status? Those coats were not normally sold at a market but hired out by the Faculty. In the end, she bought suitable material, using the old skinflint's money, and made the coat herself. And then she waited for an outcry from the old man. When she went to her mother's house he was sitting at the window, staring out. He had noticed nothing. So it's as easy as that, mused Sophie. Who would have thought it?

Then she became aware of a different problem, which she brooded on and wrestled with for days on end. For everyone in the house where she was living she must continue to be Sophie Casall. But to go to lectures she would have to leave the house as a student…the back door! The house had a back door which led out into the garden and was hardly ever used now that autumn had arrived. She could leave the house that way, secretly, wearing her student disguise and hoping that no one would be paying any attention to the back door. Or would it be better to find new lodgings where she could present herself as a student from the start? No, she rejected that idea. When she left the house in the mornings it would still be dark and nobody would see her. And in the evenings she would just have to sneak in after nightfall. She could always look for different lodgings when the days started to lengthen again next spring. She slipped the coat on, attached the beard and put on the wig, and then looked into the mirror. The apparition that confronted her was incredible—stern and austere, the small mouth compressed, very masculine. The beard and hair gave her confidence, her voice spontaneously slid down to a lower pitch, and her eyes took on a sombre and scholarly look. She was overcome by irrepressible mirth, and laughed and laughed until her beard fell off. She had better avoid laughing if she wanted to succeed in proving to them what they would never believe even if they saw it with their own eyes—that a woman, too, was capable of learning everything there was to be learnt. She felt light-hearted and carefree again for the first time since her marriage to Casall. Now, all of a sudden, she knew what she wanted. She gave no thought to the legal consequences—they could wait. Instead she thought about how to outwit the miser, who was sure to count his coins at regular intervals.

She waited. Days passed. Then one morning before sunrise she crept down the stairs. At this early hour, although the servants were already up and busying themselves in the kitchen, there was no one to look out into the overgrown garden as she darted through it. Then she was out in the street and on her way to enrol. She had decided upon a young Master whom she did not know, and intended to go and knock at his door.

An icy chill pervaded the cloister, lodging in its corners and creeping along the walls. The sun was growing gradually weaker and the days shorter. Now there was no one sitting on the College steps in the sunshine: instead the students were huddled in the few rooms that were heated, wearing heavy coats.

The first lecture that Sophie attended was with the Master whom she had chosen for her matriculation. She was freezing, for she was sitting on the floor, which was cold through and through. The lecture was on phenomena, and she busily wrote it all down, even though she could have read the book at home. I must do nothing to attract attention, assume an air of poverty and remember that I live in a miserable little room in Spielmannsgasse, because students prefer to associate with people who have money. The student sitting next to her exuded the stale smell of the previous evening's alcohol, which made Sophie feel sick. A peculiar odour of earth, sour wine and paper hung in the air. Laurien was sitting in front of her, his back bent and his paper on his lap, and once when he turned round she smiled at him. He did not recognise her. He had never seen the new student before, and she was well satisfied. If only she were not constantly afraid that the old man might decide to count his silver pennies, and perhaps beat her mother black and blue on the assumption that she was responsible...

'What's your name?' her neighbour whispered to her. For her matriculation she had adopted the name Josef Heinrich. It seemed unremarkable, the sort of name that anybody might have.

'Josef Heinrich.'

'Which scholarium do you live in?'

'I don't live in a scholarium. I have a shabby little room in Spielmannsgasse.'

The student lost interest. Anyone who lived in that street was not worth cultivating.

The Master brought the lecture to a close and turned to leave. The students rose and went their separate ways. No one paid any heed to the quiet, bearded young man who looked as if he had forgotten how to laugh, and as none of the students from the colleges knew him they preferred to pursue their own pleasures and ignore him. The solemn young man with the beard smiled contentedly to himself. I'll show you all what I can do. A lamb among wolves, and you don't even notice.

And so back to the windy cloister, which was deserted now. As she walked slowly along, some voices, gently echoing, drifted over towards her. Then she stopped dead and stood rigid and motionless. That was Steiner's voice, and the other was Lombardi's. The voices grew louder and, by craning forward a little to see past the column with its acanthus leaves, she found she could catch almost every word.

'Casall's murderer, always assuming that that's who it is, has set me a second riddle. I am to think of the *quadrivium*, and how it can happen that a dove kills a vulture.'

'And why are you telling me this? Am I no longer on your list of possible murderers?'

'Do you know, I wander around like a ghost that is everywhere and nowhere, just as the killer is everywhere and nowhere. I can trust no one except myself, and even that I sometimes doubt...'

A mocking laugh reached Sophie's ears.

'What's that about the *quadrivium*?' asked Lombardi. 'What does he mean? I've never seen a dove kill a vulture. It seems to me he's just pulling our legs. One ought to consider very seriously whether his scribblings deserve to be read at all.'

'They are the only thing we have to go on.'

'But perhaps someone else altogether is having a joke at our expense.'

Steiner said no more. Hidden between two columns in a freezing corner of the cloister, Sophie drew her coat closer around her. What sort of a riddle was that? How was it connected with the *quadrivium*? Was this a philosophical puzzle, or merely the work of an idiot who enjoyed seeing the Faculty Masters make fools of themselves? She heard footsteps. Someone was coming from one of the cellars. Needing to walk past the two Masters, she lifted her head and staked everything on a single chance. With a polite greeting she looked them full in the face. Lombardi nodded, Steiner likewise. They were as blind as bats: the first victory was won.

He had hired a horse and was out of the city before sunset. During the night he would not be allowed back into the city through this gate without paying, and he considered whether it might not be best to spend the night in one of the villages. His way to Weilersfeld took him past fields and meadows. It was a lonely area. There were hills on the horizon; the river flowed sluggishly. There was not a breath of wind.

He asked a peasant the way to the former Cistercian abbey. Where the chancel windows had lost their glass, creepers twined round the stonework, and rubble from the side aisles lay scattered about, probably serving the neighbourhood as a quarry. Not a soul was to be seen. Grains of earth came crumbling down from one of the columns as he stepped up to the altar. There he discovered fresh traces of wax on the stone surface. So they really had been here. He looked all around. The countryside was flat and empty apart from some clumps of bushes nearby. That was where they must have hidden, Laurien and Domitian. Imagining what they had seen sent cascades of shivers up and down his spine, and he felt a crackling in the roots of his hair. 'My God,' he muttered, and walked back to his horse.

He sat down on the grass and waited. He knew their rituals, and it was not by chance that he had come on this particular day. Indeed, he was familiar with all their ideas and practices, and he was afraid.

When they appeared, a curious procession in the dark, with their candles and their catlike wailing, he rose to his feet, because he had no intention of watching them perform their macabre dance. Perhaps it would have been wiser to get a look at their faces first, to make sure that they really were the people he thought they were. But that proved to be unnecessary. The chief priest was Neidhard, whose face he had never forgotten. A renegade monk who had finally found his vocation in the *sexum sacrale,* just as other people found theirs in the service of the Church, or in art. But the Church, viewing with disfavour his outlandish way of serving it, harried and persecuted him and wished him to Hell. Neidhard stood stock-still, like an animal that scents approaching danger. He turned his head and held his candle higher. Lombardi stepped closer, his knife concealed under his doublet as a precaution. The novices and nuns cried out in alarm, and their eyes shifted towards Neidhard, who with a forceful gesture called for silence. Then he smiled and beckoned Lombardi over.

'Well, if it isn't Master Lombardi. Are you feeling the urge to return to our bosom?'

'I wanted to warn you. Unbeknown to you, there are people who come here and watch you. What you are doing is folly, Neidhard, and it could cost you your lives.'

The priest in his grey habit gave a visible start. 'Who are you saying has been here? I have seen no one.'

'Oh yes. Boys from one of the villages, they were talking about it in a tavern. You must all be mad to take such a risk.'

'I know nothing of this,' said Neidhard indignantly. 'Do you suppose I would choose to put us in danger? Our first rule states...'

'I know your first rule,' Lombardi interrupted brusquely. 'And because I have no wish to be hanged, I came to warn you. If you can't be more discreet, Neidhard, you would do better to return to your monastery.'

Neidhard merely laughed. 'Where else are we to go? These are troubled times, as you well know. Ruins are not so easy to come by, nor are cellars...'

'Perhaps you should try Hell one of these days,' said Lombardi. He took his hand off his knife.

'And what's more, winter is coming,' lamented Neidhard, 'and it's getting cold outside for my flock. I can't make my little lambs lie down for me in the snow—though of course that too would have its appeal.'

He laughed again, seeming not to take the danger seriously. And then he pushed forward one of the nuns who had been following these exchanges with obvious anxiety, lifted up her habit and showed Lombardi her full breasts.

'Well, brother Siger? Would this be to your taste? You never used to be so coy, do you remember? There was a time when you would gladly have taken what was on offer, and the women loved you…'

'Just go away,' growled Lombardi.

'*You* certainly won't betray us, my friend' said Neidhard sharply. 'In a few days from now we are expecting some brothers from Flanders to join us here. But we'll watch our step, never fear.'

Lombardi turned away. He swung himself onto his horse. He could not bear the sight of them any more. A short stretch further on he hitched the stallion's reins to a tree.

It was too dark to ride home, the horse would never find the way and neither would he. So he had no choice but to sleep out here, wrapping himself in his cold, damp blanket. He lit a fire, as if he meant to guard the purity of the ruin, a purity it had already well and truly lost. But he himself had once been no better than those who were now so persistently besmirching it. He refused to let his mind dwell on that. How could he begin a new life when the shadows of the old one were always pursuing him in full cry?

*Chassez le naturel, il revient au galop.* No one can change his nature. Or, to put it another way, even if you try to drive nature away with a pitchfork, it will always come back.

He stared into the starless night.

De Swerthe was in a merry mood, for the patron of the Scholarium had decided to bestow a gift upon it. A sum of money with which the dwarf planned to set up a small library, appoint a second master and provide accommodation for more students. This would raise the prestige of the somewhat impoverished Scholarium just as it raised the canon's spirits. The individual colleges habitually recommended themselves to new students on the strength of their good masters and well-stocked libraries, but de Swerthe had never been able to offer such attractions. Until now, his benefactor had tended to be frugal with his contributions—but a wealthy man anxious for a good place in the Kingdom of Heaven must think betimes of laying its foundations while still on earth.

Having received these glad tidings, de Swerthe augmented the usual fare for that evening with roast meat, some cheese which he had ordered the cook to buy from a Dutchman at the market, and some wine from the vineyards of Eberbach abbey, with which he had good contacts. They had created a completely new type of wine there; it lay delicately upon the tongue and did not leave one's head aching like the stale-tasting wines that were to be had locally. On this occasion De Swerthe also allowed the students to talk during the meal, so that they could comment on the wonderful news, while he sat, proud and jovial, at the head of the table, letting his eyes roam around the refectory. Suddenly he noticed that one of the students was missing. Next to Laurien there was an empty seat, Domitian's place, and instantly the Prior was on his feet demanding to know where he was. Lombardi, still engrossed in his plateful of cheese, looked up and shrugged. 'Perhaps his father has returned to town.'

'But he has not applied for an *exeat*,' hissed the diminutive de Swerthe. However rich and famous his father might be, young Master Domitian could not be allowed simply to absent himself without leave. 'You will look into this,' he instructed Lombardi in an undertone, and then sat down again on his bench, vowing not to let this matter spoil his evening of glory.

Lombardi only nodded. The cheese was soft and full of flavour, the wine a revelation. Never had he tasted such a good one. Laurien, sitting opposite him, was silent as usual, eating circumspectly and drinking with moderation. When addressed, he gave brief, amiable replies, but did not seem inclined to pursue conversation further. At one point his eyes met Lombardi's, and he immediately lowered them, but then thought better of it and whispered anxiously, 'Magister Lombardi, could I have a word with you afterwards?'

'What about?'

'Domitian.'

Lombardi thought nothing of it. All the students stepped out of line once in a while. An hour later, though, sitting in his room with Laurien and holding another glass of that superb wine, he began to feel apprehensive. Laurien was perched on the stool, his hands clasped tightly together, his feet twitching as though he was on the point of running away, his eyes moving restlessly around.

'He's gone there again…'

'Where?'

'To the ruin. With Marinus from the College…'

Lombardi stood up abruptly. His face had taken on an unnatural pallor. It looked ashen. He said softly, 'It's not possible. You're saying he still goes out there?'

'Yes, he still goes. Just once more, he said. He thinks he's doing nothing wrong, it's those people who are sinning…'

'He is sinning too,' Lombardi replied vehemently. 'Anyone who gains pleasure from the sins of others incurs the same guilt.'

'Yes, sir,' mumbled Laurien, twisting his fingers as if he were trying to tie them into knots. 'But what shall we do about it? I mean, if anything has happened to him…'

'Well,' Lombardi interrupted him furiously. 'If anything has happened to him, it's his own fault. But let's think about it.'

He sat down again. His agitation added to Laurien's discomfiture. If Lombardi was worried too, then perhaps the whole thing was even worse than he himself had feared.

'You are not to say a word to anybody. Not to anybody, do you hear? I will take care of it. The best thing is for you to forget what you know, and forget that you have discussed it with me or that you confided in me before. Do you understand, Laurien? Not a word to anyone at all.'

'Yes sir. Not a word. But you really will do something about it?'

Lombardi nodded and dismissed the boy. Before his mind's eye images took shape, images he had believed were banished forever but which now obtruded themselves on his thoughts like clouds blocking out the sun. The darkness in his mind seemed to grow and grow. He felt threatened, frightened and at a loss what to do. He could not possibly tell anyone about the gatherings in the ruin and the terrible trap into which Domitian seemed to have fallen. He could reveal nothing without incriminating himself in the highest degree. He was condemned to silence and would have to wait. Wait until either Domitian returned or the vultures had picked his bones clean in the sun and the veil of oblivion had spread itself over his handsome corpse.

'Why is he pointing us towards the *quadrivium*?'

'Yes indeed. Why not the *trivium*?'

'Because the *trivium* has nothing to do with quantities. And he is pointing us towards the dove and the vulture. The one a creature noted for its gentleness, the other a repulsive devourer of carrion. Is it something to do with a moral quantity?'

Jordanus shook his head. He was weary and wanted his bed. At night the College was gloomier than ever. A building made up of windowless passageways from which the chill never lifted and of dark, unheated rooms. The library had books on chains, but there was little to be gained from leafing through them. He would not find the solution there. Steiner's eye lighted upon the little statue of the Virgin Mary standing in its niche in the wall, before it a candle that was just about to expire. Above their heads they heard the creak of footsteps: someone was pacing restlessly to and fro.

'What is the position regarding the suspects?' asked Jordanus.

'The Devil is the only one left. I cannot see Laurien as a murderer, nor Casall's wife. That leaves Domitian von Semper; there are also a few of the Bachelors and Licentiates who have no alibis. And then there are all the theologians, but one cannot treat them as suspects without making powerful enemies…'

'Do you think they would wreck their careers by killing a Master of the Faculty? Surely that is absurd.'

'And what about the canons, who have always been opposed to everything? Do you know how many canons there are in this city alone who see nominalism as the ruin of Christendom because it dares to draw a dividing-line between religion and philosophy, as Ockham postulates?'

Jordanus grinned. 'There ought surely to be some connection between the dead man and his murderer. He must at least have known him. I would be inclined to seek him among the members of the Arts Faculty. By widening the field you are dissipating your powers, like a blanket fraying at the edges. One should always start in the middle of the circle and work outwards, not *vice versa.*'

'Sometimes I think it really was the Devil,' said Steiner quietly. He gripped Jordanus's arm. 'Do you hear that?' The footsteps up above were growing louder.

'You think that's the Devil walking about up there? You should try to keep your imagination in check, esteemed Magister. You are just seeing empty shadows.'

'Yes,' Steiner muttered, 'nothing but shadows. Shadows of shadows, even: it is horrible. Someone goes and murders one of the Masters. And then sets us a philosophical riddle. That *can* only be the Devil. And we, with our habit of picking everything to pieces, have gone to the devil ourselves, because we can no longer believe in anything, since nothing is susceptible to proof. Not even God, if you ask me. There is no doubt about that, is there?'

Jordanus agreed. Quite true, there was no doubt about it. Just as there was no proving the existence of the Devil either. 'If you go about it like that, Steiner, you will never find your murderer. Devil or not, he exists. And he is watching us. Perhaps he is here in this college. Perhaps he is your neighbour. But the question is, what is he trying to achieve by putting us onto his track?'

'What if the information he is giving us is false?'

'Do you think it is?'

'No. No, I believe it to be genuine. That is precisely what makes it so diabolical. He feels superior to us. The hubris of a killer. But, Jordanus, I refuse to solve his riddles. I've had enough.'

Jordanus nodded. There was indeed something mad about

letting oneself be drawn into tackling these riddles. And yet these were the only pointers they had. So back to the *quadrivium*, to the study of quantities, dimensions, sizes. It dealt with numbers and ratios, rhombuses and ellipses, circles and straight lines, and fractions, not forgetting the stars, the moon and the sun. Clearly defined principles that one could hold on to. The doctrine of quantities was possibly the one constant that could stand up to the scrutiny of philosophers. Yet, for all that, numbers were only abstractions. No number had ever come and sat down and announced: Look, here I am. Numbers did not exist *a priori*. They existed only in man's imagination. There was no forest where a number grew alongside birch and elm and beech. No number was to be found in an ocean, nor in the clouds. The numbers could not have existed before man existed. Or could they? Jordanus sighed. It always came back to that old bone of contention: which came first, the idea or the thing? The chicken or the egg? But, as the oft-repeated saying went, you could not compare cats with trout. The human brain was a container full of invalid ideas, and if man had no eyes he might even claim that those ideas were real. That there might be a forest full of numbers, an ocean full of numbers, and numbers hanging suspended in the sky on long golden threads.

'This is nonsense,' Jordanus said at length. 'You can only go on what you can see, hear, smell, taste and feel. And calculate, perhaps: it may well be that in some way numbers are what everything is based on. Though they too can be misleading.'

'Does he want to engage in dispute with us? What is he trying to prove to us?'

'That we are wrong,' Jordanus said shortly. But in what respect they were wrong he too had no idea. 'Let us go for a walk and view the world from a different perspective. From that of a tree or a vulture. Then let us alter the dimensions. Make yourself big or small, double your size, puff yourself up like the genie released from the bottle—what do you see then? Imagine that you are an ant: a pond is the ocean, with shores that you will never reach. A tree is like the universe, and when the leaves fall in autumn they could crush you to death. You may drown in a single raindrop. A man's foot will mean certain death if you happen to be crawling in the wrong place. What *is* a man to you? You have no concept of him. Nothing. Absolutely nothing, just a shadow cast from above. Or imagine you are a vulture. Seeing the world from on high, gliding under low-hanging clouds, your gaze always directed downwards. When the smell of carrion rises, like a column of smoke, to your nostrils, you follow where the smell leads you. It will be lying somewhere down there, an animal, a human being, whatever. It is the smell of death that guides you. That is what the study of quantities and sizes tells us, namely that they are experienced differently by every individual.' Jordanus laughed softly. 'You are right, Steiner. He is here. In our immediate vicinity, otherwise he would not be so well informed. You should be careful. Perhaps he is able to deceive witnesses too…'

'So he is the Devil after all, then?'

'No. Just a cunning villain. No more than that.'

They walked slowly towards the college exit. Perhaps it was you, Jordanus, thought Steiner. Because if he is able to deceive everybody—however he does it—then I have to doubt your innocence too.

A question hovered on Steiner's lips, one that up to now he had been holding back. What about de Swerthe? Did the book of alchemy make him a possible suspect for the murder? But there was no way of proving that he had not been with his mother that evening: the neighbours affirmed that the Prior often came to visit her, though none of them could swear that he was there on that particular night. Nor was there any indication of a link between the book and Casall's death. Should he simply confront de Swerthe with his discovery in order to clarify the matter? But he choked back his question.

'Nothing but shadows,' he muttered wearily.

Even so, the thought gave him no peace, and at last he went to the Scholarium and asked to see the Prior. De Swerthe was sitting in his room, bent over a pile of bills, and seemed pleased when Steiner appeared in the doorway.

'Come and sit down,' he said pleasantly, pointing to a stool. He gathered his papers together and carefully pushed them to a corner of the table.

Steiner sat down. 'Tell me, do you know the *Libellus de alchimia*?'

Perhaps it was unwise to be so direct, though it gave him the advantage of surprise. But the Prior's angelic face showed no reaction.

'Yes, I know it. Why?'

'It doesn't represent your own views?'

'No, it doesn't. Why do you ask?'

Steiner could hardly say that he had broken into the house of de Swerthe's confused mother, and so he had to think up a different answer.

'I have heard that there are more and more books of that kind circulating in the city's colleges. Although I lecture on magic and the occult myself, I don't give practical guidance on how to produce substances, if you follow me…'

A faint flush appeared on de Swerthe's delicate, magnolia-white skin. 'Oh yes, I follow you. You mean that I should check whether there is anything of that kind here?'

Steiner made no reply. He was still watching the other's face intently. Then he said: 'Have you ever taken an interest in the subject yourself?'

De Swerthe took his time in replying. 'The Curia does not like people to involve themselves in that sort of thing,' he said at last, in a low tone. 'Yes, I've read it, if that is what you mean. But I am an ardent supporter of Thomism. Those modern schools of thought have always been anathema to me, and the catastrophes which result from that kind of magic…'

Steiner stood up. Merely possessing a book did not make someone a murderer. Besides, he could not see the slightest motive, for de Swerthe seemed wholly to share Casall's intellectual position. And yet Steiner felt a creeping unease.

'Did you have a good relationship with Casall?' he suddenly blurted out.

The Prior stared at him. 'Did I? Why? Surely you don't suspect me of having murdered Casall?'

Steiner shook his head. 'I'm asking everyone, you must be aware of that. And there are no witnesses for your visit to your mother…'

'No, and now she can't testify herself, poor woman, after falling from that accursed ladder. But seriously, Steiner, I really had no reason to get rid of Casall, though given his notorious cruelty I had no high regard for him either, but then I imagine no one had…'

Steiner abruptly took his leave. Words, nothing but words, he thought irritably. There were times when it took him days of silence to recover from the sheer meaninglessness of words. Everybody had an excess of words, even the mentally confused still had more than enough. What was he to do with this plethora of words that contrived so effectively to distort and mangle reality? The fact remained that the Prior had no witness to exonerate him. But there was none to incriminate him either.

The farmer brought his oxen to a halt and sniffed the air. He had a good nose, but not even a dead man could have missed the stench which had settled, dome-like, over the small valley, only occasionally stirring in the wind. Surely it was coming from the ruin over there! Leaving his ox-cart, the farmer climbed up the meadow towards the remains of the former Cistercian abbey. The foul smell grew stronger: perhaps it was a dead animal that had been lying for hours in the sun. Unsuspectingly he climbed over the broken masonry, heard the pigeons fly up from the empty window arches and looked around. Over there was the altar. Long shadows enveloped the choir. There was indeed something lying in front of the altar, strangely contorted. The farmer moved closer…

Over the last few days Laurien had sought the company of the new student more and more. Josef Heinrich was reserved and serious, like himself, and no doubt it was the recognition of a kindred nature that drew Laurien to him. Besides, he had lost his other friend, who had mysteriously vanished. He and Josef had sat side by side at the lecture on the soul, and afterwards strolled around the city together, although their homeward paths lay in different directions. Sophie could never go straight back to her room, and even when it was dark she still had to make certain that none of the servants was about before she could slip into the garden and from there into the house. On one of their walks they struck up a conversation, each in his own manner, he with that profound melancholy that never seemed to leave him, and Sophie of necessity acting a role which prevented her from ever behaving naturally.

She liked him. He was pleasant and approachable, but he had virtually no friends because the others were put off by his air of gloom and dismissed him as a loner who would be poor company for them.

'You're not particularly happy here, are you?' she said as they were crossing the market-place.

He stared at her. 'What gives you that impression?'

She laughed, a wry, sombre laugh that was part of her assumed manner. 'You don't exactly have many friends.'

'I had one good friend. But he's vanished without trace. And perhaps he'll never come back. In any case I don't make friends easily.' He stopped abruptly. 'You're quite different. Sometimes I feel as if I'd known you before. That does happen, you know. You meet someone who is a stranger and yet who seems very familiar…'

Sophie shrank back a little. She must be careful what she said now. 'I suppose such things may be possible,' she murmured, and said goodbye.

Pensively she walked home. Having made sure that there was no one in the garden, she hurried in through the back entrance and crept up the stairs. Once there, she removed her wig and beard, sank down on a stool and stared out of the window. She had not reckoned with this. Laurien was no fool, and he was sensitive. Would he realise that she was not the person he thought she was? But she dismissed the thought and instead revelled in the knowledge of having suc-ceeded in what she had set out to do. She had taken no one into her confidence, and if anyone asked her how she spent her time when she was not at home, she replied that the Clarisses had given her a position as a copyist, and it did not occur to anyone to suspect that this was a barefaced lie. But her situation would become impossibly difficult as time went on, she thought, for how could she keep this up for four or five years, and, what was more, find the money for the examinations? And then—but there was really no point in thinking about this—how could she maintain this disguise, which forced her to be constantly acting a part, always on her guard and never able to be herself? The pleasure of her initial triumph began to fade, for how would she ever be able to enjoy it to the full? And in the summer, when she could no longer leave her room under cover of darkness, she would have to find a new place to stay.

Nevertheless, she did not give up. Every morning at five she went off to the lecture-rooms of the Faculty, sat and wrote, conversed with Laurien, and spent the evening alone in her room. She avoided going out for a drink or a meal with the others, and this soon made her as much of an outsider as Laurien. Since during the lectures the students were not expected to say much, but only to listen and write, no one noticed that she knew more than the rest, or suspected that she had books at home which they were obliged to borrow, or read in a chained library. But she had yet another worry, a final item on the list, so to speak, and that was the matter of the coins she had stolen. So far the old man did not seem to have noticed anything amiss, but the day would come when she would have to relieve him of some more. Five coins out of a total of a hundred were barely noticeable. But ten? And he would surely count them now and again. It was just a matter of time.

One chilly October evening she opened her heart to Griseldis and told her of her metamorphosis.

'I've registered as a student of the Faculty.'

'You're having me on. You can't register. You're a woman.'

'Who says that women can't matriculate?'

'How is that possible? Have they changed the statutes specially for you?'

'No. I disguise myself as a man.'

Now Griseldis appeared to grasp the situation. Her friend was actually going into the colleges dressed as a man and studying the *artes liberales*!

'You must be mad. Do you want them to burn you as a witch on the Alter Markt?'

'Does any law prohibit women from attending the Faculty disguised as men? Is it heresy? Does God object to it?'

Griseldis said nothing. Did God object to it? No, but men did. The men who laboured to prove the existence of God—they objected to it.

'You can't do that,' Griseldis said in a low voice, and the sense of an impending threat came over her so abruptly that she closed the window as though the danger lurked outside in the street.

'Sophie, if they catch you they'll clap you in gaol. The disgrace, the derision! Can you imagine how they'll feel if you pursue this farce to the point of taking an examination? I've no idea what it says in their statutes, but I know what the Masters of the Faculty will have to say about it. And they won't be the only ones. You've sworn an oath under a false name, you've matriculated under a false name...'

'Yes,' Sophie murmured. Woman is to man as imperfection is to perfection. Woman's inferiority results from an excess of moisture and low temperature. She is a deformity of nature. *Femina est mas occasionatus*, said Aristotle, the sage whose words she so dutifully listened to in lectures: woman is a mutilated male. *Corruptio instrumenti*—when the man produces defective semen and his wife gives birth to a girl. Or *venti australes*—when the south winds produce too much water, resulting in girls instead of boys. Such a creature could not be capable of logical thought, and although the Curia tolerated convent schools for women and girls, which even taught the *trivium* and *quadrivium*, that was very different from her wish to study alongside the men.

'How did you get the money for it?' Griseldis asked.

'I took it. Out of my stepfather's purse.'

'I thought so. I'll have a mass read for you, and light a candle. May God have mercy on you.'

They sat silently at the table, drinking wine. Wine brought along by Griseldis, who was never short of funds.

'Where do the people here suppose that you go during the day?' Griseldis asked at last. The candle on the table went out, leaving them sitting in the dark.

'I've told them that I work as a copyist for the Clarisses.'

'This whole idea of yours must have been inspired by the Devil.'

'Yes, very likely. The Devil is the cause of everything. He is the midwife of philosophy, and its godfather too. This obsessive urge to know everything is his doing.'

Griseldis rose to her feet and picked up her basket. She left the remaining wine and the loaf of bread. This woman made her feel uncomfortable. 'What's the attraction of wanting to know everything? Will it buy me things? Will it dress me or feed my children? And if you know yourself that it's the Devil's work, why do you take it to the lengths of going to their lectures?'

Shaking her head in disbelief, she kissed Sophie on the forehead and left the room. Gently the door closed.

Sophie could hear her going down the stairs. Then she sat on alone in the darkness.

'Tell me what's troubling you. Come on, tell me.'

The autumn sunshine lay on the water. Laurien had decided not to attend the lecture. For days cramps had been squeezing his stomach like a bellows so that he could not take any food and he had been living on water and beer. Nothing but water and beer for three days. But now he had bought himself a big piece of cheese from the market; even if this made a large hole in his paltry budget, it would help him back onto his feet.

They were sitting on a low wall, watching the barges unloading their cargoes. The smell of herrings and pepper hung in the air, a peculiar blend of odours. Over on the opposite bank they could see the roofs of Deutz; lines of trees, radiant in their October colouring, shone brightly among the fields and meadows, and their fragmented reflections shimmered on the waves.

'Do tell me,' urged Sophie.

'I can't, Josef.'

'Why not? Why have you stopped eating and given up going to lectures?'

Laurien suddenly seized her by the hands. 'Because I simply can't. I think I know where Domitian went, and I've even told Lombardi, but he's doing nothing about it. Nothing at all. Only yesterday Steiner said that the magistrate's officers had scoured the whole city for him, they had even been to Schmierstrasse and to the Alter Graben, where you find the worst kind of riff-raff. But he wasn't hanging around in the city at all...'

Sophie could not make head or tail of this. Why should Domitian not have been in the city? And if not in the city, where had he been?

'Listen, what are you talking about?'

'About Domitian's disappearance. I know where he is, and I don't think he'll ever come back. Not because he doesn't want to but because he can't...because they've killed him.'

Sophie shook off his cold fingers that were clammy with sweat. What was all this nonsense?

'I promised Lombardi I'd keep quiet, but how can I if he does nothing? He hasn't even told Steiner where they ought to search. He's acting as if he knew absolutely nothing about it.'

'And what are you saying he does know?'

Laurien was starting to shiver. The autumn sun was not warming him, and the more he gazed at the water the more a damp chill penetrated his bones. He was waking up at night because his feet seemed to turn into blocks of ice, lumps of flesh with no feeling in them and no connection to the rest of his body. And the constant question: what should I do? Is it your business if Domitian can't keep his lust under control and gets caught in the coils of heretics who then slit his throat? What has it to do with you, Laurien?

And then, because he felt so weak that he expected at any moment to topple off the wall and into the water, and so terribly dizzy and incapable of keeping the dreadful secret to himself any longer, he leaned closer to his friend Josef Heinrich and whispered the whole story into his ear. How the sect had met there, and how he was sure that Domitian had gone to watch them again and had not come back since. How they behaved like cows and bulls in the field, shaming God and the whole of Christendom, and...

He had whispered himself hoarse. Then he slumped down and stared into the water again. Bright lights flashed before his eyes, and his stomach suddenly started to churn round like the sails of a windmill. He rushed down to the river and bent over the edge.

Sophie watched him, her mind filled with horror. Like bulls and cows in the field? But not in the field, on the altar, he had added. She saw Laurien coming back. He crouched down on the ground in front of her and took her hand again. 'Josef, you're free to go where you like, but I'm imprisoned in the Scholarium and can't get out. Please go to Weilersfeld and make some enquiries. Perhaps someone there knows something...'

She was about to stroke his hair to comfort him, but stopped herself just in time. That was not the way men behaved towards each other. 'Does he mean so much to you?'

'I'm certain that something has happened to him. I liked him, he was my friend. And it was his father who made it possible for me to study...'

Sophie nodded. 'And Lombardi? How is he involved in this?'

'Not at all. It's just...I confided in him. But he isn't taking any action. I don't think he cares whether Domitian is dead or not.'

Laurien went down to the bank again, his hands thrust deep into the pockets of his coat. Then abruptly he turned round, and his eyes fell on his friend, who was still sitting on the wall gazing abstractedly at the river. Strange—what made him suddenly think of Sophie? It seemed an eternity since he had last seen her. He had not forgotten Casall's widow, and even now he felt a small stab in his stomach whenever he thought of her. But how, or where, *could* he have seen her again? She had moved out of her former house, and he did not know where she was living now. Josef Heinrich seemed oblivious of him; his eyes were still on the water. Perhaps it was those eyes that reminded Laurien of Sophie. As if they were the same colour. An opalescent blue, varying according to the play of the sunlight in them. Harebell blue. No, lighter, much lighter, like liverwort. The most beautiful blue in the world, a delicate, bright, translucent blue amid the anthracite grey of winter.

Laurien was confused. From this distance he could not see his friend's eyes clearly at all. What nonsense this was.

But Josef's hands, too, he now remembered, had reminded him of Sophie. How strange. Small, slender hands which held a pen as if they had never done anything else. Laurien shook his head and stood up. His imagination was playing tricks on him, and he returned to his friend, who seemed to be awaking from his reverie and met his eyes.

'Come on,' he said, 'let's go.'

Sophie had an aunt living in Weilersfeld. So it would not be difficult to find out the gossip and all the latest rumours circulating there. And nothing would emerge from it anyway, Sophie thought, as she set out on her way.

Her aunt lived in a convent for poor widows, and any visitor was welcome. Around the building, a former Cistercian monastery, was a park with old trees. The ladies would often walk there, weather permitting, and that was where Sophie found her aunt, strolling along the paths with a rosary twined round her fingers.

'God has heard my prayers!' was her greeting to her niece. 'A visitor for me at last, after all this time. Your mother has stopped coming ever since she got married again.'

'She's pregnant,' Sophie said, putting a comforting arm around her aunt's shoulders. Chatting as they went, they walked through the brilliant autumn colours of the park. Her aunt grumbled about the food and her various ailments, and Sophie let her talk. Only when the bell rang for the midday meal did she ask her for the information she wanted; whether anything had happened lately in Weilersfeld. Had a dead body been found, perhaps... ?

Sophie's aunt stopped in her tracks and lowered her voice. 'Why are you asking me that? Yes, a body was found. At the ruin. But nobody knows who it is. He was young, not even twenty. But that isn't the worst of it. The farmer who found him said that his murderers had strangled him with a girdle from a monk's habit...'

Sophie was shocked. So Domitian really was dead?

'And only yesterday they found a coat lying not far from where he was discovered. The bailiff thinks he was a student from the city. And then someone else was here, asking the same question as you...'

'A young man? Dark-haired, small and slender?'

The aunt shook her head. 'He did have dark hair. But he was tall and well-built. A very handsome man, by all accounts.'

Lombardi. That must have been Lombardi, she thought at once. Why had he come here to ask the same questions that she was asking? Because he wanted to find out for himself what had happened? But if so, why make his enquiries in secret, telling no one?

She would have to go and see him. The image of the student's dead body haunted her mind, even though she had not seen it. Had he screamed but not been heard? That seemed quite possible, as the ruin was some way away from the village. How long had he lain there before death had released him?

Sophie felt grief for the student who, though a little arrogant, had always been friendly. What kind of brutes must they be to have killed him in such a horrible way?

It was a boy of about ten who entered, after giving a timid knock, and shyly laid a letter on the magistrate's table. He said that a man had pressed a gulden into his hand as payment for delivering it. The magistrate smiled at the little chap and reached for the paper.

> *If you are looking for the murderer of the student, search for the Brethren of the Free Spirit—it is they who are responsible.*

The magistrate looked up. 'What did he look like, the man who gave you this?'

The boy thought. 'Tall, bearded, and wearing a black cloak with a hood up over his head.'

The magistrate nodded. 'And you got the money?'

Beaming, the boy opened his hand to reveal the shiny coin. Then he quickly turned and ran out of the room.

The student Josef Heinrich rang the doorbell of the Scholarium. One of the housemaids opened the door and let him in. Yes, Magister Lombardi was in his room, reading. A brisk knock, and then the sound of

Lombardi's footsteps. The door opened; his face wore a friendly smile. On the table Sophie could see Ockham, the nominalists' bible.

'You're reading. Am I disturbing you?'

Lombardi shook his head and offered the student his stool. He had only one.

'You know that Domitian is dead, don't you? Another student asked me to see what I could find out about him, and as I have an aunt living near Weilersfeld I did as he asked.'

Sophie had no need to say more. Lombardi lowered his eyes and said not a word. He seemed to be thinking. Perhaps he was merely considering how to reply. At last he looked up. The expression in his slightly narrowed eyes was veiled, enigmatic. 'What do you know? And why have you come to me about it?'

'Because I heard that you had also been asking about him. So you must have had your suspicions.'

'Laurien has been talking to you, hasn't he? You two have become friends…'

'Yes. And because he is worried he confided in me.'

Lombardi gave a soft laugh. 'There seem to be a lot of people he thinks he can confide in. He should choose his confidants more carefully.'

'Oh? Should he? He thought that you would help him, and instead you make enquiries secretly, keeping your thoughts and conclusions to yourself. And meanwhile the magistrate's officers continue to search for Domitian's body within the city walls, where of course they will never find it.'

'This morning a parish officer from Weilersfeld appeared before the city council and testified that a dead body and an Arts Faculty coat had been found there. So that disposes of that. And I hear that the magistrate has received a letter accusing a heretical sect of the murder.'

Sophie studied his face. He was a cold and calculating man, that much was obvious. She could guess at his thoughts: how much should I say, how much should I withhold? What does this student know, and what business has he to poke his nose into my affairs? And why on earth did that fool Laurien pour out his troubles to him?

'Were you trying to help him?' she asked.

'What did he tell you?' Lombardi was hedging. He needed to find out how much Josef Heinrich knew. The new student responded readily to his tactics.

'That he went to the ruins once with Domitian. The poor boy is desperate; he's at his wits' end. Not only because he witnessed that sacrilege but because he is deeply anxious about his friend.'

What a simple soul, he was probably thinking. Two simple souls who have found each other. Well, then, I'll go on the offensive, I'll tell him what he wants to know.

'You have heard of these sects? There are some who worship the Devil, driving out God as other people drive out the winter. And then there are others who think they have to look for God between their thighs. Who pay homage neither to the concept of sin nor to asceticism, but instead set up their own ideal, and I can't tell you what that's like.'

'And it was they who killed Domitian?' Sophie asked softly.

'It's possible, Josef. If he was there watching them, then his life wasn't worth a bean if they caught him at it. After all, the Church denounces them as heretics.'

'And why did you keep silent? Why didn't you report what had happened?'

Lombardi smiled. 'Because I had promised Laurien that I would keep it a secret. It would have been most unwise to set the magistrate on the trail.'

No, Sophie thought. That wasn't the true reason. But then what was? That diabolical smile. He felt safe. Why had he let them search the whole city for the missing student, knowing full well that he had been murdered elsewhere?

'You're lying,' she said.

'You just mind your own business from now on, do you hear?' he answered coldly.

'Do you think that by discussing this I'm tempting the Devil to appear?'

He laughed. 'No. Though even Steiner has begun to think he has the Devil at his heels. But I don't believe that he exists in the world of real things. He belongs in the world of mental concepts, but we can't keep the two apart. Because we have never seen the Devil in the flesh, and indeed we don't even know what he looks like. He can only appear in our mind's eye in disguise, but that disguise is the image that we attribute to him. It is our own image and not the Devil's. Perhaps a person who constantly talks of the Devil may be the Devil himself, what do you think?'

'*Credo quia absurdum?*'

'You have read your Tertullian well. Casall detested him just as he detested Ockham. Casall always valued the idea and not the thing. It is easier for people like that to prove the existence of the Devil than it is for those who only believe in the existence of things. That's a belief that doesn't leave much room for imagination—it's a rather impoverished standpoint, really.'

'But the one which you have chosen to adopt.'

Lombardi nodded. He came closer, pushed the book to one side and sat on the table. 'What choice did I have? It seems I'm naturally drawn towards impoverishment.' He laughed again. He was playing on his poverty for effect. The poor Master of Arts who, far from being ashamed of his poverty, makes a virtue of it and even incorporates it into his philosophical stance.

He held the door open for her.

Yes, I'm going, Lombardi, Sophie said to herself, but I'll be back. Pity, I had imagined a somewhat different conversation. He is handsome. And clever. But even if he can't believe in the Devil, he has something to hide.

De Swerthe had installed the new library in one of the back rooms. There were rows of books attached to long chains—not a great quantity, but enough for the students' basic requirements. No more hunting in other colleges and *bursae*: now they could sit and read in the Scholarium's own library. Aristotle was represented by his *Metaphysics*, *Physics*, *Ethics*, and the first three books of the *Liber de causis*, and beside those stood Euclid's *Elements*, for geometry; then there were Boethius's *Consolation of Philosophy* and his treatise on arithmetic, and Plato's *Timaeus*. And also Virgil's *Institutiones grammaticae* and the *Theorica planetarum*. The benefactor had been very open-handed. Of course certain works were still lacking, but the little Prior was delighted, even if he was less than enthusiastic about some of the books. Although it was well known that he was no supporter of the new school of thought in philosophy—which would happily have jettisoned half of Thomas, and regarded the traditional philosophers as the ruin of Western civilization—he did not try to resist a development that was too far advanced to be halted, but made the best of a bad job. He had heard it rumoured that the Faculty intended to return to the old method of teaching and gradually abandon the via moderna. So all he could do was to wait for better times. And he would go on trying to acquire a different building, because he did not feel at ease in this district. Prostitutes and all manner of rabble still prowled the streets; all his prayers had gone unanswered, and none of his petitions for the council to impose law and order had so far borne fruit. There were not enough of the magistrate's officers to patrol the streets day and night. They had to deal with the beggars, and the thieves and murderers. His Scholarium could only be attended to when there was no trouble on other fronts. The Crown *Bursa* was similarly exposed to the influence of loose women and other undesirable elements, and in fact it suffered even more from the proximity of the whorehouse: there, too, the students' eyes were more readily drawn to the whores than to their books.

De Swerthe marked the opening of his new library with wine and a roast dinner, to which students and Masters not attached to the Scholarium were also invited. Laurien had gained permission to ask his new friend Josef to the meal. Josef ate and drank and showed his admiration for the books. By the time midnight approached—on this special occasion the main door would not be locked until then—everyone was in high spirits, and even the diminutive Prior showed signs of being merry, hiccupping contentedly after drinking too much of the wine and enjoying a good-natured squabble with Steiner about a disputation.

'Shall I show you round the Scholarium?' whispered Laurien to his friend Josef, taking hold of his arm, that fine-boned, slender arm, and immediately letting go of it again as if it had burnt him. How odd, he thought. Once again the image of Sophie flashed through his mind as he looked at his friend walking along beside him. He was beginning to feel an increasing sensation of strangeness when he was with Josef Heinrich. Perhaps it was his height, perhaps his walk. His friend crossed the cloister in long strides, with a curiously stalking gait as if he had spent his life walking on stilts. He allowed Laurien to lead him through one room after another. It was freezing cold everywhere. No fires had been lit except in the refectory where the celebration was being held. The dim tallow candle that Laurien carried gave off very little light and cast shadows into corners. This Scholarium must be a most uncomfortable place to live in, Sophie thought. The dormitories where each student had his bed, the latrines in the icy draught near the door, the small room used for individual tuition, even the library, everything seemed dank and dark and gloomy. The Scholarium was an old, run-down building that had formerly been occupied by monks who had moved to a more congenial part of the city. From one of the back rooms, once the monks' dormitorium, with massive columns and dragon-headed capitals, they now heard voices. There was a sudden clamour, and then the door flew open and three students came rushing out.

'Have you heard? They've found Domitian. He's dead! Strangled! With the girdle of a monk's habit…'

Laurien turned pale. Sophie had said nothing to him, intending to wait and see what happened, but now it pained her that he should have found out like this. He turned his gentle brown eyes towards her, and she merely nodded. 'Yes, I knew. I was going to tell you later. I'm so sorry…'

Laurien's hand, holding the candle, dropped to his side. He was still unable to utter a word.

'They brought his body back into the city this morning, and he'll be buried tomorrow,' one of the students whispered.

'What about his murderers?' stammered Laurien, his eyes glinting with anger.

'His murderers? I don't know anything about them. Apparently he was found in the Weilersfeld ruins. Why ever would he have gone there?'

Laurien turned away. He could feel the tears welling up. Whatever happened he must not start crying like a child. Go back to the refectory and act as if you know nothing, he told himself. You know the murderers, you've seen them. You can remember the face of that priest. And what about the other student, the one from the College? He must have been there too. He knows everything. And Lombardi knows everything too. And yet he remains as silent as the grave. Why?

Sophie's eyes followed him thoughtfully. He evidently felt grief for his friend, but he was also troubled by the knowledge that he possessed. What would he do with it? Was he thinking of the other student? Would he try to talk to him?

She went after him. He was sitting on the bench again, staring into his cup.

'Are you going to try and meet the other student?'

'He was there. He knows who the killers are. He probably managed to escape and is waiting in fear and trembling for them to catch up with him. If they know he's a student they'll come here—where else could he be studying but in Cologne? Or have they left the area by now?'

'I don't know,' Sophie said in a soothing tone, resting her hand on his arm. 'Laurien, there's nothing you can do without incriminating yourself. Don't do anything. Domitian is going to be buried tomorrow.'

'Yes!' he hissed furiously, 'and the murderers are going about scot-free. They'll be finding some other place to carry on their disgusting practices…'

She felt eyes on her. *He* was watching her. She turned her head. Sure enough, he was standing in the doorway, looking disdainfully at Laurien.

'Lombardi,' she said, nothing more, and stood up and left the room.

Lombardi came in and sat next to Laurien. 'Well, this *is* a nice little secret we have between us. And now, Master *scholar simplex*, I suppose you'll be wanting to avenge the death of your friend?'

Lombardi's sarcasm cut Laurien to the quick. 'What's so strange about that?' he asked, keeping his voice down. 'Isn't it my duty to say what I know?'

'Oh yes. Go ahead. Then you and the other student will be punished for not coming forward sooner, and the murderers will be out there just the same, enjoying their freedom—surely you can't imagine that they're still hanging about in Weilersfeld, waiting for the city gaoler to take them under his wing?'

Laurien stared into Lombardi's face. He hated him, he hated that coldness, those cynical blue eyes, and he despised himself for having confided in this devil.

'Wouldn't it be best to keep quiet?' Lombardi asked softly. 'Leave it to the magistrates. Either they'll find something out or they won't. What concern is it of yours?'

'And what if Marinus speaks out? How can I be sure that he'll keep his mouth shut? And how can he be sure that I will? I need to talk to him.'

'Go and see him, then. Or better still, let me go. I'll sort this out.' Lombardi lifted his cup to his lips and emptied it at one draught. 'Yes, I'll pay him a visit.'

They broke off the conversation because another student, just come from the library, joined them at the table.

Marinus lived in the biggest *bursa* in Cologne. Steiner and Theophile Jordanus taught there too, and the same spirit reigned there as in the Scholarium. But the students who lived in this *bursa* were those whose parents could afford to provide their sons with more comfortable quarters.

Lombardi approached Marinus at the end of a disputation. 'I need to talk to you, somewhere quiet where we won't be overheard.'

Marinus felt a dark premonition. Had Laurien betrayed him? Lombardi lived in the same Scholarium, so that was an obvious possibility.

They left the *bursa* and walked a little way in the direction of the harbour. Entering the cathedral, they turned towards St. Agnes's chapel, where there were no worshippers at prayer at this time of day.

Their secret would be safe here, and they could light a candle while they were about it. A hum of hushed voices, those of priests, traders and other visitors to the cathedral, was carried across to them through the high, cold air. Every footstep, every sound was drawn upwards to blend with the lingering echoes among the lofty vaults of the ceiling and to be poured out again as from a horn of plenty. And yet every whisper was as safe here as in Abraham's bosom...

Marinus was resolved to give nothing away, and even now—so he declared in the presence of St. Agnes—he would not reveal what he had seen. His father would kill him if he found out what he had been up to. But if that idiot Laurien was forcing his confessions on all and sundry, he said bitterly, then something must be done to make him hold his tongue. He thanked Lombardi for his efforts to prevent the worst from happening, and begged him again to ensure that Laurien really would keep quiet from now on. He had, after all—again a glance up at St. Agnes—sworn an oath on the Bible.

'They caught us that night,' he finally confessed, his voice husky. 'Domitian was struck down, but I managed to get away. That's all I know. But I saw them, and I saw the murderer's face. Before that we hadn't been able to shake off the vague feeling that someone had been following us on the way to the ruins. We looked round more than once, and saw a horseman some distance behind us who was obviously going the same way, but just before we reached the ruins he disappeared and we thought that it was just chance, that he was simply heading for the village. Perhaps it was a member of the sect. But it still worried me...'

Lombardi merely nodded. Without another word he let the student go on his way, and followed thoughtfully behind him.

Laurien's understanding of music had been very different from this. To him, it had consisted of notes and of harmonies, soft, or high and clear, or sombre and deep, or all mingled together. But since he had started attending this *paedagogium* on music, there had been much talk of harmonies, but he had not heard a single actual note. Instead he learned intervals and Pythagorean musical theory by heart. This was a dry kind of music, and sometimes in the middle of a lesson

Laurien wished that he were in a church, where he could listen to real singing. When he attended mass and heard a chorale, he could feel how it relieved his tension. How his unhappiness slipped from him, and something in the music whispered to him not to take life so seriously. Evil might lurk anywhere, but that was just the way life was, and it was up to each individual what he made of it. Laurien knew that he made the worst of it. Whenever there was a storm he imagined a lightning-bolt crashing into his room, if someone directed a dark, malevolent look at him he immediately saw the glint of a knife under that person's shirt. He consistently expected the worst possible conclusion even when the outcome was still in the balance. This was why he had always admired Domitian, because his attitude had been exactly the opposite: start by assuming the best and most agreeable turn of events. There would always be time for anger or disappointment later. It had done Laurien good to be with someone who took life lightly. But now, instead, he had a friend who was far too similar to himself, and this suddenly showed him all too clearly what he himself was like. Melancholy, pessimistic, like a gloomy, overcast autumn day. Josef seldom laughed, and if he did it was with restraint, as if laughter was something he did not permit himself. He spoke little, too, although he was well-read. Often when Laurien asked him some question purely in passing, he would give the kind of answer which made one think that he must have as many books lying around at home as other people had apples. As though he needed only to reach out his hand for one. He had never invited Laurien to his room; indeed, it never seemed to occur to him. As if he were ashamed of his lodgings. And justifiably so. The Spielmannsgasse was home to people who could not afford to live anywhere else, notably rogues, beggars and Polish cattlemen. His new friend no doubt had his reasons for not asking him home with him, Laurien thought, even though his lodgings were relatively close to the Scholarium.

Once again Steiner was paying a call on the physician attached to the courts of law, this time to ask him about the nature of the injury inflicted on the murdered student.

The doctor, who had performed the post-mortem, confirmed

that Domitian had been strangled with the girdle from a monk's habit, but there had been something else which he had also revealed to the magistrate. 'The deceased had an open wound on his head, as if someone had first tried to kill him with a blow. I also found haematomas there—'

'But they were not the cause of death?' Steiner interrupted, and the physician nodded.

'Precisely. The student was first felled by a blow and only afterwards strangled. Perhaps to prevent him from fighting back any more.'

Steiner merely nodded, expressed his thanks and left the house, deep in thought. Someone must have witnessed the murder and then sent the anonymous letter to the magistrate accusing the heretics. But why had he chosen to remain anonymous? Why had he not given his name? A further cause of anxiety to Steiner was the fact that he had now lost his only suspect. If Domitian von Semper had really been Casall's murderer, then the heretics had now dispatched him to Hell. So Casall's killer had evaded the long arm of the law, only to find himself before his heavenly judge instead. All the better, Steiner thought: in that case our task is at an end. But what if my suspicion was wholly unfounded and Domitian was not the murderer?

It was turning colder. Where savings had been made in the summer, there were now unavoidable outgoings. Wood for heating, though heating was kept to a minimum. So long as the temperature did not fall below freezing, the students had to make do with wearing heavy coats. Only in the rooms where they ate and where lectures were held was there a fire crackling in the hearth.

It was the day of Domitian's funeral. His parents, the Masters and the students were gathered around his grave. Josef Heinrich was there, too, wearing his Arts student's coat, which was too thin to keep out the icy wind that gusted around the cemetery walls. A marble angel on the tomb opposite looked on with blind eyes as the coffin was lowered into the earth. The Faculty had arranged for a mass to be read for the deceased, and for bread to be distributed to the poor.

Laurien stood beside Sophie. His head was bowed. No doubt

he was deeply troubled by the loss of his friend and the memory of that night at the Cistercian abbey, but when he looked at her she sometimes had the vague sense of a new danger, one that directly concerned her. He was continually scrutinising her, as if to penetrate the depths of her soul, as if he were preoccupied with something quite specific. He had never said anything, but she thought she knew what lay behind it, and it frightened her. What if he was puzzled by a resemblance between Josef Heinrich and Sophie Casall? Had he begun to suspect?

Now Laurien raised his head and she saw tears glistening in his eyes. Her hand stole towards his, and she noticed how he started at her touch.

Among the people at the graveside was one of the magistrates. He was standing back a little, so as to be better placed to observe all those present. There they all stood, mourning the unfortunate student. There must be strange things going on in this Faculty. First a Magister found dead in front of a colleague's house, and now a student strangled. Of course it could be coincidence; the one might have nothing to do with the other. But what if there was some connection which they were all reluctant to acknowledge? The magistrate was not especially fond of the university. Students were noisy, started fights and acted as if they owned the city. And the Masters strutted around superciliously, their thick folios under their arms, as if they were God's own prophets.

Why had the student been strangled? *Delictum sexuale?* What, or who, was it that the student had become involved with?

The magistrate watched them leave the graveyard, a flock of black ravens. From one of the city's churches the heavy tolling of a bell reached them. They held their heads bowed as though waiting for the executioner's sword to fall. One figure remained behind. Steiner. He looked around and, catching sight of the magistrate, came over to him. Together they watched the departing funeral procession.

'Is there a connection?'

'Between the death of the Master and that of the student?' Steiner asked in return.

'Exactly. Is it a coincidence?'

'Do you believe so?'

'Perhaps. But what I believe is not important. What was the student doing in Weilersfeld? We have spoken to the people there, but no one knew him. No one had ever seen him there before. So what was he up to? A little boy brought me an unsigned letter saying that the murderers belonged to the sect called "the Brethren of the Free Spirit". We have followed up the anonymous information, but so far it has not yielded any results. It is possible that the heretics were meeting in the ruins, but of course they have gone now.'

Steiner merely gave a nod. What had Domitian von Semper had to do with that sect? He could make no sense of it. Besides, he had another riddle to solve, he must not forget that. How can it happen that a dove kills a vulture?

'Have you solved the second riddle?'

'No. It is about a dove killing a vulture. How can that be?'

They passed through the cemetery gateway in silence, their heads still bowed.

'From the point of view of your riddler, it would be most natural to see the dove as the murderer and the vulture as its victim,' said the magistrate hesitantly. 'But that would mean standing reality on its head, for in nature it would be exactly the opposite way round. A vulture is a very strange predator, I saw one on a journey I made to the Alps. It feeds on dead animals...'

Steiner said nothing. A carrion-eater. Was that perhaps supposed to refer to the victim? Did the riddler regard his victim as a carrion-eater? As a base creature living exclusively on carrion? On the death of others?

On the door of the coach that was just passing, Steiner saw the von Semper family crest. There was a representation of an animal, but he caught no more than a glimpse of its shape. It might have been a weasel, or a marten or ermine—the creature's colouring became blurred by distance as the coach continued down the road. Steiner turned away.

Lombardi had spent the evening in one of the city's taverns. Three students had kept him company for a while, but had returned to the

Scholarium before him. So now he was strolling back alone through the moonlit streets. Walking in the direction of the Berlich, alongside the old wall behind which lay gardens and fields, he quickened his pace. The street was deserted. In a house doorway a beggar lay asleep. A cat darted across the cobbles and leaped over the wall. The moon was full, the sky clear. The shadow came out of one of the houses, sprang forward and seized Lombardi firmly by the shoulders with a practised grip which forced him to his knees, although he struggled and tried to seize hold of his assailant's hands.

'Keep quiet or you're dead,' a voice hissed in his ear, and then he felt those same strong arms dragging him off the street and into one of the houses. A door slammed shut, he could make out a dim light and a flight of steps. He was trying to turn round when a shove from behind sent him tumbling down them. Ten, twelve steps, then another feeble light in a vaulted cellar. Bare, cold walls confronted him, and four eyes watched as he struggled to his feet. The men were sitting at a table with wine and bread in front of them, and one of them, Neidhard, was smiling. Neidhard, in the grey monk's habit which he still wore to this day. Lombardi went up to him.

'Why on earth are you still here, in the lion's den?' he asked. 'Do you want to end up on the gallows?'

'On the contrary, I'm here to stave off disaster.'

Lombardi looked around. He seemed to be in a Roman cellar: there were quite a number of these to be found if you dug about in the ground long enough. An ordinary city cellar, where however much he shouted, no one would hear him. They could leave him to die of hunger and thirst down here, and no one would ever think of looking for him in this chilly dungeon.

'Yes,' Neidhard grinned, 'the past is a cast-off mistress who can never forget you. You should have told me that you are a Master at this university. I suppose the boy who ran away from us was a student of yours.'

Lombardi made no reply. Hold your tongue, keep quiet. Find out what they want.

'Those two that you told us about weren't a pair of yokels. They were students. And one of them got away. Now he's in some *bursa* or other telling everybody that we killed his fellow-student.'

Ignoring this, Lombardi asked, 'How do you know that I'm a member of the Faculty?'

'Oh, that wasn't difficult to find out. After all, you were a student when you were with us in the old days. We've kept our eye on the Faculty, and you seem to be very much a part of it. But to return to the student, do you know him?'

'No.'

Neidhard nodded. 'Very well. But you'll find out who he is.'

'So that you can do away with him?'

At this the other leapt up from his stool. 'He's spreading it around that we murdered that other student.'

'That's not true,' Lombardi said. 'He hasn't talked. The magistrate received an anonymous message, but I'm sure it didn't come from the student. And you can't really expect me to believe your protestations of innocence.'

'Please yourself. I want to know who that student is. He's about nineteen, with reddish hair, and he's fairly tall and has a scar on his neck, like a sword wound. He shouldn't be too hard to find.'

Lombardi sat rigid with horror. This was indeed a cast-off mistress coming back for revenge. A moment of folly in his youth—when he was inexperienced and thoughtless—and now his past was pursuing him for payment of debts. This one could well cost him the career he had thought he had before him. If he complied with their demands, Marinus was as good as dead. They were afraid that he would talk, and that he could identify one of them. Lombardi did not believe that they were innocent of Domitian's death, and would not have believed it if they had sworn it a hundred times over. But if he refused to coperate, what then?

'Yes, weigh your decision carefully, Magister Lombardi. We betray nobody, you know that, but we have ways and means of ruining your career without actually sending you to the stake.'

He knew their first rule: anyone who had ever been one of their number already had one foot on the bonfire. Once a person had strayed into their midst they held him in the palm of their hand, for in the eyes of the law and of the Church they were the spawn of the Devil.

'A pretty dilemma,' Neidhard said, smiling sweetly at him. 'You may go in peace. In due course someone will approach you and ask you for the information we need. Until then farewell, Magister Lombardi.'

He climbed the steps. The door was opened for him and he stepped out into the street. It was still a good five minutes' walk to the Scholarium, through Schmierstrasse to The Katzenbauch. His shoes sank into the mud. One street further on, his steps rang out on cobblestones. There was no point in continuing to pretend that that chapter in his life had never happened.

He rang the bell. De Swerthe was still up and let him in. Lombardi asked for a tankard of wine and retreated with it to his room. The window was open, and the moon was shining onto the sheets on the bed. The narrow strip of milky light slowly moved on while Lombardi stood at the window and drained his tankard. Now was the time to take stock, before he became tangled up or indeed fatally ensnared in the threads of his guilt. He had been eighteen when he had first met one of them. The same age as Domitian and Marinus. A year older than Laurien. Laurien, who probably still believed in chastity and purity, had found it repugnant, his delicate little soul besmirched. Poor little innocent! Domitian had been different, and Marinus too, evidently. But they at least had only been clandestine observers, whereas he, Lombardi, had been unable to resist the deadly attraction.

He had been a student in Prague. They had been posing as a troupe of street entertainers, appearing at fairs and performing acrobatic tricks. He had collected the money for them to earn a little extra cash for himself. Only later did he realize that they belonged to an extreme group who had broken away from the Beghards, finding even *their* heresies too tame, and intent on preaching not merely free love but something far worse. The Beghards were hunted down and either burned or drowned in the Rhine. One of the most able of them was executed in Cologne, much to the satisfaction of the Archbishop, whose aim it was to eradicate the Beghards and all who held similar views. There had been a number of trials aimed at ridding the city of them once and for all, but evidently not enough. The Beghards' most significant traits—apostolic poverty comparable to that of the mendicant orders, and a monastic life lived under a strict rule—had been turned into their opposite, at least by those into whose hands he had fallen. They had given themselves over to illicit sexual practices of the most shameful kind.

Lombardi closed the window and lay down on the bed without undressing. One evening Neidhard's group had invited him to have a drink with them in a vaulted cellar room and he had wondered what there was to celebrate. They had been careful, because they knew that they had not only the Church on their tail but also their own brethren, who did not condone their excesses. In that cellar he had watched them for the first time engaging in what they called *amor liber,* and he, torn between revulsion and arousal, had been forced to swear on the New Testament not to reveal anything to anyone. That first oath led to others, and his initial fear developed into a lifelong dread that his name might be linked to theirs. But that was not the worst of what he had done. At their next meeting they had plied him with cheap wine until he had lost all inhibition and copulated with some of the women himself. After all, when everyone was drinking and in high spirits, how could one person sit there and remain sober? If everyone was off to the carnival, how could one person stay at home, gazing gloomily at his own four walls? Fully aware that he had blundered into a heretical sect, and that running away was the only possible course of action, he had instead let himself be infected as by a dangerous disease. Even now he could summon up the image of those women in the torchlight. For them it had been a sublimely religious act, for so well had the seeds of nonsense been sown in their minds that they saw sex as a step up towards eternal life and coupled as freely as the beasts of the field. He had been indifferent to their theories. What they tried to tell him about mysticism and God left him completely cold. He did not see God in it, he saw only himself and the women and willingly threw himself down onto the straw with them. What did he care for any theological justification? His lust required none.

He was young, the women loved him, and that was all there was to it. He could still feel their hands on his body, but now it was as if they had left trails of ice all over him.

The oath that he had sworn was of no consequence, but he had been dimly aware even then that those hours of debauchery could destroy the rest of his life if his name should ever be mentioned, even once, in connection with those people. A Master's reputation had to be pure, not sullied by an association with a mystical sect. He had been attending their gatherings for almost a whole semester when he realised the seriousness of the situation and hastily moved to a different city. He went to Paris, where he gained his Bachelor's and later his Master's degree, after which he transferred to Erfurt and then to Cologne. He changed cities as often as possible, never staying anywhere for too long, just so that they should not be able to find him. And he had been here for too long. He must get away now; there was no time to be lost. And he must speak to Marinus. He would have to disappear too. If only *they* had left Cologne, but, on the contrary, they seemed to have dug themselves in and to have their eyes malevolently fixed upon him like a snake staring at a rabbit. Perhaps they really thought that they were safer in the lion's den than out in the country, and indeed, who could tell? So long as they did not preach openly they would remain unmolested because no one would be aware of their existence.

Lombardi closed his eyes. *Facies ad faciem*: now he must inform on them and go to perdition along with them, or else hold his tongue and deliver Marinus up to the Grim Reaper.

# Determinatio

It was not until some weeks later, as winter was setting in, that the first lectures were held on the teachings of that famous scholar—and former teacher in this very city—the *doctor subtilis*, Duns Scotus. It was as if the students were first allowed a period of grace in which the sun still shone and Aristotle was just the right thing for them. Then, in the winter, they were introduced to the delights of the *doctor subtilis*. After the encounter with him nothing was ever the same again. From there it was only a short step to nominalism.

Steiner was regarded as an authority on Scotus, whose writings he was said to know almost by heart. Rumour had it that if you woke him in the middle of the night and asked him to quote from a particular chapter, he could do it without a second's hesitation. Faced with a problem, it was very much in Steiner's nature to ponder at length on its substance and on the best method of approach. It was as if someone were trying to catch a bird but would never succeed because by the time he had thought about the whys and wherefores of the hunt, the bird would have flown and the hunt would have lost all purpose.

In like manner God flew away, eluding the Church, when it

became mired in dispute over the right method by which to prove His existence. Steiner was always searching for the path rather than the goal. Especially since the latter was known, while there were many possible paths to it. Sometimes while giving his lectures he himself would be filled with awe, marvelling yet again at the clarity of Scotus's thinking. Yes, this was real and true, this was genuine and convincing. 'Step outside the circle if you would know God. Consider first what path you will take to look for him. There are narrow, stony paths, paths that are paved, broad roads, routes of trade and commerce. Some lead to the west, others to the east. Some are much travelled, others rarely. On these the merchants travel, on those the beggars. If your destination is Rome, all roads lead there. That may be so. But on one you will travel for a year, on another no more than four months, even though you may start out from the same place.'

Sometimes he even had recourse to poetic images. This was not provided for in the statutes, but that did not worry him. Faced with the task of proving the existence of God, one might permit oneself a modicum of extravagance. Fundamentally, Scotus arrived at the same result as Thomas, and yet it was a different world, for if someone hit upon the right questions to ask, he would find the right answers.

The solution lay in distancing oneself from the object of investigation, a principle applicable not only to philosophy. The drop of water in the sea, the tree in the forest, the sheep in the meadow—you needed to stand back from them, adopting an external vantage-point, in order to see them aright.

It was icy cold in the room. Outside, stormy winds and snow had joined forces and a blizzard was raging around the College. It was only afternoon, but already so dark that Steiner could barely read, so he closed the book and began to quote from memory. The students hung on the movements of his lips behind his grizzled beard and gazed into his alert grey eyes.

'There are some people,' he said suddenly, 'who criticise the scholastics' method, which is to reduce everything to its component parts. Now this method is not our own but derives from the Greek philosophers. We did not invent it, though it could just as well have been of our devising. Whether that criticism is justified or not—and

I will leave that open—in the wake of Duns Scotus, at any rate, the wind seems to have been taken out of its sails. Someone who does not just fiddle about, attempting to cure a symptom but stands back and tries to discover what it signifies is more likely to be on the right path.'

He smiled. 'A doctor's findings may be too much a reflection of the doctor himself. Of course he has his repertoire of diseases that he can diagnose from this or that symptom, but one has to ask to what extent he himself is *proiectus,* and his assessment of the patient is affected by his own way of looking at him. And are we any different? We should ask ourselves about the nature of our own standpoint—how we arrived at it, how we might modify it. The murderer, too, is caught up in this dilemma.'

He paused and turned his keen gaze on the students, who had stopped writing and were looking up enquiringly. He could see what they were thinking. Why was Magister Steiner suddenly talking about the murderer? What murderer, anyway? A specific one, or murderers in general?

Steiner nodded thoughtfully. 'I mean Casall's murderer. He set me a riddle, or rather two. I solved the first one, though that proved unnecessary, because the very next day a witness came and gave me the answer that I needed. The second riddle is still lying unsolved on my desk. And I am not sure whether I feel inclined to solve it. Most likely the criminal is someone who belongs to the Faculty. Maybe he is a student. Maybe he is here in this room at this very moment, listening to me. And if that should be the case, let him listen closely to what I have to say to him.'

They were so startled that they dropped their pens. Papers rustled as they all sat up straighter. Some of them appeared nervous, others merely intrigued. If the murderer was not Domitian but one of the many other students, Steiner did not suppose that he would give himself away, even here. On the contrary, he would see this as a scholarly disputation, a kind of jousting, subject to rules of fair combat.

'Let us discuss the riddle,' Steiner said. 'Even if I am departing from the set syllabus here, let us talk about how it is possible for a dove to kill a vulture. Tell me your thoughts on the matter.'

Would he join in? Ask questions? Or just sit there listening in silence? Would his thoughts show in his face? For he too was bound by his own way of seeing things, just as Narcissus became the captive of his own image in the water.

Outside the window it had been growing increasingly grey, and thick flakes of snow were piling up on the sill.

'Well?'

Steiner watched for any clue in their eyes, their lips, their posture. The Baccalaureus sitting on the bench had leaned back and was waiting expectantly. Nothing. They were ranged in front of Steiner like sheep confronted by the wicked wolf. Just then the door opened and Lombardi came in; the allotted time was over, but Steiner had no intention of ending his class just yet. He threw a quick glance at Lombardi, who took the hint and placed himself next to the Baccalaureus, curiously eyeing the roomful of silent students. At last one of them spoke up.

'It seems to me that the symbolism of the vulture and the dove is reversed. Does he, I mean the murderer, see himself as the peace-loving dove? Do you see him in that way?'

Steiner was conscious of Lombardi's eyes boring into him from behind. What might he be thinking of this public discussion of the case?

'No,' Steiner replied, 'I do not think so. I feel rather that we must look elsewhere. That we must re-examine our approach. Let us think more abstractly, as Scotus did. That is the only way to make any progress. He is probably not referring to the qualities of the dove or the vulture, although that is what we assume because it is what immediately occurs to us. Animals are wonderful vehicles for the qualities we project on to them. We contrive to attribute almost anything to them: our frailties, our vices, our joys and also our lust. They are like the reflective surface of a lake. So I suggest that we should find a different way of looking at this.'

Now he turned to look behind him. Lombardi's handsome face still wore an amused smile. He was no doubt enjoying what Steiner was doing, for he himself had never cared much about the regulations.

'Well, now, Magister Lombardi, have you no thoughts on this famous riddle?'

'I have indeed. You want a different way of looking at it? Then let me point out that a dove never kills a vulture. Therefore the deceased was not killed by a dove.'

Steiner frowned. 'He was not killed?'

'No. At any rate not by a dove. Quite impossible.'

'So you are suggesting to me that what we have here is a totally impossible proposition?'

'Impossible, yes, but according to our method of reasoning nothing is impossible. We must try to see how it could be possible. That is presumably what the killer meant by his riddle.'

'An impossible crime?'

'Exactly. And yet it happened.'

'The perfect crime,' Steiner murmured, but Lombardi shook his head. 'The perfect crime does not exist. Unless we try to find a different meaning for the word *perfectum*. It is a construct, it exists only in our imagination. All those who speak of a perfect crime—and they are many—are attempting to apply what is merely an idea to reality. That can be done, but it requires the right perspective. So what is there that is so impossible that it ought not to exist at all?'

No one said a word. Lombardi's style of reasoning had always been remarkable: no one else possessed such a keen intelligence. Even Steiner took his hat off to the younger man.

'Well, what?' he asked.

Lombardi smiled. 'Think of one or two combinations of things that are virtually inconceivable.'

He addressed this question to the students, who now started whispering amongst themselves.

'An angel,' said one of them. 'A murdering angel.'

Lombardi nodded. '*Exemplum velut.*'

'Could Casall have been killed by a star?' another called out. And a third said that one could hardly imagine that a camel had come and felled him with one of its mighty hooves; it was also surely unthinkable that Casall had committed suicide, for presumably he had not hit himself over the head with the pot. Nor could one suppose that a branch had fallen from a tree when Casall had happened to be underneath, and that he had then dragged himself all the way to the well.

This went on for a considerable time, with the students putting forward ever more absurd ideas, until they realized that Lombardi had laid a trap for them, for suddenly he began to laugh heartily and congratulated them on their florid imaginations.

'We need to bear in mind that it must be just possible for him to have met his death in a given way. So let us leave aside the angels and stars, and the camels too, which I suspect are rather few and far between in Cologne…'

Steiner brought the session to a close. For some time the Baccalaureus, who held the statutes in great respect, had been casting venomous glances in his direction. He was probably considering whether the time had not come to instigate a disciplinary procedure to stop Steiner's misuse of lecture time for his investigations of riddles.

*In the same way the clouds of my grief dissolved, I drank in the sight of the heavens, gathered my thoughts and sought to recognise the face of my physician. As I turned my gaze upon her, [...] I saw that she was my nurse, in whose house I had dwelt from the days of my youth—Philosophy. How is this? I asked. Have you come to join me in the place of my banishment, have you descended, O mistress of all virtue, from your abode on high? Or are you my fellow-accused? Are you, too, assailed by false accusations?*

Dazzled by the thick blanket of snow which seemed to have enveloped the whole city, Lombardi closed his eyes as he listened to the laughter of children skating on a nearby pond, and the clouds of melancholy were lifted from him too. How could it be philosophy that provided consolation at times of greatest trouble? Was it not God? Or, for some people, a partner? A friend, a lover? Boethius had never seemed as close to him as now, when he had to make his decision. In the winter whiteness he sauntered through a city relaxing in Sunday repose, and suddenly he felt light-hearted and able to join in the laughter of the children on the pond. What harm could they do him, all those heretics, Beghards, Brothers of the Free Spirit, if he himself was free? Free, because he had the most beautiful, the wisest of mistresses—*Philosophia*. Seneca, Cicero, Marcus Aurelius, Boethius—they had all been captives in the prison of life and yet they had been free.

Women were well disposed towards him, and his smile could melt an iceberg. Take your decision as a free man, consider everything from all angles, or consider nothing from any angle. *Omne fluit:* what should his decision be? He would let it all go: he would apply for a post in Heidelberg, where the traditionalists had been driven out of the university years ago; they were always on the lookout for good people, especially nominalists who wanted to turn the world upside-down. They knew that every question had already been posed, every thought had already been thought, and mental constructs had been given outward form. They had long since carried through the separation between faith and knowledge, and they knew what the future held. What was he doing here, in a place full of beards that grew longer and whiter with every passing year?

At the corner stood an old man. He must have been desperately cold, for he was clothed only in rags. His eyes in their deep sockets were somnolent, weary. He held out his hand. 'A penny, kind sir.' Lombardi reached into his pocket.

'And some information about a student, sir.'

Lombardi put the coin away again.

'You ought to read Aristotle's treatise on time, then you would know that I can't tell you anything yet. So get back under your arch and come again tomorrow.'

The old man nodded resignedly. He had never heard of Aristotle, and as for reading, that was quite beyond him.

Continuing on his way, Lombardi felt uneasy. He was being watched. They were not letting him out of their sight. And they were capable of anything. He strolled down to the harbour, where people were walking beside the frozen river. A thick layer of ice covered the water, and here too children were skating. A pale sun shone in the sky. A number of people were standing by the customs house. And there he saw her: Sophie, together with her two stout sisters and her mother and stepfather. He was moaning and groaning because the glaring brightness of the snow was hurting his eyes. Lombardi drifted over to them. They greeted each other stiffly, and the old man demanded to know who he was. Sophie introduced Lombardi.

'A colleague of Casall's. A famous Magister.'

Lombardi smiled at her. 'Have you found work?'

'Yes, I have a position as a copyist with the Clarisses.'

The old man grunted. He wanted to go home. He was a man who kept a fire burning even in summer, so in winter the only way to escape the cold was to retreat to bed. And he did not like Magister Lombardi. He had an aversion to Masters. Puffed-up capons who fancied themselves because they read books. Fiddle-faddle. He turned to go, and immediately they all followed, waddling along behind him like geese. Only Sophie remained behind. 'So who was it, Magister Lombardi? Angels or stars?'

Lombardi was startled. How could she know about that? Who was spreading his ideas around the town?

'Neither. How did you come to hear about that?'

'Oh, people talk…'

The old man turned round. Why was the wretched girl not coming? Sophie motioned to him not to wait. Grumbling, he walked on.

On the river bank there was a stand selling mulled wine. 'Would you like a cup?' asked Lombardi.

The wine tasted of cinnamon, and Sophie could see her breath wafting away in the frosty air.

'Do you enjoy the work?' Lombardi asked.

Sophie beamed. Oh yes, she enjoyed it. It gave her immense pleasure to listen to his lectures, to look at his handsome face, to hear his voice, to follow his ideas.

They strolled along the bank. Across the river the sun shining on the hilltops was dazzling.

'I wish you would tell me a little about your studies,' Sophie said softly.

'I'm going to leave this city,' was his only response.

She stopped in her tracks. 'Leave? But why?'

'Because I want to go to a different university, where there are no realists teaching any more. To get away from all the antiquated stuff.'

She said nothing. She liked him. The thought of his leaving saddened her. And then she realized that what she felt for him was more than mere liking. And more now than when she had tried to seduce him. She would have liked to share her life with him. Instead of which she had married Casall.

He was looking closely at her. What did her silence signify? She still held the cup of mulled wine in both hands and was staring down into the red liquid. 'A pity,' she murmured, nothing more. He put out his hand and lightly touched her cheek. But she was not for him, she was too pure and innocent, even though one could be sure that Casall had not dealt gently with her.

'Yes, a pity,' he answered. They drank up their wine and walked on. Then he told her about Ockham and was surprised at how much she already knew. And then she took his arm and casually asked whether there was any chance of a woman's attending lectures at a Faculty. They sat down on a low wall and looked across at the children playing.

'What woman could afford it?' he asked in surprise.

'But supposing she could?'

'Then why not?' He looked into her face, amused. 'I've heard of one or two cases where women have studied at a university, though they were the exception. Just think how those clerics would shake in their shoes if women started to devise philosophical propositions. *Incredibile.* They hate women, they still have the fear of the past coursing through their veins.'

'You're not a very good Christian,' Sophie replied with a smile, and he nodded.

'No, I'm a scholar, not a priest. I seek God by a different path.'

'And what if I try all the same?'

'Have you got enough money to study? You once told me that Casall had left you nothing but debts.'

Sophie was alarmed. If she was not careful she would get herself hauled up before the magistrate for the money she had stolen. If her mask slipped, what then? Suddenly she felt an overpowering urge to tell him. What would he do? Report her to the authorities? She only wanted to see his face, his reaction. His admiration, perhaps? Or his horror?

'Do you think women are less intelligent?' She must suppress her wild impulse, which threatened to grow stronger with every moment.

'No, why should I? It's simply that it would never occur to a father to let his daughter study.'

Sophie had stood up, and was now tracing circles in the snow with her boots. Then, bending down, she formed a small snowball in her hand and threw it on to the ice.

'I'm cold,' she murmured. They walked back in silence. He accompanied her most of the way home. At the end of her street they stopped. 'When will you be leaving?' she asked.

'As soon as possible.'

They looked at each other. There were too many people around them. Any demonstrative behaviour would immediately be reported back to the old man. There could be no show of tenderness, and words were not enough. That woman on the corner, the neighbour, the children playing in the roadway.

'I'd like to see you again,' he muttered. She hesitated.

'You can visit me at any time in the Scholarium,' he went on. 'If people talk, we can say that you were bringing me another of Casall's books.'

She nodded and gave him a smile. Then she turned and ran quickly to her mother's house.

The ragged old man was standing, hidden from sight, in a house entrance nearby. His weary gaze was suddenly alert, like that of a vulture that has detected the reek of carrion. So he's got a sweetheart in the town, has he, the cold-hearted swine. Who would have thought it?

Sophie's family had arrived home an hour earlier to find the old man's three sons waiting for them. Three shoemakers, like their father, who had been a master shoemaker, though whereas he had been spurred on by his avarice, they were stupid and lazy. Why work your fingers to the bone when you could be sure that the old man had plenty of money stashed away in his stocking? The trouble was that he refused to hand any of it over, and would sooner see his sons starve than give them so much as a penny piece. Whenever he saw that their idleness and stupidity had once again brought them to the brink of destitution, he would indeed give them something—but at an extortionate rate of interest. As a result their hatred of him had become an obsession that blighted their lives, and they yearned for revenge. But they could hardly do away with him. That would certainly have been the simplest solution, but if they were caught, then on top of everything else they would end up in gaol on account of the stingy old clod. Even they were not simple-minded enough to see that as a desirable fate. So instead they would turn up on his doorstep every six months or so to complain about how little attention he paid them, considering that they were his sons, his own flesh and blood. When he remarried they grew frantic at the thought of losing their inheritance, and when, to cap it all, the new wife fell pregnant, they immediately put their heads together about what to do next. They decided to have it out with him. We're not going to let somebody else walk off with our inheritance. We just want what's ours. Then they could stop trying to hoodwink people—by this time they had hardly any customers left because their shoes were so badly made that they fell to pieces. If only the old man would kick the bucket and take himself off to the graveyard. But the old shoemaker had no such intention, because he knew that he could not take his beloved Rhenish pennies with him to the Kingdom of Heaven but would have to drop them into the gaping mouths of his greedy offspring. Such an infuriating thought was powerful enough to fend off even Death, who every so often popped his head round the door but would immediately beat a hasty retreat since there was nothing to be had there.

The sons, then, were at the door once again when the family returned from their walk. Grudgingly the old man let them in and asked them what they wanted.

'We're broke, we've got nothing left. Just look, our clothes are hanging off us in tatters because we can't afford new ones. You've got pots of money, give us what we're entitled to.'

'You're entitled to nothing. You're young and healthy, you can work, and if you aren't capable of making shoes then find another way to fish people's money out of their pockets. After all, that's what I sired you for. The true God of this world is wealth. With that you can buy yourselves anything you want. And then there are two other treasures, called cunning and avarice, they'll keep you on your toes and make you rich. And now get out of my house.'

All this time his wife with her swollen belly was standing by his side. What a trollop, and she's going to do us out of our inheritance. We're leaving now, but we'll be back. We're your conscience, old man, and damnation take your new brat.

Half an hour later the miser was sitting counting the money in his stocking. And now he noticed that five of the coins were missing. Five coins. That was impossible. Nobody knew where he kept his purse except his wife, but surely she wouldn't...

He tied the strings of his purse. The fat stepdaughters? Or had his sons crept in at night and searched the house? But they would have taken the lot while they were about it—unless they were not quite as stupid as they seemed, but actually rather crafty. So where should he put the purse now? Under the floorboards? In the attic? Yes, the attic would be a safe place. So up the stairs he went. They were awkward to climb: a chicken-coop ladder would have been easier. Clutching the heavy purse in one hand, the shoemaker clambered up the steep stairs, steadying himself against the wall with his other hand, as there was no handrail. Up above, a ray of light came in through the sky-light. He would be sure to find a good hiding-place here. Or should he go down again and entrust his treasure to a notary? He paused. No, no, they were liars and cheats, he might just as well give it to his sons for safekeeping. So the attic it must be. He came nearer and nearer to the dim light. He was almost there. On the very last step he leaned forward to put the purse down on the dusty floor. He was already looking eagerly around the attic space, searching for a good hiding place, when one of his feet slipped and he felt it dangling in mid-air. He tried to grab hold of something, but there was nothing for his hand to grasp. And then his other foot slid off the stair, and he went crashing down.

Down below they heard only a fearful bang and a metallic rattle. What was that? With an effort his wife got to her feet, groaning as she put a hand to her aching back. The pain was ever-present, and the baby never stopped kicking. She stepped out into the hallway, and suddenly saw the coins glinting on the floorboards. A carpet of shining coins. And then she saw him. He was lying at the foot of the stairs, his hand convulsively gripping the empty purse from which, one by one, the coins had tumbled before him down the stairs...

That morning Sophie had not put on her student disguise, as she planned to go to the market. As always, it was still practically night-time. Darkness and cold accompanied her down to the square, lanterns flickered, and around her were the other townsfolk of Cologne, not yet fully awake, their eyes blinking wearily, uncertainly. At the market-place the first traders were arriving and setting up their stalls. There was a smell of cheese and vegetables. Snowflakes danced in the light of the lanterns.

'A word, pretty lady...'

She stopped. A ragged old fellow was holding out his hand. She had no penny left to give him. He laughed. 'No, I'm not begging for alms. I understand you're a friend of Master Lombardi's. If you know what I mean...'

He gave a suggestive leer that made her feel uncomfortable, as everything about him did. A slimy creature.

'We need some information from him, but he doesn't seem keen to give it to us. Tell him we won't wait much longer, our patience is running out—after all, the funeral for the dead student was quite a while ago.'

She stared at him. 'Who are you?'

'Oh, you'd better ask him that yourself, he can tell you, for all that he acts the innocent. Just say one word: Weilersfeld. He knows more about the dead student than you think...'

The old man turned away and shuffled off. But she remained

rooted to the spot, wondering what that wizened old scarecrow could possibly have to do with Lombardi. When she found herself starting to shiver with cold she walked on through the snowy streets as far as the meat hall and then turned off round a windy corner.

Late in the afternoon she went to the Scholarium. She had missed lectures, because leaving the house in disguise by daylight was too risky. De Swerthe was standing at the entrance watching the tumbling snowflakes as they settled on the wall. The street was very still. The snow muffled all sound. At the end of the street people were clearing the snow in front of their houses, but this sound too was smothered as though under a woollen blanket. The whiteness was dazzling, though twilight was already descending, drawing a veil over the short day. The diminutive Prior was waving his thin arms about and lamenting the fact that it was getting dark so early and that the whole city was being buried under the snow.

Sophie smiled and asked if Magister Lombardi was there.

'Certainly, do come in.'

She found him in the deserted refectory, sitting in front of the fire and warming his chilled fingers. When she entered the room he stood up. 'I wasn't expecting to see you so soon.' In fact he had not expected this visit at all. On the contrary, he had been trying to find out where she lived, and had finally managed to extract the information from Griseldis. But simply to go and call on a widow in her own home was a delicate matter.

Her mind was still wholly occupied with what the ragged old man had said. 'I'm afraid the reason for my visit is not a very pleasant one,' she began. 'A beggar came up to me and told me to remind you that you owe him some information.'

He offered her one of the stools. He himself remained standing and merely nodded, trying to hide his alarm. How had they come to involve Sophie? Had he been too careless? And Marinus was still in the city; he must disappear, and the sooner the better. Trying to remain calm, Lombardi sat down on the table. Outside they heard the dwarf give an indignant cry—in all likelihood a sheet of snow had slid off the roof into his face. What should he do? What should he say? Of course she had not the slightest idea what was actually behind all this.

'What is your connection with these people? It's to do with Domitian's death, isn't it? Siger, you know more that you're prepared to admit, and now I want to know what is really going on. What happened in Weilersfeld?'

'And supposing I refuse to answer?'

'Then I will go to Steiner and tell him everything I know. And I will persuade Laurien to do the same.'

Yes, she would be capable of doing that, he thought, the silly little goose. Out of sheer ignorance she would put an end to his career and possibly to him too—on the scaffold. He could strangle her right now, or he could lie to her. Or else tell her the truth. He could swear her to secrecy on the Bible, but God's ears must already be aching from all the oaths sworn on the Bible which were worthless and as good as broken before they were even uttered.

'So be it,' he said under his breath. It was time to stop prevaricating, because Marinus's chances of survival were slim unless he took some decisive action very soon to save the lad's wretched life.

'You know who they are,' he began in a low voice. 'But much of it is only gossip. I couldn't say whether it's true. The people we are talking about were once with those others but then split away and adopted a new name, which is immaterial here. They are always looking out for new brothers and sisters to convert. Years ago, a young student got caught in their web. They seemed so free and independent, they sought freedom of the spirit and of the body. A seductive idea, wouldn't you say? To be able to think, and to express whatever your thoughts suggest to you, without being punished by the Church or the law? That appealed to the young student, and so did what they called free love. They sought God in physical love because they believed that he was everywhere, not least there. The young man joined them, and realised when it was too late that they were heretics who were little concerned with God. The student turned his back on them and hoped never to encounter them again, but as a result of Domitian's excursions to Weilersfeld he learned that the sect still existed, that they had not yet been burned at the stake. I presume that it was they who killed Domitian, and now they want to know the name of the student who was with him. That, my dear, is the position.'

At that moment the door flew open. De Swerthe appeared on the threshold, took a step into the room, hesitated, and immediately vanished again.

Sophie stared into the blazing fire. What were those stories she had heard, even if they were only rumours? It was said that they fornicated with their own brothers and sisters, aunts with nephews, uncles with nieces, cousins with cousins, fathers with daughters, mothers with sons. They desecrated the altars in churches. They coupled like beasts in the field, but they did it in churches, monasteries, abbeys, right in front of the cross. It wasn't possible—Siger Lombardi couldn't possibly have been one of them.

'You...' she began, but then broke off and stood up. 'No, it's not possible.'

But what would become of the unfortunate student from the *bursa* if Lombardi revealed his name?

'What are you going to do?'

'He must leave the city. He saw the murderer, and of course that's why they're worried. I'll see to it that he disappears. And if they speak to you again, tell them you don't know me.'

'Why don't you go to the magistrate and tell him what you know?'

She knew it was a foolish question. At present she was the only one who had been allowed a glimpse of his past. She could do as she chose with the information, but certainly the Curia would be only too delighted to get their hands on someone like Lombardi. Dumbly she shook her head. She could not bear to look at him. Here he was in the Scholarium, acting the impoverished Magister, like a cat masquerading as a mouse, and the fact that he had been young at the time and had turned away from them made no difference. A thing like that stuck to you as feathers stick to tar, it spread through your very bones and bowels. It took up residence in your mind, haunting it like a ghost in an empty house. But how far had he really gone? Had he merely watched, like the two students? Or had he taken part in that *danse macabre*? What had he actually done?

As if he sensed her doubts, he nodded. 'I didn't only watch. I was one of them. They found themselves derelict churches or grave-yards. They were joined by runaway monks, and copyists who had had enough of their drudgery, men and women who had spent their whole lives denying themselves any pleasure, in the belief that such self-denial was the highest purpose in life, as indeed the Church of Rome teaches. Because these people had seen the Devil in the oppo-site sex, they had avoided them in the same way as one flees from lepers and isolates them in the hospital at Melaten, well away from the citizens. But then, like a ship foundering, they suddenly heeled over to the other side. The very things that they had feared all their lives now seemed to promise salvation. It wasn't enough to take just one sexual partner, they had to have ten or twenty, and it was all the same to them with whom they did their whoring, even members of their own families. Their lives were spent in a continual ecstasy—an ecstasy of freedom but also of perdition. I am not trying to justify myself, but all the same it was salutary to discover that the Devil preached by our Church is no more than a figment of our imagina-tion, a projection of our own fears.'

'So you deny that he exists? Although you are a scholastic?'

'What I'm saying is that he may exist as a construct of the imagination, an idea, but since I am a nominalist, ideas and constructs are of only marginal interest to me.'

Lombardi smiled. She did not understand. Did he suppose that it would reassure her to know that he cared nothing for the Devil? She turned on her heel, saying that she hoped that no harm would come to the student from the college. He let her go. He knew that she would not betray him. But equally she would presumably want to have nothing more to do with him. She believed in the Devil as she believed in God. And she was right to do so. A dualistic view of the world positively compelled one to speak metaphorically of a Devil, it could not be otherwise, and the implication was that if the one did not exist, then neither did the other.

Lombardi closed the door behind her.

He had no time to lose. The following morning there was to be a class on the use of the astrolabe, on the study of the constellations and the harmony of the universe. Now he must keep a cool head. He had shown himself in public with Sophie, and from what she had said it was clear that Neidhard was having him shadowed day and night. They must be noting every step he took. And their spies could be anybody and everybody. The bone man on the corner, the knacker in Schmierstrasse, the gold-digger pushing his unsavoury, stinking load out of the city by night. Even the public executioner in the Alter Graben might be in their pocket, because all these people could be bought. For a bag of gold they would happily see the Pope broken on the wheel—they would even tie him onto it themselves.

He looked up at the sky. The sun was rising. What could he do? He quickened his pace. Marinus would probably be somewhere in the *bursa*. He found him standing at a desk in the library. 'You must get out of here as fast as you can. They're in the city, and they know all about you. They think you're going around telling everybody that they killed Domitian.'

Marinus collapsed on to a stool. His hands had begun to tremble. 'But I haven't breathed a word…'

'I know. But you must leave the city all the same. Is there anywhere you can go?'

'I don't know.'

'Then think.'

'I've got a brother-in-law in Neuss…'

'Excellent. You'll go there, then. And I'll say you've been taken ill, struck down by the sweating sickness or something. Can you leave today?'

'Is it as bad as that?'

'Much worse than you can imagine. They're watching my every move and badgering me to tell them who you are.'

'But how…?'

'I've no time for explanations. Do you need money?'

Marinus shook his head. He stood up and put back the book that he had intended to read.

'I can't go with you or they would know immediately. You must manage to get out of the city by yourself. By night, or disguised or whatever. Can you do that?'

The student nodded without a word. They had only been after a bit of pleasure, he thought bitterly. What a deadly pleasure it had proved to be. He had no need to pretend to be unwell: he felt suddenly as wretchedly ill as if he really were in the grip of a fever, or of something far worse, like leprosy.

With a parting nod, Lombardi left the library. Marinus watched him go and leaned back, exhausted, against the door.

After the lectures and the afternoon's reading he went to his room, packed a bag with his belongings and waited for darkness to fall. In two hours the gates would be closed: he must be out of the city by then. Although the *bursa* had several exits, only the main door would still be open now. So he needed to make his departure as inconspicuous as possible. He pulled his hood up over his head as he left the building. It had started to snow heavily again, and he hurried across the roadway, which already had a thin coating of frost. The driving snow was growing denser, but Marinus welcomed this because it would not seem odd to have his hood up. He hurried along Severinstrasse but every so often turned off into a side street and made a detour before returning to it again. He used this device successfully four or five times, but then lost his way. Peering through the flurries of snow, he thought he recognised the towers of St. Pantaleon's and panicked. This was the end of the built-up part of the city; he had strayed a long way from the route he had meant to take. He must retrace his steps. The snow whirled ever more wildly, the flakes hurtling into his face. There was not a soul to be seen in the street, and it was growing darker by the minute. Marinus halted. It was so silent. So uncannily silent that he could almost hear the snow falling on the cobbles. Now it was pitch dark. He shivered. What was he doing here? Wouldn't it make more sense to return to the *bursa* and have done with all the lies? Instead of trying to elude the murderers in this labyrinth of a city? He could have spoken to the Dean. Or to Steiner. Or directly to the Chancellor. And to his father, of course. There was nothing you couldn't talk about! He looked up into the greyish-black sky. His own brain, too, was in the grip of a gusting, whirling snowstorm. What folly to have thought he could escape his fate. I will explain everything, he thought. I will confess everything.

They won't kill me for it. Perhaps I'll get a few days in the lock-up, but if I calm down and think rationally about it, it's obvious that the only thing that counts is the truth...

He heaved a sigh of relief. Yes, instead of running away he would face up to the truth. He pushed his hood back a little so as to be able to see better. He was in a narrow alley, and the houses were packed closely together. Through the thick flurries of snow he could hardly see as far as the next corner, and even the light of a torch made little difference. As Marinus rounded the corner an arm fell across his throat, and he was just telling himself that only the truth counted when everything went black and he thought it was his father come to punish him....

Early one morning while he was on his way to the market, Lombardi saw a figure emerging from the garden at the back of the house where Sophie lived. A servant? An errand-boy? It was still fairly dark, and the figure was impossible to make out clearly in the half-light, even though it was only about twenty paces ahead of him. But when it came within range of a torch, Lombardi recognised a student coat. That was the home of one of Cologne's wealthy families, so it surprised him that they should let rooms to students. He thought he even recognised the student. He could have sworn it was Josef Heinrich—but surely he was supposed to have a room in Spielmannsgasse? Still, Lombardi attached little importance to what he had seen. People could live where they pleased, and if they chose to lie about it, that was their business and not his. Indeed, it would not have caught his attention at all but for the fact that he always glanced towards that house, in the hope of meeting Sophie. So he shrugged the matter off and quickly forgot all about it as he walked back to the Scholarium.

It was turning out to be a long and hard winter. This was due to the configuration of the stars and planets, which also governed the destiny of each individual man and woman. The stars were like the reins in the hands of a charioteer guiding his horse now this way, now that. Everyone in the Faculty had his personal horoscope in which he could read what lay both behind him and before him. The paths of the stars, sun and moon were described only inadequately in Sacrobosco's *De sphaera*. By contrast, the *Circulus eccentricus vel egresse cupidis*, by an unknown author, was more instructive, because it dealt with the motions of the heavenly bodies and also showed, amongst other things, the eccentrics, equants and equinoxes.

When Laurien was calculating the positions of the celestial bodies by means of his astrolabe, he imagined how an angel might be doing the same thing from above. The angel would be calculating the path taken by the earth, unaware that his own exact position was at that very moment the subject of speculation by a human being. Nonsense, thought Laurien, an angel had no fixed place. They floated in the heavens, if anywhere, invisible and holy.

Josef, sitting beside him, was deeply engrossed in the calculation, his head bent low over the paper. Why could one not construct a vehicle to travel up to the stars, Laurien wondered. According to Bacon, Alexander the Great had built machines that could be lowered into the ocean. Machines that could conquer the heavens, such as Daedalus had believed there should be…such things must be possible. It was said that Alexander the Great had descended to the bottom of a sea in a vehicle made of glass, and had studied the lives of the fish down there. But that was only hearsay; no one had ever seen the vehicle, and Alexander had taken his observations with him to the grave. What had he found? Giant octopi, dragons and serpents? Angels, perhaps? Then there must have been krakens in the heavens too, if flying things dwelt in the ocean and swimming creatures winged across the skies. Man alone, with his two puny legs, seemed to be glued to the earth. But there were the numbers, with which you could make calculations, and that was like having a glass conveyance of your own in which to sail through the seas and the heavens. It was a fascinating notion. Surely things conceived in the mind were also real? There were things that one never saw but that existed all the same. What did the nominalists have to say about that?

'Hey, what's the matter? Are you asleep?'

Laurien gave a start. He had been so immersed in his thoughts that he had not heard his friend Josef's voice. 'I believe the realists are right after all,' he whispered.

'What has put that into your mind just now?' asked Sophie.

'I was thinking about the stars, and the fact that one can do calculations about something without ever having seen it. I mean, have you ever observed them up close?'

'No.'

'There you are, then.'

'That's an odd sort of argument,' murmured Sophie. Naturally there were things that you didn't see and that existed nonetheless. The way you might see a half-moon and know that in reality it was always complete, never actually cut in half.

'We ought to set a trap for him,' said Sophie in a low voice.

'For whom?'

'For the murderer. Casall's murderer.'

Laurien lowered his sheet of paper. 'How could that be done?'

'I've just had an idea. If concepts can be made visible, for instance by means of calculations, it must surely be possible to find a way of making the murderer visible. You have to give the concept an opportunity to show itself in a form that you are capable of perceiving. Let's leave a message for him in the Scholarium. If he reads it, then we shall know he is here among us. If there is no reaction, then perhaps it isn't one of us at all.'

'What if he reads it but chooses not to reply?'

'I don't think that will happen. He is communicative by nature, and it irks him that he is unable to establish contact with anyone. Perhaps he also believes that he has committed the perfect murder and is frustrated not to be reaping admiration for it. He will reply, believe me.'

To Laurien the idea seemed absurd. What was the point of creating even more confusion than already existed? Were they proposing to enter into a correspondence with the murderer? That made no sense at all. What interest did they have, anyway, in unmasking Casall's killer? Let Steiner and the others hunt for him. Laurien felt the warmth of his friend's body beside him. And once again the memory of Sophie resurfaced. He bent across to Josef and whispered something in his ear. But his friend just shook his head and moved a little further away.

Sophie was determined to tell Steiner about her idea. After the lecture she went looking for him and found him standing outside the refectory, sniffing the air to discover what was for lunch. He could smell savoy cabbage and a substantial, fatty soup. She was brief and to the point, and he, with his stomach rumbling and his mind focusing on a good plateful of food, looked at her in incomprehension.

'Write a letter?'

'Just a few lines. We ought to set *him* a riddle, because if *he* can do it, so can we. Something like: if concepts can be constituted, then they must also be able to be calculated. That's not very clearly expressed, I know, but it could just as well be an invitation to lunch, it makes no difference. I just think we might try to establish contact with him, don't you agree?'

Steiner said nothing. This was like setting a mousetrap. But what harm could it do? The murderer might indeed be prompted to react, and any kind of reaction was better than this silence and groping around in the dark.

'Was this your own idea?'

'Yes, sir.'

'Very well. I will give it some thought.'

He sniffed the air again. In the refectory they were serving the steaming soup. His immediate need, in this biting cold, was to eat, to put some warmth, some broth glistening with beads of fat, into his empty belly.

The idea was not at all bad. Something might come of it, if one set about it intelligently and found the right words and the right place to leave the text designed to trap the killer. If he did reply, then at least they would know that Domitian had been innocent. The murderer was a man who liked to express himself; this would appeal to him and flatter his vanity. How honoured he will feel when he sees that we want to engage him in a debate! I should have thought of this idea before now. It has been lying there fallow all this time, like a field in summer. Oh yes, I shall enjoy sitting down and searching for the right words...

> *You think yourself clever, and perhaps indeed you are. For Casall's death is not yet solved. So tell me, is it correct, as Aristotle writes, and as he tells us Phaidon said, that ideas are the cause of being and becoming?*

Steiner stared at the paper. It was not a proper letter, but it was a riddle of the kind that his opponent seemed to like. A philosophical question concerning the meaningfulness or otherwise of ideas. Was his adversary a traditionalist or a modern? Or just a dullard who had been taught to write?

Steiner stood up and pocketed the paper. But now where should he put it? What was the best place to display it? He decided on the Scholarium in St. Gereonstrasse: it attracted a large number of students these days, and he himself lectured there. He would leave the note in the cloister, where the wind was least troublesome and the snow did not penetrate. Steiner nailed it in place while no one was around. Wherever the murderer lived, whether here in the Scholarium or in one of the *bursae* or colleges, this would be certain to lure him, because he was as vain as a peacock. In good spirits, Steiner set off homewards.

Next morning the piece of paper was still there. Students and Masters were crowding round it, discussing what it might signify, and then bearing news of it all round the city, so that in the space of half a day everybody knew that someone had set a question for Casall's murderer to answer. But who?

Steiner had not even told the Chancellor of his idea, and so everyone, students and Masters alike, puzzled over what the strange note could possibly mean. Only Sophie and Laurien went rushing through the teaching rooms, corridors and gardens each morning to see if a reply had appeared. And sure enough, the murderer responded. Even if he were not resident in the Scholarium he could not have failed to hear of the question, since no one was talking of anything else. Steiner ordered the *lupus* to keep a close watch, in the hope of eventually unmasking his unknown correspondent. But the *lupus*, though he had eyes like a hawk and could run like a hare, always arrived on the scene too late.

Steiner's first question was answered by his opponent with a quotation from Aristotle, '*Universalia in rebus.*' Universals reside in things. This suggested that the murderer was a man who sought a compromise between the two current schools of thought, and who accorded priority neither to concepts nor to real things. Steiner was disappointed. He had expected a radical standpoint, not such a cautious position. Nor could he tease out of that lapidary statement any indication of the murderer's personality. He therefore changed his tactics. In his next message he wrote:

> *If we do not solve the second puzzle, will you give us some assistance?*

He could almost hear his adversary laughing: it's not so very difficult, you must try harder.

The second reply was posted up on the doorway of the chapel in the Scholarium:

> *I know you, but you do not know me. What was that about concepts?*

Even no answer is an answer of sorts, thought Steiner, as he started to brood on his next question.

This late afternoon Sophie was one of the last students left in the Scholarium. The columns had remained bare, as had their capitals, there was no piece of paper attached to any of the doors or lying on a table in the refectory. Had he found a new place? And where was the *lupus*, who was always creeping along the passages?

The wind was howling round the corners, driving snowflakes into the torches like moths flying into a lamp. Sophie looked around her.

At the end of lectures Laurien had vanished into his dormitory. She did not want to bump into him. She had drawn back a little from him because the looks he gave her spoke volumes. In class some days ago he had whispered into her ear, asking her if she knew where Sophie Casall was living now, and she had recoiled, startled. Did seeing her as Josef make him think of Sophie? Might he be able to discover the truth? But she was certain that he had no solid basis for whatever he might vaguely suspect, and that he was just poking around like an angler in a murky pond, with no prospect of a catch. All the same, perhaps it was risky to spend too much time with him…

Suddenly a shadow appeared on the far side of the cloister. And yet no figure could be seen moving past the columns. There was only the sound of footsteps. The shadow lengthened, lengthened still more, became distorted and then vanished.

Sophie started running. He ought to have been beside the library door. She stopped and peered over there. Nothing. She drew closer. The bracket on the wall held a lighted lamp. Where could he possibly have disappeared to? Sophie pushed against the heavy door to the library. It was already locked. Could one get into the refectory from here? The refectory door was still open, but there was not a soul to be seen there, not even under the tables. The door to the kitchen was locked, only the small serving hatch was open. Sophie peered in. No one here either. What had become of the person whose footsteps she had unmistakably heard and whose shadow she had seen?

More footsteps. But this time it was the *lupus*.

'What are you doing here so late? The lectures finished a long time ago.'

Sophie nodded and muttered an apology. She had seen a shadow and heard footsteps, she said. And yet there had been no one in sight. An apparition? Something that existed in the mind, with no perceptible thing corresponding to it? What might the thing have been like that corresponded to that shadow? Just at this moment Laurien came round the corner holding a piece of paper.

'He was here,' Sophie said simply.

'Where?'

'I saw a shadow on the far side of the cloister.'

'A shadow? Is that all? That's as good as nothing. Even a lamp casts a shadow.'

'Yes, but not one that moves and makes a noise. Unless you've seen a lamp walking?'

Laurien bit his lip. 'How big was it, this shadow?'

'I don't know.'

'That's no good.' Laurien shook his head. 'That sounds like something in your mind, and we know the nature of things that exist only in the mind, don't we?'

Magister Steiner was coming towards them. With long strides he crossed the cloister and stopped in front of Sophie. He said nothing, but just looked at her enquiringly. She shrugged. 'I saw a shadow,' she murmured, 'but Laurien thinks that's nothing.'

Steiner smiled. 'Oh, from a metaphysical viewpoint it would be a great deal. But for the purposes of our case I would say that, regrettably, Laurien is right—it is not enough. Our adversary is cleverer than we supposed. He does not go about casually posting up his pieces of paper on the nearest wall. He waits for the right moment so that none of us ever manages to see him—not even the *lupus*, though he is stealthily patrolling the Scholarium day and night and keeping his eyes open.'

And yet I did hear footsteps, Sophie reflected bitterly. There *was* somebody there. Why had she not been able to see him?

She could not stop thinking about it. And very gradually a peculiar idea took shape in her mind. If she left the shadow to one side for the moment, since a shadow might well be deceptive, that still left the footsteps. The library had been locked and the refectory empty, and there had been no way into the kitchen. That was the sticking-point. He *had* been there. And in that case there must have been somewhere for him to disappear to. The other possibility might be a secret door known only to the initiated. Sophie rejected that idea. The riddle that the murderer had set Steiner came back into her mind. The *quadrivium*.

Before two more days had passed she had a definite suspicion. A figure that evaporated into thin air! It could either be a ghost, the soul of a dead person made manifest, or else there must be a natural explanation for it. To discover the answer she had only one option. She must go back to the Scholarium. She would let herself be locked in there overnight.

She seized her opportunity one evening when Lombardi held his first lecture in the room which had now been furnished specifically as a lecture room. Afterwards, while the students who lived there sauntered along the corridors towards the refectory, she hid in the garden in the bitter cold and passed the time by counting the icicles hanging from the roof. Then when they were all eating their supper she crept back inside and found herself a dark corner to hide in, under the stairs which led up to de Swerthe's room. Gradually everything grew quiet. The students disappeared into their dormitories, the maids left for home and the dwarf locked up behind them. At around ten he put out all the lamps and climbed the stairs. Sophie was alone.

She had brought a candle with her, but it gave off very little light. In the refectory the fire was almost out; only the embers still glowed in the hearth. Since almost all the rooms were locked, there were not many areas for her to search. She could not even get into the library. Only the door to the chapel stood open, but it was most unlikely that the murderer would have left any traces there. She could smell the scent of incense, and a gilded Madonna glinted in the candlelight.

Sophie crept up the stairs. Here too all the doors were locked, except for one. It was the door to the Prior's study. The light of the full moon, shining in through the window, fell onto a pile of papers. They were all accounts relating to the running of the Scholarium: expenditure on wood, quills, the kitchen staff, the *lupus*, and so forth. There was also a statement from the patron, and the bill for the new books. From up here one could look right over the housetops. In the distance she could make out the sleeping river, fat and wide in the moonlight. She rummaged around among the papers, but found nothing. Unsure what to do next, she tried to bring some order to her thoughts, which were fluttering like restless birds. What had she hoped to discover? Something that related to Casall? She did not know herself.

She slipped quietly back downstairs. There was still much of the night ahead of her, and tomorrow morning she would appear among the students as though nothing had happened. But until then she was stuck in here.

A strange sound made her hold her breath. It was a soft, muted rushing and gurgling, as though the river had just washed through the garden. It sounded like water, and yet there was none that could have been so close. Sophie tried to discover the source of the noise. It had come from over by the latrines. But the door to the garden was locked. A heavy padlock hung in place. Discouraged, Sophie returned to the stairs. This was leading nowhere. She crawled back into her hiding-place and snuffed out her candle. The cold penetrated her bones and kept her awake for a long time. It was only in the early hours of the morning that she finally fell into a shallow, uneasy sleep.

It was still pitch dark when Sophie awoke. One after another, candles and oil lamps were being lit in the Scholarium. The *lupus* made up the fires in the refectory and lecture room, and the women arrived and set to work in the kitchen. In an hour's time the first lecture would begin, but until then she must remain hidden under the stairs. Her legs had gone to sleep, and her whole body felt as if it were imprisoned in a block of ice. She tried to stretch out a little, but this brought her feet into the beam of a lamp, and she hastily drew them back again. De Swerthe came down the stairs, his voice ringing out through the building. Doors slammed, and the aroma of warm milk wafted over to her hiding-place. Dear God, how was she going to get through the day on an empty stomach and with these lumps of ice for feet? There was already a suspicious scratchiness in her throat, a slight shiver in her unrested, chilled limbs.

She waited. After half an hour they all left the refectory and made their way to the lecture room. A door flew open; that was Lombardi's voice. Sophie crawled out from under the stairs. Now she must straighten up cautiously; her back was as stiff as a broom. She simply must go home and warm up. She would just have to miss the lecture. She slipped out through the door and into the street. Tomorrow was another day. Tomorrow she would think where to go from here.

'You were here all night?'

Laurien gaped at her. Huddled here the whole night through, almost catching her death of cold?

'Water,' said Sophie, 'there must be water there somewhere.'

Laurien nodded. The two students had gone to the Heumarkt, which was ankle-deep in slush. Further along was the meat hall: it would be dry underfoot there.

'The *lupus* says that it's the remains of a Roman water system. When the ground water level is high, it fills up. That's all.'

Sophie was disappointed. Was it really only an old drain?

'Tell me, Josef, what is it you're really looking for?'

'I don't know.'

'And who is it you suspect? If you've got suspicions about somebody, why don't you tell Steiner?'

Why not indeed? She did not know herself. She was reluctant to accuse anyone on the basis of a mere suspicion.

'Tell me, who is it?'

She shook her head and looked around. The rank odour of meat and fresh blood overrode the usual smells of filth and urine.

'I have no evidence, apart from shadows that I was the only one to see and footsteps that I was the only one to hear. I have no witnesses, no proofs.'

Lombardi suddenly appeared opposite them with a few of his students. They met in the aisle of the meat hall, and Sophie greeted them pleasantly. Laurien entered into a conversation with one of the students, and she left him there and struggled home through the slush. Once there, she went to bed, with a heated brick for warmth. She felt as if a thousand knives were sawing at her throat. She must sleep and sweat out the illness, and then in the evening sally forth again to see what she could find at the back of the Scholarium. But what was she actually looking for? The murderer? He would not be waiting there for her, ready to hand over the proofs she wanted. She had simply got a bee in her bonnet. An irrational, groundless idea, not even a proper suspicion. A fantasy. The *quadrivium*.

She wrapped her blanket round her and closed her eyes in utter exhaustion.

When evening came she went sneaking back to the Scholarium. This time she approached the rear of the building, where the garden was. There was an empty house there, and next to it, enclosed by a wall, an orchard belonging to a monastery. A quiet, deserted area beyond which lay St. Gereon's. From the belfry of the monastery church came the faint ringing of a small bell. The snow was still thawing, forming big puddles on the road. Sophie tried to look through the window into the derelict house. Though the frost had made patterns on the glass, these had now slid down to the lower part of the panes, but there was nothing to see inside. And then she heard that rushing sound again. Yes, it could be water, a conduit deep underground, where the cellars were. Not a murderer, just water. Sophie tried the door handle but it was locked. She was about to turn away and hurry home when the chimney caught her attention. How odd. Clouds of dirty yellow smoke were curling up from it and ascending into the air, which was full of the constant drip of thawing snow. Water was dripping from the trees, the roofs, and the chimney, from which the yellow smoke was still rising. What could that be, yellow and thin and spiralling upwards until it dispersed? She sniffed the air and smelled the odour of rotten eggs, the characteristic smell of a hen-house when the housewife has forgotten to collect the eggs. And suddenly Sophie knew what that was, swirling up, mysterious as a ghost, from the chimney. Sulphur! It was sulphur, which was used to drive out pestilence. She had a moment of panic. Nonsense, she told herself in an effort to calm her fear. The plague is far away from here. There's an alchemist in there doing experiments. They brewed up all sorts of strange substances in fat-bellied flasks, trying to make gold and silver from dung. She seemed to have tracked down the wrong person—it wasn't an alchemist that she had been looking for. She peered through the dirty window once more. What was that? There, no more than a movement, a hint, a mere suggestion of a streak of light, which was now moving in a circle. And now she could see it quite distinctly. Somebody was walking round with a lighted candle in his hand. But the remarkable thing was that this somebody seemed to be holding the candle below table-level, as a child might do. There was no head to be seen, in fact it was as though a beheaded person were walking about in there. Or did the cats around here prowl about with candles to help them see better? Was it a house bewitched, where the dead rise up and walk with their heads tucked underneath their arms? Pressing her hand to her mouth in terror, Sophie inched slowly away from the window. Cold, wet drips from the guttering ran down her neck. Then she turned round again and looked upwards. The billows of yellow smoke had ceased. Above her she saw nothing but an empty, starless sky.

That night Sophie dreamt about monsters in deserted houses. A monster in every empty room. In the cellar the cyclopes and seven-headed serpents, in the attic the creatures of the air, the ghosts and witches—ghosts with empty eye-sockets and flapping coat-tails, witches who rode on crossed broomsticks and flew down people's chimneys. She had woken up bathed in sweat and had lit a lamp. Nothing was worse than fantasy when there was no reality to cut it down to size. But as for to the deserted house, even if things were as they seemed, she could go back and take another look. And if an alchemist was in fact there, secretly brewing up unspeakably disgust-ing concoctions, that need not concern her. If, on the other hand, cats were walking around holding candles, that was a matter for the magistrate or the city gaoler, but if they were not interested in what went on in that house, so be it. At any rate all this seemed to have no bearing on her suspicions. She would have to do some further searching in the Scholarium, but next time she would make sure that she was better protected against the cold.

First, however, the student Josef Heinrich went to see Steiner. He was in his garden, and was not a little astonished when Sophie not only informed him of her plan to conceal herself in the Scholarium overnight, but also told him her suspicions as to who the murderer was. The chill wind was whistling around every corner, and Steiner invited her into the house.

'That is dangerous,' he said, looking dubiously into her face.

'Yes, but you could hardly do it yourself,' Sophie responded with a smile. 'I will confide in Laurien, and if anything should happen he'll be able to help me. I just wanted you to know.'

'What you want is to make me take the responsibility for this,' grumbled Steiner testily. 'But I cannot do that. If you are right, the man is ruthless and would not hesitate to do away with you. And yet how could we stop his activities, if he actually was the murderer? You realise that it is risky to accuse someone on the basis of a mere suspicion. What sort of evidence are you looking for?'

'I've no idea. But he *must* have left some traces. Have you really never considered that he might be the killer?'

Steiner made no reply. He had indeed thought of him but had immediately cast those doubts aside. Then he remembered that business with the book of alchemy, and began to pace agitatedly to and fro. Yes, he had had a suspicion, but he had rejected it out of hand because he had been unable to see any motive. And he could still see none. And now it had taken a student to point him in this direction again. Footsteps, a shadow, and not a soul to be seen. That, nothing more, had fuelled the student's suspicion. It could have been a child. Or a restless spirit, an apparition. Or…a dwarf. There, it was out in the open, at last. An educated dwarf with a mastery of Latin, secretly nursing a possibly ungovernable hatred of Casall, who had always enjoyed ridiculing people who were different. It all fitted. Though the motive was a little thin. Too thin, really. There must be more to it than that. But what?

Steiner sent the student home, not without another earnest warning against his dangerous scheme, and then he sat for a long time in front of his kitchen fire, deeply troubled and desperately racking his brains for a better course of action than the one proposed by Josef Heinrich….

Laurien was also in a state of great agitation. It was all wrong for Josef to spend another night nosing around in the Scholarium. And then to try to rope him in too, by expecting him to get hold of the keys! That was absolutely out of the question.

'What good is it my being here if all the doors are locked? You must help me. Go back to bed afterwards if you like, but get me that bunch of keys.'

'Only if you tell me who you think it is. And anyway, go and see Steiner—he'll know what to do.'

She shook her head. She might be mistaken, she needed to be certain.

'So it's somebody from the Scholarium,' mused Laurien. 'Lombardi? Do you suspect Lombardi? But that's dreadful.'

'Are you going to get me the keys?'

Laurien was compliant by nature. The more someone urged him, the weaker his resistance grew. The *lupus* had a spare set of keys, but he was not always in the building. When he spent the night at the Scholarium he slept in the guest chamber. Laurien waited until everybody had gone to bed and then felt his way in the dark to the staircase where Sophie was waiting for him. Outside the window the moon was shining, grown almost to its full size. That was a bad omen. Everyone knew that a risky undertaking attempted at full moon was likely to go awry. One did not even go to the barber-surgeon to have a tooth pulled at full moon. This was the time when the celestial bodies conspired together to exert baneful influences on the earth. His knees knocking, Laurien slunk along to the guest chamber, opened the door and slipped inside. The *lupus* was snorting and snoring, his face turned to the wall. His hose were draped over a stool, with the keys resting on them. Laurien snatched them up and made his exit.

Outside the room Sophie stood waiting. 'Thank you. Off you go to bed now.'

He nodded. By the light of her candle she watched him go, and then climbed the stairs. De Swerthe's study stood open as before; it had nothing to offer her. But there might be something in the room next to it.

From downstairs came the sound of a door opening or closing. She froze, listening hard, but all was quiet again. On a table she found more bills, this time for a delivery of wine from the Cistercian abbey at Eberbach. Twelve bottles of the finest quality, and at a princely price too. The dwarf and Lombardi probably drank this in private while the students were having their *Gruitbier*. In a chest there were a number of coats, neatly tied in a bundle, while on a console a heavy silver candelabrum was proudly displayed. Next to it lay a sheet of paper. A list of the wages paid to the kitchen maids. Sophie hesitated. She must go downstairs and if possible continue her search in Lombardi's room. Then she heard footsteps. Someone was coming up the stairs, treading softly, and a faint ray of light became visible on the landing. Laurien, she thought, and squeezed behind the door. The light drew nearer. A broad shadow advanced into the room carrying a candle ahead of it.

It was not Laurien but the *lupus*. He halted and shone the light around the room. Was that something, behind the door there? He came closer. And then he stretched out his free arm and seized Sophie by the shoulder, dragged her out from behind the door, held the candle under her nose and pushed her up against the wall.

'Aha, who's this? What are you doing, creeping around here in the middle of the night?'

'I'm looking for a book,' she breathed, looking round for any chance of escape, but he had her firmly by the arm.

'A book? I'm more inclined to think you are a thief. There are no books here, they are in the library. Right, you just come along with me...'

He was as strong as an ox. She struggled in his arms, but he took no notice as he pushed her down the stairs and hauled her into the kitchen. There he locked her in, returning soon afterwards with a drowsy de Swerthe, who, after hearing what the *lupus* had to say, immediately started waving his arms around wildly. 'A thief? What were you hoping to steal, you rascal? Let's put him in the lock-up. We can think more about it tomorrow.'

Sophie was rigid with terror. But he had her taken down to the cellar at once, despite her resistance and her shouts for Steiner. De Swerthe laughed derisively and told the *lupus* to put the student into a cell. Then the *lupus* slammed the door shut behind her.

This whole affair would have been no concern of Steiner's—if only Josef Heinrich had not told him of his plan. When a student from a scholarium committed some misdemeanour, it was for the prior of that institution to restore order and discipline. If it was a matter affecting the Faculty, then the Dean, the Chancellor or the Rector might be called in; but finding someone prowling about in a scholarium, trying to steal money or books, did not constitute grounds for involving the Chancellor. If the intention was to expel the student, the Chancellor's advice might be sought, but this one had not even actually stolen anything. It seemed that he was talking a lot of confused nonsense as though he were delirious with fever. He was raving about murder and slaughter and about messages in the college, and nobody could make head or tail of his incoherent babble. Finally he cried out that they must fetch Steiner. On hearing this Steiner was aghast. He should never have agreed to let Josef Heinrich hide in the Scholarium—now perhaps he was in the hands of the murderer and he, Steiner, was responsible for this sorry affair. He hastened with all speed to the Scholarium and went down to the lock-up. But the plank bed had not been occupied and there was just a blanket lying on it. Apart from a startled mouse scuttling away into a crevice, the cell was empty.

The *lupus*, who had opened the cell door for him, could only shake his head. He had been there just a short while ago, it was impossible, he must be there…

One look, and another—the student was gone. 'That…that's not possible,' he stammered, and dashed off upstairs to tell the canon. He was sitting in the library, reading a book.

'The student has vanished!'

Steiner was standing in the doorway. De Swerthe raised his head. 'Nonsense! However could he get out of the lock-up?'

In no time half the Scholarium was crowding round the door in the cellar, but Josef Heinrich was still missing—the cell was empty.

'Well, see that you get him back,' rasped Steiner, leaving the building in a rage. Out in the street he tried to control his anger and calm down. What could have happened? The killer must have found an opportunity to move the student elsewhere. But where? Steiner reproached himself. How could he have allowed Josef Heinrich to put his ridiculous plan into action?

Josef Heinrich was still missing. Now Laurien had been robbed of his second friend, and he fell into an ever deeper state of melancholy. But he asked himself over and over again who had anything to gain by getting Josef out of the way. And each time the answer was the same: the murderer. Disastrously, Josef's ravings, his demand to speak to Steiner and hints that he knew something about Casall, must have caused the killer to step in and take decisive action. Laurien racked his brains, but his friend had never revealed to him whom he suspected; and so he now began to feel that he could trust no one, since anyone at all in the Scholarium might be the guilty man; Lombardi, one of the Bachelors, the bedel, the *lupus*, or even the Prior or one of the undergraduate students. It was hopeless. And Laurien had no intention of confiding in Steiner. Whenever he had looked to someone else for help he had been badly let down. No, he would keep quiet, and time would pass and somewhere in this great wide world his friend would moulder and decay, while the man who had done away with him would thrive and prosper.

When she opened her eyes it was dark all around her. There was a smell of cold damp wood, probably coming from the walls, which let the wind through. She sat up. All she could remember was being grabbed by two arms and bundled into a sack. Nothing after that. Somebody must have struck her over the head, but even that she could not now recall. She was evidently in some sort of shed. Her hands reached out to touch its wooden sides. Outside a gale howled, and somewhere she could hear the rushing of water. That must be the Roman conduit. Or was it the river? Where was she? No window, but there must surely be a door...

Slowly her eyes grew accustomed to the darkness. There was a crack in the roof where the light of the moon crept through. She looked up and felt a sense of relief. She listened intently. Nothing but the sound of the water.

So she could only wait, wait for him to come.

He was sure to be in his Scholarium now. Sooner or later he would come and check on her. Or might he just leave her here to die of hunger and thirst? Kill her, as cold-bloodedly as he had killed Casall? She had been on the right track, but now he had wrenched her off it to save his own miserable life…

Outside, footsteps approached. So he was coming after all, to see if she was still alive? She slipped back into her corner and pretended to be asleep. The bolt was drawn back on a door that she had been unable to make out in the dark, and then the hinges creaked and a beam of light filled her prison.

She opened her eyes very slightly, and in the wavering light of a torch that the wind was doing its best to blow out she saw his stunted form as he bolted the door on the inside. She caught her breath. Was he strong? She had seen his arms, and they had been well-developed and powerful. An undersized fellow like that could summon up the strength of an ox despite his physical defects…

The light moved towards her, and as though under some compulsion she opened her eyes—she had to get a look at him. She saw a smile on his girlishly soft, delicate face. His hair was tied back. A slim, well-proportioned body, but it was the body of a child. Had the circumstances of his wretched dwarfish life been different, he might have been an entertainer juggling with clubs, or a showman with a performing bear, but instead some chance or other had placed him in the care of clerics and he had received a good theological training.

'You are awake, then…. Let us consider what we are to do with you. I could drown you like a kitten. Or hit you on the head like Casall and then send Magister Steiner another nice little riddle, what do you think?'

She drew her coat closer around her. If he realised that she was a woman it was all over. But as yet she could still play the part of an ordinary, contrite student…

He seemed uncertain how to proceed, and stood there with his torch, looking down at her.

'I am not a ruthless murderer,' she heard him mutter, 'which makes this more difficult. You should have held your tongue. How much do you know? What did you mean to tell Steiner?'

She decided to speak gently to him. Perhaps he carried a deep inner wound as a result of his deformity, like many who are subjected to humiliation because they are different from other people. Perhaps what he needed was pity, or kindness and compassion, perhaps that would thaw the ice that held his heart in its grip.

'Surely it was your own intention to be identified. Why did *you* not keep quiet instead of setting your riddles? Underneath it all you wanted to be recognised, didn't you?'

He looked at her in surprise. He had not expected her to hold up a mirror to him. Yes, he had to acknowledge that she was right. He nodded. 'It's a long story. But you have not answered my question.'

'It was the reference to the *quadrivium* that gave me the idea. The allusion to sizes, dimensions. The small killing the great. And then you were creeping around in the college and I couldn't see anybody. And yet I knew there must be someone there, because I heard your footsteps. From the refectory there is only a serving hatch into the kitchen, and the kitchen was locked. Only someone small, a child *or a dwarf* could crawl through the hatch and appear to have vanished from the face of the earth. It was you, wasn't it?'

'Yes, it was. I was just going to give Steiner an answer when I saw you sneaking about. You thwarted my plan. No matter. It can't be altered, but now I need to find an acceptable solution, one that satisfies us both.'

He looked closely at her. Had he not noticed that she was a woman? He had probably shaken her out of the sack like a heap of stones and not even touched her. Had the *lupus* helped him? On his own he would have been too small, unless he possessed the strength of a giant.

'You are not going to do away with me?' she asked quietly. 'I know enough to destroy you.'

He gave a smile of angelic sweetness. 'In this city everyone is in a position to destroy everyone else. Don't you know that the city is pregnant with innumerable secrets? Everybody already has one foot on the scaffold, and those who wield the executioner's axe are no better than the accused. Go ahead and denounce me, little student, then there will be one less damned soul here among the living. But your soul is not worth much either—souls are no more than tiny stars in the firmament, wandering about and never finding rest. What does it matter if they are extinguished? But let us think carefully. In a world like this there is only one way to protect oneself. That is to let the other person in on your secrets, make him your accomplice, so that from then on he is burdened with the same guilt as yourself. That seems to me an excellent solution, don't you agree?' He smiled. The light shone on his blond hair and his handsome, pale face. How could someone like him have the face of an angel? Born, as he was, to be so small and deformed.

He came closer and held out his hand. 'Up you get, we will make a start straight away on instructing you in my art.'

She stood up. He led the way and opened the door, but whereas she had expected it to lead outside, she now saw that she had been in a lean-to shed that opened into the room of a house. Here there was a powerful stench of all manner of substances that were combined together in a pungent concoction that stung the nostrils.

Now she knew where she was. She must be in the empty house at the back of the Scholarium. So this was where the dwarf crept away to when the students were asleep. But what did he do here? On a low table stood all kinds of apparatus; she recognised a still, flasks, crucibles and jugs. De Swerthe went ahead of her, thrust his torch into a mounting on the wall and also lit an oil lamp. 'Sit down. You know what all this is?'

'Do you call yourself an alchemist? Are you searching for the philosophers' stone?'

De Swerthe laughed. 'By means of which, as with King Midas, everything is turned into gold? A pleasing idea. Yes, I am engaged in alchemy, the boldest of all branches of knowledge. Are you ambitious? I mean, do you want to be more than just a Master of the *artes liberales*? A professor of jurisprudence, perhaps?'

'No.'

'Then this is exactly the right place for you. You will be my assistant and get your hands dirty, just like me. During the daytime you will quietly continue your studies and learn what Albertus Magnus or Bacon or Aristotle said about alchemy—that can only be of benefit to you. But at night you will help me here and share my knowledge, and that will tie your hands. And now come here and skim the froth from the top of this.'

She came nearer, holding her nose. On one of the furnaces was a pan with a thick, bilious yellow mixture bubbling in it. De Swerthe handed her a ladle, with which she scooped out the sulphurous scum and transferred it to a second pan. He stood beside her, grinning. 'Now you will leave it to dry out. And now fetch that mandrake, but be careful, it is valuable…. If you want to perceive the truth, only alchemy will help you, my friend. What they teach in the Faculty is nothing but empty chatter, for who can seriously claim to be able to separate the will from the intellect? One can only separate matter, not mental constructs. Look, this is matter, this root, this boiling mixture, from which we shall make a nice little stone. The seven liberal arts…do you know to what they correspond?'

Sophie shook her head. The stench was becoming more and more acrid, and now, with the foul scum lying in its new container and drying out, she felt nausea rising inside her.

'Silver corresponds to the moon, iron to Mars, quicksilver to Mercury, tin to Jupiter, copper to Venus, lead to Saturn and, lastly, gold to the sun. Seven metals, seven planets, and seven arts. Tell me, what have you learned in the Faculty about which of the arts corresponds to which element and which star?'

She was giddy and her head would not stop spinning. She sank back on to the stool, closing her eyes.

De Swerthe laughed. 'Yes, one has to get used to it, it is all rather smelly. But you soon get over that when you realise that you are on the track of truth. It is all based on philosophical principles, for I too studied the *artes liberales* before becoming Prior of this miserable Scholarium. As you know, Aristotle himself says that all matter is derived from the four elements of earth, air, fire and water, and that they in turn are derived from the *prima materia*. Only the quantities of the constituents vary, which means that it must be possible to make noble metals from base metals, do you follow me? Oh, this will make a grand, fiery spectacle, once the froth has dried out…'

Everything swam before her eyes, and she fainted.

'So today let us turn our attention to magic or, as I prefer to call it, the occult, which is also how Thomas Aquinas habitually referred to it, because there are things which cannot be explained on the basis of their elements…'

The lectures on magic appealed to Laurien more than anything else. This was undeniably a somewhat dubious area, and the need to tolerate it gave even the Faculty a severe bellyache, but since natural philosophy did include such fields it could not be wholly ignored. After all, Aristotle and Thomas were among those who had written about the occult, and that made it legitimate to lecture on it. But if Laurien had imagined that he would witness experiments with gases and poisons and incantations, he was sadly disappointed. This area of study was presented in a dry manner, subjected to the scholastic approach which despised practical experimentation and saw the mind as the only valid instrument for the acquisition of knowledge. What was the occult? The force behind things? Steiner stood at his lectern and read from Thomas's writings. How can a magnet attract iron? How can rhubarb produce a cure? Was not a higher force necessarily lending efficacy to a lower one? Was the lower force dependent on the higher one as a plant is dependent on sun, rain and wind? What was that higher force?

Steiner looked up. One of the students suggested that it was the stars, the force of the heavenly bodies, at which Steiner gave a kindly nod and laid the book aside. He then read from Thabit ibn Qurra, so as to give the theoretical teaching the added dimension of a practical example.

'How do you rid a house of scorpions?'

The students who already knew this *exemplum* grinned, the rest just stared at Steiner and waited in silence.

'Well, then, I will tell you. You fashion an image of a scorpion from a pure metal, be it copper, silver or lead, and you do this when Scorpio is in the ascendant. You inscribe the name of the zodiacal sign on the image and bury it in the house which has the scorpions in it. Then you pronounce the words, 'I hereby bury him and all of his kind,' so that he is obliged to depart from the place. Alternatively you can make four images and bury them at the four corners of the house.'

'Can this method also be used to drive away a person you don't like?' one of the students was heard to ask, and a ripple of laughter went round the lecture-hall. Steiner shrugged. The power of the stars was great, greater than anything known to man. No doubt one could get rid of a whole host of unpopular persons in this way, but the borderline between *scientia* and *superstitio* was a fine one.

'We are not here to conduct experiments in the occult,' he admonished them. 'We are concerned with the definition of form, and with the distinction between solid wisdom and the attainments of less sagacious minds. Those who worship the planets and play about with mandragora, laurel, the brain of a hoopoe or the blood of a bat unquestionably belong to the latter category. We read *De occultis operibus naturae* so as to learn something of the indubitably real power of the heavenly bodies. For it is the stars and planets that will accompany your lives from here to the grave, and that determine your destiny...'

Laurien experienced a moment of shock. There was something horrible about that idea. Was man not free in his decisions? Did not the philosophers teach the freedom of the human will? Where was man's freedom if his fate was imposed on him by Pluto or Venus? He raised his hand and asked his question.

Steiner nodded. Yes, where was it indeed, that freedom? It was the same as with day and night, or happiness and unhappiness. It was that bane of human existence, dualism, that was present in every aspect of life and gave one no peace.

'It is true that the stars give you the power to do a thing,' said Steiner, 'but you yourself must actually do it. The first of these circumstances represents the compulsion, the other allows you the freedom that you require.'

Laurien was not satisfied. Nor was he helped by having his attention drawn to the collection of Arabic texts, the 'Picatrix'. How could the murderer be induced to release his friend? Was there some occult procedure for this, too? Should one perhaps go about it as in Steiner's *exemplum*? Or adapt it a little?

As Laurien went back to the Scholarium that evening he felt as though he were being pursued by someone with a long, sharp knife. Indulging in such hocus-pocus was almost unthinkable, but what had he to lose by making the attempt? He could not, unfortunately, get hold of a piece of metal, but for his purposes perhaps a bit of canvas would do. But how was he to perform the magical act quietly and discreetly, so that no one would notice? Was he, a student of the *artes liberales*, actually going to follow the lowest impulse that anyone could have, and experiment with magic? It was simply ridiculous! He might just as well stick pins into rag dolls! Even so, the idea would not leave him alone. Should he himself try to harness the power of the stars, should he attempt to direct fate? God preserve him! He rushed headlong through the streets; rain lashed his face and lightning flashed across the sky, as though his thoughts alone had been enough to bring the wrath of the stars down on his head. Then he chanced upon a shop that sold all manner of writing materials. Was this a sign from fate? They were sure to have canvas too, for the city's painters.

The interior was full of the smells of linen cloth and parchment. Behind a counter stood the owner.

'Do you stock canvas?' Laurien asked in a thin little voice.

'Certainly. Good canvas, the very best. Here…'

The owner pulled out a piece and laid it across the counter.

'I don't need much.'

'For a painting?'

'No, no…' stammered Laurien. 'Only very little.'

Finally the man cut him a piece only half as big as the page of a book. 'It's going to be a very small picture,' he grumbled, shaking his head after the departing youngster, who was obviously not quite right in the head.

He had pretended to be ill. Stomach pains, nausea, headache, vague symptoms that could mean anything or nothing. He was left alone in the sick-room. Venus was in the fourth house, it was a propitious time. Laurien waited for darkness to fall and then laid his piece of canvas on the floor. Then he opened the window and rested his pinewood spill on the window-seat. Now he reverently wrote his friend's name on the canvas, carried it across to the window and lit the spill. The flame leapt up brightly, licked at the edge of the canvas and then burned so vigorously that Laurien had to hold the cloth at arm's length before releasing it so that it floated down to the ground.

'Josef Heinrich, please come to the Scholarium near St. Gereon's in Cologne,' he whispered.

The cloth curled up under the action of the heat and then fell apart; the fragments lay on the ground, still glowing.

I must have taken leave of my senses, was the thought that flashed through Laurien's mind as he watched the embers die. What did I suppose would come of this magic?

He looked up at the sky, which formed a heavy black canopy above him; the twinkling stars seemed to be winking at him. With a comforting sense of having at least tried everything that lay within his power, and the power of the heavenly bodies too, he climbed into bed, hoping that his friend was already on his way back to him.

The next morning did indeed bring a Josef Heinrich, but not the one that Laurien had hoped his magic would conjure up. One of the kitchen-maids had a son called Josef Heinrich, and he appeared at the Scholarium with a sack of flour that he was to deliver. Laurien gazed after him, totally nonplussed. He must have made some mistake. Were there so many boys with the same name that the stars had not known which one he meant? Or was it just a silly coincidence that had got in the way of his pact with the stars? How was it possible that something as banal as a shared name could so greatly influence such a sacred, secret and magical pact? At the same time he felt a strong sense of apprehension. For even though it had been the wrong boy—it had worked. The magic had obviously been effective, and that was the last thing Laurien had anticipated. In fact he had only really wanted to satisfy his conscience; and youthful curiosity had also induced him to try his hand at magic. But now he saw the power of the stars confirmed, and he found this extremely disturbing. What if he were to use the same method to bring the Holy Father from Rome to the Scholarium? Would he suddenly appear like a *deus ex machina* in the fair city of Cologne and call an ecclesiastical council?

Laurien shook his head. Don't meddle with such things, it will only end in tears. You saw what happened, the wrong Josef Heinrich came, and that shows what a treacherous business it is. You don't care for the idea that fate can be influenced as easily as that. And yet the fact remains that that other Josef Heinrich did turn up here with his sack of flour, and gave you an almighty shock…

Lombardi found Steiner having a meal in the College refectory. He needed to have a word with him, Lombardi said, about the missing student.

Steiner had spoken to the Dean of the Faculty, who had instigated a search of the Scholarium in St. Gereonstrasse, but nothing had been found, not the slightest sign. Steiner was growing anxious. He had had enough of students vanishing. The strange way that they seemed to disappear into thin air was disrupting his concentration on his teaching. He had agonised over whether he ought to tell the Chancellor the truth about the canon, but had been unable to bring himself to do so for fear of putting the student's life at risk now that he was presumably in de Swerthe's hands. Even so, he could not keep it to himself for much longer.

It was important, Lombardi insisted, and asked whether anyone had yet looked for the lad in Spielmannsgasse. Steiner could only tell him that the student had most likely been lying, for everyone who rented out rooms there had been asked and nobody knew him. Lombardi nodded, and said that he possibly knew where the student lived. He had once seen him coming out of a house near to the Heumarkt, and perhaps it would be worth looking around in that locality. Steiner gave a resigned nod. He walked with Lombardi in the bitter cold as far as the Heumarkt, where, under a radiant blue sky, the cattle-drovers had assembled their beasts. A little apart from the worst of the hubbub stood the house where Sophie Casall had found lodgings. Steiner looked dubiously at Lombardi.

'Here? But this is where Casall's widow lives.'

Lombardi nodded. 'A short while ago I saw Josef Heinrich coming out of the back entrance. Perhaps he has rented a room here, too…'

'Those people don't rent out rooms to students,' answered Steiner curtly.

They rang at the door. It was opened by a maid.

'Have your master and mistress let a room to a student?' asked Steiner without preamble. The maid shook her head, startled. 'The master's out, and the mistress too...'

'But Sophie Casall lives here, does she not?'

'Yes sir. But...the thing is...she hasn't...she hasn't been seen for several days.' She looked embarrassed. There seemed to be something in her mind, but she probably felt uncertain whether she could confide in this stranger.

'Don't be frightened. I am Magister Steiner from the Faculty. We are looking for a student who has disappeared. Are you quite sure that there isn't one living here?'

She gave a shrug. 'I saw a student sneaking through the garden into the house, two or three times.... He was visiting the widow Casall. But I didn't say anything, the master and mistress might not have approved...'

Steiner threw Lombardi a quick glance. How strange for those two to be meeting! Why should an impoverished student who allegedly had a room in Spielmannsgasse, a district of thoroughly ill repute, be visiting Sophie Casall?

'I should like to see her room.'

He was firmly resolved. He felt a little uncomfortable about forcing his way into someone's private room just like that, but what was the point of sending for a constable, when the maid was sure to have a key? With downcast eyes she led them up the stairs. She seemed to find Steiner intimidating. Once they were upstairs she unlocked a door and stood aside.

Lombardi drew the curtains, admitting bright daylight. The hearth was cold: probably no fire had been lit for some time. The bed, neatly made, a deskful of books, a cupboard, a stool, a washstand. Lombardi stood there, reluctant to sully these personal objects with his gaze. What they were doing was not right. And if—just supposing it was true—*if* she had been seeing that milksop, what business was it of his? Steiner was scurrying hither and thither, apparently oblivious to the delicacy of the situation. Or perhaps this frenetic zeal was an attempt to cover up his own bad conscience. He was leafing through the books and muttering to himself.

'We ought to be going,' said Lombardi, who already regretted having told Steiner what he had seen. Steiner nodded and replaced the book. Then, however, he picked up the papers that lay in a pile next to the books and began to read them.

'"Aristotle's Metaphysics." And here, it says "Boethius's *De consolatione philosophiae*". Lombardi, these are lecture notes. Look, this was one of yours, he has noted down your commentaries too. And look here…'

Now he was flicking furiously through the pile of papers. '…this one is mine. And that is Jordanus's.'

He stopped, holding one of the sheets at arm's length. 'Can you understand this? The student must have left these notes here. What are those two doing? Is he giving her private lessons?'

Lombardi had flushed deeply. He went over to the window and opened it. From the market below came the sounds of men's shouting and the bellowing of cattle. 'She always did want to know everything,' he murmured. 'So why shouldn't the student have been teaching her something?'

Steiner hesitated, but then laid the papers back on the table. 'Yes, that would certainly be an explanation, although…'

He stared at the writing. That handwriting, small and leaning very slightly to the left, he had seen it before…. And then—he saw those few lines literally before his eyes—he remembered.

Lombardi closed the window. 'Can we go now?'

'Yes, of course.'

They squeezed past the maid, who locked the room again, and asked her not to tell Sophie Casall of their visit. Then they left the house. Lombardi returned to the Scholarium, but Steiner set off in the opposite direction, towards the Provost's House.

The Chancellor had told the servant to move his chair close to the fire. A soft lambskin rug lay over his knees. From a bloodless, waxen face—he was being regularly bled for his gout—his eyes stared fixedly at Steiner, who was leaning with his back against the door as though he did not dare to come right in. In an expressionless voice he recounted his inspection of Sophie Casall's room and his discovery there of pages of writing which had quite unmistakably been produced by Casall's widow.

'Well,' said the Chancellor rather irritably, 'she lives there. And we all know that she can write.'

'But they are notes on whole series of lectures, complete with the lecturers' commentaries.'

The Chancellor obviously did not see where this was leading. 'Then she must have copied out that student's notes,' he said perfunctorily as he toyed with the ring on his right hand, making the sapphire flash in the sun.

'And what if she didn't?'

Now the Chancellor looked up. 'Would you kindly come to the point and tell me what you mean?'

'Very well…' Steiner drew closer to the fire and sat down on a stool opposite him, leaning forward. 'The build is identical, the voice slightly altered, the colour of the eyes, the shape of the lips the same…it hadn't struck me until I recognised the writing, that's when I became aware of the likeness…'

'Likeness?' The Chancellor stretched out his hands to the fire.

'The student and Sophie Casall are one and the same person, I fear,' said Steiner.

'Nonsense!' the Chancellor instantly burst out.

'The woman and the student disappeared on the same day. The maid has not seen Sophie Casall since the day the student was abducted from the Scholarium.'

'The whole thing is beyond belief!'

The Chancellor rose abruptly from his chair. The rug slid to the floor. Still a little dizzy from his last bleeding, he placed a hand on the table to steady himself.

'You surely cannot be serious. Do you realise what that would mean? That the woman insinuated herself into the Faculty under a false name!' He was visibly agitated now, pacing rapidly to and fro and shaking his head. 'Does a sheep go to a monastery school to study Boethius? It's monstrous!'

Steiner stood up. 'I don't know what is behind the disappearance of this…this *student*, but I have absolutely no doubt that he and Sophie Casall are the same person. If she does not reappear, so much the better; but if she does, what do we do then? There is nothing in the statutes to cover a case like this.'

'No,' snorted the Chancellor, 'naturally there is nothing about it in the statutes, because it is insane. Absurd, utterly absurd. Only a madwoman would ever conceive such a notion. She must have had her matriculation interview with one of the Masters, and that donkey failed to notice anything amiss. Was that you?'

Steiner shook his head. 'No, but we can easily establish who it was. The only thing is, where does that get us?'

'You are right. He was deceived by the woman's artfulness. We cannot hold him to blame.'

'There is another thing,' said Steiner hesitantly. 'The student came and told me about a suspicion that he—she—had as to the identity of Casall's murderer. To test it, she wanted to conceal herself overnight in the Scholarium. I confess that I did not altogether discourage her, so I am probably partly to blame for all that has ensued…'

The Chancellor looked up. 'You gave your permission?'

'Yes. What she said about the murderer sounded plausible, because by that time I had also come to suspect the same man. Unfortunately I did not follow the trail any further.'

'She told you whom she suspected?'

Steiner nodded. 'Yes, but you know how it is. It is risky when there is no evidence. Too many people have been and are still being brought to trial and sometimes even put to death merely because of rumours circulating about them. That is why I delayed, but I fear that I delayed too long…'

'Then tell me the name of the man you believe to be the killer.'

'Marius de Swerthe.'

The Chancellor stared at him. 'The Prior of the Scholarium? You cannot seriously mean that…'

'I fear so. I should like to have the Scholarium searched again. And its surroundings. After all, he must have her hidden there somewhere.'

The Chancellor remained silent for a few moments as he carefully draped the rug over the back of his chair. 'You should have informed me sooner,' he said reproachfully. 'There will be a scandal if anything has happened to her. Mind you, there will be one anyway, because of her being a woman…'

Steiner said nothing. The Chancellor gave him a nod to signify that he was dismissed, and he took his leave.

The Chancellor sank back into his chair and pulled the rug around his legs once more. The fire had died down, and a bitter chill had already become perceptible in the room again. If he went on sitting here he would turn into a block of ice. He could have rung to have the fire stoked up again, but it was too much effort. A woman at a university, dressed as a man—why, his cat might as soon jump up into the pulpit and preach a sermon! About an earthly Paradise where mice dangled in front of your jaws, rivers flowed with milk and the rich, thick lakes were topped with cream. *Principiis obsta*—resist the first beginnings, or you will not be master of the outcome. This was what came of providing women with books in the convents and allowing them to read. Of what use was all that knowledge to them?

The Chancellor rubbed his hands, for they were growing increasingly cold and stiff. He would have to get up from his chair eventually. He had heard of that French female who wrote books about women's understanding of life and women's dreams. What was her name? Oh yes, Pizan, or something of the kind. He had been told about one book in particular, the one describing a city of women where everything was just as women would like it to be. Well, he, the Chancellor of this Faculty, could well imagine the kind of thing that went on there. Nothing but whoring and feasting and reading and begetting, and the devil only knew what else. The very idea froze the blood in his narrowed veins. At their universities they might read the learned philosophers, or they might just rip up their books, who could tell? And now this! A woman who had insinuated herself into the Faculty, believing that she could make her mark there just like a man. The very thought was enough to make you feel sick, it turned your stomach. And now another feeling crept up on the Chancellor as he continued on this journey of reflection. Was not this the beginning of the end? To be sure, one misguided young woman was not the same as a whole host of them, but were not women gradually forcing their way into everything? Into every nook and cranny of society? Would they not inevitably take it into their heads to try and storm the world's last remaining bastions? What if one day they really did invade the Faculties? Like a parasite, the way mistletoe grows on trees, sucking out their sap until, diseased and debilitated, the trees succumb to the next violent storm. This was *his* world, a world belonging to men. Created by God and entrusted to men, for them to fashion according to their ideas, like a cathedral. Women would never be capable of building a second Cologne Cathedral. And what would a world shaped by women be like? Children would be its kings, running around in little cloaks of ermine. Cats would sleep in people's beds, and philosophy would vanish, like a ghost, into their linen-chests. For who had ever heard of women coming up with a single intelligent idea? And yet this woman had not only sneaked into the lectures but had actually taken down a full set of notes! It could only have been from sheer overweening pride, because no woman would think of doing it out of a desire to learn, you could be sure of that!

Now the Chancellor remembered that Casall had always complained of his wife's habit of reading his books. Of course, that was where the root of the evil lay. But it was too late, women had long been allowed to share in the fruits of men's intellectual endeavours. Now they were ensconced in convents everywhere, reading and writing and composing books of their own. Dear God! The Chancellor hauled himself slowly to his feet—this cold was worse than hunger and thirst put together. Now it was certainly too late. Too late to halt this disastrous trend. The Pope himself had had no objection to giving them access to books and even guidance on which sections to read. It was like letting a wolf loose in the middle of a flock of lambs.

The Chancellor rang for the housemaid. Yes, one day women would be students in the universities, and then they would clamber up into the pulpits, and worst of all—it frightened him to death to picture it—one day they would be Masters and hold lectures, and men would listen to them with rapt attention. The maid appeared and knelt before the hearth to lay fresh firewood and rekindle the fire.

As he stretched his hands out towards the first tongues of flame, he calmed down a little. Gradually a cosy warmth began to spread once more. There was still time to do something about it. They could still be prohibited from reading and writing. But he felt like a lone voice crying in the wilderness. If even the bishops and the Holy Father were willing to let women study the *trivium* to the greater glory of God, how could he, the essentially powerless Chancellor of a university, halt this development? He could write letters to those who did have power and urge that the provision of any kind of intellectual activity for women should cease forthwith. He collapsed back into his chair, worn out. They would laugh at him. They could not see the danger. With eyes wide open, they were rushing to their destruction.

But they did not know what he knew. That in his Faculty a woman had attended classes in men's clothing. It was therefore essential to make an example of her and show them the consequences of their naïvety. But first one must catch the woman. And then put her on trial. A sensational trial that would be talked of all over the world. One that would make them see the truth. Then they would change their policy and not just burn witches at the stake but also forbid such developments as this. Prohibit the city of women, O ye men! Dissolve the convents before it is too late. Amen.

Unconsciously he had folded his hands as if in prayer. Now he leaned back, exhausted. No, that would not work. It was only in exceptional cases that women had strayed into a university, tolerated by gullible Masters and charitable Chancellors who did nothing to prevent it, since naturally women too had to pay fees. It *was* a charitable gesture, thought the Chancellor, anxious to reach a clear position on the subject by leaving no argument unrehearsed. There were no grounds for fear. He was being too pessimistic, he had lost his sense of proportion. No one would thank him for hounding this young woman. Of course she would have to stand trial, because, after all, people could not be allowed to swear oaths under a false name, or register as students under a false name. But he had better not make a ruling on fundamental principles: he might find himself isolated because no one else would understand his attitude.

He gazed into the darting flames and adjusted the rug around his legs.

She was not like the other whores in the city: for her it was only a sideline, practised in secret. She was married, childless, with her husband constantly away from home, travelling on important business to different parts of the Empire.

Lombardi wrapped a cape around his shoulders, clapped a ridiculous cap on his head and hurried through the streets to her house. One of these days she would be found out, and then she would be in for it. But that was not his problem—he was just a man visiting a whore, whoever she might be. This time, however, he was not going there for the usual reason, but because he needed information. He knew her body by heart, like Aristotle's teachings on categories: there was not an inch of it that he had not been over as thoroughly as a cow grazing her meadow.

She was already expecting him. She liked him because he was handsome, intelligent and young. She only ever took handsome and intelligent young men. When he arrived she was sitting on her bed watching the rain outside the window. He slipped his coat from his shoulders and ran his fingers through his wet hair. 'Where is she?'

'Who?'

'Sophie.'

She gave him a sidelong look. Why was he thinking of Sophie just now? 'How should I know?'

'She's your friend.'

Griseldis let herself fall onto her back on the soft, lavender-scented linen and reached out her arms. 'Come here, my love.'

'We were in her room earlier today. She can't have been there for days. And she's seeing a student. What do you know about that?'

At once she sat upright, fully alert. 'She's seeing a student?'

'I thought he had a room in the same house, but the people don't let to students. So he must go there to meet her.'

Gradually she realised that he believed Sophie and the student to be two different people. That was something, anyway. And yet it still had its dangers.

'I haven't seen Sophie for a long time,' she said cautiously, and with perfect truth.

'One of the students was snooping around in the Scholarium. He got caught and was put in the lock-up there. And the next day he had vanished without trace. It was the same student who was visiting Sophie.'

It took Griseldis a few moments to work out the real turn of events. It had been Sophie in the Scholarium, not the student, and Sophie who had disappeared, which explained why she had not been in touch for days. 'What has happened to the student?' she asked quietly.

'I've no idea. But right now what I want to know is this: what is Sophie's connection with him?'

The whole thing was quite funny, really. Yes, if you all go on looking for Sophie and the student you'll eventually find one of them, and that will just leave the other. They thought they had lost two coins, when really they were the two sides of a single coin. 'I don't know anything about a student visiting Sophie. I'm not lying to you, honestly. But *you* are the one not telling the truth. You've fallen for her, haven't you? I realised that when we slept together in that louse-ridden room at the inn. You're jealous, my friend, you don't like it when someone else visits her.'

Yes, he was having thoughts of that nature, but he was also worried. Why had she been away from home for days? The fireplace was stone-cold. Had she perhaps gone off with that weakling of a student? But that was hardly possible, given that he had been put in the lock-up and had now vanished. Lombardi's head was spinning with chaotic thoughts. Griseldis was right: a feeling of being in love, a young and tender emotion that he had never known before, had taken hold of him. He had found her attractive from the moment

Casall had first introduced her to him. But harbouring dreams of a married woman made no sense, especially when she was the wife of a colleague. There had been something playful about her, like a puppy—impetuous and high-spirited. As if she didn't take the world quite seriously. But then Casall had knocked the playfulness out of her, and he, Lombardi, had silently watched it happen. Now that she was free, it would have been possible to start life all over again. But since he had confessed the sins of his youth to her, he had better forget the whole. The memory of that night at the inn on the Alter Graben went round and round in his mind as though he were savouring a good drop of wine on his tongue…

'Are you anxious about her?' Griseldis leapt lightly off the bed and affectionately embraced him. 'She'll turn up again, don't you worry.'

He nodded. Yes, she would probably return, but it made no difference: he had lost her…

Marius de Swerthe was a highly talented alchemist. But in other ways too nature had endowed him with great intellectual gifts. Though mocked and scorned, he had distinguished himself at his monastery school by his razor-sharp intelligence. At an age when others had not even found the way from their mother's breast to a woman's lips, he was already looking for a way to compensate for his physical affliction. He had dutifully pursued his studies as a good dwarf should, but inwardly he had simply laughed at them when they attempted to separate the colour from the thing, maintaining that the colour must be an idea that existed even in the absence of the thing. Even if that were the case—and who could tell if it was or not—what relevance did that have to his infinite misery? He saw himself as the representative of all those who had, quite literally, drawn the short straw in life. He would make his mark on the world on behalf of them all, by taking the absurd *ad absurdum*. Moreover, he had a superb understanding of the workings of the mind, and was as familiar with the subtleties of human feeling as with hermeneutics. He would make the student his accomplice; there was no better way to protect his own life. Accomplices were well and truly silenced, since if they put up any resistance they were tightening the noose round their own neck. He would have the young fellow slaving away for him until his tongue was hanging out, and that was better than the most beautiful murder. De Swerthe hated violence, having often enough been the victim of it. With Casall the situation had been different. One could not transplant a tree that was old and gnarled. But a tender young plant that has only just sprouted could easily be moved and it would still thrive. The new location might even suit it far better! They would start their work this very evening. The sulphur had already been skimmed off and the mercury was ready and waiting.

'Regard this as an extension of your studies. Doesn't Steiner teach astronomy and the occult too? But what really deserves to be called the occult is the way that philosophers treat the human being, picking him apart, chopping him up, pulling him to pieces. I have always detested it, and Casall was the perfect embodiment of that tendency...'

De Swerthe was standing at his furnace, where he was crushing dried sulphur in a mortar. Next he added a few parts of the mandrake, finely ground, and crammed all of this into a crucible. A beastly stench filled the room, and the curtains covering the window prevented the smell from escaping. Sophie, somewhat reinvigorated by some soup that the dwarf had given her, was standing beside the furnace observing the strange procedure. Watching him at work had an undeniable fascination, and she could not conceal a certain curiosity. What was supposed to emerge from this? Gold? Silver? That was every alchemist's dream. He had made her invoke the seven planets and the seven metals, which seemed silly to her, but the Prior had insisted. He believed that this placed her under both his influence and that of the celestial bodies.

The night advanced; the crucible had once more been placed on the furnace and the mixture in it was bubbling gently. De Swerthe permitted himself a small glass of wine, giving Sophie one too, and seemed well content with himself and the recent turn of events. And he was right to be: by letting her into his secret he transferred a share of the guilt to her, for in times like these a plain accusation, or even as little as a suspicion, was enough to set in motion the processes of the law. No one was immune, and de Swerthe's practices occupied a murky area that the Inquisition would undoubtedly have wished to investigate. If in so doing it found a single trace of anything heretical, anything necromantic, demonic, then he would be as good as dead. And Sophie likewise.

In the hearth a bright fire crackled, stinking of sulphur. Surely the Prior must fear that someone would notice the clouds of yellow smoke billowing from his chimney? But the dwarf seemed quite unafraid. Apart from her, nobody had ever seen them, because the empty house occupied a deserted spot where there were no people around at night.

Had it not been for the smell, she would have found it almost cosy, sitting there and looking into the dwarf's shining eyes as they caught the light of the flames, drinking the wine from the Cistercian abbey at Eberbach, and waiting to see what the concoction on the furnace would yield.

'Why did you kill Casall?' She had a burning desire to know, but had found no opportunity so far to put the question to him. But perhaps the right moment had come. He felt secure, he had made her his accomplice, and now he was proudly installed on the throne of complacency that he had crafted for himself.

'Well, why do you think? It's perfectly simple. He knew about my experiments. At some point he must have chanced upon the passage leading here from the Scholarium. One night he unexpectedly knocked at the door. Oh, I detested him even before that, because he worshipped scholasticism as others worship the Holy Virgin. His whole life wasted on the sort of futile speculation that the learned faculties generate. I will explain it to you, Josef Heinrich.'

He stood up and bent over the crucible. His nose must have been completely blocked, for he seemed quite untroubled by the vapour rising straight into his face, in fact he appeared actually to inhale it as other people might inhale an infusion of camomile.

Now he turned towards her. She felt confused, looking at his lovely, almost childlike face.

'I will explain it to you, Josef Heinrich. There have always been dissenting voices—critics who have tried to show the methodology of the faculties in its proper light. Have you ever read Plato's texts? Those profoundly absurd dialogues between Socrates and Theaetetus? The one shrewd, a questioner who knows nothing and is content to know nothing because there is nothing that can be known, and the other an out and out theoretician. When you start to dismember a human being like a cow that you intend to eat, you destroy his wholeness. And man is one indivisible whole, Josef Heinrich. Mind, heart and soul, intellect and will, he is both the individual thing and the idea. He contains everything within himself. Just look at the doctors and surgeons—anything more pathetically helpless is beyond imagination. Supposing that someone has a cough that he can't get rid of: I tell you that there is a reason behind it, that he *wants* to hang on to it, because his heart tells him that it is better to live with a persistent cough than with a wife who constantly deceives him. To be sure, he is not given a choice as to which he prefers. He is no more master of the cough's coming than of the wife's going off to cuckold him, but—to return to our point of departure—what does the doctor do? He advises him to take theriac and diagnoses a diseased lung—do you see?—and this is purely because he does not recognise the connection between the lung and the whole man. He might even cut the lung out of him, except that then the entire thorax would collapse, but I ask you, is that a proper way to look at things?'

'Why did you kill Casall?' Sophie did not want to engage in a theoretical discussion. Don't let him evade the issue. He doesn't want to talk about it, but I have to know what happened. What I then decide to do is still open.

'Casall was a passionate advocate of that philosophy, and would do his best to frustrate any attempt to steer the ship of knowledge in a different direction. He lived with the delusion that he could under-stand everything because he crushed and crumbled and ground it up with his species of logic, just as all of you are trained to do by your teachers. But only real matter can be analysed and understood and separated into its components. Metals, plants, elements. That is where one must look for truth and for the possibility of really understanding something. Not in that ludicrous art of disputation which surrounds itself with a thousand constructs that no man has ever seen. Of course in public I have supported the doctrine of Thomism in order to avert suspicion, but in reality magic has always been the only thing for me. Casall's discovery of me was a grave mischance. Yes, he discovered this house, and it was immediately clear to me that there was no possibility of sealing his lips. I could not make him into an accessory, because he had a cold, hardened soul. Oh yes, he was a carrion-eater whose arrogance needed to feed on the weaknesses of others, just as the vulture can only satisfy its hunger when other creatures die...

'I implored him to keep the secret to himself, but he merely replied scornfully that he was going to denounce me for necromancy. So I sent him a letter luring him to Marzellenstrasse, and put down a lump of gold in the grass. When he bent to pick it up I jumped out from behind a tree and hit him on the head with a heavy earthenware pitcher. Then I dragged him under the elder, waited until the gold-digger who always comes along Marzellenstrasse at that time of night had gone past, undressed the body and hauled it down the street to Steiner's house, knowing that he was still in the tavern with the others. I draped the various items of clothing at intervals along the street. When I had finished, I started screaming as though the Devil were after me, and ran off. That was the way of it.'

For a moment he closed his eyes. Sophie felt a boundless pity for this ill-treated little man whose experience had been so like hers, for she too had been hurt and treated unkindly by Casall. She would dearly have liked to wipe the unshed tears from his pallid face. A kindred spirit. The same tale of woe, the same dreams, the same sufferings. And the same joy when the tormentor had finally been removed from the face of the earth.

'I know you will not understand...' muttered the canon, opening his eyes.

Oh yes, I understand, but I mustn't say so. You dear, desperate dwarf, I can well imagine what you must have felt, for I felt much the same. But now you are my oppressor and I am your prisoner. How was she to escape from these toils? She longed to tell him what she felt, but it was out of the question.

'I inserted the riddle into the book to show them that they are by no means as clever as they think,' he continued. 'Yes, it was arrogant and will not be pleasing to God, but I tell you, just as matter is the only thing that really exists, so our conception of God is an illusion. If there is a God, then, I tell you, he only has reality in some concrete form. Perhaps in a tree, or a flower, but we are not able to recognise him…. And now let us sleep,' he said amiably, pointing to a bed that he had made ready for her. 'You will stay here with me for a week while I teach you the necessary skills. After that you are free to return to the Faculty. But you will come here at night and we will study the elements and see whether we can't make something out of them after all…'

The new Magister arrived just in time for the scheduled chapter meeting. He was a stocky, bearded Austrian from the University of Vienna. His views were said to be close to those of the traditionalists, but de Swerthe cared little about that, since he liked neither of the two camps. What mattered to him was that he now had two Masters attached to his Scholarium, he possessed a library containing some impressive works, and he was thinking of adding a third dormitory so as to be able to admit still more students. The chapter meeting was being held in the refectory, where one of the maids had built up a good fire in order to encourage lively participation, for the purpose of the meeting was to bring to light transgressions or acts of meanness committed during the past year and to expose them to the view of all. Lombardi hated these meetings. He saw them as the expression of a primitive culture of denunciation, but the dwarfish canon seemed to take pleasure in this annual event. The Master from Vienna, who rejoiced in the sonorous name of Angelius Brosius, was still keeping his opinion to himself; he was altogether very reserved and would speak only when he was spoken to. The two Masters sat at one end of the table, with the students packed in along the two sides. De Swerthe was sitting at the opposite end, presiding over the meeting. Suddenly the door opened and Steiner appeared. With an apologetic smile he took a seat beside Lombardi, thereby indicating that he proposed to attend the chapter meeting. For a moment the Prior seemed a little surprised, for Steiner was not a resident of the Scholarium, but then he nodded and turned his attention back to the students.

Steiner had no intention of taking an active part in the discussions. He merely wanted to observe the dwarf. If he really had murdered Casall and abducted the student, perhaps there would be some indication of it in his behaviour. Something that would give him away. Steiner did not have much time left. That same evening the Chancellor would be sending his men to search the Scholarium once more, and by then he needed to have some evidence for his suspicion.

Laurien had been told beforehand what a chapter meeting was, but he had not given it much thought, since he found it difficult to form a clear idea of what lay in store for him.

Now the time had come, and he realised that he was totally unprepared. He hunched down lower and lower on the bench and wished he could have covered his ears. This was not something for gentle natures, it was more to the taste of those who were already hardened to this kind of thing and who hoped to improve their standing as a result of this ceremony.

One student after another took his turn. The first was able to report on nocturnal visits to a whorehouse, naming names which de Swerthe duly noted down. Those who were accused grinned, even while hanging their heads. Frequenting a whorehouse was a punishable offence, but it still somehow made one appear impressively grown-up. The Prior imposed a punishment of two days in the lock-up on bread and water, and gave a nod of thanks to the informant, who was visibly pleased with himself. The next speaker told how a fellow-student had missed confession, choosing instead to go and watch street entertainers, animal tamers and musicians in town. De Swerthe thought about it. Two days in the cell would be a heavy punishment for illicitly hanging about in the town, but probably not unduly severe for missing confession. He deferred passing sentence for the time being.

Leaning back in his seat, Lombardi gazed into the blazing fire. The room was already filled with the smoke that was not finding its way up the chimney and which stung the eyes and irritated the lungs. He caught a kindly, fatherly look from Brosius. Did he favour this method of instilling discipline? Well, chapter meetings were no less customary in Vienna than in Cologne or other university towns. Lombardi had stopped listening. He only felt sorry for those who were reluctant to denounce others even if it would bring rewards for them. What a topsy-turvy world. The words wafted past his ears like a warm wind, and he concentrated on the crackling of the fire and the beer that stood in front of him.

Suddenly his eye fell on Laurien's face, which was filled with terror. He was staring at him as though pleading for forgiveness. Lombardi had not anticipated this. How could he have done? He had not been able to arm himself against the dark recesses of the mind, and it was these that now seemed likely to prove his undoing.

One of the other students who slept in Laurien's dormitory had suddenly raised his hand. Apparently he too had thought of something with which to regale this gathering, or perhaps he just wanted to please de Swerthe, for the more names there were on his list, the more contentedly he stroked his little beard.

'Laurien talks in his sleep,' the student announced. De Swerthe looked up from his paper, to which he had just been adding another name. 'Aha, he talks in his sleep, does he? And what does he say? Is it so significant that you need to bring it up here in this chapter?'

Lombardi looked across at Laurien, who was sitting on his bench rigid with shock, completely caught off guard.

'He talks about…about nuns. About nuns on an altar. Bound with ropes. And about a priest…'

The student lowered his voice as though he could find no words for the terrible things that he was about to say. 'He also mentioned Lombardi. I couldn't make it all out, but he talked about nuns lying bound on an altar…'

De Swerthe, now thoroughly alert, leaned forward. 'Did anyone else hear this? I should think that if he speaks so loudly and clearly others must have heard it too.'

Three hands were hesitantly raised. Now was the time to show solidarity. Yes, they had all heard them, those stumbling words in the night. What had he said about bound nuns on an altar? What were they doing?

'Dreams,' de Swerthe said softly, absently playing with his pen, 'are the shadows of the soul. Who sends them to us? God? The Devil? In earlier times they were believed to be prophesies, but what of today? Are they the nocturnal mirror of our waking hours?'

His gaze wandered slowly across to Laurien, who was still staring at him in deep distress and confusion. 'So where did your dreams come from? How is it that you talk of such things in your sleep?'

'I don't know,' Laurien burst out.

'It is something you have experienced, isn't it?'

'No!'

It was a cry of despair, which went straight to Lombardi's heart.

'What do you think, Magister Brosius?' said de Swerthe, turning to him. 'Is this just imagination or something actually experienced? How would you proceed if you were in my place?'

Brosius looked at the dwarf with a mild, good-natured expression, as though none of this were of the slightest importance, as though the student had reported that Laurien had dreamt about a vast barrel of beer.

'Oh, I once dreamt of an animal that had five legs and a tail eighty feet long, and that was as hairy as an ape and loved to swim in the sea. What do you think, my dear Prior, was that something I had really experienced?'

'Of course not,' snorted the canon contemptuously. 'But that does not prove that that creature could never exist. In theory, that is.'

'Certainly,' Brosius returned, smiling. 'The idea of such a creature is possible, and so it is also conceivable that such a creature exists somewhere in this splendid world of ours. However, I had never seen it, but only dreamt of it. It seems to me that our young friend here has some wild fantasies, if you take my meaning. A young man should learn to keep these under control, but I think that dreaming is itself one good way of doing that.'

De Swerthe looked crestfallen. 'Let us leave it at that,' he growled, and closed the meeting. He sensed that Laurien and Lombardi were exchanging glances behind his back, and wheeled round. Yes, they were looking at each other, and their looks showed such relief that he knew he was right. That dream had not been the product of a vivid imagination, it was rooted in the monstrous happenings of which he had long been aware.

Steiner stood up. Without a farewell to anyone he slipped out of the door and set off to call on the Chancellor.

They were preparing to decamp. This house was no longer safe enough. Although they had been extremely careful, the city was full of rumours about them.

Lombardi was pleased to hear that piece of news. The student, he told them, had fallen seriously ill and had left the city. They gave him something to drink. Sweet wine, stolen at the harbour, or obtained by bribing one of the customs men. They were celebrating their move to new quarters: somewhere near Limburg they had found another abandoned monastery building. Enthroned at Neidhard's side was Berenice, whom Lombardi had known in the old days. A pretentious name for a louse-ridden drab, he thought, but Berenice had a way with her that men found attractive.

They had chosen this moonless night for their departure. At the city's eastern gate there was a guard to whom they had promised a large sum of money if he would let them out. But for the moment they were still here, sitting by the fire and gaining immense amusement from filling Lombardi up with this choice wine. Red-haired Berenice with her brown eyes, and her dress, if one could call it that, fitting tightly around her hips, came and sat on his lap. Now that he knew they were leaving, and having escaped disaster thanks to Brosius—God grant him a good place in heaven!—he felt at ease. In fact he was in such high spirits that he failed to notice how the wine was loosening his tongue, and his fingers too, which had begun to fiddle with Berenice's girdle. It was a devilish brew that they had given him; it tasted of sweet berries but entered the blood as speedily as the Devil finds his way into a hapless soul. After half an hour his legs began to feel heavy.

'I shall be gone tomorrow,' Berenice purred into his ear. 'We shall be off in two or three hours' time. What would you say to…'

He wanted to find out what they had done to Domitian, for

however much they protested their innocence he would never believe it. 'Tell me, Berenice, you know what happened. Everyone here knows. I can never betray you, but all of you belong to the Devil, and you most of all, for you're a real she-devil.' In a corner he caught sight of a straw mattress spread with animal hides, and now she pulled him over to it and buried him under her.

'You want to know? It's all very simple. He was watching us, and suddenly he was right there wanting to join in. He was drunk, my God, he was so drunk that Neidhard had no trouble with him at all.'

'You've made me drunk too, I must be off home. You're all murderers.' Mountains of flesh weighed down his body—by God, the woman was heavy! She was panting and groaning, trying to arouse him again. With an effort he freed himself. 'I never want to see any of you again,' he mumbled, rising unsteadily to his feet. They responded only with contemptuous grins, and let him go.

On the way to the Scholarium he passed the Heumarkt. There was no light in Sophie's window. How strange, there was a figure in a billowing cloak creeping around the house. Now it stood still, and was clearly looking up at that same window. A cleric? Lombardi could not see clearly in the darkness, but he thought he glimpsed a cassock under the cloak, and a tonsure ringed by unruly hair. He came a few steps closer. 'Who lives there?'

The other gave a start, and stared at him. 'Who are you?'

Lombardi smiled. 'Are you a lover of the widow's? I think we're both looking at the same window.'

'For God's sake,' the friar muttered. He was looking at Lombardi's coat. 'You are one of the Faculty Masters. So you know all about it?'

'What do you mean?'

'An amazing business. A case for the Faculty court. The woman insinuated herself into the Faculty under a false name. But she will have to come back here sometime, unless she is no longer in the land of the living…'

Lombardi did not understand. What was this incomprehensible stuff? What woman had insinuated herself into the Faculty? But it did not take him long to work it out. He remembered that conversation with Sophie. What was it she had asked him? Is it possible for a woman to attend lectures at a Faculty?

The scales fell from his eyes: Sophie and the student were one and the same. It was her face that he had seen before him during his lectures, and the student whom he had noticed that time emerging from the back of the house had been Sophie herself!

'Are you from the court? What will you do with her if she does come back?'

'I am only acting on the Chancellor's instructions. What he plans to do with her if she should return, I don't know. I only know that it is blasphemy to enrol in a Faculty disguised as a man. It's a bad business...'

Lombardi took a step backwards. This fellow was a spy for the Faculty, which had its eyes and ears everywhere. It was worse than a cat waiting by a mousehole: he would be keeping watch here day and night, shivering with cold, just to do his Chancellor the service of seizing this reprehensible woman when she returned, and clapping her in irons.

'Then I wish you a pleasant night, Brother,' Lombardi murmured, and turned on his heel.

De Swerthe worked with everything that superabundant Nature had provided: mercury, sulphur, phosphate, potassium, and silica, together with all manner of acids, salts, and the various compounds that the elements were capable of forming. For all these substances he had his crucibles and pans, some of them already burnt through and lying in a small heap in a corner of the room, for he thought it too risky to throw anything away. The slightest act of carelessness might betray him. There was almost nothing but open countryside between this house and St. Gereon's, where a dingy cell awaited people like him if the city magistrates and the ecclesiastical courts saw fit. Magic was an ambivalent matter even for those who had to pass judgment on it in court. For on the one hand the occult was a perfectly respectable branch of knowledge studied by renowned philosophers, but on the other hand its practitioners could all too easily fall under the suspicion of sorcery and of casting harmful spells. The boundaries were fluid. The Curia had forbidden its flock to engage in alchemical magic, but this ban seemed to have fallen upon deaf ears, for most alchemists were in fact sons of the Church.

De Swerthe instructed Sophie in the union of contraries, in the doctrine of the four elements, the four humours, the trinity of the hermetic philosophers, the stages of transmutation and the circle of symbols. *Visita Interiora Terrae Rectificando Invenies Occultum Lapidem.* She learned from him that parts of the human body were associated with the signs of the zodiac. These parts of the body could be used as symbols for the hermetic processes. So each sign of the zodiac stood for a particular procedure which the alchemist had to undertake. He reduced to ashes, he dissolved, sublimated, fermented, he exposed the substance to gentle heat, he separated, multiplied and allowed to solidify, he distilled and softened and finally united. He assayed each substance by this means or that, but in spite of everything he did, he obtained no gold or silver. He was driven by the idea of establishing matter alone as the nourishing soil of the mind, just as the philosophers relied exclusively on the intellect. His obsession gave Sophie a most uncomfortable feeling, and yet she could not help finding a certain fascination in it all. On the surface the aim was to turn base metals into precious ones, but behind that there seemed to be another, deeper idea—the quest for human perfection.

Now Sophie could also understand what lay behind the riddle that de Swerthe in his wicked arrogance had set Steiner. He had separated matter, the sleeve from the coat, the boot from the foot. He had thought himself superior to Steiner, and of course he had been proved right, in part at any rate, for the Magister was unable to solve the second riddle. He was probably still racking his brains about the *quadrivium.* And yet it could not have been simpler, for on closer examination the dwarf's riddle immediately suggested quantities, dimensions, size. But precisely this—examining things closely—was what philosophers were incapable of doing, according to de Swerthe. Essentially, he maintained, a philosopher blundered through his world as blind as a mole, believing only in what he chose to think and not in what he could see, hear or perceive through any of his other senses.

Sophie thought of Steiner. Would he be searching for Josef Heinrich? But he knew nothing of this house, he would never find her here.

In a corner of the room there was a shining metal shield with strange symbols on it. In the centre was a closed triangle, and within this a sword, and to right and left all kinds of archaic signs: one seemed to be an oil jug, another a sceptre. Around the edge of the shield were more symbols, some representing the signs of the zodiac, but also some others that meant nothing to Sophie.

'Ah,' said de Swerthe with a smile, in answer to her enquiring look, 'that is a magic circle, but that does not interest me anymore. Years ago I began to study necromancy and the art of conjuring demons, but I soon gave it up because it is only magic and has nothing to do with the investigation of nature. That shield is the only thing I have kept, for it is of some value.' He turned thoughtfully back to his crucible, in which a sulphurous mixture was once again bubbling away.

'On the other hand, philosophy as taught in the Faculties is worthless,' he continued sombrely some minutes later. 'Only scholarship that concerns itself with matter has a future, believe me. Do you know that Albertus Magnus in his *Libellus de alchimia* describes exactly how to use substances and what methods to employ? Do you see this powder here? I bought it from a trader. It is supposed to produce an effect of magic if you hold a taper to it. Combined with crushed coal and sulphur it must be not unlike gunpowder, sparking off a magic process...'

He turned round. 'Pass me the pot with the sulphur and coal. It is all prepared.'

He peered into the pot. 'Look, now it is all white. Refine it three times and it loses more and more colour. One must not add any salt, despite what the books say, for it has to be a completely volatile mixture. Give me the taper.'

Sophie came closer and stood beside him. He was holding the taper almost reverently in his hand.

'Surely you are not going to set it all alight?' she asked, as she too looked into the pot.

'The powder has to come into direct contact with the fire. Otherwise it will not vaporise.'

'But what if it catches fire?'

'It *has* to catch fire. Stand back if you are afraid.'

She retreated to the furthest corner. Was the dwarf trying to set the house on fire? Up to now the flames had only licked at the underside of his pans, but what if he now held a flame to the whole of the mixture itself?

He dropped the taper into the pot. And then she saw his contorted face. He knew exactly what he was doing. Even if this mixture summoned the Devil himself from Hell, he would have gone ahead. Now the thing was done. But the mixture did not burn. It hissed and glowed and shot upwards like a bolt of lightning. And suddenly there was an explosion. The dwarf was thrown sideways and fell to the floor. The arm that had been closer to the furnace was blackened and trembling, and he clutched it to his side. After that Sophie could see nothing more, for smoke and fumes filled the whole room. The bubbling and hissing continued, and in the midst of the smoke rose a flame-coloured column of light. It was spiralling like a whirlwind, growing more and more violent before spreading greedily, voraciously, outwards. Now the room really was ablaze. 'Marius! Marius!' screamed Sophie. But there was no possibility of reaching the producer of this evil magic. De Swerthe was beyond help. *She* must try to escape. Behind her, tongues of flame were coming ever closer. In a panic she looked around. There, on a stool in the corner, lay an axe. She reached for it, almost blindly, for the smoke and fumes were making her eyes water, and began to hack at the door. The heat became ever fiercer, the stench more acrid, shelves and tables crashed to the floor behind her, and it would not be long before the roof fell in. Mother of God, what kind of a brew had the dwarf concocted? At last some boards in the door gave way, falling onto the ground outside. A gap just big enough, and no sooner had she squeezed through than neighbours came rushing up, having evidently been awakened by all the noise.

'Somebody's come out of the house,' one of them shouted. They all stared at Sophie, until a woman, taking pity on her as she stood there sobbing and caked in soot, went over and drew her away from the house. 'Was anyone else in there?'

Sophie shook her head. Well, there was someone in there, but he was past all help. By now the dwarf was probably reduced to ashes, burnt and charred and released forever from this vale of tears.

'Who lives in that house? We thought it was empty.'

This was one of the magistrate's men, who were lowering buckets into the well.

'It's derelict,' Sophie muttered. 'There's nobody else inside.'

'And what about you? What were you doing there? You're a student, aren't you?'

She nodded. Someone held a cup of water to her lips, and she drank it thirstily. Where do you live? On the Heumarkt. Then we'll take you there. Someone was already pulling her away from the street—it was the woman who had given her the water. But they did not get far. Roused by the commotion, the students from the Scholarium came running up. The *lupus*, Lombardi, Brosius, they all stood eyeing her.

'But…that's Josef Heinrich!' cried the *lupus*, charging up to her with every intention of dragging her back to the lock-up.

'Leave him alone, you can see he can hardly stand.'

'The Chancellor of the Faculty is looking for him, he's the one who went missing.'

Now they were all tugging at her, pulling her this way and that, some wanting to take her home and others to the Scholarium. The students bombarded her with questions which she was too weak to answer. Finally it was agreed that the student should be taken back to the Scholarium for the time being and the Chancellor notified.

The magistrates examining the remains of the burnt-out house discovered that it had clearly been a laboratory where an alchemist had pursued his nefarious activities by night. There was no point in trying to deny it. The student had come out of the laboratory, so he must have been hand in glove with the alchemist, and this also explained his earlier disappearance. But who was the alchemist? The student himself? Or had he merely been his apprentice? And where was the Prior of the Scholarium? He was nowhere to be found.

The Chancellor ran his hand over the sparse hair surrounding his tonsure as he waited impatiently for Steiner, who might be able to help him answer all these questions. Furthermore, they had found, among the charred wreckage, a metal shield engraved with mysterious symbols, apparently of a highly sinister origin. Had the alchemist been dabbling in black magic? Conjuring evil spirits? Had he gone beyond mere experiments with his crucibles and pans, and conducted satanic rites? Everything was so uncertain that the Chancellor hesitated to take any action. He was at a loss as to how to proceed. Had de Swerthe murdered Casall, as Steiner had claimed? And then there was this business with the student who was not a student. Casall's widow had been taken straight to the Provost's House. A thorough interrogation would provide all the necessary answers.

Steiner too had been rummaging in the remains of the burnt-out house, clambering around among the debris looking for some clue, a piece of evidence, a pointer. And indeed he had found a cross on a chain of the kind that clerics wore around their necks. De Swerthe's cross. But nothing else remained of the Prior, and that was strange. Sophie Casall had stated that de Swerthe had abducted her and held her in this house, and that he had been the alchemist and had perished in the fire. Yet Steiner found nothing but the cross and the shield with the curious signs. Surely if the Prior had been burnt to death as a result of his experiment, Steiner would at least have found some bones. He stopped and sniffed the air. There was still a smell of rags and wood and sulphur. The constables had moved aside every beam, every brick, to make certain that nobody was buried underneath. But they too had failed to find any bones. Silently Steiner shook his head. Either Sophie Casall was lying, or the dwarf had escaped from the room and had somehow managed, amid the general confusion, to disappear from the burning house unnoticed.

'You are to search this whole piece of ground,' Steiner instructed one of the constables. 'I want to see every object you find. Any detail might be important, even a scrap of paper that is not completely burnt.'

The constable stared at him in surprise. 'Every single thing? That will take weeks!'

'What if it does?' muttered Steiner.


Falsifying documents, an oath taken under a false name, a charge of necromancy…it seemed as if the young woman had been trying to commit every offence she possibly could. Her judge was to be the Abbot of St. Martin's. He was adept at upholding and defending the law, asking the right questions and waiting patiently for the proper answers. To him Sophie Casall's case was only one of many, and so he noticed only belatedly that her trial was stirring up strong passions. This was something he had not been prepared for. Feelings obscured the essential facts, and he was amazed to see the Faculty Masters, of all people, giving way like this to the turmoil of their feelings. Should he not have suspected something of the kind, though? Days before the appointed date in early January he had heard discussions going on. Behind every door, nominalists and realists quarrelled over the merits of the case; the old conflict between the two groups seemed to have flared up violently again, like an outbreak of plague. He wanted no part in any of that. But they would be present in court and were entitled to have their say. He was beginning to see the full implications of this case that had landed on his desk.

As he crossed the entrance hall he was aware of more conversations going on all around him. Always the same arguments. They gave him sidelong looks. What might his position be? He could see the question written in their eyes, but not one of them dared ask him outright. He went on his way unmoved. Let them talk to their hearts' content and split into their different camps again. He could wait.


Steiner watched him go. He was right to keep his opinion to himself.

The mood of the Faculty had changed. Everyone knew that the widow was being held in the Provost's House pending her trial. Not a public trial, of course—God forbid! At all costs they must avoid creating a scandal among the general public, which was not especially fond of the Faculty as it was. No, the trial would be held *in camera*, among themselves. The lower level of jurisdiction within the Faculty took some time to grasp what the case was really about. Then the students came to know of it, and no doubt by now it had reached the ears of the Archbishop and of the Holy Father in Rome.

There was a sharp frost. Even inside the monastery, where he was about to hold his lecture, it was bitterly cold. The bright sun, shining invitingly through the window, seemed to belie the icy chill in the air, but two days after New Year the temperature had sunk far below freezing, and it was rumoured that numerous beggars had died of cold in the city's streets. In the harbour the ships were held fast in the ice, and the fish froze in the warehouses.

Steiner turned to the window, which was covered in frost patterns, and as he peered through the ice crystals and watched people hurrying along the street, bundled up in layers of warm clothing, he could hear, yet again, those same wretched discussions going on everywhere. Of course there was no question of keeping the Masters out of the courtroom or not allowing them to defend their points of view, but why did everything always have to bring them back to the same point? Would an eclipse of the sun have had the same effect of setting them at each other's throats again?

'Where do you stand, Steiner? We have been talking and talking for days, and you are as silent as the grave.'

Slowly he turned around. Behind him was Rüdeger, one of the keenest warriors in these verbal battles. It was really he who had started them. And Steiner would never forgive him for that.

'Why should I form an opinion? It's not really the trial that you people are talking about. You are just going over the old argument all over again: the idea *versus* the thing. Is it worth quarrelling about? Does it matter?'

Magister Rüdeger had come to Cologne from Hamburg. With his gaunt and ascetic looks he would have made a good hermit, sitting in a cell and having a bowl of food passed in to him through the bars.

'How can you suggest that it does not matter?' he hissed angrily. 'We are talking about the very foundations of our scholarship.'

'You are in the process of destroying those foundations,' Steiner answered coolly, 'by drawing up the old battle lines again. What, in God's name, has the controversy between realists and nominalists to do with this woman's trial?'

'What has it to do with it?' Rüdeger could hardly restrain himself from spitting in Steiner's face. Steiner's calm serenity was even harder to bear than a vehement defence of an opposing position. It was outrageous for one of them to hold himself aloof from the debate in this way. 'I will tell you what it has to do with it,' he hissed softly, edging Steiner closer and closer to the window. 'One of the Masters, I will name no names, was of the view that in the light of certain positions one might need carefully to prepare all the arguments to show why a woman should not be allowed to study.'

'That is rather convoluted, don't you think? What does he mean?'

Rüdeger moved ever closer to Steiner, as though planning at any moment to open the window and hurl him out of it. 'Well, to me it sounds very much like a defence of her behaviour. Don't you think so?'

Now at last Steiner understood. One of the Masters had suggested that it might be appropriate to reconsider the Faculty's objection to letting this woman continue her studies. And it was not difficult to guess whose opinion that was. It could only be one of the moderni, for the traditionalists were as firmly stuck to their Thomas Aquinas as flies to a cobweb. And now at last he could see why the quarrel had flared up again. It was not about the woman's case at all, but about the position that each of them would uphold in relation to it. Sophie Casall was no more than a symbol.

'Ah,' said Steiner, looking out of the window. He could smell Rüdeger's breath, and his eyes were searching for a way out of this window recess. 'You are perfectly right. For the present it is just one woman, and she can be forced back into her traditional role. But then there will be others, more and more of them, and it will be impossible to throw them all out of the Faculty, and so perhaps they will have to be burnt at the stake. And then there will be none of them left. That is your position, is it not?'

Rüdeger did not dare to agree. He simply stared at Steiner in silence. He attached great importance to the intellectual freedom of the universities, wherever they might be, whether in the Empire or in England or Italy. He himself welcomed any measure that made the universities more independent of the clergy and fostered academic freedom. So now he found himself in a peculiar dilemma, for he was reluctant to let Steiner put him into a category with which he would not wish to be identified.

'That's not true,' he muttered at last. 'As you very well know. Why do you say such a thing? I uphold a certain view, that is true, but I would not dream of condemning someone to death merely because he holds different ideas from mine. All the same, there are trends that should be halted. This controversy should cause us to look critically at the opinions we have held hitherto.'

Steiner smiled and detached himself a little from the window. 'If that is how you see it, then of course I welcome your enthusiasm for debate. But take care that your cannon does not backfire and that in the end you do not find yourself responsible for things that you might regret.'

At last he had regained his freedom of movement. Rüdeger stepped aside to make room for him. 'And what position will you adopt, Steiner?'

Steiner made no reply. The *moderni* were hopelessly outnumbered. Lombardi, Jordanus, and the new man, Brosius, who had suddenly declared himself to be a nominalist. Three against eighteen, that was not enough. And he himself, Steiner, would only cause irritation with his pursuit of harmony. They wanted him to take up a clear-cut position. No compromise. Where do you stand, Steiner? He looked up. Suddenly he noticed that the others had been listening to them all this time and were now looking at him. Everyone was waiting. Where do you stand, Steiner? He took a deep breath. 'I am on the side of those who have an open mind, who are genuinely asking themselves why a woman should study—a thing which, as you know, has indeed happened in other places and has caused far less of a stir there.'

He could not have formulated this more circumspectly, but even so they all knew his position now. Four against seventeen, that was still too few, but his firm, pleasant voice was always listened to with respect, and as he scrutinised them all in turn he detected no trace of derision or disappointment in their eyes. Yes, they might have guessed that he would hasten to the aid of the weaker side. Some turned wordlessly away, but even they were confirmed in what they had suspected. Steiner represented no danger to them, for they had a huge majority. They deferentially made way for him as he strode away down the corridor: it was as if by stating his position unambiguously he had induced a temporary ceasefire. The lines were now clearly drawn, and battle could commence.

The first thing to be settled was how a case of this nature should be approached. De Swerthe was still missing. However, the cross that had been found was certainly his, and was identified beyond doubt by a number of students from the Scholarium. He must have torn it from his neck and thrown it back into the room, for although slightly melted it was otherwise well preserved. So had de Swerthe been the alchemist? The accused, Sophie Casall, stated that de Swerthe had held her captive and had intended to initiate her into his alchemical operations. She also claimed that the Prior had murdered Casall, but she had no proof. Now it was Steiner's turn. He testified that the student Josef Heinrich, that is to say Sophie Casall, had confided to him her suspicion that the Prior might have been the murderer. And then Steiner also confessed that he had found the *Libellus de alchimia* in de Swerthe's mother's house, which was surely a proof of the alchemical activities of the undersized canon. Sophie Casall was to be tried on the other counts: falsification of a document and taking an oath under an assumed name. But her situation in relation to de Swerthe was still unclear. Had she really assisted him only under duress?

Then the *lupus* gave evidence. He admitted bundling the student into a sack on the Prior's instructions. However, he swore that he had had no suspicion of de Swerthe's experiments in alchemy.

They sat down together to confer. If a charge of heresy was to be brought on the grounds of Sophie's involvement in alchemy, then that should be dealt with last. It was better to begin with the less serious accusations. Were they aware, Jordanus asked, that in the fair city of Bologna, not so long ago, the daughter of a Master had herself taught at the university? His words caused general consternation, whereupon he added that the lady had delivered her lectures from behind a curtain so that none of the students should be flustered or distracted by her beauty.

That was an exception, retorted Rüdeger. In any case, the Master at Bologna had introduced his daughter into the Faculty himself, she had not slunk in stealthily like a fox into a flock of lambs.

'But if she had asked our permission, would we have accepted her?' Steiner demanded. His question met with a defiant silence. It would have depended on the Magister responsible for interviewing her. He could have decided. And, who knows, his decision might very well have gone in her favour.

'Let us be fair,' Steiner said. 'Let us conduct a just trial. I suggest that we set her three questions, and if she can answer them we will content ourselves with a reprimand.'

Renewed silence. There were some who would have liked to deprive her of her citizenship forthwith and expel her from the city. Others would have preferred to throw her into prison, where she could be treated with all due consideration but would be safely locked away.

'Three questions?' echoed Hungerland, the eldest of them, who intended to retire very soon. Early signs of dementia were causing him increasing embarrassment when he had to rack his brains for names and dates, found himself unable to remember the simplest things, or confused Aristotle with Julius Caesar.

'Yes, three questions. As to what kind of questions, we can decide that here and now, if my suggestion meets with your approval.'

'A kind of trial by ordeal?' Brosius asked, frowning.

'If you choose to view it in that light, I cannot stop you. But I think it is a more just procedure than throwing someone into the water and seeing whether or not he drowns.'

'Well,' Rüdeger interposed, 'I would approve so long as they are questions that are difficult to answer. Questions such as: how can a cannonball be fired round a corner?'

Steiner stared at him. 'That is a question which cannot be answered at all: it is wholly nonsensical and asks something impossible. For how could it be done? I must remind my worthy colleague that we have not gathered here to play the fool.'

Rüdeger laughed under his breath. On the contrary, that was exactly what they were doing, he thought. It was a ridiculous idea to ask the woman questions that she might actually be able to answer. But talk away, Steiner, you will be hopelessly outnumbered when it comes to a vote...

'What sort of questions should they be, Steiner?' The enquiry came from Hungerland, who had briefly nodded off but had woken up in time to join in the proceedings again.

Steiner shrugged his shoulders. Were they going to leave all the work to him, and then outvote him anyway?

'Think of the five questions in Boethius, the questions that *Philosophia* puts to him,' he said.

Jordanus nodded. 'Yes, but one can look up the answers in Boethius. There would be no point in that. At most it would prove that she had read the *Consolation of Philosophy*. That would be too easy.'

'Ah,' cried Hungerland, beaming now. 'The five questions of Boethius. Yes, let her answer those. She is sure to have read Boethius, and then we can set her free and she can give lectures on hermeneutics in the Faculty...' He giggled to himself in mischievous delight at the idea of the woman defeating the august Masters with their own weapons.

'The Faculty cannot tolerate that man for much longer,' Rüdeger whispered to a colleague. 'He is completely losing his wits.'

Hungerland instantly turned to face him and threw him a penetrating glance. 'I am not losing my wits,' he growled, 'but your attitude is quite ridiculous. Why must you torment the poor woman simply because she wants to learn something? Are you still afraid of women, like the prophet who fears for the salvation of his soul? My whole life long I have loved those two things, women and learning, and I tell you that it has done me no harm at all.'

He began to giggle again.

'Shall we return to the subject of our discussion, or are we more interested in the illustrious career of our colleague Hungerland?' someone called out angrily.

'Well then, think of some questions that we can put to the accused,' Steiner suggested.

They thought about it. Then they hurled their questions at Steiner, all talking at once in so chaotic a fashion that he could not understand a word and had to raise a hand to call for silence.

'One at a time, if you please,' he admonished them, turning first to Lombardi, who had said nothing so far. 'Have you an idea?'

Lombardi grinned. 'No, Steiner. Not an idea, but a question, perhaps. Should it relate to the syllabus? Is it our intention to test the woman, to find out how much she has read?'

'But that is nonsense!' exclaimed Rüdeger. 'We are not planning to conduct examinations. Whatever next?'

'Then I will make a proposal,' Steiner said, visibly exasperated. 'You are all familiar with Aristotle's *Metaphysics*. He talks there about the relationship between matter and form and links that with man and woman. That could form the basis for a good question, don't you think?'

Once again there was silence. They were all searching their memories for the passage that Steiner meant. Hungerland shook his head: the gaps in his memory were constantly expanding, encroaching like a deep, dark expanse of water upon the solid ground of his knowledge. 'He will have to read it out to me,' he murmured, whereupon Steiner reached for a book.

> ...*For whereas, according to the Platonists, matter gives rise to multiplicity but form generates only once, common experience tells us that from a given piece of wood only one table comes, whilst he who imposes the form on it, though he is only one himself, can make many tables. The same relationship pertains between male and female:*

*the female is impregnated by a single coupling, while one male can impregnate many females. And this relationship between the sexes is analogous to the relationship between those principles.*

'There is nothing there to show that a woman should not study,' Rüdeger called out.

'That is not what I am looking for,' Steiner returned, shaking his head. 'Let us ask her who wrote that and where it is to be found. And let us ask her about the relationship between matter and form, for if matter creates many things and form only one thing, it is also the case that the male principle creates many things and the female only one.'

But what, then, was the question? The others exchanged dubious looks. This was merely reciting a text, nothing more.

'I do not see a question in that,' Hungerland said in a tone of displeasure.

'Then make one out of it,' retorted Steiner.

'How is it that the female principle only ever creates one thing?'

'For example. You can go on thinking about it for a while.'

Steiner now retreated into silence and let them talk among themselves. When the time came for the vote, the minority had gained one further ally, Hungerland, who had in the meantime forgotten what the discussion was all about but was much taken with the idea of a woman lecturing on hermeneutics. For this he received angry looks from all sides, but he only laughed.

Then came the proposal from the opposing side. No questions; instead the facts should be established and then the woman's citizenship should be rescinded. Other people had been expelled from the city for lesser offences. Liars and cheats were not wanted here. And then there was the other issue, which could not be held over any longer but must be dealt with at the same time, because it was far more serious: what had Casall's widow been doing there with de Swerthe? Perhaps she was lying and had really been his willing collaborator. The shield that had been found among the wreckage was a magic mirror, an object that was clearly of demonic origin. And there had long been a suspicion that de Swerthe had had contact with the antipope, Benedict XIII, and as to him, need one say any more…?

Afterwards no one could remember who had said that. They had all sat there, aghast. The discussion seemed to be taking a dangerous turn. *The Death of the Soul.* Everyone had vaguely heard of that notorious book, which the antipope was said to keep hidden under his bed, although no one had ever been able to prove that he was a student of necromancy. That belief was founded only on rumours, but they were persistent ones. Rumours that certain Franciscans and Benedictines who were close to him conjured demons and practised magic…

'We must take care not to go a single step beyond what can be proved,' Jordanus warned them. 'Even if de Swerthe did once have contact with the antipope, that is no reason for us to start entertaining suspicions of the worst kind now. And Sophie Casall was held captive by de Swerthe, do not forget that.'

'So she says,' shouted Rüdeger angrily, 'to protect herself, obviously. And what if she collaborated with him willingly? What if the whole purpose of that disgraceful matriculation was to enable her to help de Swerthe? Perhaps that was the reason for her ridiculous disguise. The two of them were hand in glove, she and that blasphemous Prior. She is a witch transgressing against every notion of honour and morality.'

Witch. The word hung ominously in the air. Had the daughter of the professor at Bologna been a witch, too? No, of course not, but then she had entered the Faculty by honourable means. And she had not been caught fleeing from the house of an alchemist or necromancer…

'This is absurd!' Steiner shouted furiously, rising to his feet. If they were saying such things, they were no longer accessible to reasoned argument.

He left the monastery and went out into the street. Frosty cold enveloped him, and he was conscious of how tired he was of this constant shivering and the chill in his bones, which were not getting any younger and were crying out for rest. He felt depressed and world-weary as he walked down towards the river, his collar turned up. Yes, he had had enough of this cold, the coldness in the hearts of men who were seeking something which they called justice but which was nothing but a twisted kind of self-love. No one was skating anymore, and the wine sellers too had gone. A pale sun showed intermittently, white and cold, from behind thin streaks of cloud.

'Magister Steiner...'

He turned. While he had been absorbed in looking at the sky, Sophie's mother had suddenly appeared behind him.

'Have you any news of my daughter?'

'She is well. She is being treated with consideration,' he replied wearily.

'But what will happen to her? They don't tell me anything...'

'There may be a trial, but that is not certain. Put your trust in God, dear lady.'

He felt her pressing a quantity of coins into his hand. 'My husband has died. He was very wealthy. If the money can help her it will be well spent...'

His first impulse was to give the money back to her, for he was not corrupt, but then he changed his mind and accepted the money. 'If I cannot achieve anything useful with it, I will return it to you.'

She nodded. Yes, he would help her daughter. He was the only one who could help, apart from God. But God had no need of money.

The *lupus* of the Scholarium was called to give his evidence on the first day of the hearing. He testified that he had known nothing of de Swerthe's activities. De Swerthe had told him to convey the student in a sack into the store room, and this he had done. It had not been his place to question his instructions. But as for de Swerthe's having killed Casall, that he could not imagine. Then he was asked whether, on the evening concerned, de Swerthe had been in the Scholarium, to which the *lupus* repeated that de Swerthe had gone to visit his mother. But the old lady could not now be asked to confirm this because six months ago she had fallen from a ladder and her mind was now confused, as Magister Steiner could confirm. Steiner told the court about her chasing him with the broom.

The *lupus* was told to stand down.

Sophie Casall had been locked in a room in the Provost's House. Here she waited for her trial. Three times a day a monk came to bring her her food and later to remove the empty dish. The meals were excellent, which suggested that money had come from some source to pay for her maintenance. She had also been given a Bible for her edification. So the time passed, sun and moon alternated at her window and precious days of her life went by in unrelieved loneliness, hope and fear. One day, however, Lombardi appeared. He looked around. The room was clean, the Bible lay on the bed, the sheet was turned back. Sophie was standing at the window, pale, tired, hopeless.

'How are you?'

She said nothing. Not even the sight of him could cheer her.

'Your mother gave Steiner a large sum of money, and I used some of it to persuade the monk to let me see you.'

She merely nodded. So there they stood, she at the window, he at the door. For some time neither spoke a word.

'It may be that they will ask you three questions that you have to answer,' he finally managed to say.

She smiled. How wise to set me three questions, she thought bitterly. 'What are they trying to find out? Whether I have learned enough from them?'

'Look on it as an examination. It was Steiner's idea, and you know that he is very well disposed towards you.'

'Ah, Steiner…' she murmured. Good old Steiner. Always striving for justice, even now. He would have taken the same trouble over some jaded old nag. 'Whose line am I required to follow?' she asked cynically. 'The traditionalists' or the others'?'

'Which do you favour?'

'Neither,' she said in a low voice. 'You know, I have had plenty of time to think. And as I was mulling it all over, I realised that neither the one nor the other seemed to make much sense. In fact it appeared to me that we were discussing a question of no importance whatsoever. Griseldis was right. What use is it to me if I know which is superior, the thing or the idea? I was like an empty barrel being filled with water, but the barrel had a leak somewhere, so that actually it always remained empty. I wanted to prove something to you, but now I shall not be able to, because I no longer believe that the subject has any value.'

'You wanted to prove something to Casall.'

'Yes. But that whole way of thinking was not my own, but his or yours or Steiner's, or at any rate it was intrinsically masculine. Then, when I saw de Swerthe at work with his crucibles, I thought, yes, *this* is the right thing, observation of nature just as Bacon teaches. But I soon realised that that was not true either. For even if man starts to observe nature, he always believes that he can do still better. No, Lombardi, neither way is right, neither knowledge achieved through the mind, as the philosopher upholds, nor knowledge gained from nature, because the result is always something unholy. For what did de Swerthe do with his knowledge? He tried to make gold, and one can hardly imagine a more primitive motive for investigating nature than that. Oh yes, he filled his edifice of alchemical ideas with all manner of hocus-pocus, but the impulse behind it was always the same, and that was nothing more nor less than greed for material riches.'

Lombardi was anxious to contradict her. If she went to the hearing with this attitude she was lost from the start. This position was more damning than wanting to elicit the men's secrets from them, for that at least was based on a desire for a glimpse behind closed doors. But if she went along and repeated what she had just said, she would be making the men appear foolish. Nothing could be worse than to demonstrate to them that their intellectual structures meant nothing, indeed less than nothing, and were illusions of their own creating.

'You know that your view is dangerous. You had better keep it to yourself. Say what they want to hear, say that you longed to share in the fruits of their wonderful intellect. Then they will feel flattered. But if you cast doubt on their competence, they will tear you limb from limb.'

'Yes,' she murmured. 'They will tear me apart. But isn't that their intention in any case? Does it make any difference what I say?'

'You have a chance if you go about it intelligently. Butter them up, pretend to admire them, that is what they like best, for in their heart of hearts they may well suspect that everything they do has no other purpose than to pass the time.'

Sophie laughed, for the first time in days. She left the window and sat down on the bed. 'Very nicely put. I'll think about it. Perhaps I'll say that I tried to understand Aristotle but came to the conclusion that it was impossible for a stupid woman like me, that I was simply not capable of penetrating such mysteries.'

'That would be one possibility, but do you really want to deny your intelligence to that extent? It would be better to try to answer their questions, but lace your answers with large helpings of humility, and above all praise their questions. They attach greater value to asking good questions than to providing good answers, you know that.'

She nodded. Gradually she relaxed. He was trying to comfort her and to show her the right way. He and Steiner would help her. So what harm could come to her?

What Lombardi did not tell her was that the vote had not yet taken place and that there was still the risk of a charge of necromancy. Instead he came nearer, bent over her and gently stroked her cheek. Sophie blushed. 'The *lupus* has spoken in your defence. Did you see de Swerthe's shield?'

Sophie nodded. 'Yes, he told me that there had been a time when he experimented with magic but that he had rejected it as a silly, childish plaything. Why do you ask?'

He did not reply. She would work it out herself soon enough, and he did not want to add to her worries. 'Goodbye, Sophie. We shall see each other at the trial. Until then, practise showing respect for the male intellect.'

He knocked as a signal for the door to be opened. She watched him slip out and suddenly understood why he had asked about the shield.

The trial commenced early one morning in the monastery, in a chilly room heated only by a small open fire. This was the chamber where the Faculty court normally sat—an imposing room with wood-panelled walls and a richly coloured ceiling painting. This depicted Sapientia in fluttering drapery, surrounded by the figures of Justice, Rectitude and Reason, which floated like angels in the sky, spreading out their arms above the spectator below.

At the head of the massive table sat the Abbot, and beside him, lined up like beads on a string, were the Chancellor, the Rector and the Masters of the Faculty. A clerk sat in readiness at his desk. An usher brought Sophie into the courtroom, where she was made to sit on a stool. Her face had grown thin and wan, even her lips were colourless, her blonde hair limp and dull. Sitting with her hands folded, her legs placed side by side and her head turned towards the judge, she awaited her fate. The Abbot opened the proceedings by reading out the charges, which included participation in the study of alchemy. Sophie admitted everything except for the allegation of willing collaboration with de Swerthe: he had forced her into it, she protested, and hence it could not possibly be held against her.

The Abbot listened impassively. His angular, somewhat coarse features were like chiselled stone; even his hands lay absolutely still. When the accused had finished speaking he gave a slight nod. Now Steiner stepped forward. He told the court how Sophie had confided her plan to him, and how he had not tried hard enough to dissuade her from letting herself be locked into the Scholarium. Everyone looked at him, dumbfounded.

'Yes,' he said gravely. 'I know that I bear the responsibility, but there seemed a good prospect that something would come of that venture. And after all I could hardly have hidden there myself...'

'Did the accused find any proof that the Prior was the killer?' the Abbot asked with a frown.

'Well, it was his fear of being unmasked that led him to imprison her in his laboratory, and he confessed to her that he had killed Casall.'

The Abbot shook his head. 'That is not evidence, merely an assertion. How do we know that she is speaking the truth?'

'Quite right. She could be lying. But why should she?'

'Well, perhaps in order to defend herself, because she herself was the guilty one.'

'The *lupus* has stated that he dragged her into the laboratory, which proves that she was not there of her own free will. Why should the man have made such an incriminating statement to her if it was not true? I see no sense in that.'

The Abbot said nothing, but at last gave a slight nod. 'Very well, let us suppose that the Prior was Casall's murderer.' He turned to Sophie again. 'But you admit that you matriculated in this Faculty under a false name and with a false identity and then studied here. So you swore three oaths under a false name.'

Sophie nodded.

'Tell me then, what were the…' he hesitated, but then continued, '…the considerations that led you to do that?'

'I thought, what harm could it do if I learned something?'

'You could have attended this Faculty as a woman. That is unusual, but it would have been possible.'

'Perhaps. But everyone would have disapproved.'

'Where did you obtain the money to pay for your studies?'

She made no reply. The Abbot announced that there would be a short break. He nodded to the clerk and had the doors opened. The Masters streamed out, and Sophie was led away.

'I must get out of Cologne. For a whole year I have seen nothing but this city, its houses, its churches, the people who live here. As though the whole world consisted only of this city.'

A horse dealer lived opposite. On horseback, by boat or using shanks's pony, it made no difference.

'You are trying to sneak away,' Steiner said suspiciously. 'You don't like attending the trial, do you? Why is that?'

Lombardi did not know himself. He could hardly be expected to take the side of a woman who seemed certain to lose her case. And yet he did not want to enter that courtroom again.

'You are one of the Masters. You are obliged to attend.'

'Yes, but not today. I warned her. But she will ignore my advice, I know it. Steiner, I have a good friend in Kahlenberg. I'll go and visit him. Perhaps I'll be back the day after tomorrow, or perhaps not. Say that I have been taken ill, or whatever else you please. I feel I am stuck in a quagmire and can't pull myself out. At Kahlenberg there is a mountain, and one can climb it and look down from the top. Sometimes that helps one to get things back into perspective.'

Steiner merely nodded. If a person felt that he could not see clearly anymore, then this might be no bad remedy. Off you go, then, Lombardi, climb your mountain, and maybe when you look around from up there you'll see the solution. You go, and meanwhile I'll be here, trying to defend an impossibly weak position. Steiner shook his head. Sometimes he no longer knew where his adversary was or who he was. Perhaps he himself was his own worst enemy.

'Let us not deceive ourselves. Are we really interested in help-ing her? Do we want to give women the chance to study and fill our own posts? I know what the Abbot will ask her. Has a woman ever devised a philosophical proposition? Do they not merely parrot what we say, like infants learning to speak?'

'That is not true,' Lombardi said vehemently. 'There certainly are women who have ideas of their own—who even write books. I'm sure that they are capable of devising propositions.'

Steiner gave a soft laugh. 'All the same, I have to ask myself what I really want. And if I am quite honest, I want everything to stay as it is. And if you are honest, so do you. It is only your feelings that are preventing you from recognising that fact.'

'So you are one of those who would wish to see Sophie accused of sorcery, and even burned at the stake? When they start to ask questions about the meaning of the Host and of the body of Christ and such things—you know what I am talking about—then I will leave this Faculty. I thought that we had liberated ourselves from such methods.'

Steiner made no answer. The usher came to call them back to the courtroom, but Lombardi turned on his heel and left the monastery.

He had chosen an unpropitious time to ride to Kahlenberg. The first gusty winds heralding the coming of spring blew their cold breath, laden with snow and rain, into his face. Grey clouds peppered his shoulders with small hailstones, and the poplars and alders that lined his route bent and swayed. His black horse trotted stoically onwards. Dusk fell early, and so he soon stopped at an isolated, weather-beaten hostelry, where the horse was fed and stabled and its master given a room for the night and a pan of scrambled eggs and bacon. The storm raged on into the hours of darkness. The innkeeper just laughed, and said they would do well to stay awake so as not to be buried in their sleep when the roof caved in. So Lombardi lay on his hard bed, listening to the roaring of the elements and waiting for the plaster to start crumbling down onto his head. However, nothing untoward happened, and so he dragged himself out of bed the next morning, dead tired, and saddled his horse.

'Where are you bound for?' asked the innkeeper.

'To Kahlenberg. To visit the Lord of the Tower.'

The innkeeper looked skywards to where the sun was poking through the clouds. 'Be on your guard. For weeks a band of villains has been on the prowl around here—murderers, poachers, blasphemers. Do you carry a good knife?'

Lombardi nodded. He paid, thanked the man and mounted his horse.

Daylight seemed to have brought calmer weather. For the first few hours he rode under a blue sky, but then he saw more clouds rolling up from the west. Yes, this was just the weather for thieving ruffians hiding out in the woods. Carts carrying valuable goods to be traded in Cologne passed through here, offering rich pickings to anyone who could waylay them. In another three or four hours he would reach Kahlenberg. For hours now the cold had been finding its way under his cloak, while the horse was in a sweat and was trotting faster and faster as though it sensed that there was not much further to go. The woods were gloomy, almost dark, and the bank of cloud was drawing closer. The wind had risen, too, and was whistling around his ears again. Lombardi did not even take the time to stop for something to eat and drink, and so he reached the town before nightfall. The town gate was not yet closed. As he passed through, the heavens opened. Amid a torrential downpour he rode up the hill.

A quarrel had cost the Lord of the Tower half of his estate. It had been reduced to ruins, so that now all that was left to him was the tower, but this was considered impregnable. No one entered there unbidden. At Lombardi's knock, a page looked out through a small spyhole in the massive gate. Lombardi explained who he was and what he wanted. Finally, after some delay, the gate was opened. The master was expecting him, said the page. Lombardi rode up the slope. By the light of some torches he was able to make out just the lower part of the angular structure, its walls pierced by tiny windows and still narrower arrow-slits blackened by smoke and powder. The page took his horse by the reins and led it away to a shed, for the Lord of the Tower no longer possessed proper stables. The door to the tower creaked open, and soot and smoke billowed out at him. This made his eyes smart and he could see nothing through it, but he heard the voice of the Lord of the Tower ringing out, loud and cheerful, from the middle of the great hall.

'Well, if it isn't our Master of Arts! Come closer, Siger.'

In the mighty fireplace there was a huge fire, as though the Lord of the Tower had roasted a whole ox over it for his guests.

'Come here, you son of a Bernese peasant and a Breton witch.'

'My father was no peasant,' said Lombardi.

'No, of course not. He was an apothecary, but what difference does that make? The Bernese are all mad.'

'And the Bretons are all wizards and witches, aren't they?'

'Yes, I have a simple view of the world, my boy, that's what makes it all so straightforward.'

Delain laughed. His laughter drowned even the fearful crackling in the fireplace, the chimney-breast of which reached up a good thirty feet. At the long table, besides Delain, there were ten of his men and three ladies, who stood up to push a chair towards Lombardi. Young creatures about half the age of the Lord of the Tower. Who now sent a tankard of beer sliding along the table.

'To your parents, my boy, whom I expect you haven't seen for a long time.'

Lombardi deftly caught the tankard and took his seat. Delain was his uncle. He too was from Berne, and he had chanced to end up here because the Bernese had grown tired of his quarrelsomeness and had simply thrown him out of their city. Following his expulsion he had roamed the world, travelling now south of the Alps, now north of them, before taking a wife here and becoming Lord of the Tower. In Kahlenberg, too, people would have been glad if after his wife's death he had packed his bags again; but he liked it there. Black as night was his beard, black the shaggy hair which would have done credit to a ram. His stature was such that no armour would fit him, but in this new age of gunpowder he needed none. His tower sat on a veritable arsenal of powder that could be blown up whenever he gave the order, but at the moment he seemed quite peaceable and full of the sense of humour which he demonstrated in good measure when circumstances permitted.

'What are you doing here? Have you had enough of the city of cities?'

'Very possibly.'

'It won't be a longing to see me that has brought you here. Do you need a woman? Then just take your pick.' Delain reached for a large platter that was on the table. 'Here, help yourself. I'm sure they don't feed you like this in your students' hall.'

'I needed to get away. I had to see something different for a change, and I thought that your tower would be just the right place.'

'Splendid! Stay, then. Tomorrow we'll go hunting. Can you still shoot?'

Lombardi laughed. Yes, of course he could, but that was not what he had come for. Perhaps, he thought, it would be best never to return to Cologne. He could stay with Delain and join in his feuds and quarrels. Was that what he wanted? Should he opt for the Lord of the Tower instead of the ivory tower of the intellect?

Delain had lent him one of his mistresses for the night, a young girl of barely seventeen summers, if that. The two of them listened to the storm that still raged around the tower. There's a dragon that lives in the forest, the girl said, pressing herself against him in her fear of storm and monster alike. There are no dragons, my child, Lombardi said, but she shook her head indignantly. Had anyone ever seen it, Lombardi asked, to which she nodded vigorously. Oh yes, it had certainly been seen, tramping through the undergrowth, a terrifying sight, with flames coming out of its jaws. That was an apparition, Lombardi said, a figment of the imagination that has nothing to do with reality. But the girl only stared at him: were all those people who had seen it mad, then? Yes, mad, replied Lombardi, watching the glass vibrating in the window. The room was at the very top of the tower; there was nothing above it but the parapet with its commanding views over the countryside. The window was so narrow that not even a child could have squeezed through it. The dragon is so big that if it reared up on its hind legs it could see in through the window, the girl stammered, and the next thunderclap made her freeze with terror. The tower seemed to bend with the wind like an alder tree. Lombardi stood up and went over to the slit window. Outside there was nothing but pitch blackness, not the least hint of a light, even in the sky. Warm hands encircled his hips. 'Can you see it?'

He laughed. 'No, it doesn't exist, silly.'

'What does exist, then?'

'I don't know.'

In the morning he went out into the forest alone. The storm had cut a swathe through it. Trees that had been blown down blocked the narrow path. By chance Lombardi came upon a hermit who had been there for years, living on roots and berries of all kinds, and on what people brought him. The old man's cave was set in a rocky cliff, and outside it ran a limpid, murmuring stream; the hermit, a friar, was just then kneeling by it to wash himself. An austere dwelling, thought Lombardi, after glancing into the cave. Blankets on the bare earth, bars to keep out wolves and other animals, a pot, a hearth. That was all.

The friar was barefoot and was wearing a simple cloak. His beard reached down to his hips. He greeted Lombardi with a friendly smile, looking at him with clear blue eyes. Eyes as clear as the water in his stream.

Lombardi gave him a piece of bread that he had brought with him to eat on the way, and the friar beamed. He seldom had visitors, and seldom such good bread. He lit a fire and boiled water in his pot, tossed in a handful of herbs and led Lombardi into his cave. 'Sit down. Have you come from the Lord of the Tower?'

Lombardi sat down on the blankets, against the cold wall of the cave. The view was a desolate one. Bare skeletons of trees in the damp morning mist, through which the wind still prowled with a hint of menace. The mist was thickening and turning into an undulating veil which the eye could scarcely penetrate.

'You would be wise to turn back as soon as possible. In weather like this it is easy to lose one's way,' said the friar. 'People say that when the mists are gathering and the weather is on the change, that is when the dragon comes out of the forest. You may believe it or you may not, you are a man of intellect, of scholarship, but take care all the same.'

Lombardi stared out. How ludicrous to believe in a dragon which did not exist. In the night the girl had prattled about it endlessly, and he had slept fitfully and dreamt of a dragon, a huge, fleshy creature barring his way.

'So you believe in it?' he asked the friar, who had now brought a sharp knife and was starting to cut the bread.

'Does it matter? I have never seen it, so I do not believe in it. But there are things that one cannot see but that exist all the same. The peasants in the village claim to have seen it kill a lamb. Now you may object that they are all uneducated people, but even educated people have been known to ride out to slay a dragon.'

Nothing but illusions, Lombardi thought angrily, but when he looked out at the dripping fog that was growing thicker by the minute, a different feeling came over him. It was eerie. Was that not the glint of two glittering eyes? Just a cat, he reassured himself. The friar brought him a cup with an infusion of rose-hips that he had sweetened with a remnant of honey.

'Drink this, it will warm you a little.'

Lombardi drained the cup and stood up. 'Well, I suppose I had better be going.'

The friar nodded. 'Keep to the proper path, it leads to the tower. The forest is dark and endless…'

'Are you not afraid to be here all alone?'

The friar laughed. 'Oh, if thieves or robbers were to come by, I have nothing to give them. One is troubled more by fantasies, because there is no reality to act as a corrective, but so far the dragon has never taken the trouble to visit me…'

Lombardi took his leave and plunged out into the cold dampness. The mist was like moist sharp fingers running over his face; all around there was a leaden silence, heavy and chill, with never a breath of wind, never a sound. Not a bird to be seen, not a rabbit to be heard in the dark undergrowth. Suddenly he found he had strayed from the path. He stopped. Where was he? Was he lost? Which way was the hermit's cave? He turned around and strained his eyes to see through the mist. He had lost all sense of direction and no longer even knew whether he had come from the right or the left. He looked up to see if there was a pale sun piercing through the mist. Nothing. His heart began to pound wildly, and his hand went to the knife tucked into the top of his boot. He clambered through the undergrowth and all at once heard a strange creaking, as though a branch were breaking away from a tree and were about to fall. And then the shriek of a barn owl, and Lombardi suddenly saw its broad, light-coloured wings sweeping away above his head. He forced himself to remain calm: even this forest came to an end somewhere, even here he would eventually come upon some human habitation. Further away he saw a movement in the diffuse light. Something was crashing, groaning, snorting. Like a dragon! Lombardi stopped again. There are no dragons, they are only figments of our imagination to which we can assign a name, but as you know very well, Siger, not everything that has a name is made of flesh and blood or of any other kind of matter. Now he could hear it clearly—it was snorting, a long way off, where the fog was so dense that his eyes could not see nothing at all. Are they proving you wrong, Lombardi? They are right, the dragon does exist, and you have been a stupid boy, thinking you knew everything when in reality you know nothing. He turned and ran. Ran away in the opposite direction, but then, as though trapped in a labyrinth, he ran confusedly this way and that, criss-crossing the forest erratically like a ship without a compass. After some time he slowed down, sweat running down his back, and a smell of smoke found its way to his nostrils. There must be a house nearby where they had a fire burning. Or was it the smoke issuing from the dragon's jaws? Flaming tongues of fire which it spewed out at its victims before devouring them? Or did it simply trample them to death? All at once Lombardi heard the splashing of a brook in front of him. It was meandering across a clearing. A ray of sunshine broke through the clouds; the sun had moved westwards, and now Lombardi knew which way to go. He felt an infinite sense of relief. He must go a little further to the west, and then he would see the tower.

'It is your choice. Make your decision.'

Did the statutes say that they could ask a woman a question as a way of catching her out? All the same, she must be grateful to Steiner for giving her this chance, for it was a wise course of action to take. They might just as easily have thrown her into the water and waited to see if she sank.

'Ask me your question,' she said.

Jordanus had formulated it, and so he would be the one to read it out. He stood up and stepped forward, his face darkly serious, a piece of vellum in his hand.

'This is in Aristotle. Tell me where, and in what context, it says that woman creates only one thing but that man creates many things. To what principle does this relate?'

Sophie nodded, and Jordanus returned to his bench. The room was silent. If she did not know the passage she was lost. If she did not know where, in the boundless works of Aristotle, it was to be found, they would cut off her hair and put her in the pillory. She would be exposed to the cold for days and nights on end, and the passing citizens would deride her and pelt her with mud and filth. And so, little by little, her dignity would be trodden underfoot and in the end she would have to leave the city, without honour, without means, rejected by the world.

She seemed to be thinking. The question was not a simple one, and in fact there was a catch in it. The reference to Aristotle was correct, certainly, but in that passage he was commenting on

Plato's ideas rather than simply giving his own, which the wording of Jordanus's question had of course not revealed. And even if she could find the right passage in her memory, that was not the end of it. Steiner lowered his eyes. He had wanted to be just, to give her a chance, but at the same time he knew that he did not want to give active support to a trend which he would rather prevent. He stared at the toes of his shoes under the table and listened to the silence that was broken only by the crackling of the fire.

'It is in the *Metaphysics*.' Suddenly he heard Sophie's voice and looked up. The Abbot was stony-faced as ever. Jordanus sat with his hands folded together on top of the vellum.

'Yes, that is correct.'

'In the sixth chapter of the first book. Aristotle is discussing the Platonists, who see duality as the principle of matter. Matter produces the many, while form produces only the one. But Aristotle maintains the opposite: that it is matter that produces only the one while form produces many. Thus the female conceives only once, whereas the male impregnates many.'

They would all have known the answer. Some of them would have been able to recite that whole book of the *Metaphysics* by heart, all nine chapters of it. The fact that this woman was their equal in this respect pained every one of them, and yet they were conscious of the power which they possessed and which they could use to determine the outcome of this trial. What did it matter that she knew the source of those words? Even an ape could have recited the passage if it were capable of language. It meant nothing. They had thrown her into the water and she had risen to the surface again. But now came the real test. Now they would hold her under with a pole, and every time her head bobbed up they would push it down again until finally she ran out of air.

'Would you agree with that? Or would you say that a closer examination would be necessary to confirm it?'

'As he expresses it, I would agree with him,' Sophie answered tonelessly.

'So the woman creates only one thing?'

'The woman conceives only once, but does creating only mean

conceiving? Does not creation encompass much more than that? Can a woman not also create many things?'

Jordanus stood up again and placed himself in front of her. 'What is matter and what is form?'

'The woman can be identified with matter, and the man with form.'

'What is matter without form?'

'What is form without matter?'

Jordanus moved closer to her. 'Certainly they belong together. But which is the element that shapes? You would surely agree with me that it is form, would you not?'

Sophie said nothing. She was beginning to see where this was leading. Matter is a shapeless lump that lies around in the world waiting to be shaped. Form ennobles it, breathes life into it. Form creates, many times over, while matter is dull and sluggish. That was it, that was what they wanted to hear.

'What is form without matter? It would be worthless without it,' she said quietly. 'What sort of principle is it that is only an idea? Just as you separate individual things from the concepts of them.'

They leaned forward in order to hear her better. What was it that the woman had just said? Was she bringing this round to the old dispute? To their own interminable quarrel? Jordanus was taken aback. He had not anticipated this.

'Very well. Then tell me which side you are on.'

Now she had herself laid the worst trap into which she could have fallen. She saw it too late, and she knew that all was lost if she answered this question. And yet she wanted to give vent to her anger and resentment. It was absurd to drag her into this courtroom and ask her stupid questions just because she had attended their lectures. She hesitated. What had Lombardi's advice been? To be docile and full of humility, that was what these Masters liked, then they would let her off lightly. And as for the business about the money, they had postponed that item for the time being, so things did not look so very black. She could still have claimed that her stepfather had lent her the money…

The men were waiting, but she remained silent. The traditionalists were in the majority, so it would be wise to flatter them, to tell them that they had always been in the right, even if she was only a woman whose opinion counted for nothing...

But her hatred was stronger. She could feel it like bile rising in her throat. Only later, much later, would she realise that this was her hatred of Casall, a belated victory over him, a battle which she had needed to fight out with him even though he had already been dead for so long. Suddenly she saw his face before her, his eyes, his hands that had beaten her and broken her will. It was Casall whom she had hated and still hated, not these men sitting here confronting her, but she was no longer capable of making the distinction. Twenty Casalls were sitting there before her, beating her, thrashing her, abusing her, tormenting and humiliating her. It was just as it had been then. She could feel the warm blood trickling down her back...

'I am not on either side,' she said now, loudly and distinctly. 'That is not the way I think. It is your way. Continue with it if you think that there is any point in it.'

Steiner took a deep breath. He would have liked to beat a hasty retreat from the chamber. He lowered his eyes. A buzz of angry muttering rose up among the Masters, a wave of indignation spread round the room. What was this the woman was saying?

'Have I understood you correctly? You are on neither side? Of course not, how could you be, since you are only a woman. You have probably not understood the matter at all. It is like a sheep attending grammar school and pretending that it can hold a pen in its foot.'

Jordanus was furious. He had taken Steiner's side, the side of those who wanted to be merciful towards the accused. But her answers had shown him his mistake.

'You can keep your philosophy,' she went on. 'I want nothing more to do with it. It is foolish to concern oneself with it. It all takes place only in your heads and has nothing to do with reality.'

At this they all jumped up at once and leaned forward across the table, almost tipping it over. The muttering had become a furious roar, and the usher had difficulty in restraining them from hurling themselves upon her. The Abbot and the Chancellor were the only ones who had remained seated and were silently shaking their heads.

'Where did she get the money to pay for her studies?' Rüdeger shouted out angrily. 'What has she to hide by enrolling under an assumed name? What were her dealings with de Swerthe? She is lying when she claims he forced her. These are the things we should be investigating.'

He rushed around the table and would have dragged the woman from her stool if the usher had not caught hold of his arm. The Abbot was in danger of losing control of the situation. So he too stood up, and called for silence. But they shouted him down.

'In de Swerthe's laboratory they found strange symbols and characters scratched onto an iron shield and still recognisable,' Rüdeger yelled, now beyond all restraint. 'Symbols of a highly suspicious nature, of necromantic origin, if you ask me. De Swerthe was not only an alchemist, he was also a devotee of the black arts!'

Brosius, Jordanus and Hungerland sat as though turned to stone. They cast despairing looks in Steiner's direction, but he merely made a gesture of resignation. This was her own fault. A little tact, a little humility and recognition of male superiority, and they would have been able to save her from the worst. But now that she had challenged their authority and was threatening to make them look ridiculous she was beyond anyone's help. She had paved her own way to Hell.

'Silence!' The Abbot's voice cut through the uproar. 'Be silent at once, or I will have the room cleared.'

They resumed their seats on the bench. 'It's all lies, her story that she was held captive by de Swerthe. She herself is in league with the demonic powers,' one of the Masters said, giving the cue that they had all been waiting for.

'That would be a new charge,' said the Abbot.

A new charge indeed. Of consorting with demons.

'That charge cannot be sustained,' Steiner whispered to Jordanus, who nodded.

'No, provided that the witness, the *lupus*, stands firm. But what if he gives way? If he withdraws his testimony, which supports Sophie, and starts saying the opposite because there are people whose interests that would serve?'

Steiner did not reply. Where was Lombardi? What was he doing scrambling about on some mountain or other instead of being here to help her?

It was already late when a visitor knocked at his door. He had settled down with a goblet of wine and a book. The servant went to open the door. He heard footsteps. Then the door flew open and Lombardi entered. He took off his cloak, threw it over the back of a chair and seated himself, uninvited, at Steiner's table.

'You have some good wine, I see. Well, what was the outcome of the trial?'

Steiner closed the book with a snap. 'You were right. She is sillier than I thought. She said that it was foolish to concern oneself with philosophy. I need hardly say more than that.'

Lombardi gave a dejected nod. No, he need not.

'And because she set them so much against her, they are now considering a charge of necromancy. The woman has taken leave of her senses. How easily she could have extricated herself, given that she knows her Aristotle so well…' He reached for the bottle and poured some wine for Lombardi. 'She showed not a trace of contrition, she behaved as if she had a key in her pocket with which to let herself out of prison whenever she liked. Does that make any sense to you?'

Lombardi said nothing. He tasted the wine, a good, dry Rhenish wine with a hint of blackcurrant about it, and considered the situation. Was she really out of her mind, or were her anger and resentment so overpowering that they prevented her from thinking rationally?

'Where did she get the money for her studies?' he asked quietly, after a pause. 'I mean, she must have got money from somewhere.'

'She refuses to speak about that…. How did you fare in Kahlenberg?' asked Steiner.

Lombardi told him about his uncle and about the dragon that people believed in although up to now no one had actually seen it. 'Do you think that love is also something imagined?' he asked softly.

Steiner laughed. 'Like the dragon? Yes, why not? People fear the dragon even though they have never seen it. And they fear all sorts of things when they are in love, and yet no one has ever seen love. Like the dragon, it is a product of our imagination or of bad humours in our blood which give rise to the strangest kinds of behaviour. But tell me, while you were at your uncle's, did you think only about love?"

Lombardi said nothing. He had returned after realising that he had been an utter coward. 'Listen, Steiner, I must speak to her. Can I trust you?'

Steiner made a weary gesture of refusal. How much longer would he be lecturing in this Faculty? How long would he be able to maintain his position here if the Chancellor and Rector and Masters turned the clock back and drove the moderni from the city?

'Keep it to yourself, Siger, whatever it is that you have in mind. If you want to help her, try to do it while she is still in the monastery. Once the Dominicans have her in their clutches no money on earth will be able to buy her freedom.'

Lombardi stood up. With a nod to Steiner he left the house. Outside a cold drizzle received him. His boots squelched through the mire. The little house belonging to Sophie's mother stood at the corner of Lungengasse. Candlelight showed through the windows. He rang the bell, and one of Sophie's sisters opened the door. 'Can I speak to your mother?'

She stared at him, but her mother was in the hall and asked what he wanted. Money, he said, he must have money to bribe the monk who was on guard duty to let him talk to her daughter. The widow went to fetch her late husband's purse and shook the gold coins out on to the table. Ten, twenty? She had more than enough. Without a word he pocketed fifteen of them; he had never seen so much money all at once in his whole life. Then he pressed the woman's hand and left.

The next morning when he came to the Provost's House, the monks were rushing around the courtyard in great agitation. Had Sophie perhaps already been taken away from here? Might she have been thrown into one of the towers and entered in the register of prisoners as a witch? From where he had halted for the moment, waiting, he could not make out the subject of their animated talk. Was the

Pope about to descend on them? What could it be that was making them run around like startled hens? Purposefully he stepped closer and accosted one of the men, who stared at him and then pointed to the monastery building.

'Casall's widow has gone. She has vanished from her cell like a witch. Can you imagine it?'

Lombardi stood there, thunderstruck. A witch! Despite the close watch kept on her she had escaped. Just then someone came up behind him and gently laid a hand on his shoulder.

'Somebody must have helped her. What are you doing here?'

It was Jordanus.

'I happened to be passing and noticed the commotion. Has she really disappeared?'

'Yes. Someone must have come to her aid, but the monks swear that no one was here during the night.'

'Perhaps they have been paid to say that...'

'The monks? Hardly! They were all fast asleep in their cells. But how could her accomplice know where to find the keys to the widow's cell?'

At this moment the Chancellor appeared, crossed the courtyard and vanished into his residence.

'Who has an interest in freeing her and sparing her this trial?' Lombardi asked softly.

Jordanus looked him straight in the face. 'Who indeed? I do not think there are many possible candidates. How about you? I gather that you were fond of her...'

'It wasn't me. I am as surprised as you are to find her gone. I was in the Scholarium all night, and there are witnesses to prove it.'

Frowning, Jordanus observed the continuing agitation in the courtyard. 'So our little bird has flown,' he murmured. 'Fluttered away like an angel. What will happen now?'

Those who had wanted to see Sophie charged with sorcery, despite having no more than supposition and conjecture to go on, now saw their worst suspicions confirmed. Clearly she could not have escaped from her cell on her own. The monks were questioned, but they all claimed to have been asleep, and it seemed absurd to suppose that any one of them would have wanted to free the accused. The brother responsible for keeping watch over her, bringing her her food and offering her spiritual consolation, was beside himself with indignation. Like everyone else, he said, he had been in bed at the time. After Compline he had set her supper down before her and afterwards checked the lock again. The door was securely locked, he swore, and he had taken the key with him to his cell, just as he always did. And no one had come in during the night and taken the key. He was a light sleeper and would have been sure to notice.

They were standing around in the cloister, all equally at a loss. The Chancellor had sunk down on to a bench and was staring dully into space. 'We underestimated her,' he growled. 'She must have had an accomplice.... Or can you think of any other explanation?'

Jordanus was baffled. He did not believe in the Devil, and as for believing in an accomplice, that would be absurd, because there could not have been one. So how had it happened?

He left the monastery and went to the Scholarium to seek out Lombardi's witnesses.

After de Swerthe's death in the fire, Lombardi had been placed in charge of the Scholarium. Of course this was only a temporary arrangement, for he was not a cleric, and so the patron was looking for a new Prior.

Jordanus found Lombardi in the refectory, where the residents were just having their midday meal. Without a word he sat down at the table, and one of the serving-women pushed a plate and cup towards him. They all ate in silence and were about to leave the table and go to the chapel for prayers when Jordanus asked all the assembled students to stay for a moment. Sophie Casall had disappeared, he began, but everyone knew that already. He asked whether they could all prove where they had been last night. The students exchanged startled looks. The *lupus* declared that he had locked the door and put the key under his pillow. No one could have left the building during the night. Not even Lombardi? asked Jordanus. Not even Lombardi, answered the *lupus*.

Jordanus stood up, thanked them and left.

'In the city they are saying that a pillar of fire was seen hovering over the monastery in the night,' one of the students said in a low voice. 'They say that that was Sophie Casall!'

'So she really was a witch,' another murmured, his eyes cast down. 'And we never noticed. To think that she was sitting there next to us at lectures and might have done anything at all to us...'

'Rubbish,' cried a third. 'Those are just evil rumours. A human being can't simply dissolve into thin air and vanish. Of course she had help. She may have had a lover...'

'I'll wager it was one of the monks,' the first one grinned. 'He hopped into bed with her. Then, when he couldn't cope with her demands, he let her go.'

They laughed. But their laughter was muted. It was not possible for someone simply to disappear like that. Trained as they were to see the world through the clear medium of the intellect, they were convinced that there were no such things as witches and demons. But if someone came along and proved the opposite, they could only watch helplessly as their intellectual edifice tottered like an old, rotten tree. Lombardi's eyes strayed across to Laurien.

Lately he had become ever more silent and withdrawn, as though labouring once again under a dark, burdensome secret. Had it been Laurien? Lombardi caught his breath. No, not Laurien. He couldn't have left the Scholarium. No one could have, including himself.

'How was your trip to your uncle's?' Brosius suddenly asked him.

Lombardi gave a quiet laugh. 'Oh, I spent my time there trying to apprehend a dragon.'

'A dragon?'

'Yes, the peasants believe that a dragon lives in the forest there. And when I got lost in the mist I even believed in it myself for a brief moment. Oh yes, Brosius, it all fits together, don't you think? The dragon in the country, the witch in the town...'

Brosius shook his head, surprised. 'Delusions,' he murmured. 'We fall back on them when all our intellectual powers are not adequate to explain the world. In the countryside they are everywhere. Where I come from, a little place in the Lechtal Alps, the people believe in a White Lady and in spirits that inhabit the mountains, good and evil spirits, as good and as evil as the mountains themselves.'

Lombardi nodded. Yes, where he came from, too—not so very far from Brosius's native region—there were all-powerful spirits: indeed, the Alps as a whole were alive with dwarfs, trolls, fairies, nymphs, sorcerers, and white and black magicians, denizens of an insubstantial world which the simple people still had eyes to see.

'The stuff of imagination,' he said contemptuously.

Brosius smiled. 'Yes, imagination. Nothing but imagination, but we have only these three possibilities: the human mind, which creates itself from its own resources, the observation of nature as taught by Bacon, and lastly myth. Sometimes I am not sure which of them would come closest to the truth, if there were such a thing as truth.'

They left the table and went together to prayers.

In the night Lombardi heard a scratching at the barred window. His eyes still heavy with sleep, he stared into the darkness, listening. Someone had forestalled him, and he should have been grateful. He had come close to risking his life for that woman, and why? Merely for the sake of a romp in bed with her at last? For an hour of pleasure, which he could have anywhere? No, there must be more to it than that, and yet, when he really thought about it, it *was* only that. And when his lust was satisfied, what then? Would the same deadly desolation take hold of his heart again? Women had always interested him only until he was satisfied. It would never have occurred to him to want more from them than their bodies. But with Sophie he had wanted to talk, he would gladly have spent whole nights in discussion with her. Now someone else had come and was talking to her. He heard the soft scratching at the window again. He got up and peered out into the darkness. Was it the witch flying through the air and scratching at the glass? A hot, tingling shiver ran down his back. But there was nothing out there except the wind whistling around the Scholarium.

It was the sole topic of conversation in Cologne. Here at last was a new tale of truly awe-inspiring horror to gossip over with one's neighbour, who had heard something from someone else, who had gleaned a further embellishment from yet another source. And if the learned theologians could talk about angels, then there was nothing impossible about a woman using magic to escape to freedom. Every idea must at some time take on a concrete form, for once an idea existed, however and wherever it had come into being, it must eventually appear in visible shape to someone, somewhere. Yes, that was obvious even to the stupidest of Cologne's inhabitants. After all, you could not see God either, and yet he existed. You did not see the angels, and yet they existed. Probably no one had seen the Devil, but everyone knew that he was in the habit of manifesting himself in the most diverse guises. Even in a human being, in the madman who was possessed by the Devil. And the Pope had a breath of the divine spirit in him! Whatever had a name must exist, and that was that. It would be illogical to assume anything else. Magicians, devils, demons and dragons, they believed in all of them as they believed in the Last Judgment—which, after all, none of them had experienced yet either.

Steiner felt the spray on his face. He had chosen the worst possible place on the boat. His hair was wet, his coat damp and cold. The weather was good, chilly but clear, the sky a pale blue, and alongside the river, fields and villages slid past. It was peaceful and conducive to reflection, and Steiner stepped back a pace and looked around for the Baccalaureus. Hans von Stechemesser was a rising star in the Cologne Faculty, a young man who would go far. Just at present, however, he had other worries than his career, for he was leaning over the rail emptying his stomach, which could not cope with the rolling of the boat. When the worst was over for the moment, he straightened himself and turned to face Steiner. 'I'm sorry, but I have never been a good sailor…'

Steiner smiled. 'Perhaps you should go below deck?'

Stechemesser waved the suggestion away. The cabins below were no bigger than mouseholes, and the creaking of the hull made him nervous. It was better to be able to look all around you and let the spray splash up at you. If you sat centrally in the prow you could keep relatively dry and watch the castles passing by, perched on hills that were just showing the first delicate green of spring. It would be a good two hours before they would be back on *terra firma*, and in that time no doubt his stomach would have churned round a hundred times like the sails of a windmill. He would gain little enjoyment from the fine views on this little river cruise.

'You know that they are talking of nothing else in the city?' he asked Steiner, as he watched the boatmen hauling up heavy ropes over the deck rail.

'Yes. They are convinced now that she is a witch simply because of her disappearance. Shame on him, whoever it was who released her.'

'You don't believe in any of that nonsense about witchery, do you?'

'No, of course not. But you know the principle…'

'Of course.' Stechemesser was trying to concentrate on their conversation. But once again his stomach was threatening to demand another dash for the rail. He pressed his lips together.

'According to the teachings of logic, people are right to say that for every concept there must be a perceptible form,' he said at last, trying to overcome his nausea.

'No,' Steiner said dismissively. 'That is just playing with words and ideas, nothing more. Invent a word, put one together by combining existing words. And then what has come first, the thing or the name for it?'

'The thing,' said Stechemesser, astonished. God had created the world, and obviously all the things in it. Only after that did he create man. So how could a name be there first?

'In the beginning was the Word,' Steiner murmured. 'Not the thing.'

Stechemesser amused himself for a while by inventing words. Candlehorse. Buttertree. Chickencloud. Duckangel. What was a duckangel? Where in heaven's name might there be such a thing as a duckangel?

By the time they drew level with Neuss he had already invented some fifty such expressions, each more absurd than the last, but this pastime at least seemed to settle his stomach. It was as if he were keeping it under control by feeding it with ever more far-fetched concepts: shipstream, elderblond, ropemouse.

'Are you feeling ill?' Steiner asked him, seeing him staring so inanely into the water.

'Have you ever seen a duckangel?'

Steiner gaped at him. 'Whatever is that?'

'There must be such a thing, since I have found a name for it. Perhaps an angel that has the appearance of a duck, what do you think?'

Steiner stood up and went to ask the captain for a bottle of good wine.

Perhaps brandy would have provided a better cure for this peculiar mood that Stechemesser had fallen into.

'Who had an interest in releasing the girl?' Steiner murmured on his return, while Stechemesser put the bottle to his lips and took a deep draught.

'Yes, who indeed?' the Baccalaureus grinned. 'Seriously, I can't think of anyone, unless she had a lover.'

Steiner shook his head. 'He would have had to sneak into the Provost's House somehow or other. How could he have done that? No, it must be someone who lives there. Someone who could get his hands on the key, unlock the door and then see to it that Sophie Casall was able to slip out unnoticed.'

Stechemesser laughed. The wine was doing him good. Although he now felt worse than before, he no longer cared. The boat's rolling and pitching made him laugh, and when he looked at Steiner, he seemed to be rolling and pitching too.

'The Provost,' he said, relishing his own joke.

'Magister Steiner isn't here. What do you want to speak to him about?'

Laurien hesitated. He could not talk to Lombardi. Jordanus? Brosius? Hungerland? He did not trust any of them. He only trusted Steiner.

'It doesn't matter,' he mumbled and went out into the street. Steiner's servant shook her head as she watched him go. In front of the cathedral the foundlings were begging and a scavenger was rummaging among the rubbish.

'Flew out through a barred window that was too small even for a child to get through…'

He looked round. Even the old hags in the street were already talking about it.

He felt hounded, persecuted. Taking refuge in the cathedral, he leaned on a column and looked upwards—straight into the stone jaws of a slavering winged monster ornamenting the capital. Demons and phantoms wherever you turned, even in the holiest of all places, the House of God. Was Brosius right in thinking that the belief in magic was stronger than anything else? Stronger than the power of the intellect or the study of nature? If so, there would be nothing left to hold on to, for it dragged you down into an infernal realm of uttermost gloom and darkness.

'And this I tell you, when witches start passing through walls just like that, it is incumbent on us to preserve our world from such evils. Did anyone see her? Was she not a respectable widow? Was she suddenly possessed by evil, so that she fell under the sway of occult powers?'

The priest preaching from the pulpit. Laurien covered his ears. Sophie was no witch. No one in the world was less of a witch than that wondrous being. Sophie had been his friend, almost a brother to him—no, wait a minute, that was nonsense! He had never had a friend called Josef, for he had been a woman. Overcome by the realisation that his friend had deceived him and was really somebody quite different, Laurien had fallen back into the warm, comforting arms of melancholy, which seduced him into seeing the whole world as consisting of nothing but deception and illusion. And yet he felt a kind of admiration for the woman. And now this! A trial had been inevitable, but that they should now suspect her of necromancy and propose to charge her with it seemed to him a travesty. The whole city was hunting for the fugitive. Was he the only one still thinking rationally? Nobody could seriously believe that she had really and truly passed through walls. The solution was perfectly simple: someone had assisted her. But—and here Laurien too was baffled—who could it have been? Of course he himself would have helped her if he had been able to, but he had not been the one. Nor had Lombardi. Steiner? No, that was a bizarre notion. A man of such known rectitude would never have secretly contravened the statutes: any remedy he attempted would be open and above board. Who, then?

Twilight was descending upon the city. Deep red, blood-red light crept in through the lofty windows, coating the stone with a fine down of colour. The cathedral was almost empty, with none of its usual bustle. Only a handful of worshippers were still there listening to the priest's words of admonition. In the square outside, one entertainment booth after another was being set up, and people were more inclined to watch the dancing bear or the tumblers, or go to the barber-surgeon who pulled teeth—at a price, to be sure, but he came from Arabia and was selling a new medicine that was supposed to make the extraction almost painless. The cries of the showmen penetrated into the cathedral, but even they were soon lost in the high vaulting. Suddenly Laurien stared in amazement. A figure kneeling before one of the side altars had risen to its feet and was moving towards the south transept. A small figure whose walk seemed very familiar. Fair hair, wheat-blond, peeped out from under a hood; the man had a cloak wrapped round his shoulders, and a book, probably a Bible, in his hand. But that walk! It had a fluttering quality, a lightness and nerviness that could not be disguised—and yet how could anyone have recognised it? The thing was utterly impossible, for that walk belonged to a man who was dead.

'Hey!' shouted Laurien, and felt a shock of alarm when his voice resounded in the nave as though taken up by a thousand echoes. 'Stop him!'

Startled, the worshippers at the high altar looked round. At that moment the figure started running and dashed through the transept to the exit. Only then did it occur to Laurien to set off in pursuit. Outside there was a tremendous crush. He squeezed past people's bodies, pushing them aside as he searched for the apparition, which must have mingled with the crowd. At last he caught sight of him on the Alter Markt, close to the meat hall, where he had stopped, no doubt thinking that he was safe now. Laurien approached him from behind, creeping past people, keeping his head low. Whoever the man was, he was standing quite still. But when, with a swift movement, Laurien grasped his sleeve, the dwarf turned round with a yell, but then, quickly stretching out both arms, slipped out of his coat. And was gone. Laurien was so taken aback that he did not react immediately but stood there, staring bemusedly at the garment dangling from his hands, and resumed the chase too late. The dwarf had vanished. Laurien hunted around for a time among the market stalls, but soon gave up. Still, he had the coat. His one piece of evidence.

'So you're going home, to stay there for two or three months before coming back. You will have a good rest and regain your strength, won't you, Laurien?'

The new Prior—a young man still, who had been running the Scholarium for three days and was making an effort to get to know the students—shook his head. Were they all as highly-strung as this boy? Laurien was in the sick room and could not speak a word. What he had had to say, he had said when he returned to the Scholarium that evening in a state of great agitation; he had laid the coat on the table and then, quite exhausted, had taken refuge in bed. Since then he had been mute. The former Prior was dead, everyone knew that. So who was the man whose coat he had brought back with him? Probably a delusion. The coat did seem to be that of a dwarf, but there was nothing to prove that it really was de Swerthe's.

Brosius was sitting on a stool at Laurien's bedside. 'There are many dwarfs in this city. People of limited growth, whom God has blessed with other gifts than that of growing—the power of the intellect, the gift of compassion, the grace of God. It must have been another of them that you saw.'

Laurien nodded. He would go back home to the small town on the Lower Rhine. There there was no Faculty, there were no Brethren of the Free Spirit, no murderers and no dwarfs who were dead but then came back to life. There would be the peacefulness of a small town and the tranquillity of nature. He had had enough of being a student. Almost a year in this city, and nothing was left of his dreams. He would simply become a scribe like his father, he needed no degree for that. He did not intend to return. That was merely the pious hope of the Magister.

Brosius stood up and he and the Prior left the room together. They sat down in the Prior's study and remained silent for a while, each staring into space. Even they felt that they had been touched by the breath of evil, for all their reluctance to believe in it. The window was open, the curtain flapping in the wind. Birds were chirping and the air was mild, with the scent of spring.

'Nervous exhaustion,' was Brosius's verdict. 'He is unstable, that lad. He will recover once he is at home.'

The Prior said nothing. He had been told about the extraordinary events at this Faculty, the murdered Master, the two philosophical riddles, the killing of the student and, last but not least, the woman who had inexplicably disappeared from her cell. And now this. There really was never a dull moment in Cologne. 'Is it certain that de Swerthe perished in that house?' he asked softly, standing up to close the window.

'No, for not a single bone was found. Steiner thinks that de Swerthe must somehow have managed to escape. He has instructed the constables to provide him with a list of every single object that can be found on the site. They have been rummaging through the embers for days now, and cursing bitterly. De Swerthe was using gunpowder and a mixture—unfamiliar to me—of sulphur, coal and some alchemical compound. The whole house went up in the explosion.'

The Prior remained standing at the window. 'So there is no trace of the man?'

'No, nothing.'

'Then perhaps the student is not mistaken after all? An alchemist, who, I gather, was also adept at black magic, has all kinds of means at his disposal for deceiving others…'

'Nonsense,' Brosius burst out. 'We must not add fuel to the hysteria that is already rife in the city by saying that de Swerthe is not dead. What is it to us? Let him creep around in churches if he likes. Let him find a place to sleep in some doorway. If Laurien goes home tomorrow or the day after, no one need know about this. Let us draw a veil of silence over the whole disagreeable business and get back to our syllabus instead of racking our brains about ghosts.'

The Prior nodded. Yes, he was probably right. See nothing, hear nothing, say nothing.

It was still early afternoon when the constable charged with the search came to bring Steiner the list. Since he himself could not write, he had asked one of the Faculty's copyists to take on the task, and now he proudly presented Steiner with a piece of paper on which every beam, every brick was itemised. Steiner expressed his thanks, and the man then shook out onto the table a sackful of objects that had been found: scraps of charred paper, crucibles, pans, stills, an inkwell, two pairs of blackened shoes, a half-burnt hat, a ring…

Steiner froze. That ring! It seemed somehow familiar. He had seen it before. A gold ring bearing a coat of arms. The emblem had been half melted by the intense heat, but the animal was still recognisable. A badger.

'Is something not right about the ring?' asked the constable. 'We found it in a small iron box, just a moment, yes, here it is…'

He extracted an iron casket from the pile. The lid had melted. 'The ring was in this.'

Steiner was still staring at the ring. Then he thanked the man again, threw on his coat, pocketed the ring and left the house.

To the south-east of the cathedral lay the cemetery. Behind it rose the tower of St. Maria ad Gradus, gradually darkening now in the evening twilight. There was still light to see by, and Steiner enjoyed the peacefulness around him. A good friend of the Chancellor's was buried here. The mild March wind was sweeping the leaves from the graves, on which the first shoots of lungwort were beginning to show. The Chancellor was standing, his hands folded, by the grave, not moving even when he heard the rustling of leaves under Steiner's tread. Steiner stopped, so as not to disturb the other's devotions, but, without turning round, the Chancellor beckoned him on.

Steiner drew nearer. 'They are out for blood. The populace has a terrifying thirst for blood, and I wonder what we can do to incline it towards mercy.' He laughed softly. 'In ancient times it would have been placated with bread and circuses.'

The Chancellor nodded. 'Yes, there were always ways and means.'

They stood in silence, looking at the grave. A gust of wind whirled the dead leaves into the air. The sun had long since disappeared behind the mighty backdrop of the cathedral chancel, and soon the graveyard would be in darkness.

'I thought I would just ask if any new facts have come to light in relation to Sophie Casall's disappearance.'

The Chancellor gave him an enquiring look. 'Why do you come to me about it?'

'None of the monks could have helped her escape. None had an interest in doing so. And then one hears the townspeople muttering and heaping abuse on her, saying that she is a witch who will end up in the flames at Melaten. It struck me that it cannot be your wish to broaden the scope of this trial and create still more scandal.'

The Chancellor laughed softly. 'What am I to tell you, Steiner? That I let her go, because I am the only one who could possibly have done it? Of course I was extremely keen to put her on trial, for I could foresee a highly undesirable trend developing if we allowed women to study, but I found myself in a real dilemma. You know how this city has always tried to avoid being too much under the direct control of the Archbishop. What would have happened if there had been a trial against this woman for necromancy? The common folk would have insisted on having their sport...'

Turning towards Steiner, he placed his hand on his shoulder. 'Leave it at that. Ask no more questions, especially of me.'

'Very well,' murmured Steiner, 'no more questions.'

He hesitated. By now darkness had spread over the graveyard. A faint, diffuse light shone across from the cathedral precincts. And what about de Swerthe, Steiner wanted to ask. Laurien on his sickbed had confided in Steiner after all, and told him of his encounter with that apparition. He had made Steiner look at the coat, a coat which could have belonged to any canon of small stature, though there were not many such in the city.

'De Swerthe…' he said quietly, pulling his cloak more tightly around him, for with nightfall the frost and cold were returning.

'That is unimportant,' the Chancellor responded irritably. 'Laurien is a highly-strung boy who never managed to fit in here. Not everyone is suited to being a student. De Swerthe is dead. Of course the common people would love it if he were a revenant walking about among them. It is fantasy, Steiner, that causes us our worst difficulties, imaginary things which we cannot pin down to solid reality and which consequently go on haunting our minds.'

He turned to go, but stopped once more and pointed to his friend's grave. 'Only when we are down there do we stop indulging our imagination and twisting the world into the shape we would like it to be. There is something comforting about that prospect, don't you think?'

Steiner shivered. Then he took the ring from his pocket and held it out towards the Chancellor.

'Do you know whose ring this is?'

'No, I have no idea. Should I know?'

'No, of course not. But I have seen this emblem before, I just don't remember where. It was found in de Swerthe's laboratory.'

The moon slid out from behind ragged veils of cloud and filled the graveyard with its pallid light. The wind was now blowing fiercely around Steiner's ears.

'Is it of any significance?' the Chancellor asked brusquely.

'I don't know. If only I could think where I have seen this animal before. The ring is of considerable value. It is made of solid gold, and the badger's eyes are precious stones, a pair of rubies. Look.'

Deep red badger's eyes sparkled at the Chancellor. It was indeed a valuable piece. He turned away and vanished into the darkness.

It was the first really warm and sunny day in March. Only a few weeks earlier they had been driving out the winter with masks and mummery, and now it really did seem to be on its way out. Time to be moving on.

Lombardi was sitting on the wall at the river's edge, thinking about his future. Once upon a time Masters and students had brought Ockham's teachings here from Paris, but now there was a cold wind blowing against him in Cologne. Soon a decision would be taken to return to realism, and all the adherents of nominalism were already considering where they should go. Heidelberg would be a suitable place for him, Lombardi thought: the realists had been proscribed there, so that it was they who were having to look for another Faculty. And so the supporters of the two tendencies would meet somewhere in the middle of the Empire, passing each other like two caravans whose paths were always crossing.

Lombardi stood up and walked back into the city. Coming to Sophie's mother's house, he rang the bell. She opened the door herself and looked anxiously into his eyes.

'Is there any news?'

He shook his head. She had been either killed or taken somewhere else; there was no hope of her coming back, but he did not say this. Instead he bade the mother farewell and returned slowly to the Scholarium, where he packed his few possessions into a bag. Then he arranged his books in a pile on the table. He was just leafing absent-mindedly through Ockham's writings when there was a knock at the door. It was Steiner, who hesitantly came in and glanced at the open book and the bulging bag.

'So you really are going.'

'Aren't you?'

Steiner laughed. 'I am too old. You cannot transplant an old tree, it would not survive. And I have never made any secret of my readiness to teach either doctrine. Perhaps both views are correct.'

'Even if they are mutually exclusive?'

'Are they? Do you not think that there may be various truths?'

Lombardi shook his head and snapped the book shut. 'Is the argument really still about doctrine? Is it not about power? Ockham accuses the Church of being interested only in power politics, and that is why he is a thorn in its flesh. And we are caught in this quarrel like worms on the hook; in fact we are little more than the fisherman's bait...'

Steiner stepped closer and sat down wearily on the vacant stool. 'It is not merely a matter of politics or power, Siger,' he suddenly said quietly. 'It is a matter of whether one allows faith and knowledge to be regarded as two different truths. Faith and knowledge have always belonged together, and now a bond that is thousands of years old is being broken. This is a disastrous development, though of course you young ones refuse to acknowledge it. For if we begin to turn faith and knowledge into two different branches of learning, then what are the consequences? We tear the world apart. Some will take the theological path, and others the path of a doctrine which believes only in what it seems to have direct knowledge of. At present we are all united by belief in God, but that will end, for one day belief in God will not satisfy the philosopher: he will want to have concrete proofs and so will reject the Thomist doctrine. This is a most ominous change, Siger, but you young ones are unwilling to recognise that it is taking place....'

Lombardi made no reply. Steiner's prediction was right, but he was wrong about their attitude to it. The younger generation did indeed foresee that change, and in fact welcomed it. The separation of Church and secular affairs was precisely what they, the moderni, wanted and were striving for. But he did not say that, not to this man, who was watching the death throes of a scholarship based on faith and whose heart was probably bleeding at the sight.

And so he merely answered, 'Let's say no more about it, Steiner,' and demonstratively stowed the book away in his bag.

However, his bag was to stay in the corner for longer than he had intended. He had sent a letter to Heidelberg, but he would also have to go there in person.

Two days before he was due to leave, a beggar stopped him in the street and gave him a note. Assuming it meant that Neidhard had returned to the city, he hastily slipped it into his coat pocket.

The rest of the day passed, and it was evening before he summoned up the courage to read it. But when he unfolded the crumpled piece of paper, he recognised the small, dainty handwriting.

> *Before you leave the city, please come and see me once more. You will find me at the convent of the Holy Guardian Angels. Sophie*

Lombardi stared at the note.

The day on which he intended to leave Cologne for good started dull and overcast. A good day for feeling melancholy. And yet he liked setting out for pastures new. While they were trying to turn back the clocks on the church towers here, he would be advancing towards a new age. In the Neumarkt he saw Steiner but did not go over to him. As though sensing his presence, Steiner turned round and looked at him. Lombardi merely smiled.

Then he turned into Schildergasse, heading towards the Marspforte. Dark clouds hung in the sky above the church of the Clarisses, and when he stopped to look round once more three young men approached him, saying they were looking for the Faculty. He told them the way to the College and asked where they were from.

'From Heidelberg,' one of them replied. 'The realists have been unpopular there for the past three years because people are afraid of the Hussite heresy...'

Lombardi laughed. Yes, come here then, here they fear a different kind of heresy. 'Good luck to you,' he said, with a grin. 'And listen carefully to what the old professors tell you.'

He turned away again and approached the convent. At the gate a nun asked him what he wanted. He hesitated. 'Is Sophie Casall staying with you?'

She shook her head.

Then he pulled the note out of his pocket. 'I know that she is here. She sent this to me.'

The nun gave him a searching look. 'Who are you?'

'A Master of the *artes liberales*.'

The nun glanced at Sophie's message, then told him to wait and disappeared inside. A little later she returned and invited him to enter. In a windowless room lit by an oil lamp Sophie stood before him wearing the simple habit of a Clarissine novice. The nun quietly shut the door.

'It was the Chancellor. He arranged for me to be brought here.'

'To a convent? He wants you to end your life in a convent?'

'The convent or Melaten. Which would you have chosen?'

'Was the danger so great?'

Sophie nodded. 'Yes, and it was not only the clerics but the Faculty Masters who were fanning the flames. People of your kind. Is that why you were not there? So as not to dirty your own hands?'

He lowered his eyes. She was right, and she knew it.

'And what if one day someone recognises you?'

She gave a bitter laugh. 'Oh, I have adopted a different name—not for the first time. You start to get used to it.'

He felt the coldness between them. He was making good his escape, and she was left with only the worst of all choices. To be buried alive in a convent was certainly the last thing that she would have wished for. 'There might be some way for you to get out of here...' he said softly, not wanting to accept that he was losing her forever.

She reached out a hand to touch his dark curls, and looked deep into those eyes, the blue of liverwort, that she had loved so dearly. 'They are going to smuggle me out of the city tonight. Griseldis's husband came back yesterday, so the Provost said. You know that he deals in all kinds of spices. Tomorrow he is sailing to the Netherlands, and from there to Egypt. The Provost and I had a long discussion. Perhaps I owe my life to him, who knows.... And he is not at all an ignorant, obstinate old cleric with nothing but the statutes in his head—no, he could genuinely understand my reasons for what I did. In fact at times I felt as if I were talking to Steiner. I will be given a place in Griseldis's sister's convent. She has been very good and has used her influence on my behalf.'

'But,' Lombardi objected in a low voice, 'I don't want you living like a prisoner.'

'Perhaps I *shall* be a prisoner in Sicily, where they are taking me, but I gather that Griseldis's sister writes books, so it may well be a pleasant exile...'

'So they have everything organised,' murmured Lombardi. The Provost was going to rid himself of Sophie, the nightmare of his restless nights, by loading her onto a boat like a barrel of wine and sending her out into the world. Then he would be free of her at last.

Now the door opened and the nun entered. 'You must go now, Magister.'

There was no time for farewells. Lombardi turned and left.

Back at the Scholarium he met Laurien at the door, also preparing to leave.

'We could walk together,' the lad suggested, and Lombardi nodded. They were heading in the same direction, for he wanted to visit his sister in Neuss before going on to Heidelberg. So they left the city together, little suspecting that they would be back again sooner than they had hoped.

The Bell Inn was a hostelry for pilgrims making their way to the south. There, at little cost, infirm, aged and sick people could obtain a bed for the night in a spacious room; the food was good and the wine cheap. The inn was on a much-travelled road. It had the look of a smugglers' den; although pilgrims were left unmolested, many a rich innocent had lost his life here. The robber bands had a good eye for those who looked poor but had a purse full of money concealed under their coats.

When Lombardi and Laurien arrived at the inn it was early afternoon. They had been walking for only two hours, but the prospect of a hearty meal drew them inside. In the crowded taproom the pilgrims were sitting on the benches, their tired feet dangling in the air. Two women were bringing in dishes of food. The pilgrims moved up to make room for the newcomers. Lombardi and Laurien ordered beer and bread, and then each sat immersed in his own thoughts, while all around them people chatted and exchanged views and information about Christendom's holy places.

'Will you be going back to Cologne in a couple of months?' Lombardi asked at last, biting with relish into the fresh bread, still warm from the oven, that one of the serving-women had placed on the table.

Laurien shook his head. 'I don't think so. I think I would rather be a scribe like my father.'

Lombardi made no reply. He was thinking about Sophie and the fact that he had lost her forever. A sour, stale feeling had taken hold of him ever since his visit to Kahlenberg. Ever since he had run away from her trial without really knowing why. That august ideal, the pursuit of knowledge, had suddenly come to seem like a meaningless farce, like a masquerade at carnival time. Had it really achieved, changed, produced anything apart from a pointless quarrel among scholars? Was not Sophie right to claim that the Masters were fools and nothing more?

Suddenly Laurien grabbed him by the sleeve.

'Look, just look ...'

He turned his head. Three men had just come in. They had pushed back the hoods of their cloaks, looked all round and then headed for the further recesses of the room. Lombardi felt the blood rushing to his head. Laurien's fingers dug painfully into his arm.

'It's them, Domitian's murderers—I recognise them. I'm absolutely certain. That one there...'

Laurien could not stay sitting down. He jumped up and stared at the three men, who had sat down calmly on a bench at the very back and were now shouting for beer.

'Hold your tongue!' Lombardi hissed, trying to free himself from Laurien's grip.

But there was no restraining Laurien. 'I'm sure. I *saw* them. It's them...'

As ill luck would have it, Neidhard just then looked around the room. He recognised Lombardi and gave him a quick smile. This was simply too much for Laurien. The man was smiling. Why? And at whom? Lombardi's face was like stone, and yet the smile had obviously been meant for him, since they did not know Laurien. Now Neidhard was actually raising his hand in greeting, and making as though to get up and come over to them. Laurien sank back onto the bench.

And now here was Neidhard standing in front of them, bending down to speak to Lombardi, though all he said was, 'Well, have you abandoned the Faculty?' Then he laughed and turned to one of the serving-women to ask about a room for the night.

'He knows you? How is it that he knows you?' Laurien moved slightly away from Lombardi as though the Devil in person were sitting beside him and had only just shown his cloven hoof.

'We'd better leave,' Lombardi muttered, and was about to get up, but again Laurien grabbed him by the arm.

'Leave? Now, when I've found them? They killed Domitian, and you want to leave?'

Angrily Lombardi shook him off and stood up. But if he thought that Laurien would leave him in peace, he was mistaken. In a flash the lad ran after him, followed him outside and barred his way. 'If you won't do it then I will, and if I go back to Cologne and tell people where they are...'

Lombardi looked down at the puny boy. The crazy thought shot through his mind that it might be best to drag him behind the nearest bush and simply wring his neck.

'Go on, then,' he said.

'How do you come to know them? You knew all the time that it was they who killed Domitian, I see it all now. That's why you kept quiet and let Steiner and the magistrates search the whole city for him although he was lying dead in Weilersfeld. Perhaps you were even in league with them.'

There was no holding Laurien now. At last he had found an explanation for Lombardi's strange behaviour, and he was spinning a thousand bizarre threads in his mind, and prancing around on the road as if he were about to punch him.

'Be quiet!' Lombardi snapped.

'It's the *truth*!' cried Laurien. 'And you knew all along.'

'And you are determined to drag this truth, as you call it, into the light of day?' Lombardi growled under his breath.

Laurien nodded. 'Yes, I'm going back to the city. They'll be staying the night here, so the magistrate's men will have all the time in the world to come and arrest them.'

This situation was becoming really dangerous, thought Lombardi. It called for desperate measures. He could hit Laurien over the head and hide him overnight in a shed or some such place. Or even kill him and shut his mouth that way. 'If you talk, they'll put you on trial too for not having told what you knew.'

'So what, I don't care. I don't want to study anymore anyway. But what will happen to you? What is your connection with them?'

Standing on the road with Laurien leaping around in front of him, Lombardi was suddenly overcome by a feeling of utter exhaustion. All at once he saw himself as having been infinitely foolish. He had based his whole life on the absurd premises of the philosophers. Theory, all of it. Nothing real, nothing that you could grasp with your senses. If you sowed a seed, that gave rise to more seed, which was something you could see and touch. It was that sense of unreality that for days now, no, for weeks, had been stalking him like some wild beast. Invisible, glassy, reflective. The death of the soul. Yes, it was like the death of his soul.

'Very well,' he said. 'Let's go back.'

Laurien stared at him. 'You're coming too?'

'Yes, I'll come with you.'

'Of course I've no idea what connection you have with them, but the consequences may be even worse for you than for me...'

'Yes, they will. But perhaps that is a good thing. You won't understand that...'

Laurien nodded. Now he was completely calm as he stood before Lombardi. Those men inside suspected nothing, they would stuff their bellies and then fill the night with their dreams. That, too, was a good thing.

'Let's be on our way,' said Lombardi.

The plan was to take her down at nightfall to the harbour, where the ship was waiting. It was to sail the following morning. A horse stood ready, and a Franciscan would accompany her. Apart from him, the Chancellor and the Clarisses, no one knew that Sophie would be quitting the city. Together with the friar she rode down to the Alter Markt. It was a mild evening, still quite warm. The market-place was full of bustle, and people were standing together, chatting, before ending their day's work. No one took any notice of the nun and the friar crossing the market-place. At the roadside stood a spinning-woman who was waiting for her husband. At that moment the nun's horse made a sudden movement and her veil slipped. And as she happened to be caught in the light of a torch, the eye of the spinning-woman fell on the nun's face. She recognised her instantly, since she had once been her neighbour.

'Look, that's Sophie Casall—there on the horse, the witch…'

All eyes turned towards the nun. Had it been a nanny-goat riding the horse, or an angel, it would have been all the same to them. This was the witch, and at once they were all convinced that they remembered her face, even if they had never set eyes on Sophie Casall before. A cry went through the crowd. A man made a grab for the horse's rein and pulled at it, making the horse rear up. And then the mob rushed at her, trying to pull the witch to the ground. Sophie screamed, the friar attempted to catch hold of the rein, but the crowd pushed him away from her. He jumped down from his saddle and endeavoured to fight his way towards his charge, but his path was blocked. The crowd had Sophie by the arms and legs and were dragging her down the street to the Alter Markt. Filled with anguish, the friar followed behind, and then he heard their shouts, louder and louder: 'To Melaten with her! She shall burn at the stake, the witch…'

The Franciscan looked around in desperation. Then he turned westwards towards the Provost's House, where the Chancellor lived, and ran straight into the arms of an astonished Magister Steiner, who caught him by the sleeve.

'What is going on here? What is all that shouting?'

The friar, now deathly pale, his legs trembling, pointed across to the market place: 'They have dragged her from her horse and are going to take her to Melaten…'

'Whom?'

'Sophie Casall. She was to have been conveyed out of the city tonight…'

Steiner stared at him. Then he ordered him to inform the Chancellor immediately, and hurried to the market-place. By now the crowd had dragged their victim further. Constables had arrived to see what the disturbance was. They were carrying staffs to keep the mob in check. Steiner pushed his way through the angry throng. He saw Sophie being forcibly held by her hands and feet by several men. Her habit was in tatters, her legs and breasts exposed.

'What's all this about?' bellowed one of the constables, and back came the cry, as with a single voice: 'The witch, the witch, we have found the witch!'

Rigid with horror, Steiner looked around. On all sides nothing but faces contorted into grimaces, slavering and leering, and bodies squirming and straining forward to snatch a shred of clothing from the witch. Bodies bursting with pent-up rage, as if they had been carrying it around with them for years. The noise from so many throats was deafening, and there was a constant press towards the front, where the witch was being pulled to and fro, until someone happened to locate a pillory and the mob began to scream with delight. 'Lock her in it, lock her in it!' they roared, and Sophie was lifted up and her legs and arms thrust through the holes. Somebody else called for a cart, since it was too far to drag her all the way to Melaten, but the crowd were already well content, for now they could spit at the woman and pelt her with dirt and muck. At this moment a man came running up with a lighted torch and was about to hold it to the remaining shreds of the witch's clothing.

'You must stop him!' Steiner yelled to the constables, who were now wielding their staffs with a will and finally managing to clear themselves a path to the front. Now, too, the clatter of horses' hooves could be heard. Steiner turned to look: the captain of the city guard must have sent a detachment to restore order.

And as he looked anxiously down the blocked street, packed now with all the various rabble that the commotion had brought out of their holes, his frantic gaze fell upon a diminutive figure being pushed forward by the crowd and lacking the strength to resist. He was being swept along before them like mud and boulders in the grip of a raging torrent. At that moment the men of the city guard came thundering up on their horses; here and there someone was struck by a hoof and fell to the ground, which only added to the hysteria. Soon they had completely buried the dwarf beneath them, and Steiner tried desperately not to lose sight of him. When one of the constables came within reach he seized him by the sleeve and shouted into his ear that Casall's murderer was lying over there. How was he supposed to find him in this mad crush? the man yelled back. He did, however, contrive to fight his way through, dragging Steiner in his wake, to the spot where the dwarf lay on the ground. The mob had quite literally trampled him underfoot, and because of his small stature he had been unable to defend himself. De Swerthe was no longer moving. His legs were crushed and broken, and blood was seeping through the dark cloth of his cassock and running down over his ankles. More blood was trickling from a bad head wound, probably caused by a kick from a horse's hoof. People were stepping over him, some actually onto his limbs, until the constable took hold of him and dragged him into a narrow alleyway. It was a little more peaceful here, and so he laid the dwarf down on the planks lying across the street and called out to Steiner to take care of him because he himself must go back and see what was happening to the witch. De Swerthe lay motionless, except for the blood running down on to the ground, and the locks of his fair hair were coated with mud. Steiner knocked at the nearest door. There was no response. He pressed the handle down and pushed the door open.

At the end of Severinstrasse, where Lombardi and Laurien came in through the city gate, there was no sound of any disturbance. The Alter Markt was some way off, and in any case the magistrate's house was in Ulrengasse, well away from the turbulence of the frenzied mob. The magistrate, whose men were all occupied with the events at the market square, listened to what they had to say, noted down the name and location of the pilgrims' inn and promised to act that same evening, before the murderers departed again. Lombardi said little, letting Laurien do the talking. Laurien admitted to having witnessed the outrageous happenings at Weilersfeld on one occasion, and said that in view of his friend's death he felt obliged to make this statement so that Domitian's murder would at last be avenged. Then it was Lombardi's turn. Yes, he knew who they were, he had been connected with them—what was the use of denying it, for Neidhard and his brethren would be sure to accuse him, since they would inevitably assume that it was he who had betrayed them. So he revealed all the things that he had guarded for years like his very life, and the magistrate looked at him gravely and then impressed on them both that they must not leave Cologne.

Having discovered that there was no one in the house, Steiner pulled the dwarf into the kitchen. He left him lying on the floor, and scooped water out of a bucket that stood by the hearth to wipe the blood from de Swerthe's face and legs. Then he removed the man's cloak and laid him upon it on his side. At last his eyelashes began to flutter, the lids opened. His sky-blue eyes looked up into Steiner's face.

'Steiner.' The name came out as a faint croaking sound, and then his hand felt for his head and the open wound.

'Don't fall asleep,' said Steiner, 'try to stay awake.'

But de Swerthe's eyelids were closing again.

'Sophie,' he murmured, 'they found her...'

'Yes, they found her,' replied Steiner, and de Swerthe's lips puckered.

'You killed Casall,' said Steiner.

The dwarf opened his eyes again. 'I'm in a bad way, am I not?'

Steiner nodded. 'You could unburden your soul by telling me the truth.'

'You think that God's heart would be softened and he would not send me to Hell? Oh, God is not so easily fooled. He knows what I was capable of. But had he not forsaken me and abandoned me to the Devil? Who told you? The student?'

'Yes, the student.'

De Swerthe closed his eyes again. Then Steiner took the ring from his pocket.

'This was found in your laboratory, and it took me a long

time to realise whose it was. It was you, wasn't it? You took it from his finger…'

Blood started to flow again from the head wound, forming a thin veil over the Prior's forehead. Once again Steiner wiped the blood away, while the dwarf opened his eyes and looked at the ring in Steiner's free hand.

'You know whose ring that was?' he asked softly.

'I noticed the animal emblem at the funeral, but I could not precisely identify it on that occasion. It was on the von Semper family's escutcheon, on their coach, but I had forgotten it. I was only reminded of it a few days ago when I saw this ring. I had thought it was a weasel, but it was a badger. The ring belonged to Domitian. And now of course I ask myself: how did you come by this ring?'

De Swerthe closed his eyes again. 'Everyone thinks that the heretics strangled Domitian with one of those charming ropes of theirs…. Yes, it was the obvious assumption to make. He spied on them and so he was punished for it.' His eyes were mere slits, and now a smile appeared on his lips. 'You suspected Domitian of having been in Marzellenstrasse and murdering Casall. Oh, he was certainly in Marzellenstrasse, but when he arrived there Casall was already dead. He watched me dragging his body to the well and waited until I had neatly laid him out beside it. Then I put the riddle into the book, scattered the items of clothing and began to scream. I made my escape over the wall, and when I reached the Scholarium he was already there waiting for me. He had me in his power. Yes, my plan had gone awry. He was a cruel young man, I tell you, a devil in the guise of an angel. He kept me in suspense, said he needed time to think what price I should pay. So one secret succeeded another. But before he could set the price I followed him to the ruin. I had overheard a conversation between Lombardi and Laurien, who couldn't keep the secret about the sect to himself. So I followed Domitian to Weilersfeld and saw the heretics hit him on the head and then take to their heels. The opportunity could not have been better. I strangled him and sent an anonymous letter to the magistrate…. Oh yes, you would probably like to know how I escaped from the burning house. It was easy. There was another door. I left the cross behind in the house to make you think I had perished in the flames. But you never believed that, did you?'

'No. We found none of your bones, so you were clearly still alive. But why did the house explode? Were you trying to kill yourself?'

De Swerthe shook his head. 'It might have happened at any time. Unlike dealing with mere edifices of thought, working with real matter can be a dangerous undertaking.'

De Swerthe's voice had been growing weaker all the time, and now Steiner had to put his ear to the dwarf's mouth in order to catch his words. Then he stood up and fetched a clean cloth and water, for the blood had begun to run into his eyes. There would be no point in trying to get a doctor now, Steiner thought. Nevertheless he stepped outside the house. From the market-place he could still hear shouting and screaming, as though Sophie had indeed been set on fire in her pillory, but he neither saw clouds of smoke nor smelt the odour of burnt flesh. He closed the door again and went back to de Swerthe.

'And everyone thought it was the Brethren of the Free Spirit who were responsible for Domitian's death,' he murmured, looking down at the dwarf, but de Swerthe could no longer hear him.

A considerable force of constables had by now arrived at the market-place to put a stop to the mob's bloodthirsty violence. They formed a wall around the woman, who was still held fast in the pillory, while they attempted to release her from it. Sophie Casall was slumped forward, more dead than alive, over the wooden frame. Her limbs seemed as weak as melted wax when one of the constables withdrew her arms and legs from the holes. Then he gave a sign, and the door of one of the houses that fronted the market opened. A couple of his fellow officers heaved the half-dead woman on to their shoulders and carried her, amid noisy protests from the crowd, into the house. There they barred the door with a broad, heavy length of timber and kept watch at a window as the people at last dispersed, still grumbling. From the shadows at the back of the room a figure stepped forward and approached the makeshift bed where Sophie lay, an elderly woman who had shown concern for her and who now began gently to wash her face.

'You should leave the room,' the woman said to the Provost, 'I must take these torn clothes off her, you can see she's almost naked…'

The Provost nodded and was just turning to go when there was an urgent knock at the door. One of the constables opened it cautiously. It was Steiner, in a highly agitated state. De Swerthe was dying, he said with a look at Sophie, and had confessed that he was responsible not only for Casall's but also for Domitian's death.

The Provost stared at Steiner. 'De Swerthe? Why de Swerthe? I thought it was the heretics. Only an hour ago Lombardi made a statement which will cost him his career, barring a miracle…'

Lombardi's statement and confession had been wholly unnecessary. He had put his career at risk for the truth, or what he thought was the truth, and now he was forced to acknowledge that it had all been for nothing, since Neidhard and his companions had only hit Domitian on the head. Later, at their trial, they would confess to having killed the student Marinus and burying him outside the gates of the city, but Lombardi was never to know this.

So now he was sitting, close to despair, in the magistrate's house, brooding on the futility of his action and the bitter irony of life. Laurien had gone back to the Scholarium. He would have to postpone his return home for a while because he was required to give evidence at the trial of the heretics. Sophie had been taken back to the Provost's House, for her own safety; early the next morning, when emotions had subsided, she would be taken down to the harbour. Then suddenly there was a knock at the door of Lombardi's room, and Griseldis appeared. 'Come,' she said simply.

The boat that was to carry Sophie would sail to the Netherlands, where it would load its cargo on to a ship bound for Sicily. Griseldis's husband traded in everything imaginable, and taking a woman along presented no difficulty. On previous voyages he had transported pilgrims, artists and famous doctors wishing to visit the Faculty at Salerno.

To enable her to reach the harbour safely the Provost had arranged for her to be dressed in pilgrim costume. This time Griseldis was to accompany her.

'If anyone asks you, you are going to Santiago de Compostela. There are other pilgrims on board who can no longer manage the whole journey on foot, and you can attach yourself to them. And now say your farewells...'

Griseldis stood up and opened the door. A man was leaning against the wall of the corridor, and he now hesitantly entered the room.

'Griseldis has promised to give me your address, Sophie,' Lombardi began in a tone of embarrassment, 'and if they let me go free after the trial, perhaps I can...'

'Will they?'

'Probably. They can't possibly burn at the stake everybody who has ever had anything to do with those people.'

'But what will you live on if you can no longer obtain a post anywhere?'

'Oh, I could make my home with my uncle, a robber baron.'

He drew closer and took Sophie's hand. 'I will write to you, my dear. We can discuss ideas, or talk about worms caught on hooks. What do you say?'

Sophie laughed. And then she asked Griseldis to bring her a knife. With it she cut off a lock of her hair and exchanged it for a lock of his. Time was pressing again. She departed with nothing but the black lock that she held clasped in her hand.

The Chancellor was sitting pensively at his desk, inwardly railing at the hysteria that had gripped the city. The people of Cologne had rarely vented their rage in pogroms, and witch-burnings, too, had been relatively few in number. But times were changing, he thought anxiously, and the new urge to persecute any kind of outsider, which was beginning to spread throughout the Empire, now seemed to be gaining a foothold even here.

Outside the room a monk's wooden-soled sandals clattered on the floorboards. It was the beginning of spring, but the Chancellor felt only disgust and listlessness. When the birds were singing and the flowers, which normally he loved so much, began to bloom, and a blue sky looked kindly down on him, he was seized with a feeling of unrelieved despondency. Of unreality. As if he had ceased to be anything but an observer of life. He was so tired.

There was a knock at the door. Steiner entered, with Lombardi a step behind him, and they asked if they were disturbing the Chancellor, but he shook his head. They sat down on the chairs in front of the desk. Lombardi would have to make a formal statement that would be recorded in writing, but everyone, at least in the Faculty, knew what it would contain. A misguided student who must now pay for a few youthful sins with his career, unless another Faculty could be found that would employ him.

They were all thinking the same thing. 'He ought to be forgiven,' Steiner said quietly.

The Chancellor nodded. What did he care about Lombardi's lapse? Soon his own position would be occupied by another.

'You grow roses, too, don't you, Steiner,' he said with a smile, as if roses were the really important things in life. Anything to banish that sense of unreality.

'Now other people will have to worry their heads about will and understanding,' replied Steiner. 'Let us take care of the roses.'

The Chancellor laughed. 'You're right. And what about you, Lombardi?'

The sun shining in through the window lit up Lombardi's black hair. 'My father is an apothecary in Berne. Perhaps I might learn how to mix all the various powders. He never wanted me to study the *artes liberales*, he always told me that there was no money in it. Actually I am not as upset as I should be. It's only the circumstances that sadden me...the way it happened, if you see what I mean. Sacrificing everything, and all to no purpose.'

The Chancellor nodded.

'And what about de Swerthe?'

'De Swerthe is dead. The riddles have been solved, the dead

avenged. And quite soon I propose to take my retirement and concentrate my thoughts on flowers...'

'No more intellectual hair-splitting?'

'No,' murmured the Chancellor. 'No more of that. At last I will begin to study reality and nothing but reality.'

Lombardi made no reply. He had been thinking exactly the same. 'So the spectre of unreality will vanish into thin air when the constructs are finally sent packing,' he said at last, softly.

'You had better not let the other Cologne Masters hear you say that,' the Chancellor commented, smiling.

But Steiner, who had stood up and gone over to the window, shook his head. 'They are not two different things, Lombardi, they always go together, and you must never forget that, however much philosophy seems like a spectre to you just now. Even spectres are real, if only in our imagination.'

Lombardi too rose to his feet. He took his leave of the Chancellor and gave Steiner a friendly nod. Steiner watched his young colleague slip out through the door and gently close it behind him.

'The first roses are already coming into bloom,' he said, looking down into the garden.

# About the Author

*Claudia Gross*

Claudia Gross was born in 1956 in Arolsen in Hesse, Germany. She studied medieval philosophy and German. She now lives and works in Kempen on the Lower Rhine.

*The fonts used in this book are from the Garamond family*